One warrior was pierced through a house's roof.

There was another lying on the ground with all four of their limbs bending in the wrong directions.

There were ten times as many who had ___ and blacked out, as well as those who'd h___ (and extremities) broken.

Then standing at the bank of the reserv___ murderer responsible—or at the very leas___ seemed to have witnessed it.

"Ooze. Name of Psianop.
I've come to fulfill a promise.
A promise from twenty-one years ago…"

PSIANOP THE INEXHAUSTIBLE STAGNATION

An ooze martial artist who has mastered a multitude of different martial art styles. He seems to have some sort of relationship with the legendary First Party who headed off to subjugate the True Demon King, but……

The match, the largest-scale fight throughout the games, didn't defy any of the expectations of those who witnessed it, save for those of the similarly all-powerful combatants who would claim victory.

In other words, before the sun could even set, the battle was one that brought eternal destruction to the land around it.

The conclusion taught everyone exactly how terrifying the words *all-powerful* could truly be.

Alus the Star Runner versus Lucnoca the Winter.

"...You're toying with me... aren't you...?"

ALUS THE STAR RUNNER

A wyvern who obtains any and all treasure he desires. A legend-slaying champion.

"*Cyulcascarz.*"
(Wither and fall at the edge of light.)

LUCNOCA THE WINTER
The strongest of all dragons, doubted to have actually existed at all. A champion-slaying legend.

"Doing things alone is my personal policy. As a champion, I have to fulfill my obligations to this world, don't I?"

KAZUKI THE BLACK TONE

A visiting assassin who can even manipulate a bullet's trajectory on a whim. Assaulting the Free City of Okafu with a specific objective in mind.

At some point, there was a large fluctuation. Kazuki was convinced of the truth behind the change. The mystery that the bulk of those who arrived in this world in its current state were unaware of.

III

Voiceless Calamity

Keiso

ILLUSTRATION BY

Kureta

New York

III

Keiso

ILLUSTRATION BY
Kureta

Translation by David Musto

This book is a work of fiction. Names, characters, places, and incidents are the product of the author's imagination or are used fictitiously. Any resemblance to actual events, locales, or persons, living or dead, is coincidental.

ISHURA Vol. 3 ZESSOKU MUSEIKA
©Keiso 2020
First published in Japan in 2020 by KADOKAWA CORPORATION, Tokyo.
English translation rights arranged with KADOKAWA CORPORATION, Tokyo, through TUTTLE-MORI AGENCY, INC., Tokyo.

English translation © 2023 by Yen Press, LLC

Yen On
150 West 30th Street, 19th Floor
New York, NY 10001

Visit us at yenpress.com
facebook.com/yenpress
twitter.com/yenpress
yenpress.tumblr.com
instagram.com/yenpress

First Yen On Edition: March 2023
Edited by Yen On Editorial: Payton Campbell
Designed by Yen Press Design: Andy Swist

Yen On is an imprint of Yen Press, LLC.
The Yen On name and logo are trademarks of Yen Press, LLC.

The publisher is not responsible for websites (or their content) that are not owned by the publisher.

Library of Congress Cataloging-in-Publication Data
Names: Keiso (Manga author), author. | Kureta, illustrator. | Musto, David, translator.
Title: Ishura / Keiso ; illustration by Kureta ; translation by David Musto.
Other titles: Ishura. English
Description: First Yen On edition. | New York : Yen On, 2022.
Identifiers: LCCN 2021062849 | ISBN 9781975337865
    (v. 1 ; trade paperback) | ISBN 9781975337889
    (v. 2 ; trade paperback) | ISBN 9781975337902
    (v. 3 ; trade paperback) | ISBN 9781975337926
    (v. 4 ; trade paperback)
Subjects: LCGFT: Fantasy fiction. | Light novels.
Classification: LCC PL872.5.E57 I7413 2022 | DDC 895.63/6—dc23/
    eng/20220121
LC record available at https://lccn.loc.gov/2021062849

ISBNs: 978-1-9753-3790-2 (trade paperback)
       978-1-9753-3791-9 (ebook)

10 9 8 7 6 5 4 3 2 1

LSC-C

Printed in the United States of America

The identity of the one who defeated the True Demon King—the ultimate threat who gripped the world in terror—is shrouded in mystery.
Little is known about this hero.
The terror of the True Demon King abruptly came to an end.

Nevertheless, the champions born from the era of the Demon King still remain in this world.

Now, with the enemy of all life brought low,
these champions, wielding enough power to transform the world,
have begun to do as they please,
their untamed wills threatening a new era of war and strife.

To Aureatia, now the sole kingdom unifying the minian races,
the existence of these champions has become a threat.
No longer champions, they are now demons bringing ruin to all—
the shura.

To ensure peace in the new era,
it is necessary to eliminate any threat to the world's future,
and designate the True Hero to guide and protect the hopes of
the people.

Thus, the Twenty-Nine Officials, the governing administrators of Aureatia, have gathered these shura and their miraculous abilities from across the land, regardless of race, and organized an imperial competition to crown the True Hero once and for all.

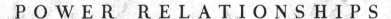

POWER RELATIONSHIPS

Country that seceded from Aureatia,
Ruled by the self-proclaimed
Demon King, Taren.
Defeated in its war against Aureatia
and annihilated.

New Principality of Lithia

defeated | victorious

Aureatia

Nation of unified minian races,
formed from merging all three
kingdoms together during the
age of the True Demon King.

??? | wary | defeat | victory

Free City of Okahu

A country formed by the largest mercenary guild
in the land.
A group of elite soldiers that deploys a military
force on par with any nation-state.
Completely independent of any outside authority.

Toghie City

Trying to restore the kingdoms of old.
The Old Kingdoms' loyalists gathered here.
And taking advantage of the Particle
Storm's attack,
declared war on Aureatia and were defeated.

GLOSSARY

❖ Word Arts

① Laws of the world that permit and establish phenomenon and living creatures that physically shouldn't be able to exist, such as the construction of a gigant's body.
② Phenomenon that conveys the intentions of a speaker's words to the listener, regardless of the speaker's race or language.
③ Or the generic term for arts that utilize this phenomenon to distort natural phenomena via "requests" to a certain target.

Something much like what would be called magic. Force, Thermal, Craft, and Life Arts compose the four core groups, but there are some who can use arts outside of these four groups. While necessary to be familiarized with the target in order to utilize these arts, powerful Word Arts users are able to offset this requirement.

❖ Force Arts

Arts that inflict directed power and speed, what is known as momentum, on a target.

❖ Craft Arts

Arts that change a target's shape.

❖ Thermal Arts

Arts that inflict undirected energy, such as heat, electrical current, and light, on a target.

❖ Life Arts

Arts that change a target's nature.

❖ Visitors

Those who possess abilities that deviate greatly from all common knowledge, and thus were transported to this world from another one known as the Beyond. Visitors are unable to use Word Arts.

❖ Enchanted Sword • Magic Items

Swords and tools that possess potent abilities. Similar to visitors, due to their mighty power, there are some objects that were transported here from another world.

❖ Aureatia Twenty-Nine Officials

The highest functionaries who govern Aureatia. Ministers are civil servants, while Generals are military officers.
There is no hierarchy-based seniority or rank among the Twenty-Nine Officials.

❖ Self-Proclaimed Demon King

A generic term for "demonic monarch" not related to the One True King among the three kingdoms. There are some cases where even those who do not proclaim themselves as a monarch, but who wield great power to threaten Aureatia, are acknowledged as self-proclaimed demon kings by Aureatia and targeted for subjugation.

❖ Sixways Exhibition

A tournament to determine the True Hero. The person who wins each one-on-one match and advances all the way through to the end will be named the True Hero. Backing from a member of the Twenty-Nine Officials is required to enter the competition.

CONTENTS

♪ *FIFTH VERSE:* VOICELESS CALAMITY ♪

♪ *SIXTH VERSE:* SIXWAYS EXHIBITION I ♪

AUREATIA TWENTY-NINE OFFICIALS

Fifth Official
VACANT SEAT

Tenth General
QWELL THE WAX FLOWER
A woman with long bangs that hide her eyes.
Sponsor for Psianop the Inexhaustible Stagnation.
Timid and always trembling in fright.

First Minister
GRASSE THE FOUNDATION MAP
A man nearing old age.
Tasked with being the chairperson who presides over Twenty-Nine Officials' meetings.
Not belonging to any of the factions in the Sixways Exhibition and maintaining neutrality.

Sixth General
HARGHENT THE STILL
A man who yearns for authority despite being ridiculed for being incompetent.
Sponsoring Lucnoca the Winter.
Has a deep connection with Alus the Star Runner.
Not part of any faction.

Eleventh Minister
NOPHTOK THE CREPUSCULE BELL
An elderly man who gives a gentle, kindly impression.
Sponsor for Kuze the Passing Disaster.
Holds jurisdiction over the Order.

Second General
ROSCLAY THE ABSOLUTE
A man who garners absolute trust as a champion.
Participates in the Sixways Exhibition, supporting himself.
The leader of the largest faction within the Twenty-Nine Officials.

Seventh Minister
FLINSUDA THE PORTENT
Corpulent woman adorned in gold and silver accessories.
A pragmatist who only believes in the power of money.
Desires a hero to sponsor in order to take negotiation bribes from both factions.

Twelfth General
SABFOM THE WHITE WEAVE
A man who covers his face with an iron mask.
Previously crossed swords with self-proclaimed demon king Morio and is currently recuperating.

Third Minister
JELKY THE SWIFT INK
A bespeckled man with the air of a shrewd bureaucrat.
Planned the Sixways Exhibition.
Belongs to Rosclay's faction.

Eighth Minister
SHEANEK THE WORD INTERMEDIARY
A man who can decipher and give accounts in a variety of different scripts.
Acts in practice as First Minister Grasse the Foundation Map's Secretary.
Maintains neutrality just like Grasse.

Thirteenth Minister
ENU THE DISTANT MIRROR
An aristocratic man with slicked-back hair.
Sponsor for Zeljirga the Abyss Web.
Infected by Linaris the Obsidian and now under her control.

Fourth Minister
KAETE THE ROUND TABLE
A man with an extremely fierce temperament.
Sponsoring Mestelexil the Box of Desperate Knowledge.
Possesses preeminent military power and authority and is resisting Rosclay's faction.

Ninth General
YANIEGIZ THE CHISEL
A sinewy man with a snaggletooth.

Fourteenth General
YUCA THE HALATION GAOL
A simple and honest man, round and plump.
Doesn't have a shred of ambition.

Fifteenth General
HAIZESTA THE GATHERING SPOT

A man in the prime of his life with a cynical smile.
Prominent for his misbehavior.

Twentieth Minister
HIDOW THE CLAMP

A haughty son of a noble family and at the same time a popular, quick-witted man.
Sponsor for Alus the Star Runner.
Sponsoring Alus to ensure he doesn't win.

Twenty-Fifth General
CAYON THE SKYTHUNDER

A one-armed man with a feminine speaking manner.
Sponsor for Mele the Horizon's Roar.

Sixteenth General
NOFELT THE SOMBER WIND

An abnormally tall man.
Sponsor for Uhak the Silent.
Originated from the same Order almshouse as Kuze.

Twenty-First General
TUTURI THE BLUE VIOLET FOAM

A woman with grizzled hair tied up behind her head.

Twenty-Sixth Minister
MEEKA THE WHISPERED

A stern woman who gives a rigid and rectangular impression.
Acting as the adjudicator of the Sixways Exhibition.

Seventeenth Minister
ELEA THE RED TAG

A young, beautiful woman who rose up from her prostitute ancestry.
Supervises Aureatia's intelligence apparatus.
Keeping Kia the World Word a secret to use as her trump card.

Twenty-Second General
MIZIAL THE IRON-PIERCING PLUMESHADE

A boy who became a member of the Twenty-Nine Officials at just sixteen years old.
Possesses a self-assured temperament.

Twenty-Seventh General
HARDY THE BULLET FLASHPOINT

A man who sincerely loves war.
Sponsor for Soujirou the Willow-Sword.
Prominent figure accompanied by the largest military faction.

Eighteenth Minister
QUEWAI THE MOON FRAGMENT

A young, gloomy man.

Twenty-Third Official
VACANT SEAT

Previously the seat of Taren the Punished.
However, it is currently vacant following her secession and defection.

Twenty-Eighth Minister
ANTEL THE ALIGNMENT

A tan-skinned man wearing dark-tinted glasses.

Nineteenth Minister
HYAKKA THE HEAT HAZE

A small-statured man who supervises the agricultural division.
Straining himself to become worthy of his position in the Twenty-Nine Officials.

Twenty-Fourth General
DANT THE HEATH FURROW

An exceedingly serious man.
Commands the northern front army, containing Old Kingdoms' loyalists' forces.
Part of the Queen's faction—and harbors ill feelings toward Rosclay's faction.

Twenty-Ninth Official
VACANT SEAT

ISHURA

Keiso

ILLUSTRATION BY **Kureta**

Fifth Verse:

VOICELESS CALAMITY

The vast Gokashae Sand Sea, on the eastern frontier. There, in that expansive, unmapped region sat a labyrinth half sunken into the sands.

It was a vault of knowledge from the Beyond, known as a "library." And if there ever came a visitor capable of transporting a large number of the tomes and actually reading them, they would say that the knowledge contained within was worth as much as an entire country. One such person accomplished this feat—a merchant woman. And by using the knowledge she gained from the seven volumes she managed to return with, she was able to rise through the societal ranks and become Central Kingdom nobility.

The sand labyrinth itself had books scattered all over the place, as it was little more than a hollow ruin lined with bookshelves. It wasn't the sort of labyrinth laced with traps and dead ends to discombobulate intruders—nevertheless, its impregnability and difficulty to traverse earned it the title of labyrinth all the same.

In the Gokashae Sand Sea, there existed those who made it

their duty to impede and interfere with any and all exploration of the sand labyrinth's depths.

Thus, an armed merchant caravan, two hundred and eight strong, was seeking this perilous knowledge. It was the first large-scale organized expedition in seven small months, and the host of bodyguards with it presumed they would be engaging with the obstructors to their plans.

There were two people spying on this massive column from a clifftop. Although they wore clothes much like minia wore, their bodies were coated in thick, coarse fur while their heads were shaped like those of wolves. They were lycans.

"......About eighteen, I'd say. I'll bet they can put up a fight, too. Must be the first big haul in a while."

The far-sight spyglass that the stout, gray-furred lycan, Heng of the Shallow Step, looked through was an item that belonged to notable adventurers and caravans of the past. An item they had plundered.

The people obstructing any exploration of the sand labyrinth were a pack of brawny and unrivaled lycans—the Zehf tribe. Every one of them sought martial prowess, having no interest in the sand labyrinth's collection of books. If anything, they considered the literary treasures to be no better than worthless garbage.

However, that was not the case for the minia and dwarves who would be periodically drawn to the sand labyrinth—and in particular, the commodities they'd bring into the barren desert to support their exploration. This was exactly why the Zehf tribe had established a base camp in the middle of the desert.

Behind Heng as he looked out that caravan was another lycan of fairly large build, with white-and-brown fur. He looked to be much younger than Heng.

"Brother, just look at them all...! The back of their l-line... I can't even see it! It goes all the way to the crags!"

"Steady, Canute. Don't be fooled by visual numbers. There are only eighteen of them that pose any real threat. The day has come for Heng of the Shallow Step to put his training to the test. I'll kill all eighteen of them myself."

"E-eighteen people..."

Canute's eyes bulged as he repeated the words of his respected elder brother.

"...A-all... All by yourself?!"

Trembling excessively, Canute forgot to pull his tongue back into his mouth again.

"Hmph...... You think I can't?"

"B...Brother! I will bear witness to your feats!"

Heng solemnly took up his specialized weapon in hand. A polearm with a curved blade affixed at both ends of the shaft.

From inspecting the enemy to forming the optimal strategy, he handled everything himself. The Zehf tribe's training began before combat even started.

"*Ngrah!*"

Heng's deep-throated bestial roar echoed. As he did, he picked up speed. Then...

◆

Heng's attack lasted about as long as it simply took for him to reach the back of the caravan. Slipping through the tight opening directly underneath the carriages, interwoven with beguiling mirages from his martial movements and dodging the hail of arrows, he gave most of the guards a moment to defend themselves before cutting them in two and ending their lives.

However, this was not so for the final two he fought.

A leprechaun wielding a strange mechanical scimitar, Rook the Shredding Trineedle.

A minia in possession of an otherworldly knife-throwing ability, Albert the Summer Rain.

Underestimating either of these powerful opponents would mean certain death. Even for Heng, if the scales of fortune tipped the other way even slightly, he would become just another corpse lying in the Gokashae.

"*Koff*, damn…you…"

Sent flying by Heng's attack, Rook the Shredding Trineedle's rent upper body was only connected by one side of her rib cage. The final result of the life-and-death battle.

"Rejoice. Your heads will be honored for seven years to come."

"Th-this technique… Where did you…? And from who…?"

"The training I've endured is far different from yours. We've been mentored and trained by Neft the Nirvana, from the First Party. An adequate explanation for when you reach the land of the dead."

"*Heh*… The First… So that's, it……"

The Zehf tribe was not a simple pack of lycans. It was, if anything, a school of thought.

Worshipping the legendary lycan Neft the Nirvana, still alive but little more than a corpse, the Zehf tribe devoted their time to studying and practicing the martial arts bequeathed by him.

This type of life-risking training was also a natural rite of passage.

The reason behind employing peerless bodyguards like Albert and Rook, as well as why a single person hadn't been able to reach the labyrinth, no matter how prepared they were for the Sand Sea's dangers, was entirely because of these Zehf lycans.

"Brother, that was incredible! You really are the strongest around! *Awooo!!*"

"Ha... I said you needn't worry... But you do the plundering. Don't let these minians escape with any of it."

Heng chuckled, despite the blood gushing from his open wound. His upper-right side was pierced with a countless number of knives.

"I—I... I'm going to become like you someday, Brother!"

"Fool... Do you have any idea how long that will take? *Ha-ha......*"

The inexperienced Canute successfully intimidated the remaining survivors, and the entire cargo of the two-hundred-strong caravan became provisions for the Zehf tribe.

The lycans, classified as members of the monstrous races, did eat minians, of course, but they didn't have a marked preference for them.

The Zehf tribe sought slaughter in part to use prominent and powerful individuals as practice to show off the results of their training, but dictated all noncombatants and the weak be released unharmed.

This area was barely the beginning of the Gokashae Sand Sea, but even then, there were likely many without the stamina to get to town before dying of thirst. Heng and the others didn't pay this possibility any mind.

As long as they stepped into these lands, even these weaklings were adventurers seeking knowledge, fully aware of the risks. Much like the lycan warriors challenging whole armies themselves, they were fated to put their own lives on the scales.

In the Gokashae Sand Sea, without any minian settlements, this was the lycans' law—survival of the fittest.

◆

"...Strange."

"What's wrong, Brother?"

The odd phenomenon came as the pair were on the way back to the village.

"You smell blood?"

"Huh, now that you mention it..."

The two suddenly broke into a run. With his wounded right leg and arm, Heng lagged slightly behind Canute, but he still ran with all his strength. Even from a distance, he could see the warriors on guard duty weren't there.

"Hrm?"

It didn't take long for Heng to figure out where the sentries had gone.

They were embedded in the stone wall. Their eyes had rolled to the backs of their heads, and they were convulsing as foam bubbled from their mouths. There were even spots where they had been slammed into the wall so hard that the thick stone itself had broken.

"What happened?"

It was clear they had been slammed at frighteningly high speeds. The possibility of explosives crossed Heng's mind, but he couldn't smell any gunpowder. Neither could he imagine that the warriors entrusted with protecting the village would let a simple explosive get the better of them.

When they passed through the gate, they were greeted with something even more frightening.

"B-Brother."

"I know. This is..."

One warrior was pierced through a house's roof.

There was another lying on the ground with all four of their limbs bending in the wrong directions.

There were ten times as many who had coughed up blood and blacked out, as well as those who'd had their weapons (and extremities) shattered.

All the warriors in the village had either lost consciousness quite a while ago or could do little more than groan in pain. Every single person that Heng checked on had been rendered unable to fight.

What in the world.

The lookouts had been totally snuffed out.

A colossal wurm, a beast that would've proved too much for a pair of their assistant instructors, lay dead and leaking an unsettling amount of grayish-brown liquid. In other words—

Whatever it was, it didn't go that far with the Zehf warriors. Does that mean this enemy can still defeat this many of our warriors at once, without killing them? Impossible. It can't be.

Lycans greatly surpassed the technical skill and physical strength of any minian race soldier. The etiquette of taking down caravans or punitive forces solo was something carried by all the warriors above Heng's level, too.

A village of such powerful warriors was submerged in a sea of blood; not a single resident was spared. Less than half a day had passed since Heng and Canute had headed off to the day's training.

Heng found one of the warriors, just barely clinging to consciousness, and slapped their cheeks.

"What happened? Can you see? It's Heng of the Shallow Step."

"...That...that thing..."

Heng's comrade answered, gasping for air through broken teeth.

"That thing's... It's not right... No living creature, should be like that..."

"Be more specific. It would be a much more serious matter if a normal living creature had been able to defeat us so."

"B-but. Th-that thing, really didn't have any proper form."

"Is it a 'guest'?"

"...Yeah, b-but not from...outside the Sand Sea, but from inside..."

Sometimes there were eccentric freaks that would aim not for the library, but arrive seeking to destroy the village itself.

Punitive expeditions sent from cities beyond the Sand Sea, for example, and similar entities were called guests, but of course there were no examples in their tribe's history of any such attempts leaving this much damage in their wake.

Not only that, but the guest had come from *within the Sand Sea.*

"Curses!"

When Heng gritted his teeth in frustration, Canute jumped up and shouted.

"...*Eek!* Master?!"

"Canute?"

"Master... Master's...floating in the pond!"

"Don't be a fool. You're talking about the master. He surely must've thought up a new method of training."

"I—I see... So this is training that you can do even with your left leg broken, then."

Heng looked to see that their terrifying instructor was indeed floating belly up in the village's central reservoir.

Just as Canute had said, their left leg had the joint twisted in the opposite direction, clearly completely broke.

That's the master I know...

It was the same aging master as always, acting on their most dreadful whims. Heng tried to convince himself.

Of course he's not...

Then, standing at the bank of the reservoir was the murderer responsible—or at the very least, someone who seemed to have witnessed it.

Though it was a light-green substance, transparent like water, and in the shape of a rough circle, it was still a living creature.

"......An ooze."

"Indeed." The creature answered. Though they were only supposed to possess a limited intelligence, the ooze effortlessly spoke in the common language. Not only that, but it was using a pseudopod to flip through the pages of what looked to be an aged and worn-out book.

"Ooze. Name of Psianop. There should be someone here who recognizes that name. I want you to lead me to them."

"Nonsense. You're free to choose your future. Be reduced to the dew on Heng of the Shallow Step's blade or leave here as fast as you can. One or the other."

"Brother......!"

"You forgot the third option."

"What?"

Before a comeback could leave his mouth, a strange sting ran through both of Heng's knees.

Then came the quiet thud of the book hitting the ground.

It was fast. Too fast. Even his nerves couldn't respond fast enough.

Psianop, an ooze, previously perceived to be an unintelligent race, had already crept by Heng and stood behind him.

Unable to turn around to face the ooze, a faint chill began to slowly shiver through Heng. He didn't have any external wounds. He could tell that his knees' ligaments—and only the ligaments—were severed in two, almost as if they had been pierced by an invisible drill.

Canute screamed.

"Brother?!"

"...I could tell by the center of gravity on your first step. A martial form that shifts one's center, then. Two steps forward, diagonally to the left. One to the right. Misdirect the trajectory of my defenses, fatal blow with left claw. Am I correct in my estimation?"

"Impossible."

One step forward, diagonally to the left. That was as far as Heng's movements had gotten.

Speed unbecoming of an ooze. Not only that, it read and saw through the flow of the combat style he had put together, one that only existed within Heng's mind—and all from a single step.

There was no doubting that the attack to Heng's knee was a blunt strike. But what sort of martial tricks did it have beyond that? Did it read his mind? Or maybe it could see into the future. No matter what the explanation may have been, the reason didn't seem consistent with any normal ooze.

"I've come to fulfill a promise. A promise from twenty-one years ago. As long as that is so, I am in the right. Brown-haired one, will you challenge me, too?"

"*Aroon...* I—I can, I can—!"

"That's enough. The fight's over."

Interrupting them was a deep murmur, as if rumbling up from the depths of the earth.

"Oh……!"

Heng suddenly cast his eyes at the ground and venerated the voice coming from the inner sanctum. Now, with their instructor killed, there was only one warrior stronger than him who came to mind.

Assuming, of course, they truly lived and could act themselves.

"Honestly, I swear. Rude, disrespectful… *Koff*, you hopeless ruffian."

The lycan that emerged out of the inner sanctum's darkness hadn't a single hair on his body.

His parched dark skin was covered in wrinkles, and his emaciated physique, looking like little more than bone, was less than two-thirds of Heng's height.

Nevertheless and even with his injuries, Heng prostrated himself before him.

Any of the Zehf tribe warriors that were still conscious did the same.

"Been a long time, Psianop."

"…Twenty-one years all told, Neft the Nirvana."

"Well, with a body like this, I don't pay attention to the months and years."

"It's unnecessary. I'm counting."

Neft the Nirvana. All the Zehf warriors had built up their training and discipline in front of this legendary cadaver.

They drilled themselves to be worthy under his unflinching

yet harsh glares, feeling his silent pressure; and with this, the Zehf tribe had been able to grow so strong.

…But how? It shouldn't have been possible.

"My lord! You're able to move?!"

"Quiet."

The living idol of worship flicked his ears, looking deeply annoyed.

Then he turned to the inferior ooze and spoke.

"Your wish?"

"Right now. Right here. You'll bear witness with me."

Neft the Nirvana.

The First Party, the very first group to face off against the True Demon King.

Of the seven who challenged the True Demon King, there were only two counted as survivors—Romzo the Star Map and Neft the Nirvana.

In that case…

What about this all-too-abnormal ooze, attempting to challenge such a living legend as equals?

Where did it come from, and who were they?

◆

"…All of you still conscious right now," Neft said, an annoyed tone in his voice.

"You all have potential… I want you to believe that."

He bore his specialized weapons, thick, semicircular blades, in each hand. They resembled axes, but with an extremely primitive design, nothing more than a handle inside the open semicircle. Though the weapons that gave birth to all the Zehf tribes' martial forms, no warrior besides the founder Neft himself could perfectly display all the techniques of prototypical dual axes.

"Surely none of you are foolish enough to choose idleness when presented with the founder's skills before your eyes..."

No longer were any of Zehf's warriors allowed to remain unconscious.

Neft the Nirvana was going to fight.

Psianop was also deeply honing his own mind. The two fighters were already within melee range.

"A low kick."

Together with Psianop's murmur, the lycan's opening move was a low sweeping kick, mowing down the ooze's *feet*, the part of its surface connected to the ground. While the movements were clearly visible, they were over in the blink of an eye.

Psianop retreated back slightly and dodged. Before Neft could start moving, he needed to be outside the trajectory of his attacks. There wasn't a trace of wasted motion in Neft's movements.

It would be too slow to watch his initial motion before dodging. Psianop readied himself to guard against the next attack.

"—or so you want me to think, before keeping the same rotation speed, you'll hit me with the axes behind you. Not once..."

Neft's combat motion wasn't over yet. In order to cleave Psianop after dodging, he launched a surprise attack with an ax he had been holding behind his back. A thick circular blade, meant to hack and chop up opponents.

Much like it was for Heng's halberd, this was the fundamental base of the Zehf tribe's martial style—a weapon that could transfer rotatory movement from the waist up to the wrist, and that could serve as a shield as well.

"But twice."

Two noises—a shrill crack and a cacophonous splash—raced across the sky.

The wild ax slashes simply slid off the ooze's surface. How it managed to block the attacks and avoid harm completely were a total mystery.

The sound of a counterattack rang out. The ooze struck as blade crossed blade, faster than the eye could catch, as though aiming for a momentary break in his opponent's spin.

The emaciated lycan was blown away like autumn leaves. He, too, was uninjured.

On the ground where Neft landed was a geometric locus, like a bizarre and complex ripple. He owed his relatively safe landing to his exemplary defense training. He had completely mitigated the impact from the terrifying blow.

"Was my estimation correct, Nirvana? You'll never defeat me, decrepit as you are. If you don't believe me, come at me with every-thing you've got."

"Big words, slimeball. You think the passage of time is enough to age me? To make me wither?"

"Are you saying you haven't? After movements such as those?"

"*Grrr...* You know nothing of the Life Arts."

The lycan spun Word Arts, his voice rumbling from the depths of hell, exacerbating tension between them.

"*Weft wogm. Wymuf wonffeer. Wwrhey wat. Wengefhornef. Wutzeiheart.*" (To Neft's pulse. Return smoke to frozen drops. Pastel fresh green. Reversed trajectory sunlight. Circulate.)

Psianop didn't use the opening during the Word Arts incantation to attack. He knew his efforts would be fruitless, and being lured in by the opponent might very well cost him his life.

...More than anything, it was meaningless if he didn't force Neft to fully exert himself and use every last ounce of his strength. If Neft didn't go all out, the victory would feel hollow.

"My lord!"

"My lord...!"

"Silence."

The other lycans venerated their master, letting out primal growls.

There had been no change in Neft's gaunt and emaciated form. Instead, as a result of regaining his usual bodily functions, his leathery skin sagged even further, and he seemed to be growing even weaker.

At least that's how it appeared *on the outside.*

The fighting spirit he radiated was another matter entirely. Not merely greater than the combined powers and fighting spirit of the rest of the Zehf tribe, but a great deal beyond that as well.

Heng of the Shallow Step looked at his little brother-in-arms. He was anxious he might be dead. Soon his apprehensions were proven true, with Canute remaining still, foam bubbling from his mouth.

"My lord…!"

It was not the sort of vital energy that was visible from the outside. Touch. Taste. Heart rate. He was willingly dulling any and all bodily functions not wholly devoted to battle.

This was the undying Life Arts user, a standout even among the rest of the First Party.

Neft the Nirvana had, over twenty long years, remained completely immobile as he stored his energy.

"You can see now… In the time it takes you to count to eight hundred and fifty, know me as the same Neft the Nirvana you knew from days past."

"Then, with everything I've got, I'm going to kill you five times."

"*Grrr.* The immortal never die—"

Shwoop.

The ooze's gelatinous body squelched across the ground.

He timed his movement with Neft's first step forward. They were within contact distance.

Then came the bombardment.

A heavy overlapping sound, that could only be described as such, echoed the moment his pseudopod made direct contact with Neft. This time, however, Neft wasn't blown away.

No—he *couldn't* be blown away.

It was as if a surging tidal wave crashed with all its might into a huge tree. Without Neft's extraordinary skills, the force would've been enough to blast a person apart, limb from limb, leaving nothing behind.

However, the giant tree that had successfully taken the full impact again withstood the destructive power and made an unbelievable move.

Every party of his body—from his left arm to his pulverized spine—contorted in unbelievable ways.

If forced to describe the noise, it sounded like a short buzzing.

It was the sound of an eighth of the ooze's body being instantly blasted away, along with the ground beneath him.

The extremely fast direct hits came one after the other, creating an awful din.

"......*Kah!*"

"......!"

The two combatants reeled, regrouping after their fierce exchange of blows.

They simultaneously condemned the other.

"*Wutzeiheart.*" (Circulate.) "Dual ax style: flicker."

"Eight Extremities, Persistent Mountain Lean."

With that single phrase, Neft's skeleton was instantly reconfigured. He had *purposefully taken* the previous attack, after all. Psianop couldn't cleanly settle things with his intense single attack because the counterattack came after an attack that would've killed any other living creature.

Neft's Life Arts, capable of this high-speed healing, both without causing any deformities or circulatory shock, were beyond the realm of comprehension for anyone who laid eyes on it.

However, the technique that Psianop produced with precision moments prior was just as much of a system that stood beyond the comprehension of anyone else.

Similarly, the technique that Psianop performed was from a martial discipline outside anyone else's understanding.

"I'm unfamiliar with that technique. *Grrr...* So that's the strength you've amassed over these twenty-one years, is it?"

"That's right. All that time, I've been learning and training inside the sand labyrinth."

For the past several dozen years, there wasn't a single minian race that had reached the sand labyrinth.

Nor did the lycans themselves show any interest whatsoever in what existed inside its walls, either.

In which case, what if *there was already someone there* in the labyrinth?

What if there was a person who never took a step outside, single-mindedly focused on amassing all the knowledge within, more valuable than an entire country?

"I spent two years on the first tome I picked up...... But I learned everything."

The intelligent creatures of this world were inferior at leaving behind written words and deciphering them.

In the past, several visitors had tried to establish a fixed, unified alphabet, but to this day, the writing used among the common people was the simple script of the Order.

Much like the people of the Beyond being unable to utilize the true power of Word Arts, for those who had lived in a natural state of being able to speak and communicate across varied linguistic systems, the establishment of a systematic written language was, in practice, an extremely difficult concept.

Though visitors of the past left behind their transgressive knowledge in book form, the ones capable of comprehending their content would be limited to a select stratum of intellectuals, like the scholars of Nagan, for example. However.

A primitive, amorphous life-form, one that normally would possess a limited degree of intelligence, had done exactly that.

"...Amusing. I admire your tenacity, Psianop!"

"I'm stronger than you!"

There was a whirring noise in the air; the sound of the dual axes rotating.

Neft was now performing his inescapable weapon techniques in peak physical condition.

Psianop did not deflect this series of attacks. His amorphous physical body was chipped away, yet despite this, he continued evading, without losing his core at the center of his viscous form.

Guarding. Parrying. Gelatinous flesh was sliced and scattered.

Taking advantage of a small gap in the onslaught, Psianop released a lethal jab. The lycan shifted his body immediately before the ooze's blow could land a vital blow. Thus, Psianop missed his mark—Neft's heart. Bits of dried skin and bloody flesh were torn from his body, but Neft's life was not yet forfeit. Both axes closed in from his blind spots. Psianop attempted to evade.

In that moment, a kick connected with his gelatinous body.

He couldn't be crushed. The pseudopod aimed at the sole of

Neft's foot, conversely shattered everything up to his waist with the impact.

Once again, Psianop had successfully predicted his opponent's move.

In the middle of a fight too quick to even catch one's breath, he remained two steps ahead.

"Cold Power."

"......*Ngh, wutzeiheart!*" (Circulate!)

Why was Neft the Nirvana of the First Party, with such an extreme degree of martial prowess, allowing the ooze to counter-attack as much as he was?

Even for Heng of the Shallow Step, it took him far too long to arrive at a conclusion.

It doesn't have any arms or legs.

It was a hard fact to accept that there could be such a terrifying martial artist.

There wasn't any visible footwork in Psianop's techniques. They were legs that generated action from the earth using his whole body's surface connected to the ground, able to step in unexpected directions without the restrictions brought by two legs.

There were no joints behind its strikes. They flowed like liquid, without any limits to its range of motion or any advance indication of the incoming blow.

Neft the Nirvana was following along with this frightening hand-to-hand combat prowess, relying entirely on his godlike sixth sense.

Before this battle, was there anyone who knew such potential dwelled within the body of the base and primitive ooze?

Without question, Psianop was the only one within the annals of history to ever be capable of exhibiting said potential.

What sort of obsession could've resulted in this degree of focused study?

"*Grrr...* Outstanding... To think that former encumbrance could progress so far..."

"It will take time to repel the left ax... In that case, another kick—"

But before Psianop could complete the thought, the ooze was blown back by an almighty strike. His flight split the two-story stone wall behind him in half.

There likely wasn't anyone alive who could perceive the course of events from Psianop deflecting the ax to being sent flying with a kick. The speed of their previous movements was on another plane of existence.

"That estimation of yours is right on the mark."

He was growing stronger. The First Party member, already at heights no other could reach, was aiming higher.

Slowly circulating the vital force he had built up over the long years, Neft the Nirvana had temporarily acquired physical abilities that surpassed his maximum potential.

Barely protecting his nucleus from being smashed or cleaved in two, the ooze dropped to the ground with a splat.

"Why? Why...?"

"...*Grrr.* Speak up now. My hearing's not great."

"......Why...did you leave me behind?"

The legendary warrior did not answer. His wrinkled face twisted even further into a sneer.

Neft believed it had been the obvious decision. He needed to make Psianop understand that once again.

Even now, after so much time had passed, Neft remembered his comrades in the First Party. He could recall the faces of those he had lost, never to return again.

...There was Alena the Benighted White Wind. Izick the Chromatic. Yugo the Guillotine.

There were friends at times, and enemies at others, but he could still remember the names and voices of the seven members, spoken of as legends. Though all their ideals and objectives were different, just once, at the end of their journey, they combined their powers. It was all for the sake of putting down the True Demon King. That's what the world believed, at least.

But it wasn't the whole story...

In truth, there was an *eighth* member of the party. Neft had never forgotten his name, not even for a moment.

"Are you going to make me repeat my past warning...? Psianop. You are absolutely no match for the True Demon King."

"*Popoperopa. Parpepy. Peep por ppe. Por pupeon. Perpipeor.*" (To Psianop's pulsation. Suspended ripple. Tie the sequence. Full large moon. Circulate.) "...That—"

The ooze chanted regenerative Word Arts. They were unmistakably the same kind of Life Arts as Neft the Nirvana's own. He had even acquired the techniques of the powerful apex master he witnessed in the past.

Twenty-one years. Neft wasn't the only one whose thoughts harkened back to the days of yore.

"That's wrong, Neft the Nirvana. Both then and now."

"……"

"……I'd be able to win. Back then… If I had been there, we would've been victorious. Isn't that right, Neft?! I want to believe so now more than ever!"

"Cretin!"

Neft dashed to pepper the ooze with more lethal ax blows.

A slightly rare, and somewhat eloquent, weakling ooze—and nothing more.

All the party members believed it was the obvious decision to come to.

"Dual-axes style—Troubled Star!"

For the one left behind by these legends, what harbored emotion made him able to continue his limitless, devoted study?

The First Party was defeated by the True Demon King. Ending up all too powerless, like the many heroes who followed after them. Simply wasted away, together with the hopes of the people of the time they carried with them.

Nevertheless, for him…for the eighth member, Psianop.

"Neft. I told you."

That battle still wasn't over.

Even now, with the True Demon King long since slain.

The bygone era still wasn't over for him and him alone.

Psianop's extended pseudopod was slashed during Neft's spin and scattered about.

No—it was a pseudopod. He could grow pseudopods, even

ones feigning attacks, ad infinitum. Hand-to-hand combat choices that demanded endless diverging paths to consider. Neft the Nirvana had fought too much under the enormous mental strain.

Did I go too far forward?

Negligence.

Reinforcing his nerves to their maximum potential, Neft could now read the flow of battle to its end point.

The leg that stepped forward tread on the pseudopod that stretched out just before it. To ensure Psianop would be unable to dodge—and blown apart with his next attack. The lunging ax in the other hand missed its mark on the ooze's vitals, as if the direction of the attack was being pulled toward his own.

Psianop, at this point, was using three arms.

For an ooze, that wasn't the end of it.

His fourth arm was now touching Neft's stomach.

"I told you I'd kill you five times!"

A staggering concussive tremor echoed throughout the lycan's body.

He was forced upward at an angle, defying gravity, as if dragged into the sky by the impact.

There was no violent striking sound nor an explosive increase in speed...

...because the full force of the impact resonated *internally*.

"*Hyaauck!*"

Neft the Nirvana coughed up a large amount of grayish-brown liquid.

With this lethal blow, unlike anything the ooze had unleashed up until that point, he realized then that Psianop had been going easy on him.

What he vomited up was his own liquified viscera.

"Spit out your brain next. Roaring Liquid Heavy Decapitation...!"

"Wutzeiheart..." (Circulate...)

Neft understood, too. For the next exchange, there would be no time to switch to the counterattack.

"Low Palm!"

"Gnnngh... Wutzeiheart." (Circulate.)

Psianop steadily remained at close range.

His opponent, Neft, continued to recover with his unreasonable Life Arts, and yet—

"Spiral Knifehand!"

"Wutzeiheart..." (Circulate......)

"Linked Leg!"

"Wutzeiheart..." (Circulate......)

"Thirteen Steps!"

"................"

The red sun was sinking red below the horizon.

That day, the warriors of the Zehf tribe witnessed two spectacles.

They witnessed a true legend, Neft the Nirvana, alive and well.

And they witnessed that very Neft...overwhelmed by an ooze appearing out of nowhere, until finally collapsing before him.

"……I've finally come to keep my promise, Neft the Nirvana," the ooze said, amid the sandy gusts.

In the past, Neft was considered one of the strongest beings in the world, and yet the ooze had laid him low.

"I promised that one day…I'd grow stronger. I promised I would catch up to you all."

The True Demon King was long gone.

The opponent who he was supposed to bring down at the end of twenty-one years of arduous training had disappeared from the world.

Psianop had learned this from a wyvern that had visited the sand labyrinth two big months prior.

The pack that Neft established to ensure this ooze's isolation, the ooze their party had set free, had long lost its meaning. Even if Psianop left the Sand Sea, he wouldn't go off to his death by challenging the Demon King.

It was an era where everything had ended.

"……Brilliant."

Lying on his back, the lycan founder's face beamed.

He looked to be savoring his defeat, making up for all the lost years.

"……"

The Zehf warriors, still able to move, gathered together to help their leader to his feet.

Even after disgracing themselves with their pitiful defeat, even though their Hero had already lost to the Demon King from the start, Neft the Nirvana was their martial arts instructor whom they respected above all others.

Psianop felt the same way as well.

"Who am I supposed to defeat now? Who's next? What can I do to wash away the regrets from that day?"

"Aureatia."

Neft answered. Even when isolated from the outside world, the rumors had reached this pack.

…According to them, the Hero who defeated the True Demon King, identity unknown to all, would appear at the Royal Games there.

"Head to Aureatia. If you believe you could beat the True Demon King…go and show…that you can defeat the one who slayed the True Demon King."

"……"

"Psianop. Do you have a second name?"

Psianop stopped briefly and answered.

"…No. Ever since that day I traveled with you seven, I've always been and have remained Psianop."

"I see."

Neft smiled as he was carried in his disciples' portable shrine.

Though covered in wrinkles, unrecognizable and withered away, it was the same smile Neft had worn on that fateful day.

"From now on, call yourself the Inexhaustible Stagnation."

Psianop didn't look back toward his master.

Picking up his dropped book, he started off toward the next opponent he needed to defeat.

Thus, his reply simply echoed out from behind him.

"......Gladly!"

He mastered the extensive and numerous martial arts of the Beyond, lost to this world.

He possessed endlessly branching combat abilities, rendering strikes, throws, chokes, and even the reading of his own moves ineffective.

He was capable of launching strikes that brought true instant death, impossible to perform with a commonplace body construction.

Among the First Party, glorified by all, he was the final member who still knew no defeat.

Grappler. Ooze.

Psianop the Inexhaustible Stagnation.

CHAPTER 2 ◀▣▶ The Gokashae Sand Sea

The silhouette of the lone minia, walking across the sea of hot sand, rose into view, outlined by the sunlight behind him.

He had a small wooden box on his back, and there was a strange instrument dangling from a belt around his neck.

His plump, round face was hidden beneath a traveler's hat to block out the sun. Though he was a part of the caravan recently raided by lycans, he had been completely left behind by the group doubling back to the nearest settlement—because among those in the caravan, he was the only one who didn't retreat from the spot of the raid, heading in *another direction* instead.

"Whew... Yeaaah, this temperature's pretty brutal. I might seriously end up dying out here. Is my body gonna last...?"

Although he dabbed his forehead with his handkerchief, largely out of habit, the sweat that appeared on his brow immediately evaporated in the hot, dry air.

"I shouldn't have come out here. Can't gather any data; the caravan's been raided... Haven't had a failure like this in a while."

"...Is that ooze all right? How can it survive in an environment like this?"

Though the man had appeared to be speaking to himself, there came a reply. The second voice rang out from the wooden box on the man's back.

This Gokashae Sand Sea was a remote area that not even radzio transmissions could reach, and the box that the bantam man shouldered wasn't even big enough for a leprechaun to fit inside. Everything about the situation seemed unusual.

"I'm not too knowledgeable myself, but oozes apparently have the same sort of perspiration system that lowers cell temperature through heat vaporization. But with ooze, that regulatory function isn't automatic, you see... Apparently, if the ooze isn't accustomed to arid climates, they won't even last half a day before shriveling up. I don't have a clue about that ooze, though."

"Hmmm. You're well-informed, aren't you?"

"I mean, I've been doing this work for a long time. I am a pro, after all."

"But didn't you fail this time?"

"*Ha-ha-ha*, well, you can expect some ups and downs when you've been at it this long."

He was looking for an ooze. A shura that surpassed the strength of the world-renowned First Party. From where the armed caravan had been attacked, he followed after the lycan's cleverly hidden tracks... And then arriving at the Zehf tribe's village, Yukiharu learned his trip to collect material would be a fool's errand.

He needed only to watch from afar to see the person he needed to question get laid low.

"...Neft the Nirvana. I was just a bit too late, huh."

"There's one other person left behind from the First Party, right? I've heard that Romzo the Star Map is living in Aureatia."

"Romzo, huh? *Ha-ha-ha.* Yeah, well... He's not gonna work."

The man laughed dryly in response to the voice from the wood box. When it came to negotiating and bargaining, Romzo the Star Map was in some ways an even more dangerous person than Neft the Nirvana. Something the man was confident about.

"If the survivors of the First Party aren't going to work......that only leaves The Land of The End, huh? Boy, I'd really like to avoid going there if I can help it..."

"If Romzo won't do, then there probably aren't any other leads on the True Demon King. I mean, witnessing the Demon King first is one thing...and then to live to safely tell the tale. No one but the First Party's done it."

"...The Land of The End is a scary place, y'know."

The Land of The End, rumored to be the final resting place of the True Demon King. A mysterious unknown monster was said to lurk there, thwarting any and all reconnaissance teams sent out by both the New Principality or Aureatia.

"You know Alimo Row? It's a village right next to The Land of The End, see. Nothing but one terrible, brutal incident after another out there... But I mean... That's really the only place we're gonna find a lead."

"Someone's a coward."

The unidentified voice coming from the wood box was tinged with exasperation.

"…But whenever you start talking like that, you usually go through with it anyway, Yukiharu."

"*Ha-ha-ha*, guess so."

A turning point for the world, with legends and champions fighting each other—and the minian realm under control by Aureatia. Arresting the advancement into this tumultuous age with an overwhelming power was something completely unknown to anyone, yet simultaneously a singular terror that no one could ever forget.

There was someone in this world who was trying to investigate the Demon King's true form.

"I'm a pro, after all."

The man was a visitor. His name was Yukiharu the Twilight Diver.

It was the day after a heavy snowfall, a very unusual event in Alimo Row.

Opening up the door, I discovered that the almshouse plaza was completely covered in white. It was unlike anything I had ever seen before; the sheer brilliance of the snowy landscape was too much for these elderly eyes.

Even now, the memories of that day are still fresh in my mind.

I woke up shortly before sunrise, but by that point, there was already a single path made in the white garden. A long, continuous path into town, shoveled out of the snow.

I've seen a great many types in my time, including gigants and dwarves, but as far I as knew, there was only one person who could manage such perseverance and strength-testing, yet honest, work. The heavy piles of snow reflected the depths of his martyrdom.

I could see the gray-skinned ogre come into view, walking into town down the road he had cleared all by himself.

Uhak. The sole family I had.

"Ah, thank you, Uhak. Were you cold?"

I always spoke to Uhak.

Though, even now, I wasn't sure if that was the correct thing to do.

Coming home, he carried a white wolf pup in his arms. A tiny life, eyes closed and trembling.

"I see... You found this little one, did you? Fantastic work, Uhak. I'm sure anyone afraid of wolves will be relieved with this."

I offered admiration at the justness of his deeds and took the pup from his large palms...

...so that I could dash it against the stone steps, killing it instantly.

I remember the sight of warm blood pouring from its split skull, melting the white snow behind.

To this day, I haven't been able to get the look in Uhak's eyes out of my head.

Why was Uhak mourning it? It was something I've continued to ponder.

It should have been the obvious outcome, extinguishing the life that would surely grow to threaten the lives of others one day.

I simply did what anyone else in this world would have done, without showing an ounce of mercy.

It was just...a soulless beast, totally unlike those of us blessed with Word Arts, so why......?

I met Uhak during the season when the air grew dry.

Everything must have started when I responded to the Alimo Row villagers' request for counsel during service.

"...Priest. I beg you, Cunodey the Ring Seat. We ask that you grant them the blessing of Word Arts in our stead."

"Of course, anything for the neighbors you've gathered together. Can I ask you to fill me in on the details?"

"An ogre appeared in the forest on the main road—a man-eating monster twice as tall as any human. We've gathered up the brave and willing, and tomorrow morning they're heading to put the ogre down. Mother Cunodey... May I ask you to use the power of the Order's Word Arts to ensure these precious lives are not lost?"

Of course, the priests of the Order studied Word Arts intimately to learn the miracles of the Word-Maker, who brought them the language universally understood by all—and not to instead use their power for combat or protection.

However, I couldn't expound on this to followers seeking my aid. During the age of the True Demon King, no one was able to escape from war and bloodshed, and everyone used this power, bested to live a moral life, for battle. The members of the Order were no exception.

This village, the closest to The Land of The End, where the Demon King perished, had been deeply scarred by the age of darkness. Priests fell amid the war and the Demon King's induced madness, the lively voices of the almshouse children went silent, and I alone remained as the only official priest in this small hamlet's church.

For the church followers, this poor old woman was their sole means of spiritual support, while for myself, their presence was the only light I had to tether my own faith.

"I understand. I don't know if these old bones can aid everyone like you all, or even I myself, hope to. However, if it will provide even the tiniest peace of mind, then I see no reason not to go."

"Oh, thank you... Thank you so much, Mother Cunodey."

Ogres. The largest, strongest, and scariest of all the monstrous races.

When I was little, I saw one up close just once. Within the forest where we were climbing trees to play, a large monster with dark-brown skin crossed entered our field of vision. It was filled with hunger and rage, enough to clearly tell from our spot up in the tree branches. If it happened to find us, its thick arms could've easily snapped our arboreal hiding place.

There was something dangling out of the sides of the ogre's mouth, and my friend hiding next to me whispered that maybe it was the hunter Jokza who had gone missing two days prior. I... simply watched the predator disappear deeper into the forest, dyed red in the setting sun, experiencing for the first time in my life the fear of imminent death.

It wasn't an evening sky back then. The morning sun cast its rays into the forest around the main road, with wild rabbits and deer off somewhere grazing on grass.

The hunters didn't seem to fear what awaited them, and I was surprised by their quick and nimble steps as they bounded over fallen trees and small streams.

For me, simply getting solid footing in the dirt without falling over took everything I had, and matching their quick gait was all but impossible.

"Ogres are really intelligent, you see."

One of the hunters appealed to his compatriots with words of warning.

"It might be waiting to ambush us. I've heard stories of some pouncing down on people from up in the trees."

The warning was unnecessary, as the hunters were paying close attention to the whole area around us and guarded me, their priest escort, from being exposed to any danger.

Thus, it was not I who first laid eyes on the figure, but one of the hunters. When I followed the hunter's sights, urging everyone to take notice, I spied a gray ogre sitting beneath a large tree.

The ogre seemed to be in the middle of a meal, sitting with their back to us.

While they looked somewhat smaller than the red ogre from my youth, even when seated, they were taller than anyone of us, and casually lying beside them was a well-worn wooden club.

"We'll shoot from here and use that tree as cover. A few of you go around to the other side to stop them from running behind the tree. Mother Cunodey... Can you protect us with Word Arts when it comes dashing our way?"

"...I can. But there's something a little bit strange about that ogre."

"What do you mean?"

"Is that really an ogre that terrorizes people?"

An ogre that terrorized the people. Even remembering my own words, I was clearly in a terrible state of confusion. After all, the word *ogre* itself was synonymous with murder.

Indeed, that was why even I couldn't explain the strange feeling I had.

I should've been just as frightened of the man-eating ogre, but at that moment, for some reason, I felt that something was off.

"Wait a moment. If I could just get a little bit closer..."

"Mother Cunodey! It's too dangerous; it'll see you!"

It was surely foolish of me to approach an ogre just to try confirming this uneasy feeling I had. I realized later that my conduct might've led the courageous villagers to sacrifice their lives to help me. It was shameful.

However, if I didn't follow my hunch in that moment, I might've never noticed.

He was eating nuts and berries. I didn't know ogres ate anything other than meat.

After all was said and done, I remembered getting glimpses of wild rabbits and deer upon entering the forest. The animals' behavior was not that of prey being pursued by a predator. That realization, though subconscious at the time, might've been what guided me to my hunch.

Unlike the ogre I saw in my youth, this one wasn't enveloped by the scent of blood and death. In fact, there were even rabbits coming and going from the burrow near where he sat.

"...He's already noticed us."

He was calm and quiet, and his back was stock-still, enough to believe he might've been sleeping, but I was confident in my hunch.

"The reason he hasn't harmed us is because we haven't harmed him. Please call back the ones you send around to the other side immediately."

"But Mother Cunodey... That thing's still an ogre. The monstrous races eat minia! It's been that way since the beginning of time."

"Nevertheless, it still has a soul."

The Orders said as much. That this was the reason the Word-Maker bestowed the miracle of Word Arts to the races of the world.

Thanks to this wonderful blessing, none of us were alone anymore. All creatures with a soul were a member of one big family.

Before I knew it, I had left the villagers behind and was now within arm's length of the ogre.

His extremely pale, almost white pupils stared back at me.

Frightened and bewildered by my own actions, I mustered up the best smile I could and addressed the ogre.

"Good day to you, our new neighbor. I'm a priest in the village just up the road from here. I, Cunodey the Ring Seat, w-wish to... to save you."

I wanted to save him. Though, at that moment, which one of us was really the one who needed to be saved?

There was no answer. The ogre didn't try to harm me, nor did he ignore me... He simply sat there in silence.

Even when I continued to speak, the only answer that came to me was silence and his watchful eyes.

The ogre tried reaching out his hand but immediately lowered it.

Almost as if my thoughts were reaching him, but he was unable to find the means to return them.

"It can't be... Can you..."

This was Uhak.

An ogre, all alone, born into the world shouldering an entirely inconceivable disability.

"...not hear me?"

◆

The first thing I attempted was explaining to everyone that no villagers had gone missing in the past big month, and there hadn't been any direct accounts of someone being attacked by an ogre.

It was not an easy course of events to make everyone trust a minia-eating ogre—especially when he couldn't understand speech or offer his own defense. Though there were examples of the monstrous races mixing in with minian society, it was almost always as either blood-drenched mercenaries or assassins. Most people couldn't possibly believe an ogre was capable of living a life totally divorced from evil and maliciousness.

Nevertheless, through the doctrine that the villagers and I followed, I patiently preached that a hand of charity should be outstretched to anyone lost and in pain, regardless of their sins, and I was able to convince them to allow him to be sheltered—or in the words of the villagers, "placed under observation"—at the almshouse.

Mysteriously, there was nothing abnormal about his sense of hearing itself, and the only thing inaudible to him was the language of Word Arts.

"Uhak. If you've lived without language all this time, then I'm going to grant you a second name right now. You shall henceforth be Uhak the Silent."

Silent. In the days of old, among a group of brothers, arrogant due to their Word Arts' abilities gifted by the Word-Maker, one of the siblings refrained from speech and was able to prevent conflict between many of the races without saying a word. His name was Melyugre the Silent. The First Party, renowned by all, including myself, also contained an individual, Fralik the Heaven, who was said to have had his throat crushed at a young age, and so he never spoke.

We had all known the essence of the Word Arts' power. That their true nature wasn't something being *said*, but Word Arts were used to communicate exactly what was in our thoughts.

"I'm sure. I'm sure there'll come a day when they'll accept it. Both that you can't speak and that you can't hear."

Just as his second name suggested, he didn't use the strength he was born with for conflict, but he faithfully helped me, handling the various jobs that an elderly woman like myself couldn't manage.

Even without being able to use language, it didn't take long for me to understand he was an ogre that showed no desire for futile conflict and was able to exhibit consideration for the hearts of others.

Citing sheltering Uhak as the excuse, the number of villagers who visited the church dropped drastically, but I wondered how many of the villagers knew that whenever someone would come to offer their prayers, Uhak would make sure to hide away somewhere, to keep from frightening them.

"You need to learn how to write. If you can't speak with your mouth, you need to learn a way to express your thoughts and feelings to others."

Teaching the Order's script to him, unable to convey anything with words, was a difficult task, unlike anything else I had experienced in my long life.

I started with silver coins. The characters for *silver coins* themselves, the characters to show how many of them to use at the market, as well as the character of *silver* itself and the one to express a circular shape. From the beginning, it was a very difficult journey.

Soaking tree bark in liquid ink and spreading old children's clothes, no longer in use, over a plank, I remember trying to teach him the script every day late into the night.

Speechless though he was, Uhak was neither stupid nor lazy, and he diligently focused on learning this new knowledge. The speed of his progress was marvelous, and he had worked through all the Order script I was able to teach him within the first three small months.

Somewhere along the way, the silent ogre had turned into the valuable family member I needed in my life.

Ina. Nofelt. Rivieh. Kuze. Imos. Nerka... The children—breaking windows every time they played, making a mess of the shrubbery and plantings the day after my pruning, always causing me headaches, making me laugh—were all gone.

The other priests who devoted themselves to their work in the Order with me, benevolently helping people in times of need, were also all asleep beneath the earth.

This eccentric ogre that showed up in my lonesome daily life was like a son to me in some ways, as well as a compatriot protecting the faith together with me.

Uhak was able to subsist without ever eating meat, having plain beans and nuts for every meal.

On the first day of every big month, he would go into the forest to gather just enough food for his own nourishment—no more, no less.

First thing every morning, he would finish cleaning the almshouse and the chapel, offer a wordless prayer to the Word-Maker, and bring in firewood and sheep's milk, always performing his tasks alone.

After he learned script, he'd get absorbed in the books left behind by the other priests, and whenever I used script to quiz him, he'd be able to immediately search for and produce the answer no matter which passage of the Word-Maker's teaching was in question.

"…You understand why exactly we all study the teachings of the Word-Maker, right?"

There was one occasion where Uhak saved a child who fell from a cliff and twisted his ankle.

However, his ogre physique terrified the child, and while he lived in this church, Uhak was ultimately never able to receive the trust and gratitude he deserved.

Whenever I'd write in script to express myself to him, I would always speak to him, too. Much like how we can speak to the wind and earth, I believed that, though he might be unable to hear me, there was a definitive power held in Word Arts spoken from the heart.

Was even that truly the right thing to do? Looking back, I wasn't sure anymore.

"Priests are people who dispel curses. Sometimes we are able to clear away the shadows that sink into a person's heart through our words…through our will. That's why language is so sacred, and Word Arts are our blessing… But, Uhak. You alone……were born without the gift of language. Despite your throat and ears working just fine."

Uhak remained bowed to the ground. I'd heard that ogres were a much more delicate race than the minia took them for. Perhaps this was true for that red ogre, too. Even on that day of my

childhood, perhaps there was someone, somewhere who could've saved his soul.

If only ogres could have been recognized as priests. Why, there wasn't any follower more modest and pious than he was.

"I don't know if that was Word-Maker's will or atonement for some sin. But even without any speech, you have a desire to help others. No one can ever take that away from you."

I was happy. I was always being soothed and comforted by the warmth in your heart.

That's why there wasn't any need to consider any of what you did as sinful.

"Uhak. You have a soul inside you. A soul just the same as anyone else's."

No matter what terrible things the embers of the Demon King brought about on that windy day.

Even if, from that day on, I lost the meaning of my own faith.

You were my precious family.

◆

Recording the events that happened that day could have served to damage Uhak's honor.

However, I knew very well that Uhak himself didn't wish to lie or cover up what happened. Furthermore, in order to leave behind a nugget of truth I accidently witnessed that day to someone, it was impossible to avoid touching on that blood-drenched incident.

Around the time the sun had progressed past its zenith, a small set of clouds had closed in on the far-off mountain outlines.

I was in the midst of drawing water from the well, when I saw a thin wisp of smoke rising off in the direction of the village.

"Uhak. Uhak, look."

Although he couldn't hear my words, he surmised something had happened by the tone and rhythm of my footsteps—the only thing Uhak couldn't hear was Word Arts speech—and immediately came out into the church courtyard.

Was it a fire or a signal? I prayed that it was simply children playfully making a bonfire as a prank. I hastened to the village, Uhak pulling my carriage along.

As we approached, the disquieting atmosphere on the main road grew denser and denser.

Birds in every direction, feathers and flesh getting caught in branches and torn off.

None of the wild rabbits were hidden in their holes, instead standing stock-still in the middle of the road, gazing at the sky.

I had seen animals in a similar state before. Back when the True Demon King was alive. That vague terror, making absolutely anything and everything go mad.

When we drew closer to the village, a stretch of bloodstains spanned across the area, as if drawn by a thick finger, and I could see the smears continue all the way into the village.

I strongly wanted to avoid thinking about what had come to the village and what was happening there, but I couldn't communicate to Uhak to stop the carriage.

"Mother Cunodey! You can't go into the village right now!"

One of the villagers who had escaped blocked the carriage, their face growing pale.

Their clothes were stained with someone's blood and flecks of soot, and they gave an account of the situation.

"I—I… I know that woman! It's Belka the Rending Quake! No one can beat her! Even she's gone mad! It's the Demon King… That's for sure…"

"…Please try to calm down. In times of distress, we all need to help each other. I have the sacred protection of Word Arts, and Uhak is with me as well. What is going on?"

"Belka… Belka the Rending Quake. The champion who went to slay the Demon King… I thought all of them had died…"

The elderly craftsman's lips trembled, and he tightly shut his eyes.

"She lied. She couldn't just die. She came back, back from The Land of The End… She came back, and now she's gone mad. She's nothing but a monster now."

I patted him on the back, and after speaking some words of comfort to calm him down, I urged Uhak to hurry with the carriage.

The dreadful spectacle came into view soon after. The blue storehouse roofs that always greeted me at the village entrance were being smashed by a palm from above, scattering into splinters.

The owner of the ginormous hand stretched up high into the sky, towering over all the buildings in the village.

Belka the Rending Quake. If the craftsman's story was right,

she was a gigant who traveled to slay the True Demon King......
now a shadow of her former self.

They say there were only two people to ever return *alive* from
an encounter with the True Demon King.

"H-help. Help. I can hear it...! I can still hear that voice! It's
awful! Help! *Aaaaugh!!*"

Her insane bellowing alone was enough to torment my ears
and mind, and her colossal straight cleaver, appearing to have
been used several times on Belka herself, was smeared with the
crushed villagers' blood and entrails, glistening with a red luster.

"*B-bbberruka io arr.*" (F-from Belka to Alimo earth.) "*Welllln
mmetttt.*" (Wriggling swarming shadow.) "*...Help...*" "*llllosse
aanettt.*" (Origin of steel.) "*Nooorstems.*" (Smashing wave.) "*...I-I'm
scared... I can't take the terror...!*" "*Uiomtestop!*" (Hatch!)

At Belka's feet, a number of small anthill-like mounds thrust
up from out of the ground.

I felt a foreboding about her frightening Word Arts and immediately hid behind the general store building...before realizing I
hadn't brought Uhak with me.

"Uhak!"

No matter how desperately I shouted, words were the only
thing Uhak couldn't hear.

He was standing near a crushed water mill...and was enveloped in the mound's destruction, exploding in horrible flames
and light.

Horse corpses were easily sent flying, and the frame of the
watchtower was broken and collapsed in half. The pools of blood

went bone-dry in an instant, and the wooden outer wall burst into flames on its own just from the heat of the aftermath.

I didn't understand what sort of Word Arts Belka the Rending Quake used, but I was sure it was some sort of Life Arts, generating something from the ground that exploded in a mix of thunder and flames.

"Uhak! Oh my... Impossible...!"

Uhak was safe. At the very middle of the destructive wave, he was totally unharmed.

Not a single scratch.

I couldn't believe my eyes. There was nothing around to shield him, and Uhak hadn't moved a single inch, yet there wasn't a single scratch, a single singe on his gray skin.

No matter how sturdy his body may have been, was such a thing even possible? I believed I had at least an understanding of what was and wasn't possible in this world.

"*A-augh... Hnaaaugh...* The voice... Make it stop... Help me...!"

The crazed gigant looked out over the survivors with murky, unfocused eyes and picked up a mother, gasping her final breaths, half her body blown off, and chewed on her.

Each time she bit down on the thing gigants generally weren't supposed to eat, she'd cough, spilling blood from her lips, and the fact that even this didn't faze Belka spoke to the depths of her madness.

"Enough! Belka the Rending Quake! The True Demon King is no longer in these lands! The thing you fear, the thing tormenting you, doesn't exist anywhere anymore!"

"...................Lies," the gigant answered as the bones of the ground-up villagers gashed the inside of her own throat.

At that moment......deep down, I could barely contain my desire to run away. Unlike my dead comrades, in truth, I was not a fine, upstanding priest in the depths of my soul.

It was simply the fact that, if Uhak stood there without running away, it compelled me to do the same myself.

"Then, this voice... Inside my head, it's still there. I can s-sense...the Demon King...! Th-they're...still alive!"

"No! There is no voice! We need to fight against the fear in our own hearts! If you doubt, fear, hate, and kill everything, then even with the True Demon King's death, it's like that era never ended! Please, you need to take back that heart of a champion! Belka!"

Belka was next to speak. They were words of murder.

"F-from Belka to Alimo earth... Wriggling swarming shadow... origin of steel. Smashing—"

"From Cunodey to Alimo wind. Waterfall flow, shadow of the eye, breaking twig! Contain!"

Before her Word Arts of destruction finished, I needed to invoke Power Arts to protect myself.

We both changed our Word Arts at the same time—and then.

Then...nothing happened at all.

I couldn't use Word Arts—an absolutely impossible, completely inconceivable occurrence.

Our Word Arts incantations hadn't failed. However, neither Belka's ground transformation nor my attempt to weave a wind force field resulted in anything. The words we both spoke were nothing more than sounds.

The fear I felt in that moment might have been difficult to explain. But...within the teachings of our Order, these Word Arts themselves served as proof of our mind's existence.

It was as if I was being confronted with the fact *that nothing like that ever existed to begin with.*

Belka's eyes widened, as if witnessing something unbelievable... And then she collapsed to her knees.

"...Belka?"

Belka didn't respond to me, trying to compel her body up again, still stirred by fright.

I watched her from nearby—watched her shoulders dislocate the more she struggled, her bones being crushed and snapped, and her flesh splitting and tearing. As if I was being shown that such a large creature like a gigant, living on land, had all been nothing but an elaborate lie.

Belka raised her head, her expression one of blood, agony, and terror. Uhak was there.

"F-from Cunodey to Alimo winds—"

I went to chant Word Arts, to protect Uhak. Or rather... because I thought my earlier failure had been some sort of mistake.

The wind didn't answer my call. My words failed to reach not only Uhak but also Belka. Solitude, as if cut off from everything else in the world, seemed to exist as a hard fact.

"*Mnnrgghh. Hnggh...ngh...*"

Belka croaked out an inarticulate groan. She had wanted help.

Even if she had been saying something, it was almost wholly indistinguishable from the growls of a mindless beast.

Uhak kept his eyes fixed on Belka, picking up a large piece of debris, a section of a broken stone fence.

He used it to smash the gigant's drooping head.

She let out a scream of grief and anger. She uttered words without meaning. Uhak raised the stone up in the air once again. Then he brought it down on her head a second time.

He looked just as diligent as always, like taking care of a necessary duty of his, as he smashed the gigant's head, and continued to smash it—breaking it open.

The gigant champion, unable to use any Word Arts, unable even to rise from the ground, was slain.

None of the villagers circling the area and watching from afar were able to stop it. Including myself.

"...Uhak?"

After everything ended, I at least realized I had regained proper speech.

Uhak didn't answer. He lived in a world without Word Arts.

...And now he was having a meal.

He quietly sat down like usual and silently picked out the insides of the gigant's crushed head and ate them.

Everyone in the village, including myself, understood it for the first time—

*   *   *

Uhak wasn't an ogre who couldn't eat people.

He simply *didn't*.

◆

The situation from there gradually grew worse.

The terror that Belka brought to the village infected the residents, and they all looked at Uhak with fear and suspicion. Though he had simply been wrapped up in it all, even if he had only done it to save someone...and even if it was an outcome no one had wished for, everyone knew that any tragedy born from the Demon King would be enough to lead to the absolute worst situation.

I had traveled back and forth to the village hoping to save those who lost family and neighbors in any way I could, but I was unable to lift the curse they harbored. Who would be next to show up, how exactly were they going to die off...and was the True Demon King actually alive somewhere?

It was exactly as the villagers had said. The sights of the people racked with fear, futures sealed in despair, these were the very sights I had witnessed during the era of the True Demon King.

As long as this terror was etched into the people's minds, the Demon King would continue to be brought back to life over and over again, filling their hearts with terror. Though they were long dead, just like they had in the past, they'd bring about misery in the future.

The clear stream of Alimo Row, walking steadily on the road

to restoration now that the world was saved from the True Demon King, was muddied red.

Those without homes wandered the town with empty eyes, and those with homes conversely shut their doors tight, to ensure no one would pass through.

If anyone, no longer able to bear the constant tension and fear, caused a violent incident, that person and their whole family would suffer a public execution administered by the rest of the village, and if any of their corpses stayed intact, they'd be hung on display at the village entrance.

Please, I asked for forgiveness. Forgiveness for being powerless, unable to save a single person as I watched them tumble down back into the era of despair.

Everyone believed that faith in the Word-Maker was powerless before the fear of the True Demon King. They were unable to accept an ogre like me. They feared they'd be carried off to the church to serve as ogre food.

This result was likely the obvious outcome. They had the right to begrudge me for being unable to save them.

Torches lit, the villagers drew close to the church, gathering to execute Uhak and me.

—These were the events of the night prior.

"Kill the Ogre." "Kill the man-eating monster." Those were the voices I heard. Cunodey the Ring Seat, for all of them, was now a vague enemy of theirs, under the blanket name of the Order.

As we studied letters together in the candlelight, I called his name.

"Uhak, nothing you did was wrong. You saved a great number of lives. Even eating Belka's corpse... That wasn't wrong, either. Monstrous races eat the flesh of minian races. It's been a fact since the beginning of our world. Despite that, you...you considered our feelings and went without eating any all this time..."

Uhak had continuously fought. A battle between his ogreborn sin and his starvation. How much faith and temperance was needed to make that possible? It was something a minia like myself couldn't begin to imagine. If one of us was destined to die, I thought it should be me, unable to save anyone and powerless as a believer.

I wrote down the words to convey them to Uhak.

"Slip through the forest and immediately cross the river... Then, in some other village somewhere, look for the Order's help. This letter I wrote should help you out somewhat. I have speech, words. I need to dispel the shadow that's fallen over the hearts of the people... The curse of fear."

Uhak took the letter and seemed to give the faintest nod. However, he pushed me aside as I went to leave the church and seek out the villagers.

"...Uhak! Don't!"

My words didn't reach Uhak. None could.

Cries of rage and fear rose up among the villagers I was supposed to protect.

They all had their own respective weapons set on Uhak. Every single one of them, down to the arrows in the air, were fended off with a flash of his club.

The bewilderment at being unable to converse with each other, at their Word Arts not performing their functions, spread through the gathered mob.

There was one who tried to flee, in fear. Uhak grabbed them on the back of their neck. Snapping it like a twig, he used the club swung over his shoulder to crush a different villager's head. A simple punch of his fist, and the villager twisted like a cloth doll and died.

When Uhak fought, nothing around him happened.

Almost as if the monolithic size of a gigant was a nonfactor.

As if Word Arts capable of calling out and communicating with the people and things of the world had been wholly impossible from the start.

Before Uhak, all the people of the world were nothing but mindless beasts, bereft of any of life's mysteries, while he himself was nothing more than a gargantuan ogre.

Not a single difference between anyone, villager or champion.

He swung his club, diligent and solemn, slowly turning the villagers into bloodstains.

"...Uhak. What was it...? What was I supposed to do...?"

The one causing the tragedy before me was my son. My comrade. My only family.

I must've wanted to run from the reality in front of me, and thus I fled alone into the woods... And then right as I felt my foot get caught on some thread, an arrow pierced my side.

The villagers had set up booby traps to kill us.

And I was caught, as if I were a beast being hunted.

My own mistake and foolishness filled me with more regret

than I could bear. I had brought the trap on myself with my weak heart, trying to abandon Uhak to escape and survive on my own.

A number of villagers who were lurking in the forest started to encircle me, sticks and hammers in their hands. This time, for sure, I was going to steel my mind and accept my fate, but I was unable to, with the terror bubbling up inside me, when…I saw one of the villagers fall to the ground.

Almost as though a path was being opened up between them, the villagers brandished their weapons at my feet one by one, without showing any sign of waking up.

Finally, once all the villagers present had collapsed—a familiar face came into view from among them. A face I could never forget.

"…Hey, Teach."

It was one of my former pupils, Kuze the Passing Disaster.

"Mother Cunodey. You still alive?"

With the heat from my arrow wound circulating through my body, his cold hand slapping against my cheeks felt pleasant.

There were many other, more important things I wanted to tell him, but with my consciousness fading, the only thing I could get out of my mouth was a simple observation.

"…You're all grown up, Kuze."

"Sorry. It's always like this for me. I'm always too late. It's my fault."

"……"

"…Don't worry, just wait there, Teach. I'll be sure to send everyone packing. All of it… I'll clean up this bad dream."

Then Kuze wrapped me up in his overcoat and laid me down in my quarters.

He tried to cheer me up, but with this wound, I wasn't going to make it to the morning.

In which case, something, anything… I wanted to try to record my thoughts like this to express my final thoughts to poor Uhak, unable to comprehend speech.

I've never been able to forget the wolf pup I killed that day.

I knew that, even now, in a corner of the garden, there was a grave for the pup, a small collection of stones surrounded with a great many flowers.

We were all born bestowed with the blessing of Word Arts. Thus, before birth, just what sort of difference was there between us and those beasts not bestowed the same gift?

Although he couldn't speak, Uhak had a heart. Considerate of others, able to endure hardships, devoted to his faith… An undeniable heart, just like our own.

Several scenes, ones I had casually witnessed from a young age, circled in my mind.

I had seen horses no longer capable of pulling carriages get butchered with axes and turned into meat.

When the children once kicked a small cat and killed it, I had simply warned them not to get too close to wild animals.

…Without showing any respect or affection to the livestock that continued to be sacrificed for us, we consumed lives like it was our natural right.

Within a world where anyone who possessed Word Arts—including beastfolk and monstrous races—was capable of expressing their minds, creatures without such a gift were nothing but tools or enemies.

Things weren't this way in the Beyond. In fact, it was possible this world was a particularly cruel one... Why had I forgotten these things, things that a traveling visitor had told my father when I was eleven years old, up until now?

Could that wolf pup have been the same as Uhak?

Possessing a clearly established heart but simply without any method to communicate its words?

If that was indeed the case, what a truly terrible and awful sin it would be.

As long as we continued to live in this world, we were sure to continue piling more and more on this horrifying sin of ours.

Ever since that day, I've been tormented by thoughts unbecoming a priest.

Were Word Arts an absolute law of nature?

Dragons fly, gigants walk, minia communicate with words, and Word Arts give birth to phenomena.

Do all these things we take for granted really just exist without any reason behind them?

...Uhak. In your eyes, you must have always looked at us mindless beasts as one and the same. You were the only one capable of loving everything equally, judging all things impartially, and confronting life on your own.

I was sure that eating a life you killed was your way of taking responsibility for the life you took.

You stole the lives of many of the villagers. Much like how I killed that wolf pup.

But that isn't your sin to bear.

We're the ones who're wrong. We're exactly like Melyugre the Silent's siblings, addicted to their Word Arts and destroyed.

I taught you this at some point, I'm sure.

Priests needed to be people who can lift curses.

Uhak the Silent. From tomorrow on, I want you to throw away all the teachings I gave you.

Without being bound by the morals the minian races created, I want you to live as you feel is right, treating all lives as equal.

...I cannot endure the sins of living any longer. I don't think I'll be able to atone for them. It's far too much for a single person to bear.

If I die, I want you to eat my flesh.

◆

The Sixteenth General of Aureatia, Nofelt the Somber Wind, and his troops arrived the next morning, after the tragedy had passed.

The villagers who attacked the church were all smashed to a pulp, pieces of them bitten off and eaten. Additionally, they discovered others hiding in the forest who were now all corpses, with their vitals gouged out by some small dagger. Nofelt was readily able to discover the ogre responsible for the massacre.

Nofelt put down the farewell testament the old woman had left behind.

"Funny."

Everything was too late. It was always like this with incidents related to the Order. Even when it concerned the very almshouse he was born in, it took a day's time for military personnel to get permission to save it.

"...How stupid. Granny Cunodey's definitely got some screws loose... Even went and croaked on me without a word to me about it."

The heart of the abnormally tall swordsman was filled with hatred, in contrast to the flippant smile on his lips.

Aureatia abandoning his birthplace. The Word-Maker, unable to save anyone. A world manipulated by the True Demon King.

Neither the Hero nor the nobility, not a single one, gave a damn about the weak who continued to die.

"Yo, Uhak. So if you're one of Granny's disciples, see, that basically means you're my junior, right? That's enough, don'cha think? I don't really care. Let's ruin everything."

The ogre was silently sitting with his back turned, facing the altar.

He didn't express it with words, but he was performing his daily prayers.

"All right, Uhak. Hero time."

*　　*　　*

A mountain of flowers was placed at her body, lying in the cathedral.

He perceived the world even though he could not comprehend Word Arts.

He possessed the true power of disenchantment, thrusting the same reality he saw on others.

He commanded, as the strongest of all minian-shaped creatures, strength and size that existed as authoritative reality.

An axiom-denying monster, ever in uncommunicative silence, that overturned the basic premise of the world.

Oracle. Ogre.

Uhak the Silent.

The second tragedy that assailed Alimo Row perfectly aligned with the man's arrival at the village, a wood box slung over his back. The main road that led into the village was blockaded by a large number of Aureatian soldiers, but the detours around the blockade only led to a small church, or The Land of The End. That region, feared by living creatures far and wide, was exactly where the man was heading.

"Really showed up at a strange time, huh."

The Aureatian soldiers coming and going from the road in front of the town appeared to be trying to cover up the very existence of the incident from the eyes of the people around them.

The reporter carrying the wooden box was a man named Yukiharu the Twilight Diver.

"...Something really stinky going on here."

He was a small-framed, round-faced man. Wrapped up in trim, neat apparel, his dress was completely different from when he had visited the Gokashae Sand Sea.

His most distinctive feature was the instrument hanging from his neck. It was equipped with a monocular lens, but its large base and bellows construction made it vastly different from the monocles familiar to this world.

A strange voice answered from inside the wooden box on his back.

"Seems like a lot of people died, after all. They're probably piling them up in a lumberyard or something nearby. If there were some large buildings, they'd probably use those, but a village this tiny isn't going to have any of those, after all."

"Not like that, I mean that this whole incident smells fishy to me... Take this, for example—"

Yukiharu looked down at the freshly dug wheel rut at his feet. Opportunities to use this narrow road detouring around Alimo Row should have been very limited.

"At the very least, within the past two days, a large number of carriages have been coming back and forth down this path here. They're heading for Alimo Row...... While these are *foot tracks* leading out from the village. There are all these footprints heading out, but none coming back."

"I mean, you say that, Yukiharu..."

A troubled voice came out of the wooden box.

"But I can't see any of that from inside this box, you know."

"*Ha-ha-ha*, forgot about that, sorry. Anyway, that's what's going on. You want a peek? I could open up and show you. I don't really sense anyone around that'd get a glimpse of you."

"...I'm fine; it's fine. So then, do the footprints tell you something?"

"I mean, it's a simple story. A large group of villagers walked out of the village and didn't come back for some time. When they did eventually return, they were wheeled in on carriages. Carriages that weren't used when they first left."

He adeptly manipulated the instrument around his neck and photographed the tracks in the area.

"Basically, that'll mean the villagers were all killed up ahead of here and had their corpses carried back to the village."

The glass dry plate camera, at the present moment, hadn't spread to Aureatia yet.

It was his own personal machine, allowing him to do everything from focusing to aperture adjustments with only one hand. His supernatural skills to take a series of pictures all while holding it in his hands—or really, the mere fact he was taking photographic pictures at all—was something no one in this world could comprehend.

"...Yukiharu. It was one of the Twenty-Nine Officials who mentioned they were cleaning up after that massacre, right? Um...... Nofelt the Somber Wind, was it? Isn't he the one behind it all, then?"

"There's no question that Nofelt was the one to dispose of the large pile of bodies. But Nofelt's troops themselves aren't the perpetrators here. The time line has the radzio transmission about the incident coming to them from the neighboring town—and then arriving at Alimo Row with his unit a day after that. So after the massacre. If they had ordered the perpetrator from the start to carry out the massacre, then their plans should've moved forward with a lot more speed. In other words... Nofelt doesn't have any direct link with the perpetrator, but he seems to be covering up the criminal he *did* find."

The true criminal must have been at the end of the road Yukiharu was currently heading down. There were only two destinations at the end of the road skirting Alimo Row. The Land of The End, where the True Demon King perished, or the small church.

"Yukiharu. You really asked all over about the church, right? That there was this strange ogre living with an old woman...... You didn't know from the start, did you?"

"*Ha-ha-ha*, oh, no, no, no. That's in my nature, really. If something interests me, I end up asking all about it. I'd regret not being able to ask everything I want to ask when given the chance, right? But...... Things have gotten interesting thanks to that."

He heard this ogre was incapable of using the language of Word Arts and had silenced a fearsome gigant.

Meanwhile, Nofelt's squad, dispatched to the frontier beyond the eyes of Aureatia proper, was actively trying to cover up the crime. They were proceeding with plans to muzzle anyone who knew of Uhak the Silent's existence. He wondered if the residents in the other village Yukiharu had gathered information from would've been so open with him had he arrived a day later.

Nofelt's actions were his own. Was there a reason to go so far for just a single ogre?

"There are going to be Royal Games. If Nofelt does put him as a hero, then that'll confirm this story. This'll sell for sure."

Coincidently arriving right on time, Yukiharu alone had

gotten ahold of information regarding a powerful fighter who was still unknown to anyone else.

"Seriously, Aureatia's way of doing things is as nasty... Uh-oh."

Noticing something, the wooden box lowered their voice.

"There are soldiers coming out in front. They're not walking like Aureatian soldiers."

"From out in front?"

They were *coming from* the direction of The Land of The End. Yukiharu went on high alert and paid close attention in their direction.

Climbing up the hill and showing themselves was a group of five merchants. They were leading a one-horse carriage solely for carrying their belongings.

"They're all soldiers. Don't let their disguises fool you," the wooden box warned in a whisper.

Yukiharu put on a bright smile and walked up to the group directly.

"Well, well, good day! Honestly, it's been quite the rough going for you and me both, I'm sure!"

The peddlers came to a stop, a bit at a loss at Yukiharu's confident attitude.

"Oh, and who're you? Doing some work involved with the latest incident, I'm guessing?"

"Yes, I'm a reporter. Yukiharu the Twilight Diver. A pleasure to make your acquaintance."

"...Twilight Diver!"

A tall, lanky younger man reacted at hearing Yukiharu's second name. He filled in the details to the muscular man who seemed to be their commanding officer.

"He's a shrewd reporter! Twenty percent of the incident reports that come in have Twilight Diver written on it."

"Calm yourself." The muscular man commanded his excited subordinate with a wave of his hand.

"...That so? I had no idea. That means we've made acquaintances with a celebrity. Gathering material about the slaughter at the village, then?"

Yukiharu understood the significance of the commander's behavior. The tall subordinate lad's comments were clearly a slip of the tongue. The commanding officer cut him off before he accidently revealed anything beyond that.

The articles that Yukiharu the Twilight Diver mainly specialized in were primarily incidents of large-scale death and tragedy— or foresight of such events. He was a war reporter.

Additionally, he had a complete grasp on what percentage of the information he leaked himself ended up in which city. Twenty percent. A city with an extremely high demand for reports on ongoing battleground situations, even when limited to Yukiharu's articles alone.

...*Free City of Okafu. I see; so these are mercenaries with the self-proclaimed demon king Morio.*

"That said, best not to keep going any farther. Up ahead's The Land of The End, after all. What the hell're you heading there for?"

"Huh? Is it really?"

Yukiharu constructed an expression as if he was honestly surprised and then scratched his head.

…The Land of The End, where the True Demon King perished. The reason he purposefully came all the way out to this frontier was solely because he was making for this region, the only clue to discovering the True Demon King's true identity.

"Whoops. I must've gotten lost somewhere along the way. I've never really been out this way's the thing."

"*Ha*, now that's quite the misfortune to find yourself in. It's embarrassing, but we're in the same boat. Just on our way back. Seriously, the Aureatian bastards are always blocking up the roads like that; it's a damn headache."

…*I see. Then they must've not been expecting to encounter anyone, either.*

Never dropping his superficial smile, Yukiharu's train of thought continued forward.

They were using the same excuse as Yukiharu, that they got lost, because they hadn't anticipated beforehand that they'd be getting into a dialogue with someone they met along the way. They had *borrowed* Yukiharu's reply.

This was likely why this officer had taken the initiative to ask first. But more than that—

…*They're investigating something. Wait. Maybe it's something else here…*

Yukiharu closely observed the gazes of the four mercenaries. Their peripheral vision was focused far wider than the average person.

They're standing guard.

"The rumor is that the with this recent massacre, it was the work of someone who came out of The Land of The End. After all, this story involves the Demon King, so even Lord Nofelt has to dispose of everything in secret, right? I came out all this way to get details, and instead I can't even get into the village."

"A monster from The Land of The End. There was the incident with Belka the Rending Quake, too, for one. Stands to reason they'd do that."

"In secret." With that description in mind, Nofelt's unit likely leaked information on purpose. Precisely because of the incident with Belka, they're able to frame *someone like her* as the criminal behind the recent massacre.

"The True Demon King really is terrifying, aren't they? They died a long time ago, right? To still have such an influence, even from the grave... Just what in the world were they?"

"Who knows. You curious?"

"Oh, come now. I mean, who wouldn't be? Better question: Are they actually dead in the first place?"

In that brief moment, he could tell all five of the men's breath caught in their throats. The reaction suggested they didn't want to entertain the possibility, even for a moment.

Yukiharu spoke cheerfully.

"After all, no one's ever confirmed the True Demon King's corpse for themselves, right? It's something I've always wondered. Why does everyone believe some rumor that the Hero brought them down? Always a chance—even now that they've been alive in The Land of The End the whole time and *could come out* at any moment."

It was said there was some unidentified presence that attacked anyone who came to The Land of The End to investigate. Aureatia. The New Principality of Lithia. The Free City of Okafu. Various powers continued to dispatch reconnaissance units after the Demon King's death, but they were all warded off by this mysterious assailant, and this unknown presence was called the Demon King's Bastard. *It wasn't considered the actual True Demon King itself.*

"We know."

The officer replied with a strained smile.

"They definitely died. That much is very clear... When that thing was alive, *things were much worse.* Not just here, either. The whole world, all of it, was... It was terrifying just knowing the True Demon King existed. Even you gotta understand that much."

"......"

Yukiharu, of course, knew as well. That the True Demon King was definitely dead.

Knew that on top of their enormous power, they were a real demonic king, their very existence itself bringing fear.

"......That said, I'm still a reporter, after all. I need to pay close attention to everything, even the things no one else is concerned about."

He needed to confirm the facts. No matter how frightening it may have been to close in on them. The twilight everyone else was scared to step through was exactly where he'd tread. Thus, his second name—Yukiharu the Twilight Diver.

"Demon King… Aye, D-demon King. Killed 'em."

The elderly man among the five mercenaries, sitting in the bed of the carriage, cut in with inarticulate words.

"…Killed 'em, all right. The Benighted White Wind, Alena, must've killed 'em. That brat was a real genius. D-didja know? He… A spear, he hits with the spearhead. The very tip of his thrust, see."

"Hey, Gramps, that's enough."

The officer admonished him, looking utterly fed up. On the left side of the old man's head was a deep scar.

"*Heh-heh-heh.* That hero, y'know… Now that's some real courage… The First Party…"

"Alena the Benighted White Wind. They were one of the seven members of the First Party. I've heard plenty about his legend. Is that older one there acquainted with Alena?"

"Pretty much. Used to be students together or something, and he'll always find a reason to start talking about them. Even though Alena's been dead a loooong time, now… Even though everyone in the First Party ended up losing."

The First Party—the first and last hope during that lost age of terror. The seven people said to be the strongest the world had to offer came together to challenge the Demon King all at once, and they were mercilessly defeated.

So, too, was their glory now all part of the past.

Then, in the end, even the True Demon King was killed by some unknown force.

"…Ended up talking a while on the roadside here. You'll have to sit next to Gramps, but want a ride back to town? I wanna hear all the stories a legendary reporter like you has to share."

"Oh no, please, I'll have to politely decline. Truth is: I've got an appointment with Aureatia's unit to gather material on the massacre. I was thinking I'd just stop by Alimo."

The commander replied with a smile.

"That so? A real shame."

From the moment Yukiharu encountered the men, he understood.

They're planning on killing me.

Mercenaries from the Free City of Okafu are here. On a road with nothing but The Land of The End awaiting them. Not only Yukiharu the Twilight Diver, but the Free City of Okafu was also investigating The Land of The End. These five were standing guard. To ensure no one else got the information before Okafu.

"Well then, at least let us hear some stories on the road back, Twilight Diver."

The soldiers around him, save the commander talking, put their hands in their breast packs or the bags they carried. They were getting ready to draw their daggers.

In an attempt to stall them, Yukiharu abruptly spoke up.

"Um, excuse me? It's Twilight Diver here, per our arrangement! I got a bit lost on the way, see? The soldiers gave me directions, and well, I'm on a road somewhere on the way to the church right now…"

His words were directed to the radzio transmitter extending up out of the wooden box. The five mercenaries stopped moving.

While they might have needed to kill Yukiharu, they had no other choice.

"......This is Asnes the Veering. What happened? You were supposed to meet me in Alimo Row. The soldiers should know you're coming, too."

The reply came from the wooden box itself. However, to the eyes of the five mercenaries, it looked as if there was a radzio transmitter hidden inside the wooden box... He was scheduled to gather news from the Aureatia unit stationed in Alimo Row. A lie to prevent the men in front of him from trying to harm him.

Yukiharu conveyed his present location to the voice on the other side of the radzio with his initial message. The mercenaries couldn't afford to kill him anymore.

"Sure, I get that, but they told me to take this road, so what was I supposed to do? Can't you use your authority, Commander Asnes, and say something to them? Oh, actually, was it Lord Nofelt in command right now?"

"Forget it; just stop wandering around. I'll send a unit to find you. You don't have anyone else with you, right? This operation's classified. I can't have you screwing things up with your stupid reporter antics."

With the hollow and functionless transmitter in his hand, Yukiharu winked to the five mercenaries.

".........Oh no. Just me here. All right then, I'll wait here for your escort."

When Yukiharu ended his radzio performance, the wooden box once again fell silent.

As he turned back to face the five mercenaries, he waved his hands back and forth.

"You don't need to worry. I won't say a word to the Aureatia folks. We both got ourselves lost out here after all, right?"

"...Yeah, right. Thanks."

The commanding officer lowered his head and passed by Yukiharu. Though they had planned on killing Yukiharu, as long as that could possibly lead to engaging a squad of Aureatian soldiers, they couldn't afford to do so.

Yukiharu the Twilight Diver was a man who had continued to survive across numerous battlefields thanks to his quick wits.

"Don't make me improvise on the spot like that."

A tone of displeasure rang out from the wooden box.

"*Ha-ha-ha*, sorry, sorry. Still, you did great. I think you and I make a surprisingly good team if you ask me. Asnes the Veering? *Bwah-ha-ha-ha!*"

"...Who cares what the name was. That was really close, you know."

"Pretty much. Thanks to that, though, I learned something very important—Okafu's probing The Land of The End, too. They're trying to exclude anyone trying to get information on it. There's a chance they might have a lead on the True Demon King, too. But, man, the self-proclaimed demon king Morio is scary! Those five just now were quite strong in their own right. They never let their guard down."

"...If The Land of The End's a bust, does that mean a trip to

Okafu? This basically suggests that if there are any leftover clues about the True Demon King, that would be the only place that'd have them, right?"

"Weeeell, I'm not so sure."

There was one other lie in the previous performance. He was not alone, after all.

With Yukiharu the Twilight Diver, there was always an unidentified presence inside the wooden box that moved together with him.

Additionally, seeing that he was undertaking an investigation of The Land of The End, and everyone who had come before him had failed......he contrived a meetup with a separately acting group that was already deployed on sight.

"That decision really depends on the inclination of our *client*, wouldn't you say?"

At that moment, four different things were visible in Milieu the Hemp Drop's narrow eyes.

First, the mercenary who was quarreling near the counter—from what he could make out, he said something along the lines of "*Who cares about a damn contract?*" and "*I quit.*" It wasn't anything important, but he was eventually shot with a crossbow. A fight within the Free City of Okafu, and especially inside the walls of The Goose, meant that either side was drunk, so the arrows missed their mark by a wide margin, destroying two liquor bottles on the counter. The contents then trickled down to where Milieu and the others were. An all-too-common sight.

The next event came from the chair in the corner. He saw it out of the corner of his eye. A man covered in rags reacted with lightning speed to the stray arrow closing in. He twisted his body slightly. A bolt pierced his chest. The arrow stabbed perfectly through the area near his heart and stuck itself in the pillar behind him.

After it was all over, the waitress near the man in rags finally realized the situation at hand. Together with a high-pitched shriek, she let the water jug slip out of her hands. Milieu could also follow the trajectory of the spray as it scattered in midair.

However, when the jug left the waitress's hand, the hand of the man in rags caught the bottom of it. With the subtlest of moves, he captured all the water back inside the jug.

"I'm all set on the water, thanks."

The man, his heart freshly pierced through, handed the water jug back to the waitress.

"Since it looks like my seat's got a bit of a target on it."

Milieu also clearly saw the state of the fingers poking out from the gaps in the man's rags.

"Hey there, you a mercenary as well?"

Milieu was now in a merry mood for the first time in a long time and nearly skipped over to take the seat across from the man. Normally, Milieu would've liked to treat the man to a drink, but considering who he was talking to, he knew his kindness would be meaningless.

"I'm Milieu the Hemp Drop. Instead of water, maybe you need some tobacco or something?"

"......Nah. I've heard booze and tobacco aren't great if you want to live a long time, so I abstain."

"*Pfffft*, that's a tasteless joke. In that case, you must be here looking for work."

The Free City of Okafu was an independent city created by the self-proclaimed demon king Morio, where mercenary services were the city's main business...

The war between the kingdom and the self-proclaimed demon kings—or possibly the struggle for existence between the minian and monstrous races—raged on. It was fueled by applying military force to conflicts of any size—so much so that these territories were no different than mercenary headquarters.

Now, with the fall of the New Principality, the proficiency and number of soldiers gathered there from the far reaches of the realm surpassed all other nations besides Aureatia. They came due to its specialized logistical support beyond an individual mercenary's reach—aggregating jobs and information, loaning out cutting-edge weaponry like guns and cannons or peacetime training.

Of course, during the end of the True Demon King era, they were only given jobs that involved getting rid of the Demon King Army, and the mercenaries lost any room to freely choose who were their friends and foes.

This was still true, even now.

"I came here this morning. I have business with the people trying to crush Okafu. Don't give a damn what happens to this country, but they might be the ones who know something about me."

"That part about knowing something about you sounds suspicious to me. Right now, at the very least, I don't know you at all."

"Sound Slicer."

The man put his right hand on the table. It had neither muscle nor skin. It was a smoothly polished, jewel-like, skeletal minian hand.

"Shalk the Sound Slicer. But that's not my real name. I'm just calling myself that."

"...The lost memories from when you were living, then. Or rather, they say that skeletons are totally different creatures, personality-wise, from their previous living forms... How many years since you came alive?"

"Alive? Don't be silly. It'll be two years soon. I've *been dead* for two years. To be honest, I don't even know much about this world in general, let alone about myself."

Milieu was already convinced. That stray arrow from earlier that pierced through the man's chest wasn't because he hadn't dodged in time. With minimal movement, he dodged to ensure the arrow would slip through the gaps in his rib cage. He had matched the speed of the arrow's flight to do so.

Skeletons. Like golems and mimics, their existence was totally different from life birthed in nature, instead of created with Demon Arts. In minian society, they were feared more than the monstrous races; they were abominations to be avoided.

However, given that skeletons and revenants used corpses for their base materials, there was someone living who existed before them. Though they didn't have memories and souls of their previous forms, it was natural for them to discover things regarding their former lives.

Though realizing it to be an idle endeavor, there were some who pursued the memories of their previous lifetime in order to fill in their vacant selves.

"Sounds to me like you could use a guide, eh? Someone with the same goal in mind, with the know-how and skills, to boot. A guy like me, for example. Though, well..."

Milieu looked over his shoulder toward the counter. A man with a bottle smashed over his head collapsed, covered in blood, and the remaining mercenaries had run off in separate directions.

For the past several days, it was this scene repeated over and over again. Not a rare sight at all.

"Can't say it looks like a very favorable state of affairs at the moment."

"...I want to know about my enemy. How many people he's brought with him, for instance."

"Go on."

Milieu shrugged and smiled with his narrow eyes.

"Hasn't brought anyone. Plans on eradicating all of them by themselves. Ridiculous, huh?"

What was laughable was the fact that their enemy truly did possess the strength to keep their word.

This was still a world where the strength of an individual could sway a battle. Even examples like this, of an inconceivably powerful individual causing the destruction of large military forces, weren't rare—anyone resolved to the path of the warrior hoped to reach such limits, pouring themselves into polishing their skills, and a small number among those then joined the ranks of the strong. Such examples were called champions.

Okafu currently was under attack from just such a champion. It was said she was a visitor who had a long-standing feud with their lord, Morio the Sentinel, but given their status as mercenaries, they weren't privy to any more details than that.

"Kazuki the Black Tone is coming."

In the span of a single big month, and at frightening speed, Okafu's elite had met their end. Doment the Green Sash. Inezin the Ophidian Measurer. Larky the Hemotidings Bullet. All of them taken out by a single person.

"That'll make things quick. We'll figure out which of us is stronger, and that'll be the end of it."

"Whoa, whoa, and here I was thinking up until now it'd be all about who's stronger between Kazuki and *me*, instead."

"...You might be right."

The skeleton's hollow sight dropped. He was staring at the weapon hanging from Milieu's waist.

It was a commonplace rapier, if anything an abnormal sight within The Goose's walls, overflowing with dangerous mechanized or heavy weaponry.

"Is it better if a new recruit like me stays out of it? This is a mercenary's pride issue, isn't it?"

"Can you even handle it—is probably the better question. We've more or less got our strategy all figured out, but if you come out of nowhere to throw a wrench in the works, I feel like you're the one who'll end up having a bad time."

"Got it. In that case, I'll just remain on defense...... I'm the new guy, after all."

"*Ah-ha-ha*, I love it. You're real confident, aren't you? If that's not enough for you, you could join the other side, if you'd like. After all, we're heading into a new era. Defending a self-proclaimed demon king's country is going out of style."

"Well, as you can see, I'm dead. I exist in the past tense, as it were."

It was then that the door behind the counter opened, and the pair both turned to look at the same time.

The proprietor drew a simple line across the chalkboard to display a reward sum and announced the gathered men's new job.

"We got a mission, mercs! Gathering people to fortify the area around Great Bridge Gate! Hold the enemy back until tomorrow morning and keep them outside the second outer wall! Paid in full up front, whether there's an attack or not! It's a mission straight from Lord Morio himself! Any ungrateful bastard fixing to challenge him, huh?!"

Six of the men responded to the hoarse shout.

"I'll take today's job, too. I still haven't earned enough for my sister's treatment."

The huge man, gigantic two-handed swords strapped to either side of his waist, had deeply tanned skin, like black ink. His name was Hilca the Shadow's Ship.

"Whoa, hold up here—the pay today's got an extra damn digit tacked on!! Lord Morio's gonna spend up all his popularity!"

The elf, wearing a wide-brimmed hat low on his head, hollered while stretched out on the couch. He was said to use a staff in battle, but no one had ever seen him carry one before. Leforgid the Woven Trail.

"I'm in, of course."

The calm, elderly ogre was a veteran even to the other gathered mercenaries. He answered while making adjustments to the cogwheel on the inside of his round shield, appearing to be some sort of mechanical weapon. Wint the Astonishment.

"...I'd like clarification on some of the conditions. What happens if we put this threat down?"

The tall zmeu woman fiddled with a slender instrument in her hand, resembling a medical bottle. She was Pagireshe the Quivering Toes, former second-formation rear guard in Obsidian Eyes.

"Well, obviously I'm in."

"I'll be joining up with you today, Shalk the Sound Slicer."

Two minia. One elf. One ogre. One zmeu. And one skeleton.

In this town, where power was the measure for everything, no one was treated differently, even monstrous and construct races. Fight, get results, and be rewarded. For Shalk, living as a mercenary, it was a very simple arrangement—and one he was long familiar with.

"Well now, Shalk. My name's Leforgid. I can tell even with that cloth covering you up. You're a skeleton, right? How the heck're you moving if you don't eat nothing?"

"Sorry, that's a secret."

Shalk dealt with the elven mercenary who was first to chat with him.

"I was thinking I could give you that juicy info in exchange for hearing why you can't move an inch without food, see."

"*Heh*, funny guy, huh? Well, how 'bout we have even more fun, eh?"

"…Quit while you can. Shalk's not just talk. I saw his moves a bit earlier. He could probably dodge your techniques, too."

"Even without any muscle? Well, I hope so, I guess…"

Milieu arbitrated the situation, and the elf shrugged before stepping back.

Shalk said nothing more, but he did feel a twinge of nostalgia. When he was a mercenary for the New Principality, he recalled someone trying to rile him up like this on his first there day there, too.

A carriage was likely to be along soon to take them to their post. A harsh mission, where from now until the following morning, they'd need to be on constant guard against an attack, completely unsure when it might come.

While each of them prepared for battle, Shalk, too, took his own weapon in his hand. It was a white short spear. The shaft seemed to be made of bone, as white and smooth as Shalk's own body.

"Are these lot the only fighting power we got? Seemed like there were quite a lot of mercenaries back at the citadel."

"Each shop is in charge of defending different positions. Morio's personal troops, well… They'll probably provide supporting fire from the citadel—but can't rely on them for much. The enemy'll attack under the cover of night, so they'll only be able to fire at random. You'll get caught up in the fire and shot yourself if you're not careful."

"If you're worried about our fighting power, the plan's that three of our proudest fighters are returning from Aureatia today, but…"

"Hey, don't go looking at me, Hilca. I tried to stop 'em."

"…Wanna take bets on if they'll make it back alive or not?"

"They must have been wiped out."

"Yeah, definitely."

"Not even worth the wager."

Under the current situation, even coming in and out of the Free City of Okafu was a game of pure luck.

Not only that, but with how it was, the ones who managed to get through the gate unscathed were considerably blessed by fortune.

In Shalk's particular case, though, entering the city without his carriage coming under attack at all, it had been a considerably *misfortunate* outcome instead.

"That reminds me, I haven't asked yet. Have any of you here seen the Hero's bones before?"

"What's that question about?"

"Some code or something? What about you, Hilca?"

"I don't even know their face; how am I supposed to know what their bones look like?"

"*Ha-ha*, good point!"

Shalk looked at the ogre drinking his booze, the only one yet to answer. He shook his head, just like the others.

It appeared Shalk's only option to find his answers was to ask their enemy that night.

"I don't have any proof, but… I'll take the bet that they're still alive."

◆

The setting sun, like a bright flame, cast defined shadows on the ground.

The main road that led them to Okafu had even terrain until, as it approached closer and closer to the city, it changed into a mountain slope. The Free City of Okafu was an impregnable fortress cast into a huge rocky outcropping.

Within the carriage, wrapped in red shadows as it returned home, there were people engaged in conversation.

One zmeu. Two ogres. Including the driver, the three were all Okafu mercenaries—and confident in their skills and prowess.

"From here to Okafu... A bunch of places that menace could be waiting to ambush us."

With their work in Aureatia finished, they chose to return to the Free City amid its current state of danger. Up until a few days prior, Aureatia itself was facing a similar crisis as the Particle Storm disaster approached their borders. Although they heard that Aureatia had already warded off the threat, there were plenty of people, even beyond other mercenaries like them, who would choose to return to their home city.

"You think Kazuki the Black Tone's coming this way? A swordsman like you is at a disadvantage against a gunfighter, right?"

"Yeah... I've dodged bullets...four times, I think? One time, I didn't dodge and got a wound in my side. It must've just grazed me, because it only took one large month to heal," the ogre in the passenger carriage replied. The blade he carried was short but as thick as a shield.

Lifting up his clothes, the scar he showed was cut deep into his skin, and if he were minian, it'd likely have been a fatal shot to his inner organs, but for an ogre with extremely thick muscles and fat covering his body, it wasn't even enough to incapacitate him. They were the most terrifying monster race of all, combining horns, a massive body, and an intellect on par with the minian races.

"I'm intrigued. How'd you manage to dodge 'em? You must've caught their look and hand movements, right?"

The zmeu linked both her claws. This reptilian race was counted among the minian races because unlike the monstrous ones, they did not eat minians.

"You think you'll be able to dodge *after* your enemy sets their sights on you? Bullets fly at you like this—"

The ogre mercenary slapped both his hands together.

"In the blink of an eye, without any prior warning. I guess if you focus hard enough, you'll know the second it happens, but that's it. Your body won't be able to react."

"Huh. Well then, what d'you do?"

"Same as always. I move my enemy. If I cover my head, they'll want to aim for my easier-to-hit torso. If they're already in motion, then that brief second where they stop moving and drop their sights is the perfect chance. Imagine where your opponent's sights are set—and manipulate the moment they fire and where they aim."

"Sheesh, those reflexes you ogres have are absurd. I'd go with a nice, clean bomb, I think."

When weapons were involved, the zmeu's were much more large-scale than the ogre's. The complex mechanical launcher was curiously fitted with a fuse-lit explosive. The functionality allowed them to sync the moment the bomb went off with the moment it hit the ground, by using a cogwheel to rearrange the launch angle and ignition point for the fuse.

"………Hey."

The ogre driver cut into their conversation. His senses were far more sensitive than the two riding in the passenger carriage.

"I heard it just now. A song."

The mercenaries in the carriage instantly moved. A finger brushed a sword hilt…and another sat itself on a firearm's grip, before stopping in its tracks with a spray of blood. It came almost exactly as the stray sound of a gunshot rang out.

"……"

The driver instantly crushed the horse's neck, toppling the carriage over. It needed to serve as a shield from the gunfire.

A sea of blood flowed from the sideways carriage. The zmeu and ogre pair were already shot dead.

There had been only one gunshot.

Went through the damn eardrum, did ya?

Even while covered with a thick armor of muscle and flesh, the ogres had one spot that was completely defenseless. Nevertheless, the shot came in the middle of a twisting mountain road, through a carriage…and pierced a zmeu's lungs at the same time?

"*Taaaah, tah, taaah. Tah-taaah.*"

He could tell the song was getting closer. It was completely irrational behavior and only served to give away their position.

"Dammit. Visitors. Accursed visitor psycho…"

He looked down at his own weapon, thrown out of the carriage and on the ground nearby. Just how much of a fight could he put up with this iron rod? It was impossible think that an ogre would lose to a minia. As long as it was an ordinary, commonplace minia.

"*Taaaah, ta-taaah…*"

"You're dead meat."

He lunged and tried to grab his weapon…and that was as far as he got.

Aiming at the smallest inch of his head bending forward, the bullet *circumvented* the downed carriage and pierced him through the eye.

◆

"*Ta-taaaaah…taaah, tah. Ta-taaah.*"

The high-pitched, clear voice spun a melody across the unpopulated wilderness.

Along the mountain road, skirt flapping in the sunset, a single figure twirled the muskets in each of their hands.

The person who had finished up killing the three mercenaries was a woman. In her midtwenties, she wore a girlish skirt that seemed to clash with her boorish military coat.

"*Taaah, taaah, ta-taaah, taaah, ta-ta-tah. Finished them off~! What a scene~!*"

"…Miss Kazuki Mizumura. Are you always singing that?"

There was one other, sitting on the downed carriage. A young boy, seemingly in his early teens. However, his grizzled hair imparted a bizarrely mature demeanor.

"*Before inevitability, tears everythiiiiing away……* Yup. Is it weird? You have a problem with me?"

"Oh no. I just thought you haven't changed very much from thirty years ago."

The two conversing people were still young. At the very least, that's how they looked on the outside.

"That goes for both of us, right? Visitors don't age, after all."

"…I suppose you're right. This is based off the research I've had done, but… An ancient royal family in this world also governed for far longer than one generation would conceivably be able to. It lends a lot of credibility to the story that all the first people in this world were visitors."

"Huh. So then, what's the reason why we don't age?"

"Hard to say. This is entirely speculation, but…it might, for example, be to make us leave an impact here."

The young boy locked his fingers together and looked toward the sky.

The blue-tinged large moon and the red small moon. Several circumstances were the same here; nevertheless, it looked quite different from the Beyond—a reality far off in the distance.

"Take you and me, for example—we may be deviants, and such humans are abandoned here in this world without anything…… but to go from that point to leaving some sort of impact on society here takes even longer. Innate natural talent may rust and crumble away over such an extended time. Passing on techniques and knowledge onto others could end up only impacting one generation... But right now, neither you nor your age, nor your skills, at the very least, have withered at all, Kazuki."

"Hmmm. I don't really care, to be honest. So basically the whole reason we drifted over here is because the World-Maker or whatever is trying to change this place?"

"...The opposite. I think that it was originally to support and maintain this world. In the beginning, there were only visitors. In order to take root and establish an ecosystem here, their original genetic life span wasn't enough—in other words, dragons and gigants are races that still possess long life spans because of the mutants they originated from...from the longevity of their visitor ancestors. At the very least, that's my hypothesis."

The "visitors" in this world were not only minia.

It wasn't hard to imagine that the dragons were the offspring of a large reptile deviant far in the distant past that had been sent to this world. It was similar for oozes, creatures that shouldn't, according to wisdom from the Beyond, have senses or any intellect, as well as mandrakes, plants that behaved like animals—everything must have originated from an original deviant of some kind.

The entities spoken of in the stories of the Beyond must have actually existed in the past, before being banished here.

In this world, which lacked an abundance of written documents or records, the mere search for the truths of history proved difficult.

"Anyway, you didn't come for a chat, right? Out all this way. Aren't you supposed to be busy working with those Old Kingdoms' guys? War's gonna break out there, too, you know. Heard that Particle Storm thing didn't even reach Aureatia, so you must have a rough time ahead of you, huh?"

"Once all the preparations are in place, there's nothing else I can do. Chatting is my job, after all."

"You're really impossible to trust. Is that a bit of a fatal flaw for your work?"

"...You really think so?"

The young boy smiled, looking a bit troubled.

"Now then, let's say I've dropped by to check on how the situation's progressing, then. I need to integrate the period I'll be backing you up into my schedule, after all."

"Progressing? It's basically the same as always. Heck, these three weren't even that strong."

Her black boots kicked a corpse. The leather, fully immersed in the pool of blood, was discolored all the way up to the ankle.

"At this point, as far as mercs worth worrying about, Okafu's pretty down to just Milieu the Hemp Drop, right? Choke them out by blocking the flow of people and goods in and out of the city, and I'd say they have one small month left in them? Maybe less?"

"I'm not asking about the enemy's limits. Why, right now, it's amazing in and of itself that you've been able to keep up your activity like this without any rest, Kazuki. Fighting nonstop for a whole big month already, six whole days. Even if someone had power rivaling an army, there aren't many who could *fight continuously* with unlimited concentration. That's why armies gather so many numbers together, to compensate for that with an increase in overall endurance and the number of eyes on watch."

"Really? I mean, that's what I'm managing to do right now."

The course she chose to capture Okafu wasn't a blitzkrieg, but a battle of attrition through unconventional combat. To be able to take that upon oneself with just individual fighting power held an unimaginable strategic mean, beyond just a prodigious strength in combat itself.

"…You know what happened with the New Principality of Lithia's downfall, yes? A mighty nation that established this world's only air force, erased in a single night."

"Hmph. That had to be Aureatia's doing, too, right? For a long time now, they've been getting up to shady nonsense without telling me anything."

"Suppose, if you will, they utilized outstanding individual fighting skills like yours when they conquered the New Principality, too? That'd mean they would have no need to operate a giant armed force and could conquer all the nations in the world. They could accomplish everything without needing funds for equipment or training, without making logistical considerations, and without anything being revealed to either the enemy or their own citizen, too. A war superiority that never would have existed in that other world."

"……And you're saying I have some relationship with Aureatia?"

"Just a few days prior, Aureatia devoted all their might to

defending their homeland from the Particle Storm. Given the need to split their military forces up to also engage the Old Kingdoms' loyalists, if they did see a need to keep the Free City of Okafu in check with as little of a deployment as possible… If I were in their shoes, I'd send such an outstanding individual to do so."

"I've had enough of your baseless conjecture, thanks. Does that story of yours have anything to do with my job here?"

"Don't you think such outstanding individuals pose the same threat to Aureatia, too?"

"……"

"During the operation on the New Principality, the commander of their wyvern army, Regnejee the Wings of Sunset, died. Another visitor like us, Dakai the Magpie, too. Toroa the Awful, and the almost one-thousand-year-old Vikeon the Smoldering, both killed one right after another… I believe all these incidents should be seen as having circumstances beyond my understanding of them. It's possible…these champions are purposefully being disposed of."

Aureatia, too, was utilizing outstanding individuals to suppress hostile forces. It was a type of warfare that made it possible to avoid consuming any of their own national strength.

From a more long-term perspective, they were thinking of erasing such threats from this world as well, as eventually they could easily threaten Aureatia's destruction. The Gray-Haired Child could understand that. What they wanted, what they feared.

"…For the ones who attacked the New Principality, the assault likely served as *preliminaries* to the Royal Games. The Royal

Games themselves are festivities in order to establish Aureatia's hegemony, while simultaneously being used before they start as a means to send champions to the battlefield. You're planning on participating in the Royal Games, too, aren't you, Kazuki?"

"…"

"In other words, you, too, are in danger. Why would they send one person to conquer Okafu?"

"…I'm not alone, though. That's why I have you lot here backing me up, right?"

"No, I don't mean like that. The fact that you're here keeping up a fight solo like this… I'm wondering if, more so than Aureatia's military operation, you yourself have a goal you're after *out here where Aureatia's eyes can't reach you*."

"You little…… Are you serious?"

She immediately aimed a gun barrel at the young boy. Kazuki wore a faint smile that was visible through her long hair.

"If by any chance…you're asking me something I'd find inconvenient, you best know I could shoot you dead right where you stand."

"If you have some goal you're hiding from Aureatia's side, I can work with you in secret."

With the gun barrel pointed at him, the boy raised his hands into the air. In this world where shura ran rampant, he didn't possess any fighting prowess whatsoever. He was a visitor who'd drifted to this world for a deviancy that existed beyond the battlefield.

"You have business with Mr. Morio Ariyama…rather, the self-proclaimed demon king Morio, yes? This is purely conjecture, but your condition for this operation was being present at the postwar negotiations. Without the backing of Aureatia, it would be difficult to create an opportunity to have a confidential conversation with the ruler of a nation. As a fellow visitor, perhaps you have some business you wish to discuss with him?"

"Hmmmm. You're certainly well-informed, aren't you? Even you know that Morio's a visitor, too."

Self-proclaimed demon kings. Individuals with excessive systematic, or Word Arts, power. Mutants who try to establish a new species. Visitors who brought heretical political concepts to the world. The ruler of the Free City of Okafu was unquestionably one of such deviants.

"Okafu is supplying military power that includes provisioning weapons, along with peacetime drilling and training. Although they disguise themselves as a mercenary guild, their business structure is clearly that of a private military company. That alone is enough of a factor to surmise that Morio is a visitor."

"Well then, let's say my goal here's this—to bring you in, too, and have the three of us wax nostalgic over our far-off homeland. How's that sound?"

"Oh yes, when that time comes, I'd love an invite."

The boy looked up at the Okafu fortress with a face of mixed feelings.

"Do you truly plan to bring down Okafu through force of arms? You've demonstrated your strength to them plenty by now. There's a chance Mr. Morio would be receptive to bargaining with you individually, without waiting to reconcile peace with Aureatia."

"What a stupid idea. He'd never agree to those kinds of negotiations while he has the food stores prepared for a siege. Besides, aren't you the one developing new models of guns to kill people like me?"

"Originally, I was making them for you, Miss Kazuki. Reaching production stability was a difficult road."

"You get that I was being sarcastic with that, right?"

Part of Kazuki's mission included neutralizing Morio. Even if there was a path to avoid battle, her status as a champion came to her precisely because she continued to produce desired military achievements.

"Your goal is information, right? Mr. Morio's position allows him to pull and collect all the information from the mercenaries he has stationed across the world."

"That's right. But you wouldn't get anything out of it. Just looking for personal confirmation."

"That's...quite intriguing. All the more so if it's enough to pique your interests, Miss Kazuki."

"Yugo the Moving Decapitation Blade. Yukiharu the Twilight Diver. Morio the Sentinel. Hiroto the Paradox."

"......"

"Pfft. That's a good look for you. Those are the names of all the recent visitors who have shown up here. I'm sure you've picked up on it already. They all came from the same country we did."

It couldn't have been so in the past. Simply from the naming conventions for the different races and the cultural styles, there had to have been a large number of people arriving here not from their own homeland, but a cultural sphere far off to the west.

At some point, there was a large fluctuation. Kazuki was convinced of the truth behind the change. The mystery that the bulk of those who arrived in this world in its current state were unaware of.

"...True, there may be some bias at play. Though, rather than declare that based on the handful of known examples, I feel it's necessary to view things long-term and gather data."

"I have no idea how many hundreds of years *long-term* is for you."

Kazuki twirled the muskets in each of her hands, spinning herself around with them. Her coat and skirt fluttered with her.

"*Taaah. Ta-taaah. Taah, taaah......*"

"I take that to mean you don't plan on asking for my help yet, then?"

"Beyond paying for your goods anyway. I'm a champion, aren't I? Even if I'm just a plain old murderer."

She smiled as she danced in the light of the setting sun.

"Doing things alone is my personal policy. As a champion, I have to fulfill my obligations to this world, don't I?"

Nine years earlier, when the True Demon King still lived, there was a vivid legend formed amid that age of darkness.

A musketeer, touching down from a different world, deftly wielded a weapon that, at the time, no one had ever seen before, a "gun," and all by herself, liberated a northern city turned into a labyrinth by a self-proclaimed demon king, called the Great Ice Bastion.

The Free City of Okafu's assailant was a visitor. Kazuki the Black Tone.

◆

The high outer wall looking down over the mountain ridge. Past it on the other side was another wall. With another wall behind that one, too. The road through the space in between the walls skirted around like a maze, forming the town......and making any spot within the meandering road always exposed to long-range fire from the central citadel.

On top of this, each and every one of the mercenaries stationed there had equipment and training on par with Aureatia's regular soldiers, making an easy invasion impossible. However, Kazuki the Black Tone was a champion in the shadows, better versed in this type of unconventional warfare than any other.

Kazuki was going to achieve her goal without any meddling from Aureatia. Meanwhile, Aureatia could avoid an all-out war with Okafu while praying for the visitors' mutual demise.

Kazuki the Black Tone whittled away at Okafu's military strength, and using relief as a pretext, Aureatia would dispatch their army, negotiating from an advantageous position. That was the plan Aureatia had devised. If possible, after the two visitors involved had been killed.

Kazuki was well aware of Aureatia's attempts to get rid of all deviant combat powers from the world.

A veteran visitor like Kazuki the Black Tone could also use such world affairs for her own purposes.

She firmly brushed away her long hair. She squinted her eyes in the final brilliance of the setting sun.

Turning his sights on the small carriage that appeared to escort him away, the Gray-Haired Child muttered to her.

"Looks like it's time to go. Sad to go our separate ways, but be well."

"When will I get to see you again, then?"

"It might be another ten... No, I'm sure I'll end up seeing you again before long, Miss Kazuki Mizumura. I'm glad to see you haven't changed at all."

"Right. And you were just as shady as always, yourself."

Kazuki smiled a little. Then she nimbly jumped into the car she had bought from the Gray-Haired Child.

It was called an automobile. A vehicle that was powered by steam. She needed a mode of transport without an expendable life span in order to ensure the day's strategy for storming the fortress would succeed.

Now that their first meeting in thirty years was finished, the young boy's carriage grew smaller and smaller in the distance. The horse kicked the earth, running.

Horses. This world had horses, too. There were times when she'd suddenly think back on it nostalgically.

A world that was clearly connected to her homeland yet was unquestionably different.

"*Ta-taaah, taaaah, taaah. Ta-taaaah......*"

Inside the car, Kazuki hummed to herself as she fiddled with several muskets.

The night would be her time. The many gunners positioned in the citadel would be unable to hit their proper target in the darkness and the light of the kerosene lamps. At the very least, not Kazuki the Black Tone and her perfect understanding of everything involving guns.

The steam engine started up. Currently, her position was on a slope looking down on the drawbridge spanning the ravine. It meant she'd descend an incline so sharp it physically felt like a straight drop, with the speed of the steam-powered automobile.

The car's mass won't change. Unlike horses' legs, the wheel rotations are fixed, too...

It wasn't equipped with the steering functionality of cars in the Beyond. Kazuki didn't need it.

If its hit any sudden obstacles, it'll be repelled and fly back at the appropriate angle—just like a bullet.

She felt the speed increase as she descended the hill. In the driver's seat, she didn't do a thing.

Much like how no gunner touched their bullet after setting their line of fire.

The drawbridge closed in. She continued rushing forward. Getting wind of the assault, the bridge was in the middle of being drawn up. She could tell the bows and guns at the citadel all had their sights trained on her.

Steam-powered automobiles felt no fear. Its speed neither accelerated nor slowed. A storm of gunshots. A hail of slaughter relying solely on sheer volume. The metal plating installed around the driver's seat would guard her against the hail only once. It was accelerating plenty. It didn't stop. The car collided into a mass of rock. The car body was launched up into the air at exactly the angle Kazuki wanted—tumbling diagonally toward the end of the rising drawbridge. The cargo bed was crushed, and the load of muskets inside scattered out of it like rain.

Similarly launched into the air, she readied her two muskets.

"Impact."

It was as if she had known her sacrificial gamble would succeed from the very start. She cleared the bottomless ravine and had invaded the Free City. She breached the first outer wall.

In midair, she made out a shield-wielding ogre guarding the tightly shut gate.

A correct judgment to make. Supposing she was able to step inside the second outer wall and could utilize cover and her mobility, the ragtag mercenaries had no hope of winning. For the first three days, she had massacred her enemies to ensure just that.

"...*Taaah, ta-ta-tah, finished them off~! What a scene~!*"

First, she would kill the ogre guarding the gate. Instantly, as she crossed her arms to unsheathe her guns, two gunpowder flashes occurred at once.

A shrill metallic sound rang out.

"…What?"

Kazuki was puzzled as her lithe knees dulled the impact of her high-speed landing. The ogre didn't appear to have reacted to her shots at all. Yet her target still lived.

She was certain the previous sound had been both of her bullets being stopped at tremendous speed.

They weren't normal bullets. The muskets mass-produced in this world had remarkably improved accuracy compared to their historical equivalents in the Beyond—but the bullets had curved at a speed only Kazuki was able to see.

Their trajectory was aimed at the ogre's carotid artery, wrapping around both flanks of the shield to pierce it. It was no work of Power Arts. Her supreme technique brought the air resistance and rotation of the bullet itself under her willful control. Kazuki the Black Tone was always running through these calculations as she readied her shot.

"You've got a lovely voice. You should become a singer."

"……*Fiiingers out of reaaach. One on top of theeeee other… Tah, tah.*"

There was another mercenary in hiding. An abnormally thin body, able to hid behind the ogre's large frame. A skeleton.

Skeletons were fast. Without either muscle or organs, they possessed an extremely lightweight body, lighter than would've been possible for any living being, and that was even combined with the physical strength and technical skills they had possessed in life, too.

That being said...

She had never before seen any being like him. Speed on an entirely different level that the simple racial difference couldn't explain. Even in the darkness, how he had managed to react so deftly?

The two bullets she had fired simultaneously hadn't been cut nor reflected.

The wide side of his spearhead had *knocked them down* to the ground.

What kind of speed was that, seriously?

Kazuki grew annoyed.

"...What, you're just hiding behind the gate?"

"My job's defense. I have some things I'd like to ask you. I'll keep you company till you run out of bullets."

"Oh? Suit yourself."

A projectile came at her from the side, trying to catch her off guard. She pulled her body back and avoided it like it was nothing.

A thin medicinal vial landed on the ground and exploded in an irritative acrid black smoke.

"Kazuki the Black Tone. You must be sick of being the hunter, right? Today you're the prey."

The zmeu's reptilian face, after launching the medicinal vial from some sort of mechanical device, was gravely solemn.

A correct judgment. Even if she forced her way past the drawbridge, right here, before she could step within boundaries of the second inner wall...it was possible to surround Kazuki with several mastered hands and create this advantageous position—as long as she hadn't prepared for such a situation.

"*Hilca io ocaf. Formia ora. Nel cloza.*" (From Hilca to Okafu soil. Power of hoarfrost, cliff face.)

Reinforcements. A black-skinned minian was chanting Word Arts.

Using the momentum from her dodge, she rotated just barely over the ground, catching two of the muskets she had scattered all around, using her finger's first knuckle joint. The guns that had been fully loaded into the car were the groundwork she laid for the fight. This area had already been turned in her combat domain.

She rotated. Took aim. She wasn't firing at the zmeu in front of her or the chanting minia. She fired at the latest new reinforcement.

"*Enzeham nort! Nazelcthuk!*" (Stop heartbeats! Come to pass!)

On her right, she shot the thigh of the elf coming through the smoke screen, slashing at her.

The shot missed the head because their follow-through with their low-positioned iron rod protected their vitals. As proficient as their reputation suggested.

"*Hngah... Augh!*"

"......She got Leforgid!"

"Damn, how's she reacting so fast...?!"

In the drug-wielding zmeu's direction, an abruptly risen stone wall cut off her line of fire. Protective Craft Arts from the black-skinned minia. Supposing she had been shooting at the zmeu, then the elf's attack, cloaked in the smoke screen, would have split her head in two.

Correct judgments, each and every one of them.

Too bad it's all meaningless, though.

Taking on several mastered hands and fighting them at once. Fighting continuously.

To Kazuki the Black Tone, it wasn't anything special at all.

She would admit her opponents had the upper hand. Their judgment had been precise, and she could tell that their coordination was quite high.

Nevertheless, Kazuki had *become completely accustomed* to such situations and opponents. Even if the mercenaries compiled every possible optimal solution together, they wouldn't be able to match her talent. Without question.

"*Tah, ta-taaah. Taaah, taaah. I don't believe anymore...... I feeeel, myself, meeeeelting awaaay.*"

She spun her muskets in rhythm with her song. With it, she applied centrifugal force to them.

"*......Ta-ahn!*"

The metallic click came after Kazuki threw the musket in her right hand.

The next vial discharged from the zmeu's launcher machine was intercepted by the gunstock of the thrown musket long before it landed, and the smoke screen from the explosion enveloped the zmeu and the minia Word Arts user.

She kicked one of the muskets scattered at her feet and broke into a dash. The gun spun on the ground, sliding as it sped into the black smoke cloud. Kazuki's straight advance came faster than the black-skinned minia could incant the first stanza of their Word Arts.

"*Hilca io ocaf.*" (From Hilca to Okafu soil.) "*...Hng!*"

"*Taaah, tah.*"

She pulled out the left musket from within the smoke. Her gun was simultaneously also a bayonet spear. An enormous amount of blood drenched the bayonet, and the minia's Word Arts ended incompletely. The intercepting stab from their two-handed sword also failed to reach her.

"Beforeeee, inevitabilityyyy. Tears everything awaaaay."

She spun the musket she pulled up behind her. The blood scattered in a clean arc.

There was a sound of a shot from behind. Launched from the shield of the ogre defending the gate, the four metal rivets were blocked with her wooden gunstock. She had already picked up that this mechanism in the shield was the ogre's trump card.

Throwing one away and using the other for defense, now, both of the muskets she'd had in her hands were rendered useless......
Suddenly, the first enemy popped up in the back of her mind.

...That expert fighter. If the spear-wielding skeleton...picked this moment to make his move, then what?

"Shhhaaaaa!"

The vial-launching zmeu was at close quarters. Her claws were threatening to tear out her throat. A deafening boom pierced through the zmeu's mouth and passed through her skull. Kazuki threw away the small gun she pulled out of her coat. An armament of hers she hadn't revealed to them up until now.

"Ta-taaah..."

The moment that Kazuki the Black Tone took her hands off all the guns she had, including her hidden weapons—

It was the perfect opportunity he had been aiming for.

A minia wielding a rapier came up from behind Kazuki.

The man was Milieu the Hemp Drop.

He had perfectly hidden his presence during the exchange of blows up until that moment. A silver streak, straight at her heart—

"Aw, close one."

She kicked up a musket at her feet with the tip of foot. The gun she had sent to this position with a kick before her charge.

The bayonet's intercepting thrust, digging into his flank, reached out longer than the rapier.

"......!"

Piercing through his abdomen, she then pulled the trigger.

His innards exploding, the rapier wielder went flying from the shock.

"And you had the best chance, too. What a shame."

She hadn't read the situation—Kazuki herself simply maintained a position where she was capable of responding to anything.

Kazuki twirled around, moving like a dancer, and smiled down at the people she killed.

Four of them were snuffed out. Her fighting brought everything to a close in an instant.

She kicked two guns up into the air to pick them up. She was unscarred.

During the high-speed battle, she had constantly used her opponents to cut off the line of fire from the citadel. The rain of gunfire was never going to reach her. When it came to both combat and tactical strategy, the mercenaries were no match for the champion.

Left over were the two guarding the gate. A shield-wielding

ogre. With him was the skeleton spearman. Even if she assumed there were a number of traps and troops waiting for her behind them, the Free City of Okafu's military power was definitely growing weaker and weaker.

"I was only just hired by Okafu today, but…"

The skeleton looked at Milieu's pathetic corpse.

"…This guy said he'd show me around, see. Guess that's what they call the mercenary problem, but…I shouldn't have gone and made a promise like that."

"What? But I had him go on ahead so he could show you around the next life better."

The skeleton stepped forward. Black rags, reminiscent of a reaper. A full body of bone, treated with some unknown technique to polish them pure white.

"Shalk. Fall back."

The ogre gave a brief warning to the skeleton mercenary.

"You can tell, right? Anyone that challenges her probably has a death wish."

"Well, I've been dead for a long time now. Got nothing to lose, really."

Shalk brandished his white spear.

"Kazuki the Black Tone. You the Hero?"

"…Nope. Been mistaken for them before, but it's not me."

"Really now. Well then, first off, if I win, I want you to pass your entry for Aureatia's Royal Games to me."

"Is that right…?"

She herself hadn't considered the Royal Games to decide the

Hero as anything more than whimsical entertainment. The firm promise that she'd be rewarded for taking down Okafu with the right to enter was, from the very start, nothing but a *bonus* for making contact with Morio the Sentinel.

However, she never expected anyone out there would challenge her to a duel for such a reward.

"Makes no difference to me. You can have it."

One-on-one. The prospect of competing against the speed that first stopped her bullets gave her a bit of a thrill.

Or perhaps, maybe this skeleton had hoped for this very situation, and that was why he hadn't gotten involved in the fight until now.

"Second question. This one I'd like the answer to now."

"...You know, you're quite a bit pushier than you look, huh."

"You've visited The Land of The End. As part of that very first search party to confirm the Demon King had disappeared."

"And?"

Kazuki was looking at Shalk's center of gravity. He held his spear out straight ahead. He was trying to kill her with a maximum-range thrust.

This skeleton was likely able to dodge faster than her bullets flew, even if he waited until after seeing where she aimed.

Nevertheless, for Kazuki, reacting after seeing her aim was still too slow. She could fire in a completely different direction than where her gun barrel was aimed by using the spin and inertia she gave to the bullet inside the barrel. Even if he compiled together all the optimal solutions to her attacks, he wouldn't be able to match her talent.

"If the Demon King really was defeated... Did you see the Hero there? And if they happened to be dead, did you see their bones? If you did, then—"

The future up until the final moments was settled. With both guns, she would simultaneously send a bullet straight ahead and an indirect shot to cut off his route of escape. Kazuki's bullets would land five paces before the spear could reach her.

"Did they look anything like these bones?"

"Sorry, but..."

Kazuki's long hair waved in the night breeze.

In this world, there was a skeleton who was brought to life without any idea who they were.

Surely it must have been similar to the loneliness felt by visitors, exiled in another world for their deviance.

"I don't know a damn thing about you."

"I see."

Dust and sand flittered in the air. She pulled the trig—

CHAPTER 5
Kazuki the Black Tone

CHAPTER 5
Shalk the Sound Slicer

"Huh?"

It was after the spearhead had been pulled out of her windpipe.

Shalk was five paces outside his spear's range. Exactly as the preternatural champion, Kazuki, had estimated.

The visitor, capable of watching a bullet's path with her naked eye, was only barely able to capture the exact second that he nigh instantaneously returned his grotesquely extended and rearranged right arm back to normal—it was supernatural speed.

Much more—the speed of his spear thrust.

...Impossible...? What...?

She couldn't sing.

The strength drained from one of her legs, and her body twisted as it collapsed.

Shalk the Sound Slicer was looking down at her as she writhed. Both in the New Principality of Lithia and here in the Free City of Okafu, he was after the same thing. The truth behind the Hero and the Demon King of this world.

Or a powerful someone who could tell him who he was.

"Aaah, this...wasn't the one, either."

The hollow skeleton spat out bitterly, walking off into the wilderness. Who was he? Where did he come from? Why was he as strong as he was?

Even the skeleton himself didn't understand.

"......Who, am I?"

He possessed a deceased, suprarational physical form, rendering both thrusts and fired shots meaningless.

He knew spear techniques capable of surmounting champions, while being completely ignorant of his own origins.

He voided the perceivable concept of range as meaningless with instantaneous separation and conjugation.

A monstrosity abruptly born into this world. The fastest undead in the land.

Spearhead. Skeleton.

Shalk the Sound Slicer.

CHAPTER 6 ◈ The Age of the Demon King

Four years ago, in an age when the Demon King's reign of terror darkened the very skies…

It lay a half-day's walk from Kuta Silver City, where the volunteer army to block the Demon King's invasion gathered. The man had crossed beyond the minian races' final line of defense and stood there.

He carried no weapon.

His eyes drooped beneath a wide-brimmed hat, and his face seemed gaunt. He carried a large wooden box on his back, containing what was presumably his travel equipment.

He wasn't a warrior. Supposing he did join up with the volunteer defense army, the man would've had no prospects of returning alive. He inherited a stout physique from his father and had dreamed of becoming the kingdom's greatest bowman, but it didn't take long to realize he had no talent for archery. He could have reluctantly shifted his focus to becoming a swordsman, but he knew this wouldn't work out, either. He wasted two whole years simply confirming for himself that he had no strength for combat. And now, here he was.

"Sakaoe Great Bridge Town. Must be the place."

Narrowing his eyes, he could finally discern the city emblem shown on the town guide board, dirtied with blood. It was supposed to be a trading city, well-known in the east and west. After hearing about it, the man never would have thought this would be how he'd end up paying it a visit.

"It really got this bad in just one small month, huh? I'll b—"

His frivolous chatter stopped when he caught an elderly woman squatting beside a watermill along the road.

"I-it's okay. You're still alive. You're still alive, okay? You're not dead yet. Okay? It'll—it'll all be over soon. Just a little more..."

The woman was mumbling incoherently, half smiling and half crying.

She continued to raise a blunt instrument of some kind in the air, striking it hard into a young girl who was long dead.

The jerky convulsions in her leg that came with each blow were malfunctions caused by what remained of her brain, largely smashed and scattered on the ground.

"*Haaah, haaah...* I-it'll be okay. This'll make it all better. I'm scared. I'm so scared...... *Auugh......*"

"......"

The wooden box–laden man didn't say a word or lend a hand, simply continuing on ahead. In this era, there were countless stories of people who invited even greater tragedy from getting involved with such people who had fallen so far.

When he passed by her, he got a good look at the blunt object she was single-mindedly bringing down repeatedly on the dead girl. It had been reduced to nothing but a deformed dark-red shape, but it had very tiny arms. Gripped firmly in the woman's hand appeared to be a foot.

Curse the Demon King Army.

Heading *toward* the Demon King Army was sheer madness.

At this point, no one had ever thought about purposefully venturing into the Demon King Army.

Everyone knew that the "volunteer defense force" existed in name only. All they could manage was driving out the maddened citizenry and their deeds from the defense line and pray that the True Demon King never unpredictably crossed it.

The man himself had no guarantees he would return from his journey with his sanity intact. It was a reckless challenge.

Around the time his surroundings started to grow denser with buildings, three silhouettes, then a fourth, aimlessly appeared on the town streets.

Each one brandished a weapon that could hardly be called one. A rotted piece of lumber. An iron butter knife. One of the men even gripped down tight on the sharp edge of a rusted ax blade.

"Heh-heh. Eh-heh, hee-hee-hee-hee…"

"No… Please… Help meee. Someone, kill me…"

"Brother… It—it's not my fault, okay? All this… It's a dream… just a dream…"

The survivors who hid themselves in fear sensed the visitor and must've come reaching out to him for help—at the very least, the man figured that's what he would've done.

"No… *A-aauuuuuuuuugh! Aaaaaaah!*"

A young girl flew at the lumber-wielding man and, together with a scream, gouged out his eye with a fork. Drilling the handle all the way down into the eye socket, she persistently kept up her destruction, tearfully screaming as she went.

"……"

The wooden box–laden man didn't move, simply watching from a removed position. If he tried to stop them, he'd get swept up in it, too. Even for this young girl, so much more delicate than him, there was nothing he could do.

"I'm sorry, I'm sorry… I'm sor—"

The girl's apology was interrupted. The back of her head was bashed in by another man.

Even while the girl's neck was twisted down in a strange angle, she still continued to scoop out her victim's eyeball. With the second blow of the blunt object, her head was completely crushed. Another person was lured into the tragedy from a back alley somewhere, and the two killed each other. Yet another person came after. *These people were seeking someone to help them*, after all, then.

The man with the wooden box had stopped breathing at some point while he looked on.

He needed to stifle the part of his mind that found it all so terrifying.

I get it now. That's why, then, that no one ever comes to save these people anymore.

The one still breathing was a middle-aged man who already had one of his thighs bitten off.

Simply having someone get close causes them to start slaughtering each other.

The man with one thigh torn off shakily walked and shoved both his hands right into the center of a pool of blood.

Those hands had killed his neighbor for no reason whatsoever. He was on the verge of death himself. A truth that pleased no one.

"Heh-heh."

The man was laughing.

"Heh, heh, heh, heh, heh, heh......"

Laughing in despair. No words could reach him.

He was a simple minia, no different from the man with the box. He must've lived a quiet life, celebrating happiness and lamenting misfortune.

This was the military force that comprised the Demon King Army.

"...Forgive me, old man. I ain't the hero here."

"I can't take it... I'm scared... I want to relax... Aaaah......"

Even as a tragedy unfolded right before his very eyes, he absolutely couldn't get himself involved. He understood that.

But at least once, he needed to test his own power.

"Hang on a sec, there."

The man lowered the wooden box on his back to the ground. He took out his trusty instrument from inside when—

"HALT."

It wasn't one person. It sounded like several people all speaking as one.

An aberrant presence looked down on the men from the roof of what was once a church. It looked in part like an enormous wolf, but its coat of fur, gleaming blue and silver, was nothing like a wolf's natural fur.

The man raised his hands up while still seated on the ground.

"...I've stopped."

"YOU. YOU TRIED TO ADVANCE BEYOND THIS POINT."

"And? Did you make your nest up ahead or something?"

"...DO YOU WISH TO STAND AGAINST THE TRUE DEMON KING?"

Anyone who visited this hellish place likely wouldn't have any other reason.

"NO MATTER WHAT MEANS OR IDEAS YOU MAY POSSESS—THEY ARE FOOLISH DELUSIONS. ABANDON YOUR AMBITION AND RETURN WHENCE YOU CAME. OR BECOME MY SUSTENANCE. THESE ARE YOUR OPTIONS. NO MATTER WHICH YOU CHOOSE... IT SHALL BE A MORE MERCIFUL FATE THAN CHALLENGING THE DEMON KING."

"Pretty impudent right off the bat, huh? Ominous, too. You a barghest? Definitely not a lycan, right?"

If it was a beastfolk that understood Word Arts, and with a wolf-like form, then it had to be a barghest. However, seeing its colossal frame and eight legs instead of four, it also appeared like something different entirely.

"I AM A CHIMERA. OZONEZMA."

"A chimera...? No way. As if there'd ever be a chimera as cleanly put together as you. Also, eating me before I get the chance to meet the True Demon King is your idea of kindness? That's messed up."

"...EAT YOU? ...YOU ARE FREE TO BELIEVE THAT I AM HERE TO EAT MINIA, IF YOU WISH. YOU SHALL NOT HEAR MY WARNING, THEN."

"Nope. If you're planning on killing me, get it over with. See, I don't got any fighting skills to my name."

The man smacked the back of his head.

Wholly free of deception, the man didn't have any combat means at his disposal.

"......IN WHICH CASE, WHY DO YOU ADVANCE FORWARD? INDEED...... YOUR BODY POSSESSES MUSCLES WITH EXTREME AMOUNTS OF STAMINA. JUDGING BY YOUR DEFENSIVE BODY MOVEMENTS, A FIGHTER YOU ARE NOT..."

"Never met a wolf that blabbers on like you before... Come on, then, what're you waiting for? You going to kill me or not?"

"WANTON SLAUGHTER IS NOT WHAT I SEEK."

"*Pfft...* You look like a demon king straight out of a poem, and you're playing the Goody Two-shoes act? I'm nothing but a bard. I just wanted to have this old man listen to my song."

The beast shifted his eyes to the man's personal treasure. It was a type of five-stringed instrument, but Ozonezma possessed no knowledge of it.

"So, Ozonezma, you've killed all the champions who've come here, acting the part of the Demon King's gatekeeper like this? The thing is: I'm a bit different than all of them, see."

Running his boorish fingers over the stringed surface, a sound played.

"The brilliance of his justice... A return to the field of corpses... The twin moons cross paths—"

"......?! WAIT."

Ozonezma's perplexed voice interrupted the singer's voice.

"What is it?"

"WHY ARE YOU SINGING?"

"What else is a bard supposed to do?"

"BUT WHY ARE YOU SINGING *HERE*?"

The man grinned. A smile that showed a glimpse of the confidence at the root of the powerless man's impudence and grit.

He sang.

"In the verdant morning... The valiant true king... Drinks deep of honor eternal..."

"................."

The song, and the music, continued.

It was verse that sang the tale of an ancient king long ago, one even children would recognize.

The music he played conveyed as much. The exceedingly simple sound of his voice, and his strings, quivered as to stir the depths of the soul.

Beauty. Touching—singular words were unable to fully express the delight, the sorrow, the hope, the rage, the resignation, the hatred, the joy...... It was as if all the emotions constituting one's heart simultaneously blossomed at once.

They were neither Word Arts nor a superpower, but it was the sort of song that penetrated deep into every corner of the parched scene of despair.

"......"

Even the man with one of his thighs bitten off had stopped laughing.

As if the song had abated the waves of sadness and terror, he silently stared at the bard.

"...WHAT IS THAT?"

Even the giant beast listened with rapt attention.

It was stimulus from the turbulent world, the first he had known after surviving his life of bloodshed.

"CAN THAT DEFEAT THE DEMON KING?"

"Of course it can't. Still though, plenty of people have disappeared trying to kill them with more direct methods. Needs to be someone out there who tries something a bit more unorthodox. With my music... *Pfft.*"

He couldn't help laughing at the sheer absurdity of his words.

"I'm going to touch the True Demon King's heart."

"IMPOSSIBLE."

Ozonezma shook his head. The man was taking on the True Demon King. No matter how wonderful his music may have been, it was obvious from the start that it was impossible.

"A FOOLISH ATTEMPT. INDEED, YOU ARE YET ANOTHER GOING TOWARD THEIR DEATH."

"Think so? What about you then, Ozonezma? You don't want to become the hero?"

The man didn't think this Ozonezma in front of him was one of the True Demon King's followers.

Everyone knew that the True Demon King didn't have anyone like that with them.

No one could become their companion. Because they were the enemy of all living things.

In which case, the chimera's warning was unquestionably true. Death was the only option to stem those who sought to stand up to the madness and perish in futility—such was the complete and total despair that awaited up ahead.

"IT IS IMPOSSIBLE FOR ME. THAT IS PRECISELY WHY I REMAIN HERE. I... I DO NOT WISH TO TASTE THE DESPAIR OF THOSE WHO HAVE MOVED ON."

"Hey, it's not impossible. Even an idiot like me is trying to defeat the True Demon King. You're telling me you can't muster up the same amount of courage?"

"......"

"Even if you stay back here for now, the fight's gonna find you eventually."

He stood up and shouldered the injured man.

With his song, he had successfully pacified a single person. However, their mind might never fully return. So immense was the terror the True Demon King induced.

"However, was there a power out there in this world capable of reaching them, however slightly, in their hearts?"

He was imagining one possible future.

"...No need to get all worked up. My work here's done. I'll head back now."

"WORK...? WHAT WAS YOUR WORK?"

"Y'know, you had a point. You're totally right—it's utter madness to be singing in a dangerous place like this. Since you were kind enough to watch me, I was finally able to test things. There aren't too many guys out there who can capture the Demon King Army alive, see. Very few. Up until now, I've only ever been able to test it on a girl with her eyeballs crushed, really..."

"......WAIT."

Ozonezma elegantly dropped down from the rooftop. Landing without a sound, despite his huge frame, his perfectly joined body made it impossible to determine what part of it was chimera.

The beast followed after the man as he walked off.

"YOU ARE IN SO MUCH DANGER I CANNOT SIT AND WATCH. WHY DO YOU NOT HAVE A SINGLE GUARD ALONG WITH YOU?"

"Well, well, did you really like my song that much?"

"...THAT IS NOT MY POINT."

It was preposterous ambition that even the man himself found hard to believe.

A traveling bard who simply sung his songs and an unknown champion-slaying beast.

Perhaps that was what made it all the more interesting.

At least one person needed to try an unorthodox method.

"Well, you're free to come with me for as long as you'd like; I don't mind. Even you'd start feeling depressed if you stayed behind in a place like that."

"…TOWN ISN'T TOO FAR AWAY NOW. ALSO, I HAVE YET TO ASK YOU YOUR NAME."

"Olukt the Drifting Compass Needle. I'm gonna do something so amazing that they're gonna be writing songs praising *me* one day, just you wait."

It was two years before the Demon King's subjugation. There was a man named Olukt the Drifting Compass Needle.

It was an era of darkness. He was nothing more than another victim of the True Demon King, another amid the masses of victims. There were plenty of others like him.

Without making anyone hear his mentally soothing singing, he died without leaving a name for himself behind.

However…

In the past, there was a town known as Kuta Silver City. Located at a pivotal point for trade east to west, it was a large metropolis that prospered mainly from the tourism industry. The activity in the city could have held its own with current Aureatia, particularly the trade quarter, which had a new building popping up with every visit, leading it to be called the shape-shifting city.

In modern times, it went by a different name—The Land of The End.

"...A goblin?"

Rique the Misfortune cast doubt on his trading partner as they appeared in the abandoned fortress ruins.

A hideous split mouth with a small frame. Pale sallow skin. Slim ears. A goblin—he didn't look like anything else.

He grabbed his familiar short bow while he lifted himself up. The room was formerly a soldier guardroom. He had been able to make sure the area right next to the bed was furnished with a weapon.

"Stop right there. I'm Rique the Misfortune. What's your second name?"

"…You seem quite guarded. Well, I suppose you don't become a notorious mercenary without being cautious. I am the Thousandth. Zigita Zogi the Thousandth. Pleasure to make your acquaintance."

Surprisingly, the goblin spoke with eloquence.

Goblins—from what Rique had heard from his father and grandfather; before the True Demon King appeared, their race had run rampant across the land. Savage and breeding in large numbers, goblins often invaded minian domains, threatening their safety, and were the main target for extermination, together with wyverns, as a necessity of civilization as a whole.

As a result, while the wyverns survived, individually strong and capable of flight, goblins on the other hand—with their low intellect and vulnerability to simple attacks with water and fire, numbers as their sole advantage—were said to have disappeared at one point.

"…Zigita Zogi the Thousandth. Our dealings together didn't just start yesterday. I thought the intermediary would be a minia, but… Are there any minia that would cooperate with goblins?"

"Who's to say? You mention that I have the minian collaborator Rique, but you have a dwarven collaborator yourself, yes? In other words, there are *plenty* of ways to negotiate a deal without showing your face. Plenty of ways to fight without showing your face, too."

"Suppose so. But you're showing me your face today."

"That's because you hired me for a considerable sum, Rique. Please accept my show of good faith. Perhaps you hate goblins; is that it?"

"……"

Rique sighed and sat down where he stood.

He wasn't sure. In truth, he didn't really have anything against goblins. As he was relatively young, he didn't remember the time when goblins were around. He hadn't personally witnessed them destroying crops or stealing children.

His longtime business partner belonged to a rare species. Really, that was all there was to it.

"The request this time has come from the Lana Farmlands. To stamp out all the living creatures in The Land of The End. That small farming village's really thrown an outrageous job out there, and I doubt they will pay much for it, as well."

"…Actually, there have been two recent tragedies to hit Alimo Row that were due to beasts wandering out of The Land of The End. Whether it's a small town or a bustling city, the fear is the same."

"But by subcontracting me here, you must be putting yourself deep in the red, Rique."

"Don't need to worry about me. Can you actually fight on your own?"

"Fight? That would honestly be a tall order right now… Per our contract, I can only provide the same level of logistical support I've offered you in the past."

"I'm not asking for you to save me. I'm asking if you can protect yourself. Given that you've come out all this way to see me, surely you know what I'm hunting, right?"

"…My goodness. I didn't mean to snub your thoughtful consideration. I have heard the rumors, though."

As he spread out his camping tools inside the uninhabited stronghold, Zigita Zogi added more wood to the fireplace.

When he cast simple Thermal Arts at the igniting stone, the fire illuminated his face.

"That the Demon King's Bastard is here."

The area where the True Demon King was, even now, a region consumed with terror and danger, rejecting all normal life—making anything that haunted the area abnormal.

The maddened beasts that wandered out from The Land of The End very rarely attacked settlements.

At the same time, The Land of The End was also the sole clue for pursuing the truth behind the Demon King's death. The powers that dispatched research expeditions there were too numerous to mention. They were naturally from Aureatia, but also from Taren the Punished in the New Principality of Lithia, and more. However, an unidentified monster frequented the region, and all attempts at surveying the area or bringing the monster down had ended in failure.

"If its reputation's to be believed, the enemy's the same species as the Demon King. I'll already have my hands full taking care of myself and won't be able to give any attention to defending you... I think."

"...You're much too modest. Right now, between the Old Kingdoms' loyalists in Toghie City and the attacks on the Free City of Okafu, surely there's plenty of up-front and well-paying jobs you could've chosen over this."

"I'm not an Old Kingdoms' loyalist, and I definitely don't

think I have the skills to fight Kazuki the Black Tone for a job……
Also, it's not good, either."

"What isn't good?"

"That there's someone menacing the beasts in The Land of The End."

Zigita Zogi cast his eyes around the room. There wasn't another soul on the first floor of the guardroom.

"I hate to say it, but it appears you're the only one who feels that way, Rique."

Rique the Misfortune often let his innate goodness and honest disposition lead him to working at a loss. He was a rare breed for a mercenary in the current age, but it also showed he had the clear skills necessary to hold fast to his own will.

"There isn't much information about the Demon King's Bastard, but have you devised some means to defeat them all by yourself?"

"By myself…? Of course not. Who said anything about that?"

"Ohhh. In that case…"

Midway through his words, Zigita Zogi looked farther into the guardroom. A specter of a man appeared, coming down the stone-work stairs.

"…Your voices…echo up to the second floor, Rique."

"W-well… This *is* a surprise. I never would have imagined someone such as yourself would be here for a job like this."

"Goblin. Do not interfere with us. Get in our way, and I kill you. Your first warning."

Placing all his weight on his cane as he walked, he had an elderly man's frailty. However, the face hidden under his dark-blue robe was enveloped in a darkness blacker than night, leaving both his race and expression a mystery.

"Thermal Arts. Power Arts. Craft Arts. Life Arts."

For Word Arts, there were four schools known systematically throughout the world, and Word Arts that lay outside these four schools were collectively known as Demon Arts. However, in the current age, there existed just one individual who boasted about discovering a fifth school of Word Arts from within these Demon Arts. Arts that no other had been able to analyze before.

His name was Krafnir the Hatch of Truth.

"...Stamping out all the living creatures dwelling in The Land of The End. Together, Krafnir and I will conquer The Land of The End."

◆

A mysterious dust blackened the sky, and there was a vague lukewarm moisture in the blowing wind. The trees and grass grew in an unnatural direction as well, as if trying to avoid the area that cursed any and all living organisms.

Riding together in the new style of carriage, the three arrived in The Land of The End.

Extremely accurate arrows of light metal and various types of medicines. Logistical provisioning to the ruined fortress, in anticipation of a drawn-out conquest. Finally, once he had finished the arrangements for their comings and goings like this, for the timing being, Zigita Zogi's first role was over.

"The Demon King's Bastard. Can the True Demon King even have children?"

"Good question. Who knows, really. Regular demon kings, the self-proclaimed kind, sometimes make their own constructs. I mean, no one knows the truth behind that thing's identity. Save for, of course......the True Hero."

"What of the idea that it's a remnant of the Demon King Army? Even for this latest job, it all originated with this Belka the Rending Quake person attacking a town, right?"

"This enemy is rational. It's clearly targeting research expeditions and ambushing them."

Krafnir cut in, sitting back deep in his seat.

"EITHER THAT, OR IT COULD BE SOME SORT OF CONSTRUCT TAKING SUCH ACTIONS AUTOMATICALLY."

"...That's why I don't think it's the Demon King Army. If there were any others still alive like Belka, and if they were truly part of the Demon King Army, they'd never target the research teams sent here over and over again and send them packing, nor could they."

The Demon King Army had no leadership, nor did it even have an objective.

The *weakest and wickedest* military force that once completely covered the whole land.

Exterminating the Demon King Army, huh. I wonder what Krafnir's up to.

Krafnir the Hatch of Truth. An arts caster said to be the greatest of the modern age. Rique thought the meager reward of a poor farming village wasn't enough to encourage a champion like him to act, but the man's thoughts were completely opaque.

"…Is that a survivor?"

Krafnir picked up on a presence ahead of where the carriage was heading.

A round, clear, and faintly crimson-colored creature was blocking the road. An ooze.

"Maybe, Zigita Zogi. Can you wait here?"

"You intend to get out of the carriage, then? I imagine with your bow, Rique, you should be able to aim at it from our current position, no? Besides, if you take your eyes off me, I might run away and leave you behind, after all."

"I wonder. I can tell you aren't the type to do something like that. At any rate, don't come any farther."

Leaving the carriage, Krafnir and Rique carefully closed the distance. The soil was strangely moist, an ominous sign.

When the two drew closer, the ooze was mumbling incoherently.

"Sorry, I-I'm sorry… I'm sorry. I'm sorry."

"…Almost none of the soldiers who encountered the Demon King's spawn saw what the enemy looked like. Probably because they moved too fast. The extent of their injuries was pretty varied, too."

"Hmm…… You think this ooze is the same?"

"I'm not sure."

The two continued to keep their distance from the ooze, trembling in terror—when suddenly the ground directly below it split open.

"……!"

An enormous maw burst up from the earth and devoured the ooze before it could say a word. Behind the surfacing head was its horrifyingly long body.

The strongest terrestrial creature in the land, a wurm. Even more terrifying, parts of it had been reinforced with gold wire, with crystals set in both of its eye sockets. Not an organic creature of the natural world—it was a construct.

"What the hell, Krafnir!"

"......Yes? This is the fastest way to handle things... If speed is our enemy's weapon, then my Mighamud will swallow this bastard up even faster."

"That's not the problem here... Other creatures nearby're gonna notice the sound and tremors. You know what'll happen next? They'll *come looking for someone to help them.* That's the kinda place we're at right now."

"Naturally, that was my intention. We are exterminating the Demon King Army. In which case, it would be easier to bring them all together and take them out at once."

The bizarre wurm was named Mighamud. Krafnir had singled out the carcass of an especially large wurm and breathed life into it to create his revenant masterpiece.

While Krafnir himself never received the actual demon king designation from the kingdom, his construct-creation skills were on par with those who were. Far beyond it, he was the only one capable of reproducing constructs, something thought to only be capable through atheoretical emotional sensibility, from an actual theoretical framework.

"...Or perhaps, you aren't confident you can take on a swarm with your lone minian body, Rique the Misfortune? I would be willing to give a lesson......and teach you about my Mind Arts."

"Of course not. Just brings more trouble's all. If your stunt sends you to your death, don't expect me to help."

"Kwah, hah, hah, hah, hah...... Spare me your juvenile prattling."

Next, another person appeared. Pitifully emaciated and wrapped up in rags. They seemed to be minia. Mighamud's reflexes moved faster than a snake's—but far faster than it could act, the minia's chest was shot through with an arrow. Collapsing from the singular shot, they showed no signs of getting up.

Rique still had a large number of arrows readied in his hand when he shouted.

"They're still more of them coming. Krafnir!"

"......Do not act ahead of me. This is my first warning."

Gravitating toward them one by one, and then mostly beginning to devour each other, the maddened army began to be shot down by Rique's accurate bow fire.

A group of leprechauns reduced to a nauseating state appeared as well, but before they could try anything, they were all swallowed up in Mighamud's massive jaw.

Voices of madness and resentment. A ceaseless, unending nightmare.

Even for two men of such tenacious mental fortitude, it was

enough to *tempt their minds*, regardless of their knowledge of the Demon King's death. It was considered best not to involve oneself with the Demon King Army. For many people across the land, this was just as true now as it was then.

"Why...why're they living in such an awful place?!"

"......That's the True Demon King. The power of terror. The more one wants to run, the more impossible it becomes. They're long dead at this point. You know this well enough."

"Cursed Demon King... They've been dead for so long already...!"

Rique nocked his next arrow.

At the same moment, an intense red premonition flittered in the back of the man's mind.

One of the reasons he had lived and survived through countless battles was because he could sense warnings of threats approaching him with visions of the color red.

"Ooh?!"

Rique jumped, throwing his whole body forward. He hadn't an inch to spare.

From somewhere on the horizon, something attacked like a lightning bolt. Penetrating through all the debris along its path, it dug into the earth, drawing a line of destruction far outside the range of his bow.

"No way...!"

A small backlit silhouette appeared in the direction of the setting sun. It wasn't the silhouette of any of the large-size races.

The shadow moved. Rique had never before felt such a vivid and clear red premonition before. Who was this person?

He would dodge the red. Could he line up his arrow for when they crossed?

Im—

This time, he could clearly hear the supersonic sound of movement, splitting through the air with a loud crack.

—possible!

However, Rique's innate skill let his arrow fly with the barest of movements, making a direct hit. Exquisite skill, simultaneously done while dodging another of the straightforward attacks.

A direct hit at reverse velocity. No matter where the shot hit his mark, it would have a relatively fearsome amount of power in it. Yet…

"The arrow's broken…"

"Did it hit?!"

"It didn't get through! To the right!"

He looked to the right. An attack was incoming. Was he going to be in time?

Mighamud's colossal form cut in to protect Rique. Its thick flesh, protected by strong scales harder than steel, was effortlessly gouged open. Overcoming Mighamud and dashing forward, the figure continued under its momentum, grazing Rique's body.

…This is it.

A presence whose true form had been impossible for the various survey teams to see.

It had only launched three attacks at that point, but the average expedition would've been annihilated before they could even take another breath.

"Who are you?!"

The red color ran. He evaded. The figure passed by, bringing destruction with it.

"I should ask you!"

The voice came from behind as it passed him by. In a total twist of surprise, the unidentified monster replied to his question with one of its own.

A high-pitched voice, clear and resonant.

"Who exactly are *you*, then?! Showing up here and killing all those weakened people! Didn't anyone ever teach you…? Teach you that you shouldn't kill people like that!"

Rique couldn't help but look back behind him.

"……?!"

Fortunately at that moment, there was no follow-up attack, and Rique laid his eyes on something astonishing.

The figure, standing on tiptoe on a resident's crumbled chimney was a girl, of nineteen or twenty years.

A thin chestnut braid, swaying in the aftermath of her movement. The luster of her hair and skin was far too healthy to consider her part of the Demon King Army. Porcelain legs peeked out of her skirt, and she was also barefoot.

It didn't make any sense.

Her movements thus far had all been so forceful that a single dash would crack the ground beneath her feet.

"Everyone's in so much pain... They need help more than anyone else! Because of people like you!"

"...What's with this girl......?"

This was The Land of The End.

Her face, her words and mannerisms, her abnormal power... *Nothing like it* should have been in a place like this.

She had physical abilities far more frightening than any gigant or wurm. Rique, having experienced combat with such enemies many times before, actually couldn't even figure out when she would attack.

"...I'VE GOT HER. *CRAFFNIL IO MAGMA. NEXOPENES.*" (FROM KRAFNIR TO MIGHAMUD'S CORPSE. HOLE OF MUD BALL.)

"Your name?"

Now that he had seen her form, at the very least, he couldn't attack her indiscriminately anymore. With Krafnir's Word Arts incanting behind him, Rique said to the figure while training his short bow her way, "My name's Rique the Misfortune. So you're the Demon King's Bastard, huh?"

"The Demon King's...Bastard?! No... That's not it!" the girl shouted. She appeared to be enraged, but Rique found it eerie that she totally lacked the bloodlust and domineering attitude that naturally accompanied all fighters.

Aureatia. The New Principality. Their investigations had all been warded off by this one girl.

An unidentified roaming beast that inhabited The Land of The End.

"Oh, I'll tell you! My name's—"

The girl bent forward. The clothes she wore were torn along the side, and her flawless, uninjured skin was plainly visible.

Rique was sure that was where he had shot his arrow.

In all likelihood, Rique was superior in simple terms of skill. It was nonsensical to think her Word Arts could match Krafnir's. He could dodge. He could hit her. However.

...Am I gonna be able to kill this girl?!

"Tu the Magic!"

◆

Her mother choked to death.

Mother still had her butter knife gripped in her hand. With the dull blade, she cut open the stomach of her own son—the girl's young brother, barely three years old—stuffing her face full of his entrails until she choked and died.

Both of their expressions remained frozen in unimaginable agony. Filled with terror and despair up until their final moments, both mother and younger brother died a hopeless death.

She herself had no wounds at all. Her body was still intact. Her eyes, praised for their clear twinkle, and her expensive clothes she had once laughed about being too stiff for her were perfectly fine.

She was the only one left behind in this waking nightmare, in a country where everything had sank into the maws of hell.

The soles of her shoes were seeped in blood, and while she wandered vacantly through the building, she gazed at the town down below. This kingdom hadn't been razed in flames. Nor was it overrun by some colossal monster.

Nevertheless, everything was dead. Everyone finished in bottomless despair and terror, tormented by tragedies before perishing, similar or worse than what befell her beloved flesh and blood. They all died like this, one by one.

The True Demon King was nowhere to be found. They had already left.

Everything was over. Yet the young girl was the only one still alive. She was driven into despair.

"No, no, no, no, no, no..."

Her hands picked up a sword cast down on the floor. Someone must have dropped it. A dull sword with an awful number of nicks in the blade. Struggling under its weight, she tried to split open her own stomach with the sword. It was time.

"A-auugh... It hurts, it hurts...... I'm scared...... I can't take it anymore......"

The chipped blade scraped away at her skin like a saw. She could see bright-red blood pour out of her. It was her own body. Nauseating. Painful. Agonizing.

What's going to happen to me? What's going to happen to me? What's going to happen to me? What's going to happen to me? What's going to happen to me? What's going to happen to me? What's going to happen to me?

She went to shove the blade, kept back by her skin, deep into her abdomen. Into her very own body.

Was she going to be forced to taste this agonizing pain for the absurdly protracted time until her death? Why was she doing something so horrifying? What was going to happen to her?

"I—I...... *Sniff...!* I—I—"

Tears came.

"I'm scared."

Frightening. Terrifying. Neither she, nor anyone else, should've wanted to do anything like this. *Yet they weren't able to stand it all if they didn't.*

The Demon King was watching. She could hear that voice. Her arms kept moving.

"Help...... I don't want this..."

A wet, squelching noise. It must have been her skin tearing, the blade reaching inside.

"Stop!"

Suddenly, someone interrupted her, grabbing the sword out of her hand.

A long chestnut-colored braid hung from her head, the most striking aspect of the girl's appearance.

"Fool! You're still a young girl...... What if that leaves behind a horrible scar?! Didn't anyone teach you to take care of your body?!"

It was a lovely young girl. Around nineteen or twenty years of age. She looked about as old as her second eldest sister.

Amid the hellish nightmare......this young girl alone, appearing out of the blue, was the only one who wasn't smeared in blood or misery.

"Wh-what……?"

She looked at her own hands. The girl was holding them. She could feel her body heat.

The girl with the braid paid no mind to the filth of her hands and held them tight in warm hands of her own.

"……Who are you?"

"Tu. Tu the Magic, just passing by. Um…er, why?"

The braided girl looked at the sword lying on the floor. She seemed to be truly and utterly bewildered.

"…Why would you do something like this?"

"……"

"I was looking 'round town before I came here… Everyone was suffering; everyone was dying. It didn't make any sense at all. All of them were still alive! Everyone…… It's too horrible… I can't let something like this stand."

"That's not it…! That's not… I-it isn't… It isn't my fault."

Within the young girl's heart, filled with terror, it seemed like all of existence was condemning her.

She was the only one who survived. Despite everyone else dying, she alone survived.

"……!"

The braided girl, Tu, shook her head, as if throwing off all misery with it.

"Of course not! Let's go!"

Tu vigorously rose to her feet, her hands still tightly gripping the girl's, raising her on her tiptoes. She blinked rapidly, eyes that had been forced open for so long.

"Go?"

"We're running outta here! I'll take you with me!"

"......Ah."

Running away.

The idea hadn't crossed her mind up until that moment.

If someone hadn't said that to her, would she have aimlessly wandered about the ruined kingdom forever?

She was positive she would've. It was terrifying.

However, it was a different terror than what she had felt earlier—a *person's* fear.

"I... I want......to run away. I want to get away. But—but where......?"

"Doesn't matter where! You'll go crazy staying in a place like this! Get on my back!"

She did as she was told, letting Tu carry her...when she noticed how her own tears were dirtying Tu's clothes.

Oh no, I—I... I'm being saved like this; I can't...

It was then she learned she had been so terrified that she couldn't even afford to cry.

"I'm sorry."

"For what? Here we go—I'll run slow, okay?"

Tu started running. Completely contrary to what she had said, the landscape drifted by faster than even the finest steed could hope to match.

Flying out of a window, she freely bounded over towers, walls, gardens.

The girl couldn't believe it. It seemed like a lie. This young girl's words and her strength were both as if one of the champions, romanticized in poetry, had slipped out into the real world.

"...It'll be okay!"

The braid, fluttering behind her, was like the tail of a shooting star.

"The world's not cruel! I've heard it myself. There's all sorts of possibilities, no matter what the times're like... All sorts of color out there! So in that case, there's gotta be a future where you'll be able to smile and laugh, too!"

Among the tragic scenery, there was a girl capable of declaring such bright things without any hesitation.

Suddenly showing up, suddenly saving her—why was she able to remain so cheerful?

Tu and the girl's encounter that day was the only one they had. Like a hallucination that couldn't be shared with anyone.

No one else knew the truth of the day when she alone survived.

"Who......who are you?"

"Tu the Magic. Outside of that...... *Ha-ha-ha!* Honestly, I don't really know much myself! But it's okay!"

Tu laughed, leaving the hellish scene far in the distance behind them.

"The important stuff I've known from the beginning. Everything 'cept your name anyway! Mind if I ask?"

"...........Sephite."

The name of the last member of the royal family, unable to protect the citizens who needed their protection.

The day she could give her name with pride would likely never come.

However, Tu looked back and gave a blossoming smile.

"Nice to meet ya! I'm positive a smile would suit ya."

"What are you talking about?"

"I mean you'd look a whole lot cuter with a smile on your face, Sephite! Don't you think?"

◆

In parallel to the electric fistfight at hand, Rique etched the surrounding environs into his consciousness.

A destroyed tower three steps away, to the right. A stone fence, almost fully intact, twelve paces behind him.

Debris was scattered everywhere as vestiges of past destruction, including Mighamud's battle and Tu's recent charge. He needed to piece together some lightning-fast footing for himself.

"You're going to be sorry..."

Tu jumped up slightly from atop the residential building. Her movements were light enough to make him doubt her body really was capable of causing such destruction.

"For kicking them like that!"

She vanished, leaving a brief sound behind.

She kicked the wall to come from a different direction—no. Rique couldn't see the red warning flash.

There was an ominous crunching sound of some moist hard substance being smashed.

A right arm flew through the air. Krafnir's arm, ripped off and sent flying. Far beyond him in the distance, he could make out Tu's silhouette, digging into the earth to break speed.

It was possible for Rique to evade her attacks by himself. He could just barely capture her initial motion.

Nevertheless, it was an attack he couldn't afford to be hit by, even once.

I don't have the flexibility to protect someone else. If I don't continue to keep focused on myself, I won't be able to dodge her at that speed.

Krafnir's body lurched like a falling tree, and after two shaky steps, he picked up his fallen right arm with his left. His left hand was abnormally thin and parched an amber yellow.

"Aiming for me, is she?"

The veteran arts caster spat, offended.

He wasn't just skinny. The body he had kept hidden under his thick robe up to that point had all of its flesh completely chipped away. It was the body of a skeleton.

The man who had discovered the source of construct creation.

"I've got you figured out! Your body's somewhere else, isn't it?!"

"Just from figuring that out......what do you think you can do? Do you think a constructor like me would

EASILY REVEAL THEIR TRUE FORM? *CRAFFNIL IO SEYV. IMHOVEST. YUUSHUWEM NEO.*" (FROM KRAFNIR TO SAYV'S CORPSE. VIOLET STEM, TORN MEMBRANE.)

"D-don't even think about it!"

Reacting instantly, Tu's bare feet smashed the remaining torso. The vessel Krafnir manipulated remotely was lifted up and scattered into the air, together with its navy-blue robe.

A fragment of...its lower jaw continued the Word Arts incantation. *"MUQIMNART. PEGTILYRIA."* (RING OF WATER. HARM.)

From within the smashed-up corpse gushed forth a dirty greenish haze, which enveloped the area.

Tu immediately jumped away, but the haze blocked her vision, resulting in the three arrows fired at her from the flank to squarely hit their mark.

Chest. Left eye. Right thigh. Rique the Misfortune's masterfully skilled shots didn't miss their targets even when aimed through a cloud of fog.

"*Auugh...* Dammit! I let down my guard!"

She had indeed let down her guard. Under the standards of an average fighter.

...None of them penetrated. Not even a layer of skin gone...

Aiming for the gap in her ribs at point-blank range, he had assumed it wouldn't be able to pierce through her chest.

With precision enough to fire a shot through the eye of a needle, he also made a direct hit on her left eye. It hit but was repelled. He was sure what he saw.

If he aimed at her eye, and his attacks still couldn't hurt her, what other methods were left?

"Sorry, Krafnir, but I'm leaving the offense up to you. I'm going aim for her eyes. I'll make her keep her guard up to defend them. I'm guessing you're the better thinker here... Figure out a way to get through her defenses for me."

"I'VE ALREADY FINISHED DOING THAT."

Answering Rique's call was not the skeleton body scattered in every direction, but a metal bug that flew up close to his right ear.

While Tu was wiping her eyes—alone an unthinkable opening for a fighter to show her opponent—the pair needed to exchange fighting tactics.

"It's a poison mist that paralyzes the nerves and inhibits respiration... If arrows won't pierce her, then obviously it's time to try this...... Though."

Tu's eyes were once again fixed on the pair.

Her eyeballs took on an ominous green phosphorescence. She wasn't a minia......at the very least.

"Is the poison working on her? You're the one to judge."

"...What am I supposed to do...?!"

Tu's feet kicked up dust. A lightning-speed kick was coming.

He twisted his body. He fired his arrow straight in front of him to slam into her charge. Rique was moving at such a blinding speed that the fabric of her clothes began to tear.

"Impressive. Gotten used to it, eh?"

"I've seen it four times now!"

She was simply accelerating at top speeds and kicking. Either that or punching. That was the extent of the young girl's moves.

Tu's charges had destructive power and speed that could surpass a cannonball, but as long as he didn't miss her tell, he could dodge her attack, even if its speed broke the sound barrier.

Naturally, this was predicated on his special ability to sense incoming threats—and a vision honed through experience. Above it all, it required him to keep himself engrossed in complete concentration.

"...Enough with the dodging already!"

Tu expressed her dissatisfaction. The arrow that must have hit her square in the face didn't leave a single scratch.

"If you keep dodging me like this...I'm gonna have to run at full speed, you know."

In what seemed like a meaningless act, she began stretching where she stood. Rique's instant follow-up arrows hit her, but even as he focused the shots at her eyes, she didn't even flinch.

"I'm! Serious now! A full power kick from me! Will blast you to pieces!"

"Wait! What in the world—?"

He dodged the threatening red flash. The terrifying kick ended up grazing Rique narrowly as it passed him by.

A cloud of dust. His vision turned upside down. He already factored it all in. He caught the girl in his sights and aimed his bow. He could tell his body would soon fall back down. He focused his strength in his thighs.

Firing a shot, to keep her in check. Meaningless. There wasn't any attack that could keep this girl back.

A concussive roar.

Rique jumped into the air. A black wind crossed right under his feet, gouging the earth.

The track of her green pupils drew a curved line and smashed a stone wall. She continued running right through it.

He collapsed to the ground to dodge Tu's charge. Everything from her reactions to her attacks were too fast. It was all he could manage.

The ground was deeply gouged. The hollowed-out ditch continued all the way across the city. He didn't have any time to get back up.

An explosive blast. A dull noise echoed. Then it stopped.

Reactivated Mighamud threw its body at her from the side. Blocking the blow from the giant mass, several times larger than herself, pushed her three steps back.

Digging her bare feet into the ground and placing her hand on Mighamud's head, she suddenly murmured to it.

"...Do you have a heart?"

Unlike with Krafnir's proxy body earlier, the girl didn't crush the revenant's head.

The chance gave Rique barely enough time to get up off the ground.

The girl again set her sights on him. She lowered her body, her initial tell.

A charging stance.

It's all the same.

The girl's combat tactics were composed solely of the exact same straightforward charge, over and over again.

It had tremendous power behind it, but with Rique's superpowered eyes and experience, evading it wasn't completely impossible. He couldn't even call it a technique, instead she was simply throwing her body's physical abilities at him. However.

An explosive blast.

"Hrnaugh!"

He was narrowly dodging it the same as always, but the balance was gradually beginning to shift.

Rique's heels stopped. They touched a piece of rubble he hadn't been aware of. It was a horrifying moment. His grasp of the surrounding topography was becoming negligent.

What was the next direction he needed to step in? The timing? Tu once again stamped her foot.

An explosive sound.

How long—?

Rique kept dodging. He was concentrating his thoughts on defense, but he couldn't help having the question pass through his mind.

How long are these attacks going to continue?!

Despite how much she moved around, Tu the Magic didn't show the slightest hint of exhaustion. He couldn't even see any signs that she had discerned her tactics were useless and was changing her simple, repetitive approach. He could dodge. She was just launching herself at him.

However, the slightest hit from her attack would mean an immediate knockout.

There was no pause between her attacks. Counterattacks were ineffective.

"Hey, robe guy! Where are you?! You're leaving all the fighting up to Rique?! Lose your nerve, that it?!"

Did this girl have unlimited stamina?

Was he going to have to continue evading these attacks forever?

Right at the moment Tu took her stance to attack again—

"Lose my nerve?"

The golden wire on Mighamud's flank split open, and a countless number of cannons poked up from inside its open body.

"Me?"

The simultaneous explosion and light shook the earth. Five stonework buildings were blown apart—a cone-shaped chunk of the land itself had been carved away. The vegetation that came into contact with the smoke from the barrage changed into fine black bubbles and dissolved away.

An explosion. Debris scattered. A whole area erupted in flames.

The ruinous destruction was spreading out farther.

Rique immediately covered his mouth with his scarf and put as much distance between himself and the center of the attack as possible.

"Krafnir...... You've gone too far!"

"DISEASE. PROPELLANT. ACID. I JUST DID WHAT YOU SAID AND GATHERED ALL THE METHODS THAT'LL BREAK THROUGH HER DEFENSES."

From the start, Krafnir had hidden a countless number of cannon golems inside Mighamud's body.

A lifeless military force capable of utilizing noxious biological weapons against the living. Creating constructs with identical standards was the true pinnacle of Krafnir's skills.

"THIS IS THE TRUE METHOD OF FIGHTING WITH MIND ARTS. I'VE SURPASSED EVEN IZICK THE CHROMATIC..."

The red premonition of death. The smoke split open.

Rique evaded. A green afterglow flowed through. The color of Tu's eyes.

Seeing this before him, Krafnir's voice trembled in fear.

"TH-THIS GIRL...!"

Landing on top of a faraway stone wall, Tu slowly turned back around.

"............"

A large portion of her clothes had dissolved, and the flames from the incendiary agent that clung to her continued to torment her.

In an epicenter of destruction, bringing death a thousand times over to the average person, her fair skin was totally unscarred.

With her unobstructed body, it was only her eyes that gleamed a fiery green.

She was beautiful, despite being nothing less than a reason-defying monster.

Backlit against the sun...... It was fantastical, as beautiful as any painting.

"......What are you?" he muttered, finally finding his words.

At this point, Rique doubted whether he had enough stamina left over to dodge the next attack. The only possibility left to him was conversing with her to buy time to recover.

"You haven't gone mad... Right?! If murder...and fighting to protect yourself isn't justice, then what...?! The beast, the Demon King Army, will attack other settlements!"

"...Where those ones you killed doing that, too?"

"..."

"The fact that they're here means they couldn't leave this area even if they wanted, right?! That's why they're in so much pain. No matter how much I try to save them... It's no use. They struggle, bite their tongues...suffocate themselves... Even break their own bones."

They understood each other. Though a monster far beyond himself, she still wasn't a beast incapable of understanding Word Arts, either.

...In which case, just who was Tu the Magic? Where did she come from?

Was she not even a product of the laws of Word Arts, the world's basic foundation, but instead, like her name suggested, something ripped from a fairy tale, a being of true, real magic?

"Whenever someone comes here, they all come out. Because *they want someone to help them.* But everyone kills them. Excusing it by saying it's because they're the 'Demon King Army.'"

"That's right. They're too far gone to be able to go back. That's the disaster assaulting this land. They're bound to leave here eventually and attack others! Will you take responsibility for that?!"

"What if they don't attack anyone, then?! What about *your* responsibility?! If it's the same either way, then I'm gonna try to help the wretched and pitiful! Th-that's the champion's... You know! Er, when someone......when they do the right thing, what's it called again...?"

"Moral code," Krafnir's bug pointed out.

"A moral code!"

Rique dropped his bow to the ground. Then he raised both hands, empty, into the air. A stance of surrender.

He likely could've continued to fight. Enough to dodge one or two more of her attacks, at least.

However, he clearly saw how his bout with the Demon King's Bastard would end.

"It's over."

"Whoa, wait, don't just up and surrender on me! I—I won't know what I'm supposed to do anymore..."

"...You're the one who's more in the right here, honestly."

Rique realized. He didn't have any right to unilaterally slaughter a group of sentient beings just because they lived in The Land of The End.

This fight was meaningless already, and Rique was clearly still inexperienced if he hadn't been able to realize something so simple before he encountered this girl.

Rique pointed over toward the minia he first shot down with his bow.

"Check to see if they're breathing."

"……?"

Despite finding the true meaning of his words suspicious, Tu obediently approached the minia and put her hand on their chest.

Then she blinked in shock.

"He's...alive...?"

"A custom-ordered drug I had Thousandth prep for me. They'll be asleep for half a day, and there's not many side effects, either. These hollow arrows have undergone a highly precise processing and can release the medicine from the impact pressure."

"WAIT, RIQUE, YOU—?"

"Right, I guess I didn't tell you, Krafnir. A small farming village's reward money isn't enough to get me to employ Thousandth. Even for a guy like me, see. My other employer is the Free City of Okafu. *Recovering survivors* from The Land of The End. The commission to exterminate everyone just said, *'Don't leave any living creature behind,'* right?"

Tu's expression lit up instantly.

This mannerism of hers, too, seemed just like any other girl her age.

"Then, Rique, to make sure everyone survived and escaped...!"

"...Since Krafnir made his constructs go wild, I ended up having to pretend we were competing with each other. At the very least, I held back to try to make sure no one died... Except with you. I get that this might not be enough of a reason to lay down your arms, but—"

A soft body came flying toward him, cutting him off, and he collapsed.

Rique didn't have the stamina left over to dodge.

Green eyes smiled like a blossoming flower, right up close to his face.

"Amazing! That's incredible! I never would've thought you could protect someone like that!"

"…Er, I mean…"

"……"

Unable to directly look at her bare chest, Rique compelled himself to direct his attention elsewhere.

As a result, his follow-up comments were mostly the first thing that came into his head.

"……K-Krafnir, it was the same deal with you, right?"

"……?! What're you talking about?"

"Inside of Mighamud. Going through such a large-scale reconstruction like that, you didn't leave the digestive organs behind on purpose, right? Why's a champion of your renown taking on a low-paying job like this? You planned on letting them all live and taking them out of here… Right?"

"You too?!"

"……Hmph! Save me your false accusations!"

Rique looked at the revenant lying down on the ground. Within the leftover space in Mighamud's open flank, where the golems had been released, there seemed to be plenty of room to do just as he said.

He was also competing with Rique...hurriedly recovering the survivors, trying not to kill them in the process.

Then if he considered that Krafnir's initial action to gather the region's living creatures to him was so he could swallow them all up at once—and protect them from Rique's arrows in the process...

"Even if that was true, still... It was simply because, I needed, materials for my construct creation; that's it! Nonsense... Absolute drivel!"

"It doesn't matter either way! You're still taking everyone away from here, right?! So the two of you were good guys, after all! This'll save everyone! Whoo-hoo!"

"...I'm telling you, you've got it all wrong!"

His excuses didn't seem to be reaching the young girl.

She wanted to save these people that no one would reach out to try to help. Had that sole determination really been behind her continued defense of The Land of The End? Tu the Magic was all too naive, yet as a fighter, all too warped.

"...For now, put this on? A young girl shouldn't be walking around in such a state."

"Mm-hmm! Thanks!"

Tu smiled, putting on the overcoat Rique handed her.

Where did she come from? How did someone with so much power get born into their world?

…The monster in The Land of The End was known as the Demon King's Bastard.

"I'm so glad, though. With this, I won't have to drive off all the people who show up here anymore."

"What are you going to do from here on out?"

"If I'm free to move as I'd like, then there's one place I want to go... For a long time. Perhaps if you and Krafnir could take me there..."

"...Me? You think I'd do that?"

He wasn't sure. When he thought about it, he hadn't had any prejudicial biases against goblins.

Then what were his thoughts toward a girl of a totally unknown and never-before-seen race like her?

Could Rique take responsibility for the Demon King's Bastard after she left this Final Land behind?

"I guess I'll help you out. I think it's something I need to do."

"I want to go to Aureatia."

"Aureatia, you say? Hmph... I see."

Krafnir reacted to the name. He should've earned his right to participate in the Royal Games occurring in Aureatia.

Rique could spend his lifetime and still never reach him, an arts caster standing in the realm of champions.

They started walking, and it wasn't long before Zigita Zogi's carriage came into view.

Although he must've witnessed the fierce fighting from where he was, he still hadn't run away.

Perhaps he stayed out of pride for his merchant dependability—either that, or perhaps he was concealing some unfathomable power from Rique, too.

In this world, there were many powerful individuals.

Faced with such limitless heights, Rique the Misfortune still felt young and inexperienced.

"Rique! And Krafnir is...?"

"Right here."

"Huh. You've shrank down quite a bit now, haven't you? And you've added another to the group, I see."

"Once we finish up things here, I want to bring this girl to Aureatia. Can you arrange for our transport back?"

"But of course. I'll still need to prepare some number of additional carriages anyway...... Assuming I have things right?"

"We're going to be carrying a lot of people outta here, after all."

Rique grinned.

Ultimately, this job had been a charade, with all of them being complicit.

Sometimes things ended up like this, too.

"Why do you want to go to Aureatia?"

"I mean, it's the biggest minian city, right?! I like places that're all sparkling and vibrant, too! I want some cute clothes, and I can't wait to try all different types of food! That and..."

Pressing down her overcoat to her chest, Tu looked slightly sheepish as she smiled.

A terribly carefree mind, inside an inconceivably abnormal body.

"There's a young girl there I wanna see smile!"

She possessed overwhelming physical ability, wrenching superiority from any skill or technique.

Her endurance was infinite.

She boasted wholly unrivaled defensive capabilities, rendering even poison and cannon fire meaningless.

An incarnation of true magic, appearing out of a land filled with nightmares, her origin was a mystery.

Juggernaut. ███████████.

Tu the Magic.

Right as the grand battle between the Demon King's Bastard and Rique the Misfortune and Krafnir the Hatch of Truth was unfolding—

In a different direction from the three of them, there was another person who successfully infiltrated The Land of The End, coming out between a gap in the warped and distorted trees without any proper road through them.

A man, short-statured with a round face. On his back, he shouldered a small wooden box.

"Well, I'll be."

Yukiharu the Twilight Diver put his hand up to his forehead, shading his eyes. A loud rumbling like cannon fire continued to ring out from far off at the edge of his line of sight.

What made it truly terrifying was that the sound hadn't come from any gunpowder or explosive. It was the sound of something, which Yukiharu was unable to catch with his naked eye, smashing the terrain using just their physical strength.

He guessed it was probably the Demon King's Bastard.

"That's incredible stuff! A little ol' guy like me'd be smashed to bits in an instant if I got wrapped up in that."

"……"

Yukiharu continued talking to himself as he took his first step into The Land of The End and walked over the earth, filled with a damp silence.

"The research teams that come here meet one of a few possible fates. The first one is their carriages are totally destroyed, and they're instantly knocked unconscious, then they decide there's no hope for them and flee back home. That already sounds a bit strange, don't you think?"

"…Strange how?"

"The fact that there's eyewitness accounts of the Demon King's Bastard spreading around. It means that they *survived The Land of The End and got back home.* Even after getting knocked out right smack-dab in the middle of the Demon's King Army wandering around in droves."

"…You're right. If everyone died, there'd be no one to pass on the information."

"That means this someone or other is taking down the research teams but, at the same time, also sends them back somewhere safer afterward, too. My thinking is: This pattern of events…is all from that Demon King's Bastard person."

There were happenings from within Final Land, a place that already gnawed at that sanity of all who stepped within its borders. The eyewitness accounts of the survivors thrown into chaos by these enigmatic attacks would likely be intermingled with a mix of truth and fiction. It was fair to say that Yukiharu's position alone, able to compare all the results brought by the many research teams, made him able to notice the two divergent trends.

"What's the other?"

"Everyone is killed."

A reasonable result that anyone could imagine as the fate of those who stepped foot in The Land of The End. Thus, it was difficult to get information about the area out there, with exceptional stories about encountering the Demon King's Bastard being the only ones circulating.

"The other pattern is that all members of the research team are confirmed dead. Don't you think this is still strange, too?"

"...I get it. The dead shouldn't be able to *confirm themselves as being dead*."

"Thaaaat's the rub. If everyone ends up getting killed in The Land of The End, they'd be labeled missing. No one out there is going all the way to The Land of The End to identify the bodies. Sort of like how the surviving research teams get driven out of the region, the murdered teams must be getting killed outside The Land of The End's borders, too."

Perhaps these two examples coincided on purpose. Supposing that after the Demon King's Bastard wiped out their team, if there were some among them who had their lives taken while they were unconscious, accounts would come out that the mass killings were also caused by the Demon King's Bastard's attacks.

"......Who's doing it, then?"

"You just met them, right?" Yukiharu replied while unhesitatingly prying open the door to a residence. His voice didn't betray any unrest as he looked around at the remnants of the nightmarish tragedies that occurred to the people who once lived there.

"It's the Free City of Okafu. They're thorough. Trying to make sure that no one gets out with any information on The Land of The End. They circulated the rumors of the 'Demon King's Bastard,' disposed of anyone trying to investigate, and ensured no one arrived at the answers behind the True Demon King. There's definitely something here that'd inconvenience them if it got out."

Even as he fished through the rotten and blood-drenched house, a big grin gradually began stretching across his face.

"A national-level scandal, *just like you.*"

"............"

At the very least, he had been able to dodge their hounding on the way in. However, the trip home was definitely not going to go as smoothly.

Back when he ran into the mercenaries, perhaps it would have been better if he pretended to have absolutely no interest at all in The Land of The End or the True Demon King, instead. Yukiharu the Twilight Diver knew for a fact that wasn't something he could do, though.

"Yukiharu."

His current search wasn't only for material proof. To Yukiharu, the people's reactions when the topic of the Demon King came up, and even their deceitful replies, were all material for his reporting.

"Hey."

"Here in this world, no one's taken any pictures before, huh. In that case, a piece of a corpse..."

He wanted to know more. Every single one of the world's secrets were endearing to him.

Anything he had yet to see. Anything unimaginably gruesome and cruel.

Far more than could ever fit in his old world.

That's why someone must have *prepared a whole other world* for Yukiharu to investigate.

The feeling that he was truly closing in on the essence of the world was more important to him than anything.

"...Yukiharu. You didn't... I can't see, but—"

"*U-urrgh*, n-nooo, help, help..."

He heard a minia's weeping voice come from the area to his flank.

No, he might've heard it the whole time. He felt hot.

"*You've been stabbed, haven't you?!*"

"Aaah..."

Fully absorbed in his investigation, Yukiharu at last turned to look behind him.

A victim of the Demon King...... A wretched woman, her whole body damaged, was crawling on the floor and jabbed a rusted kitchen knife into Yukiharu's stomach.

He must've been so excited that he hadn't noticed her until she got close. No, that wasn't it. Throughout all his field investigations up until now, Yukiharu had never neglected such rudimentary precautions.

"I get it. I... I see. So that's it. *Ha-ha*. This is incredible!"

Yukiharu vigorously scratched at the wound in his flank, left behind after the knife slipped down to the floor. He was laughing.

It was said once anyone got themselves caught up in the tragedy of the Demon King Army, it was already too late for them.

"...Dread. I'm scared. I get it. That's why m-my curiosity and terror, took over my mind, and w-without knowing......I lost my, my composure... This has never happened to me before...!"

"Yukiharu!"

"Help, help, please help me. M-my husband, I—I ate my husband."

"*Ha-ha. Ha-ha-ha-ha-ha...* Well now, miss, well, well, well... You really did me a number..."

For a brief moment, Yukiharu laughed while staggering on his feet. Laughing while blood poured out of him was definitely not the mark of a sane mind. However, there wasn't a single soul in this abandoned land to point this out to him.

The woman slowly dragged herself along and gripped on the knife once more. She had grabbed it by the blade.

"Help."

A leather shoe pounded her face.

"......You're in the way."

Still smiling, Yukiharu brought his foot down on her face again.

"You're a nuisance. A real pain, truly. You're interrupting my investigation. It's...it's so interesting, and you had to interrupt me."

A second time. A third time.

That was enough to stop the languid and debilitated woman's breathing, but Yukiharu struck her with several more kicks.

"...*Phew.* Okay. Theeere we go... Nice and calm again."

"Hey. I know I'm not really one to talk, but...you're not really in a good spot, Yukiharu."

"*Ha-ha-ha!* Maybe. But as long as we're in The Land of The End, you don't have any proof that you haven't gone loony, either, right? Hell, truth is, you're not even the type to get scared or worry yourself over a minian life anyway, right?"

"......"

"See? Totally calm and clearheaded. Supposing... Supposing I wasn't, you and I are still in the same boat together. I'm gonna be thorough with everything, right up to the end, got it?"

There was a compulsive elation in Yukiharu's tone. Fear—and curiosity.

"...That's true. If you really sought to abandon everything, you'd throw me away first. I'll do my best to keep you company, then, at least until you end up dead."

"*Ha-ha-ha*, thanks. Seriously...... You're a big help. I really do feel that way...... Yeah."

He wiped off the tips of his shoes as he answered the wooden box.

This was still the first house. Until the moment he got his hands on the truth, a truth whose very existence was uncertain, he needed to keep struggling through this nucleus of fear and madness.

◆

"Hello there, Twilight Diver...... We meet again."

Exiting The Land of The End, Yukiharu was greeted with a gun barrel.

The sun had long since set, and he had severe wounds all over his body that gave him no guarantee he'd be able to walk back to civilization.

"Ha-ha-ha... Well, hello...my merchant friend. I didn't catch your name on the road in... How unbecoming of me."

"Oh please. I'm not someone worth mentioning, see."

He was the mercenary captain from the Free City of Okafu he had encountered on his way into The Land of The End.

He appeared to have joined up with another small group before sunset, with now ten of them total. After continuing his investigation within the ceaseless madness and terror, until all his stamina was spent, this development all but eradicated his hopes of returning home.

"You find anything special? Not that it'll change things."

"......It seems to me...that you couldn't immediately......get a larger-scale force into action, huh? Nofelt's troops are right over there in Alimo Row, I guess......since Aureatia's curbing Okafu's military movements..."

Words were only going to buy him a small amount of time. The mercenaries had no reason to entertain Yukiharu's attempts at conversation.

This mercenary squad wasn't trying to steal information about

The Land of The End, after all—from the start, their goal was simply ensuring Yukiharu's silence.

"Ha-ha-ha...... S-still, though......"

"I'm not trying to apologize or anything, but I don't really bear you any ill will. Sorry about this."

"...There's one, though. One person who can get a large number of troops into action."

—Suddenly.

Arrows flew in and pushed aside the tips of the mercenaries' barrels. Sniper fire from deep within the darkness. Hit with the unexpected assault, many of the soldiers dropped their weapons. The captain immediately went to draw his short sword.

A carriage, rushing at high speed, forced its way in between the two of them.

One of the mercenaries had their breastplate smashed and sent flying by the horse's hooves. This wasn't the only carriage that burst in, either. Several carriages followed after it, one after another.

Yukiharu smiled as he covered his bloodied face in his hands.

"...A commission to exterminate the Demon King Army... from the Lana Farmlands. *A commission from a settlement within Aureatia's sphere of influence, in order to preserve their peace and order.* Aureatia doesn't have—especially not under Nofelt's personal authority—the resources to intervene."

Even as he spoke, the lights of the carriages continued to gather, coming to a halt and circling around Yukiharu. The mercenaries cloaked as merchants were simply outnumbered, unable to stand against them.

"Twilight Diver......!"

One among the contained mercenary squad stirred.

It was the old man in the carriage bed, with the large scar on his forehead. The elderly man who had been staring vacantly at the sky earlier stepped forward faster than a flying arrow and tried to run Yukiharu through with his spear.

"First. Piercing slash...!"

"Gramps, wait!"

Even the mercenary troop captain's attempt to restrain him was too late for the wholly unexpected display of masterful speed.

However, a finger cutting in between them firmly gripped the spearhead and used the momentum to slam the elderly man to the ground.

"Stop it!"

It was a young girl, hiding her bare skin under a large overcoat.

Even as the long delicate finger clenched the rough blade, not a single drop of blood fell from her skin. Facing toward the elderly man, dumbfounded that his full-powered thrust had been stopped, the young girl shouted a comment terribly out of step with the situation.

"This person could've died, you know!"

The mercenary captain was perplexed at the sequence of events that had just played out in front of him.

"D-dammit! What the...what the hell is this?! Rique the Misfortune?! Damn you!"

A young dwarf descended from the head carriage. The man who had interrupted the mercenaries' attacks with his volley of arrows.

Having accepted the commission from the Lana Farmlands, Rique the Misfortune must have had, on the other hand, a contract with the Free City of Okafu to clean up the aftermath. Capturing all of the Demon King Army in The Land of The End and eliminating all potential threats, including the Demon King's Bastard, were coinciding interests.

"I'm the one who should be asking what's going on here," Rique flatly declared as he kept his short bow at the ready.

"The conditions of my agreement with Okafu...were to guard the remnants of the Demon King Army we recovered. As long as you're trying to kill Twilight Diver here to ensure his silence, who's to say you won't do the same to the Demon King Army folks we captured? You're going to have to travel with us to settle things with whoever's responsible."

"Dammit. You naive and ignorant punk... So we're the ones made out to be the fools here. Did you hear there was a unit like ours here...from Twilight Diver over there?"

No average person was capable of approaching The Land of The End. Even for the mercenaries trying to protect the region's secrets, they were only capable of attacking people along their way either into The Land of The End or on their way out.

Therefore.

"...Nah. I had Thousandth serve as the intermediary."

"Rique. I don't really think it's necessary to answer that honestly."

If they had come in contact *inside* The Land of The End, there was no way anyone could know.

Zigita Zogi the Thousandth. He was a logistics specialist, origins unknown, who was accompanying Rique the Misfortune this far as a subcontractor. However, from the very beginning, he had devised a way to mobilize a large-scale transport caravan and slip it past the Free City of Okafu's vigilance and make Yukiharu the Twilight Diver, continuing his investigation of the True Demon King, meet up with Rique in The Land of The End.

"…Well, there you have it."

Yukiharu stood his wound-riddled body up and shakily boarded one of the carriages.

"Thousandth. He was one of my clients."

This time, it was the mercenaries' turn to raise their hands up in surrender.

"We've been duped, all right. All those guys were supposed to cleanly disappear from the Final Land…and today'd finally be our last day stuck doing this dirty work."

"*Ha-ha-ha-ha.* Well, I can sympathize. But having everything get wrapped up all at once like that……doesn't happen very often, after all."

At last getting a firm sense that he had escaped the terror, Yukiharu smiled and sunk his body into the carriage passenger seat.

"Well, no. I wouldn't say that's always true."

Zigita Zogi answered from the seat across from him.

"The story of the True Demon King. And Okafu the Free City. And the Old Kingdoms' loyalists. As well as the Royal Games preliminaries—perhaps, everything is going to get settled all at once."

"*Ha-ha-ha-ha......*" Yukiharu answered with a dry laugh. The wooden box slung on his back stayed silent the whole while.

"A torn piece of fabric's going to do all that?"

"That's right. Very well done, Master Yukiharu."

Zigita Zogi peered through a magnifying glass inside the carriage at the item Yukiharu the Twilight Diver had risked his life to recover—a torn piece of clothing, the size of his finger.

It was a definitive and decisive piece of information.

"...With this one item, I've assembled all the material I need for the negotiations with Okafu."

The central citadel of the Free City of Okafu.

Excluding the self-proclaimed demon king Morio's personal guards, people were rarely allowed inside its walls, but once one took a step inside, they were surrounded in a solemn atmosphere, completely opposite from the mood of the city below, thick with the sordid air of thriving mercenaries and scoundrels.

Hiroto the Paradox was invited into a room known as the "command room." A self-proclaimed demon king consultation, one that would greatly affect the grand plan that had consumed his life.

"Save the formalities."

Though only of average size, the mustached man had a brawny build, like a tiger.

He wore stiff khaki-colored clothes, reminiscent of the military uniforms in the Beyond. These weren't clothes from the Beyond themselves, of course, but they must've been tailored to reproduce the same look.

Many visitors were attached to their original clothes from the

Beyond—and fancied the otherworldly apparel. For all of them, that alone was their link to their original world.

"So we finally get to meet, eh? Hiroto the Paradox."

On the other hand, Hiroto was small. More than his stature however, his outward features were that of a child.

His face, too, made him appear to be in his early teens, but his grizzled hair gave him a strangely mature air. It was this outward appearance that earned him his other moniker, the Gray-Haired Child.

Looking over his guest, sizing him up, Morio the Sentinel cut off the end of a new cigar.

Hiroto always had proper posture. Though, this perfection was solely to present himself to those he was negotiating with.

Lightly crossing his hands over his knee, he leaned forward slightly as he spoke.

"I'm honored that you'd regard me so highly. I've long looked forward to the day I'd get the chance to meet with you, Mr. Morio Ariyama."

"I said to skip the formalities. You've been taking care of us for a long time, but you don't really think that I don't know where Kazuki the Black Tone got her guns from, do you? If it wasn't for this latest information at hand, I wouldn't have met you during a time like this in the first place."

"……"

Hiroto recalled what Kazuki looked like when he'd first met her. An old visitor companion of his. When he offered her help back in the ravine, he spoke with completely honest intentions.

Someone who far surpassed any of Hiroto's estimations killed her not far from where he sat. If things went as he originally planned, then Kazuki would've surely been here with him for these negotiations.

"Of course not. However, surely you know better than most that's how things work in the arms business. If there's a demand, I sell weapons. If there's demand from both opposing sides, all the better for me."

"Logical reasoning and personal feelings are a different story. My soldiers were killed by her guerilla attacks. Wasn't just about the numbers, either. All of them were part of the Free City's family."

"Fair enough—"

Hiroto detected a slight shift in Morio's expression and searched for an opening to cut in.

A dissatisfied, yet slightly mournful, grimace.

Soldiers were family. A military man who worked his way up to where he was now. The man who built this mercenary city from the ground up after being banished here from the Beyond. Morio appeared to esteem dignity and justice, but the truth was much different.

"I admit that, without our supply of logistics and guns, Miss Kazuki Mizumura might have indeed given up on her conquest of Okafu. The people who dispatched her would've likely gone with a different approach, instead."

"Aureatia. I know that much. Those bastards've finally decided we're getting in their way."

"Now that you've crushed Miss Kazuki Mizumura, the Free

City of Okafu has become their greatest threat. Next time, the Aureatian army is sure to get involved, I would say."

"...Doesn't sit right with me. Kazuki cut down our best soldiers. We go at it with our current military strength, Okafu will lose. I need reinforcements to prevent that. And those reinforcements are going to come from your army. No matter how things fall, it'll probably all be according to your plans, won't it?"

Bringing his hands together on top of the desk, Morio scowled at Hiroto. The conversation was flowing in a promising direction.

If he was completely refusing Hiroto, he wouldn't feel like the idea "didn't sit right with him" at all. The words signaled friction between his emotions and his logic. Morio was far from an emotionless man, but he was still clearheaded enough to weigh the two ideas against each other.

"I am always acting in service of my own profits, of course. I even used the Free City of Okafu itself for said profit. But the personal profits I'm speaking of also include profits for my allies. If you permit me to offer my assistance, I'll ensure you don't suffer any more losses."

"And that means what, specifically?"

"It's your turn to be the seller here. I will *hire the entirety* of the Free City of Okafu."

"......You can't be serious."

Morio was at a loss for words. He had known that the Gray-Haired Child had amassed a tremendous amount of capital, but...

"You intend to buy an entire country? And what sort of benefit does Okafu gain from agreeing to this?"

"There isn't a future for the private military-contracting business in this world going forward. With the New Principality of Lithia's fall into the defeat of the Old Kingdoms' loyalists, the demand for the mercenary trade itself disappeared. Essentially, I will be taking over that demand for the time being. If I had to give the specific merits for you, then...it'd be finishing your war with Aureatia without losing a single soldier. I'll explain the concrete details at a later date, but I've already devised a way to advantageously proceed with the Aureatia postwar negotiations. If I may speak even further into the future... I can provide a battlefield that befits your soldiers."

"...A battlefield?"

"Yes. Conflict is the lifeblood of the mercenaries of Okafu. You yourself built up such a city to provide a place where they can belong, am I wrong? I promise they will have their battlefield."

The interest in providing a battlefield that Hiroto included at the end was a benefit for Morio *the individual*.

More than dignity and justice, he was a commander who treasured his family. There was some truth to that.

However, he truly wasn't scared of them dying in combat. He sought to ensure his family lived out their lives as soldiers. Choosing the words *guerilla attacks* to criticize Kazuki's fighting described his thoughts on the matter.

"Even I know what sort of situation this country's currently being placed in. Hiroto the Paradox...... A fixer of your caliber must be able to get some large-scale strategy going, I suppose. Besides, if you publicize *that information*, we're both going to be annihilated… That being said, I can't easily trust you, either. You get that, right?"

"……Yes."

"We've dealt with each for a long time, but ultimately, I haven't seen your own power for myself. You were the first to develop guns in this world. You have some connections to technology that's fifty years ahead of its time here, and you've established business relations with any and every power—that's it. With that money, is there any army you could hire that'd outclass the one here in Okafu? What can you even do if you're going to avoid losing a single soldier up against a huge army like Aureatia's? I want proof. That you can be relied on. That you're up to the task of having our backs."

"…Fair enough. I suppose the day's come to show what sort of power I hold—and what I've accomplished."

Hiroto shifted his eyes to the citadel window. From the tiny window, installed only to allow for sniper fire from within, it was possible to look down over the mercenaries coming and going on the city streets below.

Around half the residents here were mercenaries. Such was the city Morio created.

"Mr. Morio Ariyama. To you, your true power doesn't lie in the mercenaries gathered in town, does it? Your personal troops, though, were handpicked and taught in the latest military training that you've learned in the Beyond. You've never once showed off their strength to the world, so they must be your true trump card, yes?"

"...Obviously, I'm going to be the one training my own soldiers. What of it?"

"These mercenaries...including those personal soldiers of yours. I'll gain control of all of them, by myself."

"I wondered about this earlier, but... Are you mad?"

Visitors, having strayed beyond proper natural law and rules, weren't guaranteed to have the same amount of fighting strength their outward appearance would suggest. For example, as it was with Kazuki the Black Tone, there were even some who lightly handled multiple rifles with slender arms, and others who moved faster than the eye could see.

This Hiroto the Paradox was unmistakably not one of these types of visitors. His movements and mannerisms made his skills apparent. Not only his obvious physical ability, but the way he showed his unguarded moments, and when he tried to conceal them, too, made it clear that all of it was inferior to the average person.

Supposing Morio did intend to kill him, he would've been able to snap off his neck at any moment during their conversation.

"I won't bring any harm to your soldiers, of course. I wouldn't want anything to happen to my would-be allies, after all. I won't use blades or guns. How do those conditions sound?"

"...I don't need to turn a mere game of tag into some big deal, thanks. I'm not trying to surround and kill you, for one, and I can't let my soldiers' lives get thrown out of order. If you're truly serious, I'll just tell my soldiers, should you get discovered, to simply capture you unharmed. Allow me to add that to your conditions."

"I couldn't ask for anything better. In that case, by the end of the day."

Assuming Hiroto the Paradox had prepared some ruse to control all of Okafu's forces, practically speaking, it would be impossible for him to make it a reality.

A number of bodyguards would be glued to him at all times, just as when he was brought to the control room the first time. To make sure he was immediately apprehended the first moment he looked ready to strike.

Nevertheless, Morio understood he wasn't the type of man to wordlessly pummel a negotiating partner he had come to proposition. Supposing that did happen, though, Hiroto had no hopes of winning.

That's why he hadn't said "you" to the person in front of him, but used a distant "them," instead. A roundabout phrasing to suggest that Morio and his troops, bodyguard detail included, were unconcerned parties in his gamble.

It was as if he was convincing them that it wouldn't even get to the point where Hiroto would reveal himself openly and confront Morio's soldiers...or try to challenge them with an ambush. With this, in order to match the conditions Hiroto first presented, Morio's side would try to capture Hiroto unarmed instead.

Thus, he was able to make his preparations.

He exited into the hallway and opened his bag. Seeing one of the bodyguards slightly tense up, Hiroto smiled.

"It's not a weapon. Would you like to give it another search?"

"……"

It wasn't a weapon, of course. Judging solely from its appearance, it appeared to be a type of radzio.

However, he was also lying. For in Hiroto's hands, it changed into a weapon more powerful than any other.

He inquired of the bodyguard directly behind him, as if making simple small talk. "…Now, then. I can take that path over there to get to the observation tower, yes?"

"What are you planning on doing there?"

"*Hee-hee.* Do I look like I'm going to snipe anyone right now?"

"…No. Not at all."

Hiroto moved through the citadel, making for the roof of the observation tower. The bodyguards followed after him, keeping their distance without losing him.

With his poor physical stamina, Hiroto had some trouble getting up all the way to the top of the stairs after completing the long walk to the observation tower.

"Phew, that was tough. You all go up and down these stairs every day?"

"…You're the first person I've seen to run out of breath just from climbing some stairs, Master Hiroto."

The guard smiled sarcastically. He was probably appalled at the sight.

"I'm quite ashamed."

As his appearance suggested, he was a powerless man equipped only with his big talk. Anyone would look down and make little of Hiroto—

Until he stood up on top of the observation deck, looking down over the ground, and began.

"…Ahem. Aaaah. Ah-aaaah."

Grabbing his throat, he tested his vocal cords. Then he readied the instrument he brought with him.

When Hiroto the Paradox was transported to this world, more than any gun or car, this tool was the item he wanted most of all.

The machine had a very simple construction. Over a base of a tanned wyvern wing membrane, a coil wrapped in gold wire linked together. Inside was a magnet, which produced electromotive force through vocal vibrations. That current passed to an amplifier circuit made from radzio crystal, the input being connected to an output with an exact reverse construction. This would vibrate the wing membrane and spit the sound back out through the funnel-shaped mouth.

The item was called a megaphone.

"People of the Free City of Okafu!"

His amplified voice boomed across the whole city.

Everyone was startled by the words coming down from the heavens, with some readying their weapons as they focused on the man standing on top of the observation tower.

"I am sure my face and name are well-known to you all! I am the visitor that Master Morio commanded you to capture, Hiroto the Paradox! Allow me to greet you all once again! Thank you for listening!"

By getting out ahead and revealing his identity to them all, he stalled the several soldiers who turned and promptly fixed their aim at the suspicious individual. Morio had ordered them all to capture Hiroto the Paradox without harming him.

On the other hand, this also made the guards watching over his every move unable to act, as well.

While the machine he used surprised the people below, Hiroto clearly wasn't making any sort of offensive movement. Visitors couldn't use Word Arts, either. It was almost physically impossible for him to attack any of the far-off mercenaries below.

"First, there is something I'd like to make clear. I imagine it was evident with your orders, but I'd like to be sure. I have promised Morio that I would win out against all of you. That was the condition on forming an alliance between myself and the Free City of Okafu! Now. I did make such a boasting claim, but...... Did any of you really think you'd lose to someone like me? An obvious weakling, bereft of any skill? Let me begin here. For starters... By 'winning,' I'm talking about achieving my goals. With that in mind, what does 'losing' then usually mean?

He was lying. Morio had simply asked to show him proof of his powers and hadn't given any definitive promise based on such a display. Viewed from another perspective, it was a statement that could be distorted in many different ways depending on the interpretation. There was enough latitude to convince even Morio himself of such an interpretation.

Therefore, by brazenly asserting it as such in front of a large number of people, he was making them believe it was already an established fact. That if Hiroto won, their cooperative alliance was a done deal.

"For example, since I am sure most of you are soldiers, you probably think that the clear loss of all your liberty, as in, one's death itself, is the most universal form a defeat can take. However, when it comes to the idea of a 'struggle to survive,' what should be a direct expression of a fight between life-and-death, an individual's death isn't synonymous with defeat. Interesting, isn't it?"

He continued to speak while incorporating grandiose gesticulation. He was holding their attention.

In order to wear down the will to use violence among these people who made violence their trade, he needed to give them a story to focus on.

"There exists no living creatures that can best a dragon, however, the minian races have clearly claimed victory over dragons in the struggle for survival. A peerless individual is not guaranteed to be the final victor. I saw much the same in my past world of the Beyond."

The audience still scorned Hiroto. He was a curious target, purposefully exposing himself in a location easily shot at by bows and arrows before suddenly launching into a strange speech. He was fine with that.

The most important factor of all was to ensure *they couldn't remain apathetic*. Therein lay the meaning behind establishing himself as a target to all the inhabitants through Morio's commands.

"Let me tell you about myself. I've sojourned in the Free City of Okafu for three days. During my time, both as one who knows the Beyond and as one who knows minian society, I admired the splendor here. In this town, there is no discrimination between races! In the Beyond, one is limited to feuding with your fellow minia, yet here both minia and monstrous races live together, fight together as brothers-in-arms, and use the same money to trade! Even with such bustling activity, this city is host to a natural system of discipline!"

Hiroto was fully aware. Okafu's atmosphere was assuredly not born from any tepid ideals of equality. Theirs was simply the natural outcome of their liberalism and economic activities.

Ogres and lycans were generally warriors that far outstripped the physical and mental abilities of minia. If they were only employed as mercenaries in wartime, there wouldn't be any of the dangers from training a standing army of minian-eating soldiers. This was a point where the Free City of Okafu differed from the New Principality of Lithia, who tried to utilize a wyvern army as their own domestic air force.

There was a high demand for the monstrous race mercenaries that Okafu commanded, and by traveling from battlefield to battlefield, they were easily able to supply themselves with their "food." As a result, the monstrous races in Okafu weren't driven out like in other minian cities. That was simply the extent of it.

However, Hiroto used that fact. If he lauded the group they all belonged to, people would be naturally uplifted and release the caution in their hearts. Anyone with a mind of their own was always starved for pride.

"Now then, I ask those who have seen Aureatia to think about them for a moment. How was it in Aureatia? Not only do they not accept the monstrous races themselves, could you say that the warriors wounded in the campaign against the Demon King were properly compensated in the end? Would you say their long-held minia supremacy—their aristocratic reverence—is a natural method of governance, worthy of a world where anyone can communicate their will to another via Word Arts? Neft the Nirvana, from the First Party, was a lycan. Yet after returning from his battle against the True Demon King with his sanity intact, a triumphant achievement to be sure, he was forced to live in exile in the Gokashae Sand Sea. When the people of Aureatia tell tales of the First Party, does the name of Lumelly the Poisoned Ground ever get mentioned? Though not a minia, she should still be remembered as a grand champion, one that none should be ashamed to recognize!"

He paused. He wasn't unleashing a continuous rapid-fire stream of words, but guiding his audience's subconscious along a particular track.

The soldiers themselves all understood their current situation, where worsening relations with Aureatia had put Okafu in a precarious state. He would use that enmity. While he himself remained their target, he would guide the focus of their hostility toward Aureatia.

"...Yes, it goes without saying, I am a minia myself. Am I even qualified to expound on a prosperous coexistence among all races? I am sure some among you harbor such questions. Let me tell you about myself... I said I would do just that mere moments ago. 'Who is this child anyway?' 'What's he going on about after popping up out of nowhere?' 'Did this buffoon mistake that roof for a church confessional, and hasn't he realized it yet?'"

He confirmed there was sparse stifled laughter escaping from the audience. Now that he had turned their hostility toward a different target, he returned their *attention* back to himself.

"Allow me to introduce myself again. I imagine that there was some among you who have heard the name Hiroto the Paradox while bargaining for a musket. Do you know where those things you carry in your hands day in, day out, are made? Aureatia? The ruined Nagan Labyrinth City? Or the Hakeena Microregion perhaps?"

He gestured to one of the guards to come over and stood him in front of his audience. Originally meant to keep Hiroto in check, he was unable to resist Hiroto's skill with words and the attention from the audience. Hiroto gave him a new role, separate from his close observation of Hiroto's movements, right on the spot.

Directing the guard with a simple wave, he had him hold up the musket in his hands. It would be vital to show that it was not Hiroto himself, but someone the mercenaries considered one of their own, who held up the musket—and instill that idea in their state of mind.

"None of those places, in fact. The guns I make are not produced here on this continent. Then they're from the Beyond, you ask? That, too, is not the answer. Yes, now then, here I shall introduce myself to you all! I am Hiroto the Paradox! Over sixty-nine long years, I have created another world, a *third* world! A world unbeknownst to you all!"

A wave of amazement and disbelief was rippling through the audience.

From the beginning, there had been preparations in place for this series of events Hiroto had incited. Allies who had already infiltrated Okafu stirred the audience with their own cheering and, with their regulated and trained attention, guided everyone's focus on to Hiroto.

"At the edge of the world! Beyond the sea! I have created a country of goblins! Look for yourselves and see; they are my compatriots!"

His words the signal, a concealed group advanced forward. With their faces covered up by their cloaks, they resembled short leprechauns. A group of goblins he had slip into the city while he was bargaining with Morio. Hiroto's preparations had begun before he had been invited that day, before venturing into the city for negotiations.

Signs of confusion and caution rose up among the crowd. An obvious reaction to see a group of goblins, thought to be already extinct, right before their eyes. Nevertheless, it had been necessary to burn some type of definitive proof into them. A degree of fluctuation between anxiety and excitement was what truly allowed for his words to impress themselves in the minds of his audience.

It was a risky method, to be sure. He needed to bring the

situation under his control faster than their dormant feelings of hostility toward these goblins could make their return.

"People of Okafu! Can you believe me?! That it's possible to continue across the oceans where krakens dwell, to the end of the world! That there is already someone who has discovered such a water route?! That goblins, reviled as lower and base, have a civilization capable of producing such high-quality firearms! That they are now in fact synonymous with the word *guns* itself! That they could create a nation, form a society......and are able to coexist with a minia like myself! Of course you can! You are bearing witness to such a society right before your very eyes!"

Clenching his fist, he looked fiercely down over the crowd.

Hiroto the Paradox was serious.

It would never be possible to make others believe his words if he didn't firmly believe in them himself.

"I'm sure you all know! That it's possible for the monstrous and the minian to coexist! That the monstrous races have power that is far more outstanding than the minian races believe! More than anything else, all of you, even those in Aureatia, have placed your lives in the hands of goblin-made weapons and have survived by doing so! You must've seen plenty of proof with your own eyes! Let me say once more! This Free City of Okafu, it is a wonderful city!"

Hiroto could hear the sound of someone climbing the tower steps...... Morio the Sentinel had come to put an end to his speech.

Even if Morio had an inkling of the purpose behind the speech, Hiroto had chosen this specific observation tower, far removed from the command room, to ensure Morio couldn't quickly stop him. Despite this, the man's intuition and speed were beyond Hiroto's original prognosis. He likely had left the command room immediately after the speech began.

He even came personally instead of leaving things up to his men. This man won't be the type to be won over with simple smooth talk.

He needed to make several revisions to the staging he had prepared around his speech. Hiroto continued to speak.

"Now, however, Aureatia threatens this land! This system of shared prosperity that Lord Morio built is on the verge of being lost! But because of that, now is when I wish to help you all! For my profit? That's right! For my own self-protection! Indeed! I am no upright and pure man, and I do not intend to wax on about ideals and peace! Nevertheless, I can promise you results! I promise that, just as I saved the goblins previously driven from these lands, I will save each and every one of you! The Hiroto the Paradox you see before you, and this large goblin army, will be your allies from here on out! Just as I've promised Lord Morio, I will lend you all my strength!"

That was as far as he got. The wooden tower door opened, and Morio appeared.

Matching up perfectly with his calculations, timed at the exact moment Hiroto brought up his name.

"Drop the megaphone."

Morio ordered, still just as calm and levelheaded. Smoke wafted up from his cigar.

Hiroto couldn't surpass Morio with violence. If he thought to do so, Morio could've slit Hiroto's throat with a knife on the spot. Hiroto took his mouth away from the megaphone and came up beside Morio.

"Yes, I understand. It's a bit heavy, so could you take it for me?"

Morio didn't let down his guard for a moment, but when he reached to take the loudspeaker—Hiroto forcefully grabbed his outstretched hand. Without a moment's pause, he shouted into the loudspeaker.

"Here now, I pledge my fellowship to you, Free City of Okafu!"

It was a trap to draw out Morio's handshake.

A cheer erupted from the audience. This time, it wasn't from the goblins he had previously hid among the crowd, but a cheer rising as a natural result of his speech. The thunderous applause continued.

Morio loathsomely glared at Hiroto. Hiroto, too, stared hard into the eyes in front of him with a solemn look of his own.

"You little…!"

"It is exactly as I first said. I absolutely won't let you suffer any losses."

If Morio felt like it, he could have killed Hiroto at any moment. Now though, it was too late.

Even the self-proclaimed demon king Morio—in fact, precisely *because* he was a self-proclaimed demon king—was a statesman whose position stood entirely on his people's trust in him, and he couldn't ignore their disposition no matter what he may have wished to do.

Taking a deep breath, Hiroto once again called out to the audience.

"People of the Free City of Okafu! I have made a promise to Lord Morio! That with my victory, my army, my weapons, and I will be your strength! I pledge to you civilization and progress beyond what has ever come before it! What say you? Allow Hiroto the Paradox to bring you victory! I assure you that it absolutely does not signify your defeat!"

Lowering his loudspeaker at long last, he shouted with his unamplified voice. It was all his own staging.

At this point, his voice would travel clearly to the ears of the audience, their attention now completely focused on the man.

"So that I and, more importantly, you all can claim victory! So Lord Morio can claim victory! I, Hiroto the Paradox, ask you all! Please, let me win for you!"

The applause reverberated. It was more reserved than when Morio had made his appearance, but it clearly gave affirmation to Hiroto's words.

Hiroto bowed deeply and turned to face Morio, unable to do anything but watch the situation unfold from behind him.

"…So this is what you were after, huh?"

"That's right. And just like I said, I was able to overcome everyone here."

"So whether I trust you or not, now I'm forced to join forces with you, then… Well, I don't have any choice. I don't particularly want to let myself get hung up with foolish pride, either."

The self-proclaimed demon king Morio. Hiro's judgments about what sort of man he was turning out to be right after all.

During the fight that lay waiting on the horizon, the man's popularity was sure to become an indispensable boon.

"Well then, advantageous postwar negotiations, without any of my soldiers getting hurt. Must have some plan to turn things in your favor, then."

"Of course. I'm going to make use of the Old Kingdoms' loyalists in Toghie City, while they're staring down Aureatia's northern army."

"You can't be planning on allying with them, are you? With the Particle Storm crushed, those guys aren't going last much longer."

"No."

Hiroto's smiling face never faltered. He was always overflowing with confidence. If he didn't, he wouldn't be able to subdue the populace.

"Zigita Zogi."

Hiroto snapped his fingers. A small shadow jumped down from atop the rooftop's entrance.

"A goblin? Having them slip into the city is one thing, but they've gotten into my citadel, too?"

"It is an honor to make your acquaintance, Master Morio."

Even a veteran warrior of Morio's caliber wasn't able to sense this goblin's presence nearby.

"Introductions are in order. This here is Zigita Zogi the Thousandth. He is my most reliable adviser... The arrangements have been made, then?"

"But of course. At this stage, we're just waiting for them to make their move."

Zigita Zogi flashed an audacious smile.

Hiroto the Paradox was a man without an ounce of brute strength to his name. However, he could still *fight*.

He faced Morio and gently brought his hands together.

"We can annihilate them whenever we'd like."

◆

The northern army confronting the Old Kingdoms' loyalists. Their commanding officer was the Twenty-Fourth General of Aureatia, Dant the Heath Furrow.

I don't like it.

The Imag North Flats had the perfect topography to set up camp. To the east, there was a large canal. In front of them, in the direction of Toghie City, was a thick forest. Behind them on their southern flank was Imag City, assuring that they wouldn't have any trouble with their supplies. As long as they were able to handle this plateau, conveniently free from harmful insects and fauna, Imag City wouldn't fall.

…However. All of this only served to make Dant feel like the ease of their position was being exploited.

On the other side of the forest, the Old Kingdoms' army, from their base in Toghie City, was still recruiting participants from the frontier beyond Aureatia's reach, and they were growing in numbers. Up until only a few days prior, the calamitous Particle

Storm threatened Aureatian home soil, and the necessary division of their large forces here left them unable to expect any reinforcements for the time being.

Doesn't seem right. My forces alone can't keep them in check forever. So I'm supposed to throw my troops at them little by little and try to get them out by attrition? Royal games, Particle Storm... Every single one of them going on about heroes and champions, spouting absolute hogwash. Am I the only one who can see the real problem right in front of us?

The general commanding this northern army was Twenty-Fourth General, Dant. With him was the Ninth General, Yaniegiz. If they were solely holding out and keeping the enemy in check, they had enough military power to do so—that much was certain. There was a difference in both equipment and training between Aureatia and the Old Kingdoms' army. However, given their strategy to use the Particle Storm to attack Aureatia without using any of their troops ended in failure, it was all but assured they would quickly attempt a show of force. The Old Kingdoms needed to bring the war with Aureatia to a close in as advantageous a position as possible. If there was a target they could set their sights on for such a task, it would be Dant's troops, facing off against them as one of Aureatia's main frontline forces.

Holding out against an attack isn't enough. If we're going to win, we need to completely stamp them out. Aimlessly drawing out the conflict is going to exhaust our own troops and drain the resources of the territory we're trying to take back in Toghie City.

Troop strength had been divided to help with the evacuation of the Gumana Trading Post, where the Particle Storm was set to pass through, but conversely there were no reinforcements for this region, where a clash of arms was all but guaranteed. Dant believed this rigid troop placement was linked with the management of the Royal Games.

Sixth General Harghent and the like had cast aside any appearances of being a military officer and were off searching for candidates to become the True Hero. An appalling state of affairs.

No reinforcements are coming here. Yet Gilnes plans to make his move in a few days. Taking command of the front lines is that Caneeya the Fruit Trimming...... So it'll all depend on her tactical approach, then?

He heard Caneeya the Fruit Trimming was a valiant woman of Herculean strength, no less than Gilnes himself, and born with an extremely large physique. If this current deadlock was something she intentionally set up herself, then he couldn't afford to make light of her tactical ingenuity, either.

The Imag North Flats were suited for defense. The same was true for offense, however.

In addition to the narrow road utilized for merchant travel built to pass through the lowland forest, the marsh that circumvented the forest was a wurm habitat, making it impossible for even an army like Aureatia's to avoid enormous losses.

A forest that restricted a large army's freedom of movement—and a marshland that carried the danger of wurms. There was no means to skillfully deploy the massive force of arms defending Aureatia.

Nevertheless, if necessary, they could easily retreat back and hole up inside Imag City. If it came to this, they would likely be able to hold out for a considerable period of time.

Though, the burden placed on Imag City would be substantial. It could possibly cause a decline in Imag's support for the Aureatia Council. Once there's a negative effect on the people, they were quick to turn hostile.

At the moment, with the Royal Games close at hand, Dant wouldn't be let off lightly if he prolonged Aureatia's plans.

When his thoughts had reached this conclusion, a messenger made their return to camp headquarters to give their report.

"Commander, sir. Regarding the scouts sent to try breaking through the woods—three were killed in action, and another's been heavily wounded. Traps and skilled guerilla soldiers lay waiting in ambush, making an advance through the forest difficult."

"...I see. Safe to assume the forest's been fully fortified. Send the scouts who made it back to headquarters. Once I've gathered all the info on the current state of affairs, I'll share it with everyone."

The soldiers, fed up with the deadlock, had recruited volunteers to attempt a reconnaissance mission, but things ended exactly as Dant expected they would. Would these four sacrifices be enough to check the soldiers' impatience?

Charging through with brute force would lead to heavy losses. Though it wouldn't be totally impossible, this should be enough to make them think twice about any aggression on our part.

Burning down the entire forest surrounding the main road was likely the quickest method.

However, surely their enemy was aware that wasn't something they could do easily.

This forest was a valuable asset for Imag's lumber industry, and if Aureatia burned down the forest, he'd have to bear in mind the several years of compensation they'd need to pay the city for their loss.

On the other hand, the Old Kingdoms' loyalists did not have such shackles placed on them. Their foe could burn down this protective barrier and come attacking them as soon as they finished making the necessary preparations.

Advance forward and sacrifice the forest or fall back and place the burden on Imag City. If we'll be criticized either way, it'd be better to act fast, but...

If they could hold out until Aureatia dispatched reinforcements, they could send a large, detached force around, avoiding the marshlands while they traveled, and besiege the Old Kingdoms' loyalists while Dant kept things under control where they were. This was currently the role Dant's assistant was asked to play.

If their reinforcements made it there faster than the enemy army could make their move, there'd be no need to take any risks. However, that truth also served to make them hesitant to act at all.

"...Commander, reporting, sir! An army believed to be with the Free City of Okafu is currently advancing this way!"

"Okafu?!"

"Two thousand strong! Currently, they're marching down the Kameeke Highway!"

Dant quickly spread out a map. The arrangement was supposed have Twenty-Seventh General Hardy keeping Okafu's movements in check. In fact, they had suffered significant losses from the attacks of Kazuki the Black Tone, who Hardy had dispatched to handle things, and Dant had assumed they'd be unable to make any moves.

That wasn't it, though. First of all, why were they purposefully making their way to Dant's encampment? Even if they did have plans to make an attack on Aureatia, there were a number of other important positions it would be better to attack first.

"Mercenary bastards... Are they trying to join up with the Old Kingdoms' loyalists?! Muster all the unit captains together. We're turning back to Imag City!"

"You're saying to abandon the plan?!"

"That's right! They're charting a course to split the battle lines from the flank! If our retreat path is blocked off, and they restrict our link to Imag City, this plateau'll turn into nothing but a weather-beaten tomb! We need to withdraw as soon as possible, or we're all going to dry up!"

There was time to withdraw the entire army, judging from the Okafu army's position. As long as they had the forest blocking their advance, the Old Kingdoms' army wouldn't be able to charge down Dant's retreating forces.

Nevertheless, Dant had ultimately been driven into choosing to retreat.

Did this mean Okafu's schemes had gotten the best of that old man Hardy? If the Old Kingdoms' loyalists anticipated reinforcements from the Free City of Okafu, then just how much were they playing into their hands?

Dant gnashed his teeth.

I don't like it.

◆

"Really."

Commander of the front lines, Caneeya the Fruit Trimming, smiled and nodded, just as she would've in peacetime.

The soldiers' eyes weren't able judge whether she was truly smiling, but even when standing on a blood-drenched battlefield, no one had ever seen this expression of hers waver.

"What exactly is Okafu's goal here?"

"Maybe they intend on gift wrapping Aureatia's destruction before surrendering to our forces. Whatever it is, right now they're neither our enemy nor our ally…"

Caneeya's thick arms twirled her sword, shaped like a thick cleaver.

She had a hunch a fight was coming. This hunch wasn't of an intense battle where both sides straddled the line between life and death, either, but instead of a ravaging overrun bringing victory.

"But we can use them."

"If now's the time our enemy makes their move, then now's the time we should make ours."

"Indeed. We'll pass through the forest."

The Old Kingdoms' army placed their elite troops in the forest, blocking reconnaissance attempts from the Aureatian side.

They were waiting for the moment Dant's army withdrew. The Aureatia army, taking the high ground on the plateau, thought they could look out over the entire forest. However, as long as they were only looking at the forest from the Imag City side, they were bound to have blind spots. It was information even the Aureatian spy unit infiltrating Toghie City wouldn't have picked up on from their position.

"Passing through the path we cleared, of course."

The dense forest had been largely carved out on the Toghie City side.

The impenetrable wood that blocked any invaders was deforested except for the single defensive stretch—and carried by the canal to the east side of the forest. From the moment she had created a deadlock with Aureatia's force, Caneeya had begun planning for this moment.

Without the dense forested terrain, their cavalry troops wouldn't have their mobility limited. Quickly launching a large force was possible. Using this defensive opening, they would charge into Aureatia's retreating forces with everything they had.

None of the Aureatia army would be safely arriving in Imag alive.

"Let's go. Gilnes is sure to be happy, too."

"Yes, ma'am!"

Thus, Caneeya placed the cavalry unit under her command on the vanguard, and the large army made the ground quake.

Most of those who gathered in Toghie City were ragtag foot soldiers, but that wasn't true of Caneeya's troops. They were all battle-proven warriors, once part of the Central Kingdom's regular army, and all regulated under one idea.

"Onward, cavalry troops! I'll prove there's no ambush waiting for us!"

With Caneeya's battle cry came a loud response echoing over it.

The thunderous sound of hooves trampling over the earth. The entire army flowed into the empty stretch of forest under the enemy's blind spot. As they charged forward, Caneeya's smile widened even further.

The enemy general remained unaware that such a massive host was closing in right behind them. She envisioned her enemy awakening to their tactical defeat and dying amid complete bewilderment.

"All right, all right, all right! Twenty-Fourth General Dant. Your head's mine!"

She charged up the hill at full speed. Naturally, there was no ambush after she exited the forest. In response to the Free City of Okafu's movement from the flank, Dant must have acted to ensure the smallest number of casualties. Since he had always had a secure path of retreat, there was also no reason to risk his troops' lives by placing some of them in the rear guard.

When she created the deadlock, that terrain became the winds that would drive her army and her army alone to victory, as if she had personally ordered it made that way herself—

…Suddenly.

A suspicion flashed in the back of Caneeya's mind.

…*As if I ordered it myself?*

It was at that exact moment.

A terrifying rumbling, different from the kind made by soldiers and horses, sounded along with agonized cries at her back.

The soldiers charging alongside stopped their horses one after another, looking to their comrades behind them. Caneeya saw it last. Disaster had struck.

Turbid waters flowed out from the canal like a powerful dragon, fully swallowing up all the soldiers left behind in the lowlands.

As if she ordered it herself.

The trees that originally would have prevented any flooding, Caneeya had cut down herself.

"It can't be… The levee!"

Right as the large force behind Caneeya passed through the lowlands, the levees on the eastern canal were destroyed. Why?

There shouldn't have been any elements of the deforestation that had been leaked. At the very least, not to Aureatia.

…*Who? It was someone. Not Aureatia's army.*

It couldn't have possibly been Aureatia. She could see from atop the hill.

There were people lying in ambush on the higher ground,

shooting down and killing the soldiers as they fled piecemeal from the floodwaters pouring in.

A small, nimble, and unseen—or at least, not seen in the past several decades—race of creatures.

Goblins appeared from within the forest and killed her soldiers. A trap. Battle strategy. Group tactics. Her elite guerilla troops, completely and unilaterally bested by base, inferior goblins.

"......Rescue those who lagged behind. Any objections?"

"...General Caneeya! Wh-what is that?!"

Instead of answering her, the staff officer pointed at the hill. Caneeya looked at the individual up in front of them.

A grotesque monster was waiting for them.

As if it had known somehow that Caneeya's troops would show up at this spot.

"ANYONE. ANYONE HAS, IN THEIR BODY, THE GROUNDING OF A HERO."

It looked like a massive wolf, but its gleaming silver-and-blue fur was nothing like a wolf's natural fur.

The creature slowly moved its head and looked at the young new recruit.

"THE TENDONS OF THAT MAN'S FEET POSSESS WONDERFUL INSTANTANEOUS FORCE. JUST HIS LEG STRENGTH ALONE...HAVE TALENTS EVEN RIVALING DOMENT THE GREEN SASH."

The soldier didn't wait for any orders before aiming his bow at the wolf. A dangerous creature, beyond any doubt.

The wolf didn't move. It seemed to be sizing up the people in front of it.

"...........YOU, OVER THERE...... YOU POSSESS A BODY ILL-SUITED FOR ARCHERY. THE CONDITION OF YOUR BRACHIAL MUSCLES SUGGESTS AN UP-AND-DOWN MOTION. TECHNIQUES THAT INVOLVE SWINGING DOWNWARD— SWORDPLAY, FOR EXAMPLE."

There was the *twang* of an arrow being loosed, and the monster violently shook its body.

However, that was the extent of it. The beast tossed the arrow it had stopped with its teeth to the ground before continuing to speak.

"...OTHERWISE, THIS IS ALL YOU CAN MUSTER."

"I'm going to bring this thing down," Caneeya muttered as she twirled her massive sword.

With eyes betraying none of its emotions, the monster replied, "IT IS REGRETTABLE TO BE MET WITH HOSTILE BEHAVIOR... THOUGH, I AM AS MUCH TO BLAME. LET ME TELL YOU MY NAME."

With a loud smacking sound—its colossal back spread open.

It was an indescribable transformation, an inconceivable shift from its elegant wolf form.

Sprouting up in droves from within its body's cavity were an innumerable number of arms.

"I AM OZONEZMA."

Patched together with tendons and gold wire, each one

carrying sharp medical instruments...the white arms of minian corpses.

"I AM A CHIMERA."

◆

Shortly after wiping out the Old Kingdoms' army, an Okafu army messenger contacted Dant the Heath Furrow. The contact came promptly, as if they had foreseen Aureatia's path of retreat.

"......What's going on?!"

He thought it was a trap, attacking from their flank to cut off their retreat, but given that the Old Kingdoms' army was annihilated in an instant, it was clear to Dant that they weren't a military force he had originally taken them for.

"Okafu made their move! The Old Kingdoms' army is destroyed! None of this makes sense!"

"......A pleasure to make your acquaintance, Milord Dant."

The messenger coolly began to speak. A lone goblin followed at his side.

His name was Hiroto the Paradox. The musket distributor, the Gray-Haired Child. An enigmatic visitor.

"Hiroto the Paradox...! What...? Just what are you plotting?! Working for Okafu, are you?!"

"Not at all. This is not under Okafu's orders, but rather, my own idea. I came calling because I felt it best to assist you, Milord Dant."

"…You think I'll believe those words? Trying to make feel me indebted by stepping into a battle out of the blue and saving us? Your pretext for conquering Aureatia, is it, then?!"

"Milord Dant. Please think over it carefully."

Hiroto casually leaned over while lacing his fingers together.

"How does the Aureatia homeland view this situation? I imagine they don't want you making any unnecessary moves during this deadlock with Toghie City and are planning to suppress them with reinforcements from the homeland as soon as the aftermath of the Particle Storm is dealt with. Wouldn't these current events be viewed as you making negotiations without permission from General Hardy, tasked with suppressing Okafu, and utilizing their mercenaries as your reinforcements?"

"And from that situation, I'm saying that this all must be some trickery of yours! Do you think I won't arrest you right here and make you tell me the truth?!"

"I'm not speaking about the truth here. I'm talking about *whether there's any room for interpretation.* Why, Milord Dant, are you delaying reinforcements during this most difficult turning point in the war? The other general commanding the northern army… Ninth General Yaniegiz is behind in Imag City, yes? He isn't standing on the front lines himself, as the one in charge?"

"……"

"Milord Dant, you're part of the *Queen's faction* that doesn't wish to see a Hero-led reformation, yes? From the outset, I think it's very likely that your stationing here was something directed by the reformation faction organizing the Royal Games…to drive you into being routed back to Imag City and diminish your position and political influence. You must have realized this yourself, though."

The circumstances around the response to the Particle Storm had been different compared to a response to a onetime disaster. A *military operation* that incorporated multiple end goals.

There was an acceptable reason behind the delay in reinforcements from the Aureatia homeland—they were dealing with an unprecedented calamity, the Particle Storm. However, because it was such an understandable reason, it also prevented any criticism about the excessive division of troop strength between the homeland defense forces and the Particle Storm operation.

If they were just keeping the Old Kingdoms' loyalists subdued, Dant's army alone was enough for the job. However, maybe, if Caneeya the Fruit Trimming's stratagem to utilize the terrain had actually been realized in this battle...

"It will be all too easy for the reformation faction to trap you by claiming you hired Okafu to snag an expedited victory for yourself. With that in mind...we would like to aid not Aureatia, but the Queen and you yourself, Milord Dant."

"……"

In front of Dant, unable to give his answer, Hiroto used his open, outstretched palm to indicate the goblin standing beside his chair.

"Let me introduce you. His name is Zigita Zogi. During my dealing with Toghie City, I manipulated the market craftsman contractors for cheap, while conversely buying lumber at high prices. Everything was based on his ideas. The shape of that deadlock, with the forest in the middle, was simply Caneeya the Fruit Trimming turning the image she conceptualized into a reality."

"It was natural to think, from the Old Kingdoms' loyalists' perspective, they'd want to use the delay in reinforcements caused by the Particle Storm to their advantage to settle things quickly. In truth, the forest was blocking their march and getting in their way, as well. I *made them consider* what the quickest way for them would be to clear out that obstacle. *Kwah-ha-ha-ha.*"

Zigita Zogi let out a chuckle, his mouth twisting hideously.

"Really, with military strategy......the more you think you've hit on some brilliant idea on your own, the easier it is to fall right into the trap laid out for you."

"......"

"What do you think? Your army is unscathed. Furthermore, our goblin army is filled entirely with his personally trained soldiers. Behind them still is the army of the Free City of Okafu. I can lend it all to you."

"A-are you trying to instigate...a revolt? Or is that intimidation?"

His outward appearance was of a boy in his early teens. His grizzled hair was the only thing that aged him.

This man was weak; that was much was certain. Weaker than both Caneeya the Fruit Trimming and Dant the Heath Furrow.

Despite it all... This man...

"Well, then. Who's to say, really. You're the ones who can decide the answer for yourselves."

"What the hell do you take me for? I... I am not a shameless man who would sell out Aureatia like this. Nor do I plan on pulling the trigger on starting a civil war, either."

"In that case, I can arrange a path forward for you that involves neither option. A path where the Free City of Okafu's army is dissolved, and they are placed completely under Aureatia's jurisdiction. I will present you the achievement of brokering such negotiations."

Even in Dant's present circumstances, appearing to have moved forward with Okafu negotiations entirely of his own accord, there was only one path that would let the man escape being a target of criticism. It was having *the threat that the Free City of Okafu posed vanish entirely.*

"It doesn't make sense. What benefit do you all get out of that?"

"You seem to be gathering heroes yes? Aureatia's Twenty-Nine Officials are searching for them, I've heard."

Heroes, yet again. It was the only thing anyone was concerning themselves with.

Dant didn't like it. From the very start, nothing about this battle had sat right with him. What rubbed Dant the wrong way more than anything, though, was that he himself was getting caught up in the tide, too.

"Now…what would happen if, say, there was, in fact, more than one hero? No one has yet to confirm for themselves how exactly the True Demon King died. What if, for example, there was an allegation that someone with a huge army at their command defeated that same True Demon King with that said troop strength?"

"That'd be totally impossible...! Have you ever seen the True Demon King's power to drive anyone mad with fear?! The power to bring death, the weaker you are, the more numbers you amass, the more you face off against, the more you're driven into insanely killing each other! It'd be absolutely impossible there'd be more than one Hero! Even a child can understand that!"

"That's not something anybody is able to prove. I'm talking about *whether there is enough left up in the air for that interpretation*. If that hero had a nation behind them, for Aureatia, or perhaps for a majority of this world's population, could the residents of said nation be considered enemies?"

"...The Royal Games. So you lot are after the Royal Games, too?"

"I'd like to dispatch him as a possible Hero. Zigita Zogi the Thousandth. He's received the support of a goblin army and Okafu's army—and defeated a Demon King. They are champions of a shared fate."

Sweat slowly began to bead on Dant's forehead.

The meaning here was not only limited to the right to appear in the Royal Games.

As long as there was a chance they had some relation to the Hero, Aureatia would no longer be able to make any moves against Okafu. At the very least, their public position would be forced to abide by that. Hiroto the Paradox. From the very start, this man was aiming for a participation slot in the Royal Games. If he had been the one to guide every part of the situation to this end, then......

"I'll take two of the slots."

"...Two...?!"

"Yes. I'd like you to give a recommendation to a member of the Twenty-Nine Officials you find easy to manipulate and who you have some rapport with. I'm sure a general of your renown has at least one person who can fit. I'd like you and this other official to back two of our choices."

He agitated the Old Kingdoms' loyalists using both material and immaterial information, driving them to their doom.

He ended the battle without spilling a single drop of Okafu soldier blood.

He entered into an advantageous peace between Aureatia and the Free City of Okafu.

And finally...he prepared the newest battlefield.

Hiroto the Paradox had carried out all his promises to the Okafu public.

"HIROTO."

A giant silhouette landed from inside the encampment walls without a sound. It looked a bit like a wolf, but the beast's appearance was unlike anything Dant had ever seen before. There had been no voices from outside that forewarned the threatening infiltration. No one had even noticed.

"YOU ARE STILL GOING? I HAVE ALREADY FINISHED MY DUTY."

"I see. Thank you for your help as always, Ozonezma."

"...I AM NOT HELPING YOU OUT. OUR RELATIONSHIP IS NOTHING MORE THAN EQUAL COLLABORATORS."

…He didn't know when things had shifted.

Dant was no longer able to kill the frail boy where he stood.

While keeping his attention rapt with their negotiations, the boy summoned two types of brute force to his side. What was there Dant could do now? Okafu's army would be dissolved, the achievement would be credited to him, clearing him of any doubt, and in exchange, he would back the two in front of him as hero candidates. Could Dant think up any other solution right here on the spot that would surpass Hiroto's demands?

"Two slots. These two here, are my hero candidates."

Tactician. Goblin. Zigita Zogi the Thousandth.

Medic. Chimera. Ozonezma the Capricious.

And finally.

"You… Damn you… Hiroto the Paradox! Just what in the world are you?!"

Standing before Dant as he smacked his desk and jumped to his feet, Hiroto spread out his hands.

Now, shouldering the control over all of this military force, he gave a flawless smile.

"You're the ones who can decide the answer for yourselves."

He possessed world-transcending speech and negotiating gifts that sealed away any deviating choices in his audience.

He was able to understand one's mind with a simple glance, fully learning all of his enemy's wants and fears.

He birthed an unknown nation, achieving a degree of development that outstripped minian civilization.

A cultural invader who twisted all the olden logic according to his otherworldly logic.

Statesman. Minia.

Hiroto the Paradox.

The glow of a single camp light flickered along the roadway.

Even without a horse, as long as you skillfully divided up the distance, the trip to Aureatia didn't require an overnight camp. That day, however, the calculations were thrown off a little bit.

Yuno the Distant Talon still wasn't accustomed to traveling. Journeying together with a visitor who couldn't adapt to the common sense of this world, Soujirou the Willow-Sword, they were wandering through various regions under Aureatia's orders.

This time, Soujirou was apparently nominated to act in Kazuki the Black Tone's stead, after she failed to conquer the Free City of Okafu, and headed out to present himself to the Twenty-Seventh General Hardy, in command of said operation. However, as soon as the two arrived, there had been some sort of understanding reached higher up the command chain, and Soujirou never had the chance to participate in the operation to conquer the city. A complete waste of a trip, for Yuno as well.

The man she shared her journey with was covered up with a simple sleeping bag, a bit removed from where she was. Beside him, a Nagan training sword was offhandedly lying on the ground.

"…I wish I had studied more. About what tools you need to make camp or about gathering plants and berries… I never had left Nagan before, after all."

"Hmm? Don't seem like a big deal to me. Ain't no beasts around, neither. Just relax and get some sleep; it'll do ya good."

Soujirou seemed very accustomed to suddenly setting up camp like this. For Yuno, having heard the civilization of the Beyond was far more advanced than in her world, it was a rather surprising fact about him.

Yuno asked a question that suddenly popped into her mind.

"…What was it like before you came to this world?"

"Huh?"

"You've taught me about it before, didn't you? The M1 Abrams… You said it was a tank from another country, right? I just wondered what the Beyond was like…including that tank stuff, too."

"Ah well, see… Truth is, I ain't really know much myself."

"……?"

◆

Twenty-one years earlier.

The True Demon King appeared, spreading despair across the land, and it was the final era where people held some hope that, someday, someone would appear to end their torment.

"S-stop… Stop, please! I'll die! I'm going to die! You'll kill me!"

There were ruins where the voices of the living had long died out. A crazed wurm chased after a young boy, its rough scales smashing through the ruins of the city like a fire. The other residents who had lived there up until a small month ago, though still minian in appearance, were no longer minian in their hearts and minds.

Up ahead of where the boy desperately tried to make his escape, a mountain of crumbling debris blocked his path.

"*Aaaaaaah?!*"

He roughly scratched at his vibrant red hair.

This was going to be the end. He truly believed this was it.

The wurm, exuding a stench of blood and rotten flesh, opened its mouth wide...and it was impossible to hope that any help would come to his aid. This land was under the control of the True Demon Lord, after all.

"*Aaah... Gaaah*, enough! I really will die!"

A track of light rushed in far faster than the wurm could consume its prey. The spearhead seemed to have grazed the inside of the wurm's mouth as it flew by it.

The young boy landed, pulling a small trail of blood spatter behind him, and the colossus, still under the momentum of its attack, dug into the earth before it came to halt.

"*Hah...hahhh...* Dammit.........! What the hell am I supposed to do if I die, huh?! I'm doing my damn best out here, too, you know... Right? I'm working hard. Nothing but this, every day! Everyone under the stars comes at me trying to kill me... What reason is there to do this to me?!"

Using his red spear to prop himself up, he panted. A young

genius of spear craft. At the time, there weren't many who knew the name Alena the Benighted White Wind.

"Hwah, hee-hee-hee-hee!"

On top of a stone fence was a young girl who had watched over the fight sequence. She remained seated as she clapped her hands together and laughed.

"Whew, you're as impressive as ever, huh! You really sure you're a minia?!"

"Lu...Lumelly... Were you watching the whole time?! Watching me?! As I almost died?!"

"'Almost died'? Gimme a break."

Her black hair, giving her a sense of composure, swayed as a nasty smile crept across her face.

She was a young elf girl known as Lumelly the Poisoned Ground. She didn't appear to be too far apart in age from Alena. Though, elves were a race that maintained an outwardly youthful appearance for a long period of time, so even her traveling companion Alena had no idea if they were close in age.

What he did know was that Lumelly was an arts caster of truly unfathomable ability, and that was apparently the reason why she was driven out of the village she was raised in—and nothing more than that.

"You start groaning, 'No, no, I'm gonna die' whether you're facing off against a dragon or a damn mouse. Who the hell's gonna take that seriously, huh? Go really get yourself killed for a change, will ya."

"Hey... I'm always fighting for my life out there. I don't want to die, and that's why I trained every day, let out one hundred percent of my full power nonstop, until I was finally able to move this fast, okay? It always feels like I'm shaving off two or three years of my life every time. I'm not some carefree genius like you, Lumelly."

"Oh, you got the gall to treat me like some genius, huh? Dang, you are a helluva funny guy! Ah well, maybe it's better if you think of me like that, eh? *Hwah-hee-hee-hee-hee!*"

Lumelly the Poisoned Ground was, without a doubt, a genius.

The legend that she had fought a Word Arts battle against Izick the Chromatic, said to be the strongest and most wicked demon king, was common knowledge to everyone in the Western Kingdom by that point. There wasn't anyone else who could manage such an extraordinary deed.

He had seen the light of the Thermal Arts she casted, black and corrosive.

She was a girl who used an irreplicable superpower, interfering and overwriting the Word Arts of others.

"If you're here, I'm guessing the others are, too?"

"Yup. That damn Izick was dragging his feet about some stupid preparations of his or whatever, so I came to flush him out myself... Finally."

Still squatting on top of the fence, she was glaring at one of the fortresses.

She must have hated them more than anyone else in the party.

"The True Demon King. Finally be able to kill 'em dead."

The young girl seemed to sneer at justice, morality, and all the values esteemed by general society. Like Alena himself, she also didn't appear to be fighting with the sort of aspirations befitting a champion.

Why was Lumelly trying to challenge such a terrifying opponent as the True Demon King?

Alena wondered if the day would ever come where he could ask her. Maybe if they truly managed to defeat the Demon King.

"...Hmph. A wurm is dead."

A different voice.

"Get mixed up in another fight, young Alena?"

Casually turning out of an alley was a man of unrefined features, wearing round glasses.

He was named Romzo the Star Map, another one of their traveling companions.

"C'mon, Master, these aren't petty little scraps we're talking about here! Would any sane minia pick a fight with a wurm?! Everyone under the sun says not to get involved with the Demon King Army, and I even tried to run away, too, but I... Today I really did think I was seriously going die for real, honest!"

"It's all the same."

Behind Romzo, there were residents scattered on the ground, fallen and without any power to stand back up.

He was a veteran master, capable of neutralizing those at the edge of madness, fully transformed into the Demon King Army like this, without causing any harm...and more importantly, without ever being swallowed up by the fear.

"Whether it's a brawl on the outskirts of town or a Demon King Army riot. Lay your troubled mind bare, and it will simply fan the emotional flames of your opponent. That's why it's so easy for you to get wrapped up in misfortune."

"Th-that's got nothing to do with it, though. I can't do anything about being scared, can I? I should've stayed behind with Psianop, too..."

"That's true. You had that option. In that case, why are you trying to take on the True Demon King?"

"Well..."

He wondered why. Some in this world had to do it. There was no doubt of that. But did Alena the Benighted White Wind possess the convictions necessary for the deeds of a champion?

Even now, he couldn't help wondering. Despite his journey coming to an end where he stood, right at the True Demon King's doorstep.

"All right, the three of us can go together. Izick's getting impatient."

"...Okay. Let's go."

"He's the one who's kept us waiting this whole damn time! Guess that bastard's not gonna learn unless I beat the piss outta of him, huh?!"

Twenty-one years ago. There were seven people, known as the First Party.

Going from servant to champion solely off his skills with a bow, Fralik the Heaven.

A fighter who mastered the martial arts of his tribe, passed down uninterrupted through the ages, Neft the Nirvana.

A black-hearted arts caster, forsaken by the world, Lumelly the Poisoned Ground.

An unparalleled child prodigy with a spear, clad in trouble and bad luck, Alena the Benighted White Wind.

A self-proclaimed demon king feared for performing the evilest deeds the land had seen, Izick the Chromatic.

A visitor who controlled dark arts handed down from the underworld, Yugo the Moving Decapitation Blade.

A pioneer in medical techniques who understood all the meridians of the body, Romzo the Star Map.

They were the hope of all life that still breathed in this land. The seven who first harbored the courage to challenge the True Demon King. Each of them transcendental champions, possessing equal strength, they sometimes squared off against one another and sometimes joined forces to fight against the Demon King Army, but at long last, today was the day they would head for their final battle.

A man with a black scarf covering his mouth came to meet Lumelly and the others as they arrived.

"Lumelly. Haven't seen you since our fight in Tileet Ravine."

"Yugo…! I still remember that promise you made, you know. I'll be a big help, I swear. 'Conceal the blade of your heart.' You said that to me, didn't you?"

Yugo the Moving Decapitation Blade nodded mildly at his former enemy's words.

He wasn't the only one. Right now, every one of them except for Psianop was assembling in front of the Demon King's castle.

There was only one among them who was sitting cross-legged on the ground. He was a middle-aged man wearing a green overcoat, appearing to have seen better days.

He was peering into the castle with a window he made with his fingers. With the same aloof and detached attitude he always had.

"Hrmm, hoo boy, this is baaaad news! Oh yeah, this is gonna be a reeeeal tough one."

"Hey, Izick! You asshole!"

"Ow!"

Lumelly mercilessly kicked him in the back. Her demeanor the complete opposite of how she had spoken to Yugo.

"What did I tell you this morning?! Quit moaning and whining about every damn little thing! No chickening out now, asshole!"

"Now, now, Lumelly dear, I'm not scared at all, you know. Uh... Ahhh, actually, I might've lied. I might be a bit scared honestly. Strange, isn't it? Cold and heartless Izick the Chromatic, scared."

The True Demon King, their mere presence enough to stain a whole area with madness.

No one had seen their true form before. Anyone who approached them, and those they approached, were all driven insane.

Courage was needed to face off against the unknown terror. Without true power that could sustain oneself, like the seven gathered here together, they wouldn't have been able to get this far.

There was a terror that made one want to turn away and run.

It should've been a completely normal fortress of a local lord, and yet one look made it clear that the True Demon King was there...

So powerful was the clear terror given physical form that lurked inside its walls.

"What should we do, Fralik? Attack or not? If a man of Izick's caliber is saying so, truth may be that our chances aren't good. I'm fine either way, myself," Yugo asked, still with his arms crossed.

"......Mrm."

Fralik the Heaven only replied with a brief momentary grunt, his gaze fixed hard on the castle.

His throat hadn't been functional ever since it was crushed while he was still young. Short verbalizations were the only way the man could express his will to others.

"Ah."

"Fralik's saying he'll go. Then, I'm going, too."

"*Grrrrrf...* Killing them today is our only option. A city lies just ahead. If we let the Demon King invade, it'll be ruined. Surely none of you here intend for that to happen."

Neft the Nirvana. The last hero of a lycan village as their race was slowly being ousted by the minian races.

Izick reluctantly stood up.

"Whatever, guess it doesn't matter to me. I've been doing whatever horrible thing I've wanted to make sure I don't die with regrets for a while now! *Ha-ha-ha-ha-ha!* If it's kill or be killed then, I want the end to be as flashy as it can be! Let's have some fun, eh?!"

"Mhn."

Fralik smiled. He didn't speak with his words, but he was always the center of their party.

They then all stepped into the castle. Into the jaws of death.

* * *

Indeed. It was the jaws of death. Much like everyone in later eras knew, the First Party was defeated.

Completely powerless, just like many of the champions who would follow in their footsteps. They were completely destroyed, along with the hopes of everyone of that age. Of course, the current seven were unaware that this future lay ahead of them.

"……I can tell. The True Demon King…… They're up ahead here."

Izick guided the party, using a homunculus he created to scout ahead. The homunculus, no bigger than one's ankle, went terminally insane just from approaching the room. Any beings with a soul, even constructs, would meet such an end.

Every one of the seven could feel a mysterious and unknown premonition of death.

Alena the Benighted White Wind was the one to put their hands on the door in front of them.

"I'm opening it."

He concluded that was what he needed to do. He needed to open up a line of fire for Fralik's arrows and Lumelly's Word Arts.

Everyone had received Rozmo's pressure point technique and was now capable of displaying powers of concentration beyond their normal limits. Nevertheless, this technique wasn't enough to endure the intense pressure of the terror facing them, capable of driving an ordinary person instantly insane.

His heart pounded; the inside of his mouth went dry.

It was cold. He had a hard time breathing. He was terrified.

Alena trembled from fright. He had only ended up here because he had gone along with the flow. Surely the other champions, who had reasons for being there, didn't feel this way.

...*The True Demon King.*

The door opened. A shivering cold air caressed his nerves.

The chant of Lumelly's Word Arts that reduced all to ash raced out of her mouth. The gem on her finger grew more radiant. That was how things should have went.

"Rumeyry io halese. Hamsuwaka baal, morteka zuorurg." (From Lumelly to Haresept's eyes. Strumming verdant ripples, of hollow light.)

Her incantation stopped.

Fralik's bowstring, which should've twanged faster than anyone could act, didn't move.

Yugo, who should've exploited the shadows to sunder everything in two, was also frozen where he stood.

Why?

As he feared the ceaseless throbbing of his own heart, Alena tried to look for the reason why.

A reason so apparent that no search was even necessary.

They were terrified.

"Oh. Do I have guests?"

Alena thought that it was a pretty voice. Its owner sat rather normally in a chair within the bedroom, reading a book just like a typical minian scholar would.

A breeze blew into the room. Just like what blew in the world outside...the same wind from a world without this enormous dread in front of them.

The long black hair smoothly swayed, and the pitch-black pupils looked at the party.

She smiled.

The terrifying Demon King. A ruinous demon that crushed all behind them.

Or perhaps a shapeless phenomenon of pure destruction itself.

It was none of the above.

It was simply a young girl.

The True Demon King was different from the seven gathered there in only one regard.

A white line running over simple, machine-sewn black fabric. A red scarf prominent on her chest.

...It was the clothing of a different culture from someone far, far beyond their own.

"Hello."

It was known as a schoolgirl sailor uniform.

◆

"You don't know? About your own world?"

Yuno was suspicious of Soujirou's vague reply.

Was he seriously trying to tell her he didn't understand anything about his own world?

"…What's that supposed to mean?"

"Hmmm, I dunno how to put it, but my country, right? It got really messed up a long, long time ago, with all these guys from a bunch of other countries showing up, see. It was nonstop fighting, so I don't really know."

"Wait, so…there was a war then… Right? So your country was already…"

"Yeah. I guess that's what it was. Things were like that since I was a kid, so I only heard 'bout it."

Of course. When Yuno thought it over, it was obvious. Soujirou had fought against another country's weapons. She didn't need to hear from him to know what his situation was like.

This swordsman from another world had long ago tasted the type of ruin Yuno had experienced in Labyrinth City.

"This girl called Shiki Aihara, 'pparently she destroyed it all."

◆

The sun over the Free City of Okafu was low in the sky, and the lights of bustling nighttime activity began to pop up here and there below him.

Looking down at the scene from the terrace of the central citadel, Hiroto the Paradox suddenly muttered.

"Miss Kazuki Mizumura said something."

At long last, even Kazuki the Black Tone had come to meet her end.

Thirty years ago. She was the champion who Hiroto saw potential in, already having shifted his base of activities to another continent and entrusting her with his guns.

"Mr. Morio Ariyama. She said she had something she wanted to inquire of you. Now I know...what she was frightened of and what she wanted to ask you."

"...To us here in Okafu, Kazuki the Black Tone was a mortal enemy up until the very end. At that point, any sort of bargaining with her would've been totally impossible."

"She probably thought as much, too. That was likely why she tried to fight against you as an enemy until the bitter end."

Hiroto's calculations didn't always play out perfectly.

He thought: If only he had prepared a place for negotiations on that last day he saw Kazuki.

For these past several decades, there were far fewer instances where he had been able to handle matters without losing anything than those where he hadn't.

"So then, what did that woman want to know?"

"She only gave me a few hints to go on. Why exactly have all the visitors who've shown up here recently been people from our country? Or perhaps, she might have been thinking that the conclusion my surmising has led me to was dangerous information."

"......That's right. You might have a point. You're different, but Kazuki, Yukiharu the Twilight Diver, and I—we've all arrived in these past twenty years."

"And that's why I had Mr. Yukiharu investigate things for me."

He placed a scrap of torn fabric on the desk. Almost all the inhabitants of the world would be unable to grasp the meaning behind the article.

Morio looked at him with a complex expression, not quite anger nor animosity.

A rotted section of a student uniform—a schoolgirl's sailor uniform.

"I likely don't need to go into the full account of how this was obtained from The Land of The End. Mr. Yukiharu Shijima. Zigita Zogi. I was the one who sent them both there. I took the liberty of joining in on Okafu's operation."

"......Information on the True Demon King...... Kazuki was after it, too, then."

"That's right, Mr. Morio Ariyama. I believe you wanted to ensure that one piece of information *wasn't known by anyone else*, yes? That's why you feared The Land of The End the most of all. You were always tense, enough to intervene with a small farming village's request to clear out the land."

Hiroto immediately used the light of a candlestick to set the scrap of cloth on fire.

"Didn't hesitate to light it on fire, huh."

"Indeed. I felt that was the best thing to be done."

The existence of this material evidence had been his final trump card to get the self-proclaimed demon king Morio to agree to direct negotiations.

However, it was no longer necessary. It was an all-too-dangerous fact not only to Morio, but to Hiroto himself as well.

"The True Demon King was a visitor, weren't they?"

From a certain period of time onward, it was only individuals from their country who were transported to this world as deviants.

…Hiroto had knowledge concerning the superhumans who were introduced here from the Beyond.

Pilots and soldiers who left inconceivable military exploits in the wars there. Or warriors in history who performed superhuman and unbelievably strenuous feats of battle. Drawing on individual concrete examples was beyond necessary. Even if their abnormality didn't reach the level of total world divergence, it still meant there was an environment there that birthed superhumans who eclipsed all human understanding.

Both Morio the Sentinel and Kazuki the Black Tone had been soldiers in the Beyond. It was these very wars, bringing chaos and death, these ages of chaos where no one would take any notice if someone disappeared entirely, that gave birth to these deviants from the world—these visitors, these shura.

In which case, it would mean the Beyond had to be in a continuous widespread maelstrom of war, beyond anything Hiroto could imagine.

"Let me make it clear that, even in this country, I'm the only one who knows. Even those guys I had sealing off The Land of The End weren't filled in on anything outside of the scope of their mission. I erased any of them who tried to find out themselves. Since this is something that concerns *all of us*."

"I know."

The True Demon King was a visitor.

This single fact being brought to light would be enough to upend the world once again.

The Word-Maker who guided visitors from another world and established the heavens and earth. The knowledge of visitors who had already permeated this society's civilization in various forms. The foundational base behind the sense of values held by all the current living beings in this world would be feared and expelled.

As a result, at the very least, it would no longer be a world where the Order or visitors could live.

Miss Kazuki Mizumura didn't intend on telling anyone about it, either, then.

I'm just fulfilling my obligations to this world. As a champion.

Hiroto no longer had any way of knowing how exactly, when faced with this fact, in what way Kazuki planned to carry out her atonement to this world.

He knew, however, that in the face of a monumental disaster like the True Demon King, thinking so nobly was a very difficult thing to do.

...Miss Kazuki Mizumura. You were exactly the champion I expected you to be after all.

To Hiroto the Paradox, unable to become champion himself, it was impossible.

Though, I'm sure you would deny it yourself.

The True Demon King.

Yugo the Moving Decapitation Blade understood the moves he needed to bring an end to his enemy.

Throw his short sword low, skimming the ground, and cut her ankle. From his low throwing stance, like he was crawling on the ground, immediately jump to the ceiling. Force her attention on the ground and use that chance to split her skull with a descending sword slice. A technique he called Smoke. That would kill her.

If she tried slashing at him from the front, he'd be able to take the initiative. He had a technique, Darkness, where he slashed sideways while deceiving his enemy to think he was swinging his sword down from above. That could kill her, too.

In the back of his mind, he imagined his various moves. Opening. Soot. Sleep. None of the numerous techniques Yugo had mastered would fail to kill this girl in front of him……

I should be able… to kill her.

Yugo the Moving Decapitation Blade's feet weren't budging a single inch.

It wasn't that they were restrained. Nor was it from pain or exhaustion. He stayed kneeling down on one knee and wasn't able to fully stand up. He was supposed to move faster than anyone else in the party, and yet he hadn't at all.

"C'mon, now… I mean, c'mon, guys."

From behind him, Izick the Chromatic was mumbling.

"Say something, would you?! For this whole damn time, I was acting weird, wasn't I?!"

His voice was mixed with laughter like usual, however, he was emphatically terrified.

"Why...didn't any of you notice? It's strange, right? I mean, the moment I realized where the enemy was... Why didn't I, y'know... tear down the whole town with locust revenants or something?! I'd totally do that, right?! Of course I would, you all know!"

"...Izick."

"I-it's almost like... *Ha-ha*...... Like I got cold f-feet or something... Must've thought trying would've been pointless, that it'd be the end for me, and chickened out... Right?! Quit screwing with me!"

He tried to send out a fleshy tentacle from the inside of his sleeve. A living weapon that corroded any living creature and disintegrated them—but this, too, came to a stop without reaching the girl.

She hadn't done anything. It was Izick himself who prevented it from reaching his target.

Though the tentacle had no will of its own, its wielder dreaded it.

"......Gotta be kidding...... Impossible..."

Lumelly was also dumbfounded by the scene in front of her. Even while seven champions stood before the True Demon King, not a single one of them could even attempt a single, misguided attack.

None of them was capable of doing what they needed to do.

As if they were nothing more than a gathering of fools.

"Word Arts!"

The shouting voice seemed to belong to Alena.

"Lumelly, overwrite things with your Word Arts! With you Word Arts, just maybe!"

"Th-that's not it… That's not what this is! What're we even supposed to do…?! This—this isn't from Word Arts at all!"

Yugo's thoughts raced as he desperately tried to bring his breathing under control.

That's right. This isn't Word Arts or any kind of special technique. This phenomenon isn't some compelling force. It's simply…… our minds feeling this terror. That's all there is to it.

He could move his body. He could feel hostility toward the True Demon King.

Just my fingertips is enough. Two fingers to lob a needle at her. That's enough to kill her. It's clear now that the True Demon King possesses no fighting abilities. This is the perfect chance. Right now… I have to kill her quick.

Yugo's physical constitution would have revealed if this was the result of a vampire infection or any type of poison or illusion. Naturally, it wasn't Word Arts, either. There wasn't a single reason why he couldn't kill the True Demon King on the spot.

"…Hey, you there."

The True Demon King bent down in front of him and looked up into his eyes.

She had approached him with the footsteps of any normal young girl. In the time it took for her to stand up from her chair and walk over… What had Yugo been doing while he watched her?

Her thin fingertips gripped his hand, and she handed over a small metallic rod.

Into the hands of a man who boasted of speed faster than the eye could see, who had never let any enemy get close to him, into Yugo the Moving Decapitation Blade's hand.

"You want to try stabbing with this?"

Yugo looked at the item lying in his own palm. It was some sort of something, its point crushed and stained with blood and brain fluids. It was an implement originally known as a ballpoint pen, however, even for someone with knowledge of the items of the Beyond like Yugo, it was difficult to identify it at all.

If I'm this close. Her eye. My weapon's in my hand. Finger… I just need to move one finger. Then I can kill her. Her black eyes. Her voice. Kill… Kill the True Demon King. The true. Terrifying, terrifying. She's terrifying.

His breathing was staccato. He couldn't maintain his breath control. He couldn't hear the world around him. He could see, and yet it was only her dark pupils that were visible. Terrifying. He wanted to escape. There shouldn't have been any reason to feel such dread. She was looking at him. She was smiling. It was frightening enough to tear out the back of his brain, to make him go mad. Scary. Horrifying. Terr—

A sensation of something popping open ran through his body.

At some point, without him realizing it, he had stabbed the ballpoint pen into his own eye socket. He gouged the live eyeball and scraped it out with his own hands.

Despite knowing it was horrifying, even though his conscience was screaming that he needed to stop, he continued, unmistakably doing so of his own volition.

Frightening. Terrifying. Why exactly did he have to do something like this?

"*Ah, aaaah... Aaaaaaaah! Hngaack! Aaaaaaah?!*"

"There we go. I'm glad. *Tee-hee.*"

The True Demon King looked at him and laughed, whatever she found so amusing an absolute mystery.

It wasn't from relief or joy, but an innocent and pure laugh, like a child's.

"Y-you... What the hell're you...?! Dammit, d-dirty coward... If I just... If I could just use Word Arts! M-my voice, so hoarse, dammit... Daaaaamn you...!"

Lumelly's voice hadn't actually gone hoarse at all.

It was but a very mundane phenomenon—her voice caught in her throat from her dread.

The True Demon King strolled among the champions, frozen where they stood.

"I'm just human."

She then turned her sights on Neft.

"It's okay. You don't need to be scared at all. Feel free to relax...... Okay?"

"Stay away. *Grrngh...* Stay away......! Stop! D-don't look at meeee!"

Neft rent his stomach with his arms. Not even using his axes, completely with his bare hands. He spat up blood, regenerated with Life Arts, and tortured his body even further.

His live viscera dribbled onto the floor, and as he continued to reduce his cellular life span by his own hands, Neft continued to writhe in the anguish and fear his own immortality tormented him with.

"Hraaaah! G-gahk, gwaah... Aaaah...!"

"Aw. And what do you want to do?"

"Ah... Eek...!"

The black pupils turned Alena's way next. He couldn't even sit himself down, still with his spear in his hand. He simply remained standing, looking at the True Demon King.

With a giggle, she took his hand.

"Look. You can do whatever you'd like. You all are my guests here."

"F-Fralik... I—I want..."

Alena raised his spear. Despite knowing he definitely didn't want to do anything like it. That a simple thrust of his spear would put an end to the terror for good.

The fact that he didn't do so in front of her... That he couldn't stop himself from being tainted by the greatest despair and tragedy he could think of—was terrifying.

"...t-to kill him... Help... L-let me, kill him..."

"...Is that so? Well then, go right ahead."

The True Demon King gently smiled.

She never gave a single order.

It would have been so much more of a saving grace for them all if she compelled them with commands like "kill yourself," or "kill your comrades."

Izick the Chromatic was making his own revenant's tentacle choke up his windpipe, and he didn't move.

Yugo the Moving Decapitation Blade continued gouging out both of his eyes with the ballpoint pen he was handed.

Romzo the Star Map crushed Lumelly's bones as she remained unable to move.

Every one of them was in tears shrieking. Driven mad under their own will, they injured themselves.

"Hnngh...! Mrn...unh......"

Even Fralik the Heaven was crying, his voice unable to scream.

Alena tore the honorable man to pieces, turning him into eternally unspeaking flesh. The one performing such a deed was none other than himself. It all felt like a nightmare. Alena was terrified.

Aaah. Why—why did people *convince themselves to try being brave*?

Why did they know the terror and still try to confront it? Even when they themselves knew most of all that terror was there waiting for them?

They went and actually reached their destination. Despite every single instinct as a living being shouting at them nonstop to avoid it, not to come in contact with it.

"Sorry... I'm sorry, Fralik! *E-eeaaaugh...!*"

"Mnnnh! Mng, aaugh! Augh!"

"No, no... I hate it, I hate it, I hate it... I can't take it anymooore! *Aaaaaaugh!*"

*　　*　　*

The sensation that came to him through his spear shaft was unmistakably Fralik's flesh. It was fat. The spinal cord and blood vessels tangled around his red spear were severed.

Alena possessed the skills necessary to avoid killing someone in one stroke, to make them suffer as long as possible before they died.

It was hell. He wished that the always righteous Romzo would guide him once again.

"Aaah... Aaaah... Easy. Easy. Easy. Easy. Easy."

The Romzo who still continued to punch Lumelly long after her head had been torn off.

The elf, the ultimate Word Arts caster as far as Alena knew, died unable to do anything whatsoever.

Neft continued to die in unending toil. Izick's cursing was long gone.

Terror. Terror was all there was.

Terror. Terror. Terror. Terror. Terror. Terror. Terror.

"Oh, that's right. I need to read what happens next in my book," the True Demon King said as though nothing had happened.

Amid a scene of complete waking hell, she alone remained a normal young girl.

There had to be some reason.

Some thoroughly mastered psychological technique—an undiscovered system of Word Arts or superpower would have been enough.

It must've just been because they weren't strong enough. *That's why* they wanted to believe they could lose. There was some unfathomable contrivance at work, that she herself had some sinister motive, and was thus spreading terror over the whole world.

That was what it had to be. There was assuredly some reason to it all.

If there wasn't, *then what could anyone hope to do*?

◆

"Psianop."

The body that had preserved its youth long past its prime in a single day was pushed to the limits of decrepitude and senile decay.

Romzo. Alena. Izick. Even bringing the others—who weren't beyond saving—with him as he escaped, he had been able to survive. Since the True Demon King hadn't even tried to finish them off.

However, he wouldn't be able to escape for the rest of his life.

The True Demon King's terror would always haunt his mind.

Forever sullying his champion's pride and heart… A genuine terror too hideous to speak of.

"You shall not challenge her. You cannot beat her. That monster……"

He measured the vitality of the cells that were being continuously revived with his Life Arts. Two years, no, less than one year left.

"…Th-there isn't anyone who can beat her anymore…"

Neft the Nirvana. He went on to stand watch in the Gokashae Sand Sea and protect the only comrade he had left in this world.

Protecting him not from outside enemies. He was protecting him from the same hopeless death they met, challenging an opponent he had no chance of defeating.

◆

There was the shabby-looking figure of a man wandering on the outskirts of the Assiel Fiefdom.

"Piss off... Ha-ha...! I... I'm the Demon King Izick, dammit...! *Hrnk*, y-you think this is enough to make me give up?!"

It was a self-proclaimed demon king, at one point called the evilest in all the land.

He continued on aimlessly, the whole while vomiting up the viscera he had burned raw with his own techniques.

What he could do by not giving up, no one knew.

"I'm still alive... I-I'm... I'm gonna kill you, got it...? Ha-ha... I'll create the strongest construct of all time...! Next time... N-next time, for sure...! *Koff, bleeeerg.*"

Coming out from the mountain road appeared a group with a similar appearance as Izick.

Stained in the blood of their own family, smeared with tears of despair, they were monsters wearing the same expression Izick now had on his own face. All of them were originally minia. They were still minia even now.

"Ha-ha-ha... Don't play with me..."

He wore a stiff, twitching smile.

As if drawn in by his fear, the Demon King Army flocked to him.

"Come on! Come and get it! Like some ignorant gutter trash like you, don't make me... *Ngh, hahk, gauuuuuuuuugh!*"

◆

"Oh... Easy. To think it was s-so easy...... *Hee-hee. Hee-hee-hee-hee.*"

Romzo the Star Map returned to the city, looking hollow and empty.

No one's words seemed to reach him, and he simply repeated the same mumblings over and over again.

He was the only one who returned back to civilization from the fight with the True Demon King without any injuries. Together with Neft the Nirvana, they were designated the only two survivors of the First Party.

However, unknown to others, in Romzo's case, his psyche had broken down.

Three years later, and despite outwardly appearing to have recovered his senses on the surface, this remained so.

"It was—it was this easy."

Ever since that day, any minian coherence had disappeared from his heart.

As it was gradually reduced to the heart of an unruly beast, unable to believe in any sort of faith or justice, he eventually began living a life of retirement, casting away everything.

"K-killing one's comrades, was so easy. *Tee-hee*."

Within Romzo's eyes, he always saw his own hands, stained with blood.

◆

"I'm scared. Scared. Scared. Scared. Scared. Scared. Scared. Scared—"

A sole silhouette tottered along as he walked through the lifeless ruins.

His mouth was dirtied with human flesh and blood, telling a story of a fall into depravity he could never recover from.

He had been reduced to the same state as every other living creature in this land. Dragging a red spear wrapped up in entrails behind him, it let out a hollow rattling sound.

"Scared... I'm scared. Help. Someone...... Someone!"

Save for the two sole survivors, none of the champions who challenged the True Demon King were considered to have survived. All wound up like him.

Those whose true genuine courage led them to be confronted with true genuine terror.

"Scared... I'm scared! Scared! The Demon King's watching! I can hear that voice!"

Therefore, there was nothing more to be told about this man's story.

The whereabouts of Alena the Benighted White Wind were unknown to all.

◆

She was without any past or motive, endowed with no power or skills.

She didn't possess any Word Arts or superpowers, without even the power of magic tools at her disposal.

She was just one single minia, and not every and all phenomena had a reason behind them.

Nothing more than a ghost from the past, long since defeated. She was already dead.

Archenemy. Minia.

Shiki, Enemy of All.

ISHURA
Keiso
ILLUSTRATION BY Kureta

Sixth Verse:

SIXWAYS EXHIBITION I

A pure-white field of ice, as if the stars in the sky were twinkling.

Quiet and still to the far reaches of the horizon, without any enemies to battle or friends to exchange conversation with.

She serenely closed her eyes.

Battle. Ah, what a wonderful thing.

Beyond the Igania Ice Lake, conflict still continued on within the realms of men.

Long ago in the past, another dragon had described it. Saying the conflicts of men were terribly ugly and asinine. That they do harm to others of their own race, their own species, was proof of the depths of their wickedness.

Lucnoca didn't think so.

Those not of humankind didn't know. They didn't know how venerable and noble it was to challenge others unlike oneself, while trying to stay true to themselves with the power and knowledge they were able to possess.

Hope. Emotion. Animosity. Conviction. Any of them would work.

All in order to prove that the inner realm of the heart was something far bigger than the reality seen in one's eyes.

As long as all the living creatures across the horizon hadn't given up for good, conflict was undying.

Even beyond this far-off and frozen land, that alone remained ever unchanging for her.

As long as the spiral of strife continued on, eventually someone would appear to challenge Lucnoca.

Within the endless repetition, someday, someone she could fight would appear.

Someday.

When would Harghent, the man who had promised combat today, appear again?

He might have come tomorrow. He could never appear again, too. Lucnoca had known more people who had kept her waiting like that than she could count.

Someday. Someday.

Nevertheless. As long as there was the possibility, however small, her life wouldn't be empty.

She wanted an opponent. She wanted victory. She wanted defeat.

—She wanted to fight like the champions she had watched expend everything while fighting her.

◆

"Listen. The Twenty-Nine Officials of Aureatia are the highest authority of the minian races. They're the ones who keep Aureatia moving. Make sure not to offend them at all and knock before entering just like I taught you."

"Yeah, leave it to me! I practiced a whole bunch!"

A manor in an affluent and high-class residential area. A strange pair advanced down the brightly illuminated nighttime corridor. A bizarre man cloaked in a full-body robe, who seemed to drag his feet behind him as he walked. A young girl walking with short steps while her attention was drawn restlessly left and right, her long soft braid of chestnut hair swaying with it.

The pair was Krafnir the Hatch of Truth, pioneer of the fifth system of Word Arts, and the Demon King's Bastard, Tu the Magic. A combination that anyone was likely to find incomprehensible, whether privy to the identities of the two or not.

"Look, look, Krafnir! What a cool sculpture! What d'ya think it is? The sun, maybe?"

"You damn—!! That sculpture was on the door, wasn't it?! Why did you break it?!"

"Wait—this wasn't supposed to come off? Uh, um…"

The bronze sculpture ornamenting the door was made with a mold from Craft Arts and certainly wasn't something that could be torn off with a minia's physical strength.

"Krafnir, take it!"

"No. You hold on to it."

"But—but they'll revoke my entry!"

"Pay them for the damages, then! I don't care!"

Gathering the eyes and ears of the servants with their banter as they went, the two finally arrived at the room they were searching for—the room of the Seventh Minister of Aureatia, Flinsuda the Portent. The civil servant sponsoring Krafnir the Hatch of Truth's participation in the Royal Games.

"Um… Hello and good evening…"

Tu timidly entered the room, conspicuously hiding something in her hand behind her back as she entered.

Krafnir bowed, appearing exasperated with the girl's behavior beside him.

"…IT'S BEEN SOME TIME, FLINSUDA. THIS GIRL…IS TU THE MAGIC. AS I MENTIONED IN MY CORRESPONDENCE PRIOR TO ARRIVING, I WOULD LIKE TO RECOMMEND THIS GIRL TO BE A HERO CANDIDATE."

"*Hoh-hoh-hoh-hoh-hoh!* Young little Tu, then? Nervous? I'm Flinsuda the Portent. We'll be great friends, I'm sure."

Flinsuda the Portent was an extremely corpulent woman, decked out in extravagant clothes with ornaments of gold and silver. Blowing on her beautiful nails she had been tending to, she gazed at the two with a beaming smile.

"Relax, relax~! Feel free to sit; I don't mind. Shall I have them bring some tea? Tu, dear, which would you prefer, amber tea or orange tea?"

"Oh, um, I… I wanna drink both!"

"WHAT DID YOU SAY?"

"Oh no, it's fine, it's fine! In that case, I'll have them bring both. You don't need anything, right, Krafnir? Misanthrope you may be, it's awful sad that I can only ever talk to you through a construct like this, you know."

"Yeah! Krafnir, you coward!"

"C-coward... This isn't cowardice! Remote construct synchronization! In order to show, not keep secret, this unrivaled technique to the masses and make them recognize the utility of Mind Arts, I—"

"We don't need to get all technical now, Krafnir. Now, what were you here to talk about, then?"

Flinsuda's cheerful smile never faltered as she hastened the conversation along.

"...The Sixways Exhibition. You need to back an unparalleled fighter, one who's certain to win out over the other candidates, yes? Of course, I don't plan on losing myself...... But."

"...And you're saying little Tu here is stronger than you?"

Behind Krafnir, Tu carried one cup of each of the different teas in her hands and looked to be alternating between them, but she ended up finishing both in the blink of an eye.

"That's right. None of the methods I can think of can defeat her."

"No injuries no matter what sort of attack she's hit with, and neither poison nor fire have any effect on her. If that is indeed true, it's quite unbelievable, isn't it? *Hoh-hoh-hoh-hoh-hoh!* Now who's sturdier, I wonder, her or the Vortical Stampede."

"The Vortical Stampede ultimately died. She may've been a construct with a high degree of perfection, but...I think that given her pilot requirement, that left behind room for weakness."

"And what about Tu? Can you definitively say that the girl has no weakness you can think of?"

"...Look into her yourself. I'm leaving Tu with you."

"What?"

Stuffing her face with a tea cake, Tu looked at Krafnir with surprise.

"She should be left in your hands so you can inspect her. There's plenty of lead time before the matches start for that."

"If you're so insistent, Krafnir, then I think perhaps it is indeed worth a try."

"Um... What am I supposed to do here exactly?"

Tu didn't understand most of the conversation going on in front of her. She was brought along to this manor today similarly under the vague pretext of "consulting about the next steps forward."

"Don't you worry now, Tu dear. If you come here to this mansion, I'll treat you to whatever sweets or teas you'd like, every day."

"...I'm happy to hear that and all, but..."

She dropped her eyes down to the plate still sitting in her palm.

"Will I be able to meet with Sephite?"

"...With the Queen?"

"She's the girl I wanted to see. I came to Aureatia believing I'd get the chance to meet her here... If I participate in the games, will I get to see Sephite, too?"

Sephite. It was the name of the queen who sat at the top of Aureatia, not a person some mysterious unknown being called the

Demon King's Bastard could get an audience with—as long as said being wasn't a potential hero candidate.

"I'd say so. As long as you keep on winning and advancing, dear."

"…! I'll give it my all, Flinsuda!"

Although he gazed at Tu as a smile blossomed on her face, Krafnir's inner thoughts were spinning.

…*With this, I've removed myself as a candidate.*

Krafnir was very well acquainted with Flinsuda's overall character. She was a pragmatist who only believed in financial power, instead of her longtime friend Krafnir or the power of heroes. She also needed a peerless candidate for the games herself. Unmatched enough to *compel the other powers at play into trying to court her as an ally.*

With the money she gained from this, she was planning on expanding her own influence even further and solidify her authority for generations. There were some like her among the Twenty-Nine Officials, simply using their hero candidate for their own political goals.

If it was only being manipulated as part of Flinsuda's schemes, that would be one thing. This Sixways Exhibition……is dangerous. It's all preliminary groundwork for the era that will continue afterward. These true duel contests, both candidates struggling for their life, have to be nothing more than a plot to get rid of Aureatia's foreign elements, these deviant individuals.

If Krafnir was going to survive, he couldn't afford to get himself involved in such a plot.

At the very least, he was different from Tu. He wasn't a truly invincible being like her.

◆

"......The Gray-Haired Child has wormed his way into the Sixways Exhibition."

A meeting room in the Aureatia Central Assembly Hall. Rosclay the Absolute spoke to the room filled with his main supporters.

Golden hair with red eyes. The beautiful features that charmed all the citizenry didn't currently wear the smiling face he could present to the nation.

"Not only is he simply appointing a hero candidate, but he's forcing us to accept the entirety of the Free City of Okafu itself as a *hero*—an interpretative use of the 'hero' idea beyond our expectations."

Now, at the stage where Aureatia could no longer stop their machinations ahead of the Sixways Exhibition, the Gray-Haired Child had made his move.

He skillfully used information control to create a threat out of the Old Kingdoms' loyalists, using the Particle Storm to their advantage, and then through his eloquence and negotiations to influence the Free City of Okafu's movements, he personally destroyed the Old Kingdom loyalists himself.

The New Principality of Lithia. The Particle Storm. An inevitable result of these priority threats to Aureatia piling up one after another, he had led them into this final state. The Gray-Haired Child's aim from the very beginning had been to take part in the Sixways Exhibition using the power of an entire nation itself.

"Rosclay. There's no need to accept them. They're foreign enemies of Aureatia."

Immediately replying was a tan-skinned man wearing dark tinted glasses. The Twenty-Eighth Minister of Aureatia, Antel the Alignment.

"If we accept their demands, they'll trample us all, best they can. Right now, while we were forced to concentrate our focus on the Sixways Exhibition, the whole of Aureatia might be swallowed up by the Gray-Haired Child."

"...Another concerning factor is that the Gray-Haired Child went and colluded with that idiot Dant. Now that they count an entire nation among their allies—who's to say how much the Queen's faction is going to try to get in our way."

The snaggletoothed and wiry man was the Ninth General, Yaniegiz the Chisel.

On the front lines against the Old Kingdoms' loyalists, he was the general, together with Dant, tasked with defending the nation.

"Yaniegiz, it was your role to begin with to watch over Dant and make sure he didn't get caught up in any of the enemy's schemes. Why did you so easily let him make contact with their messenger?"

"...I definitely kept a close eye on him. However, they carefully aimed for the moment he was in the middle of a sudden retreat to contact him, so there wasn't anything I could do. The agents I had watching him were all mid-retreat, too, see. What, are you saying you would've been able to stop it, Antel?"

"That's enough, Yaniegiz."

Rosclay reined in Yaniegiz's provocation.

"...Nevertheless, he's right. The Gray-Haired Child choosing Dant's retreat to make contact means that was all a part of his calculations, too."

By *showing* the Okafu military force, who never actually fought at all, he had made both the Old Kingdoms' loyalists and Dant's forces move all at once. It signaled that he had a perfect understanding of the current internal factions within Aureatia.

Antel pushed up his tinted glasses with his middle finger.

"At the very least, though, our moves going forward are pretty cut-and-dried. We shouldn't recognize his participation as a hero candidate. Okafu's already exhausted their national resources from the Black Tone's unconventional warfare. We need to move forward with negotiations while we hold the advantage."

"That is—," a shrewd-looking man wearing thin glasses replied. Third Minister, Jelky the Swift Ink.

"—impossible. We can't prepare any material that will draw out concessions from Okafu beyond the current status quo. You are quite right, Antel, we could defeat them in open war. Nevertheless, we mustn't force them to surrender. We don't have the economic reserves *to simply govern* Okafu after its surrender. Allowing Morio the Sentinel to continue governing Okafu would become an absolute condition of the negotiations. There's nothing we can make a move on here.

"I get all of that well enough! I'm saying that we need to present them with an alternative condition and block their involvement as a potential hero…! If we acknowledge their twisted interpretation here, there's no way to know what sort of moves the other Twenty-Nine Officials will start to make!"

"And what would you do for that alternate condition? As long as we recognize their participation in the games as a potential hero, we'll be able to avoid providing any financial compensation to Okafu regarding their recent intervention on the Toghie City battlefront. I'll say it again, but we don't have any public funds to spare. That includes both the budget for hosting the Sixways Exhibition as well as the losses we're anticipating to occur from the games themselves. Disaster relief to the cities damaged by the Particle Storm and the reconstruction support to Lithia. Our enemy's ascertained the limits of our support capabilities and is now trying to force things to go his way. What I can say, as the man responsible for our finances, is that it's impossible. Simple as that."

If they were simply going to war, the very best option would to be hit their enemy head-on with their overwhelming troop strength.

Therefore, there was a reason behind Aureatia's mobilization of individual champions to combat the New Principality of Lithia and the Particle Storm, beyond simple fighting strength and covering up the truth—champions *didn't cost them any money.*

No matter how high the rewards to the different individuals involved may have been, it was immaterial compared to the total cost to mobilize an army's worth of soldiers. It was necessary for them to do so in order to expel the hostile powers while preparing for their large-scale and prioritized political policy, the Sixways Exhibition.

Antel put his hand up to his chin and searched for some other measure.

"…Then why don't we prolong the negotiations with Okafu and stipulate a deferral until the Sixways Exhibition is over. That would… Wait, that's all the more reason for the hero candidacy… I see."

"Exactly. As long as there is an undecided hero candidate, the Sixways Exhibition itself *can't get underway*. Much like the New Principality situation, assuming we directly eliminate the Gray-Haired Child or Morio the Sentinel ourselves, the enormous burden of governing the completely resourceless Free City of Okafu will be levied on us. It's not about whether to accept their hero candidacy, Antel. The opinions we need here right now are what we're going to do about it."

On top of it all, the circumstances around the Free City of Okafu were different from the conquered New Principality of Lithia and Toghie City. Okafu was a city that reflected the ideas of the visitor, Morio the Sentinel, from its point of inception. A city for the mercenary trade, constructed in a desolate mountain crag without any sort of resources to speak of outside of its military superiority. Even if they were defeated, given that there was nothing to be gained from occupying the city, they wouldn't be truly defeated.

"…Let's transfer them to Aureatia," Rosclay posited. Bringing his hands together before his forehead, he contemplated.

"We'll give Aureatia city citizenship to the mercenary industry that abandons the Okafu homeland and allow them to pursue their profession. Given that they are going to name themselves as heroes and participate in the Sixways Exhibition, our enemy's accepted the dissolution of their army as one of the conditions already. We'll assign Morio the Sentinel to govern Okafu, and the Gray-Haired Child will be allowed to work with Dant."

"That's...Rosclay. You're basically saying to open up our gates and invite an enemy army right inside our walls."

"We can't compleeeetely ban mercenary work anyway, right? We won't be able to stop contracts on an individual basis."

"...Naturally, I don't think this will totally keep their threat in check, either. What we need is to divide up their forces between their homeland and Aureatia... Then for all intents and purposes, we will be holding Okafu's only current source of capital, the Gray-Haired Child, hostage."

The wrinkles in Jelky's brow furrowed deeper as he replied.

"...So we'll be the ones pressuring Okafu's finances instead. In exchange for allowing them to infiltrate the heart of our country, we won't allow them to raise the funds to wage an organized war. The Gray-Haired Child's assets and Okafu's coffers... Since the Sixways Exhibition's overall duration isn't set, it'll turn into a contest of resilience, then."

"That's right. I don't believe that by operating solely off their mercenary trade, the Free City of Okafu has anticipated this type of situation and amassed the capital to deal with it. However, the budget for everything involving the Sixways Exhibition has already been fully appropriated *on our end*, isn't that right, Jelky?"

"Yes. Just as I mentioned earlier."

"…With both sides stopping each other's attempts at war, then that means the Sixways Exhibition will ultimately decide things, after all."

Antel bitterly nodded.

"I think some serious consideration is necessary, but Rosclay's proposal might be the only way to go… If the money's not there, not much can be done about it."

"I think we're favored enough," Rosclay asserted as the one shouldered with the name Absolute.

"As long as they fight in Aureatia—they won't have the power of the people on their side."

There were too many threats that exceeded all possible estimations, and they couldn't wield unrestricted power. Despite this, their only option was to expend all their strength to maintain order. Until peace eventually came.

Aureatia. The largest and strongest minian nation, seizing control of the shura that threatened the very continuation of the world itself, plotted to use the power of the people to bring the world under their control.

◆

Okafu's movements were unexpected.

Within the same assembly hall, there was someone forming a different plot based on the actions of the Free City of Okafu.

While waiting inside the room for the contact from his

one-person radzio, the Fourth Minister, Kaete the Round Table, was deep in thought.

But the fact that they're drawing the attention of Rosclay and his lackeys isn't a bad thing. Make Rosclay and the Gray-Haired Child fight among themselves, and I'll be the one to create a new main faction. I'll reform this history from the ground up.

He had already decided on a candidate to sponsor—Mestelexil the Box of Desperate Knowledge.

An abnormal and irregular being compared to all the other champions—even compared to Lucnoca the Winter and Alus the Star Runner.

An inexhaustible reproduction of technology from the Beyond. This went far beyond the realm of mere fighting strength. Even when limited to military functions, his power alone could grant a superiority far beyond even that of the New Principality of Lithia's air force.

Mestelexil's presence was likely to advance the hands on this world's clock several hundred years into the future.

Demon King. Cursed True Demon King. As long as I breathe, I won't let things stagnate. New technology, new knowledge... I'll show this world true power, like nothing anyone has ever seen before.

This reformation was fundamentally different from abolition of monarchal rule that Rosclay and Jelky's so-called reformation faction was aiming for. What Kaete wished for was a much bigger, and longer-term, reformation. An unpredictable future of possibilities, rendering the remaining deficiencies and conflicts of the world meaningless.

I, Kaete, will expel all terror from the land.

A short while later, his radzio received a signal.

<Kaete, you snot-nosed brat! Send someone to meet us, dammit! These Aureatian soldiers came and surrounded us!>

Kaete's thoughts were forcefully interrupted.

"Gah……"

The old woman behind the voice was none other than Kiyazuna the Axle. The ultimate golem creator who birthed Mestelexil into this world and now, with Izick the Chromatic dead, known as the most terrifying self-proclaimed demon king in the land.

"You've gotten that close already?! Why didn't you contact me first?!"

<Well, Mestelexil said he wanted to hurry and see Aureatia! Here I thought these dim-witted Aureatian imbeciles wouldn't notice us anyway, but now's the time for you to do your damn job for once!>

"Like hell you weren't getting spotted! Listen now, you absolutely can't lay a hand on anyone until I get there! You kill anyone, and any talk of supporting Mestelexil goes up in smoke!"

<What a pain in the ass! Better not make us wait long. Eh, Mestelexil?!>

<Ha-ha-ha-ha-ha-ha-! It's been, a while, Kaete!>

"I don't care! Behave nice until I get there! Got it?!"

The Fourth Minister, reputed to be the sternest and fiercest civil servant of all, immediately began getting himself ready.

He needed to go and meet her fast, before the woman could get herself wrapped up in anything.

"Swear I'm surrounded by…nothing but pains in my ass…!"

Early morning. Inside an Aureatia spire, Alus the Star Runner opened his eyes and, with a light flap of his wings, climbed up to the window. He had sensed the presence of a visitor.

The white cityscape he looked down on was still asleep.

"............Who?"

His voice was quiet, barely a whisper that only those with keen hearing would be able to hear, yet there was a reply.

"Psianop. Psianop the Inexhaustible Stagnation."

Alus tilted his head slightly. The presence he had sensed at the base of the tower belonged to a single ooze.

Normally, a race that would never exchange words with a wyvern like Alus. Oozes feared wyverns.

"Psianop. Who was that again......?"

"Came across each other in the sand labyrinth. I remember."

"...Ah. The sand labyrinth. Wasn't really much there..."

Alus finally managed to recall the singular insignificant memory.

The title of labyrinth was nothing more than a designation made by the standards of the minian races. Although it was in the middle of fiery, unforgiving desert sands, for Alus, easily managing to reach it directly without any interference from the terrain or the lycan tribe there, the sand labyrinth wasn't worthy of the moniker.

"I learned about the True Demon King's death through you. Since I've come to visit Aureatia, I thought I should come and say hello, at least."

"…Whatever… I don't care about any greetings from an ooze… I didn't even, remember, either…"

"How about that Toroa the Awful, then?"

That name elicited a reaction from Alus, though it was little more than a slight raise of his head.

"There's rumors that the enchanted sword monster you were supposed to have killed has come to Aureatia. He might be planning to *get his revenge* on his killer in the Sixways Exhibition. I wanted to hear what your thoughts were on it."

"……They're a fake," Alus quietly, yet firmly, declared. "……If they want to get revenge, they should come by right now to cut me down… Why aren't they…? They can't because……unlike the real Toroa, they're weak…"

"Could be because they're strong," Psianop replied matter-of-factly.

"May be thinking that a fight to the death between you two would destroy this whole town with it."

"…I wonder if the same would happen, if you and I fought, each other."

Alus looked down at the small ooze below him. He didn't have any interest in fighting against powerful opponents, but this Psianop was clearly strong. He understood that much.

Psianop opened up the book he was carrying with his pseudopod.

"Hard to say. Want to find out right now?"

"…………"

The ooze's emotions were impossible to read, even more so

than expressionless Alus's own. Even after opening his book, it was impossible to judge if his eyes really were pointed down at the pages.

"...........Sounds like a pain."

"Hmph. Too bad. My business here is concluded."

Psianop decided to take his leave and return, from what Alus could tell.

"There's one thing I'd like to ask before I go," Psianop said as he made his departure.

"You knew that the Demon King was dead, didn't you? Why were you able to say that so confidently?"

"..........."

"Or maybe you're..."

...actually the hero after all?

The survivor of the First Party left the final part of his inquiry unsaid.

◆

Aureatia old town. Following the Particle Storm incident, Toroa the Awful's path led him to find shelter in a worker's slum in this section of the city, voluntarily helping out with cargo transport and other physical labor.

As he didn't have official citizenship, there were no guarantees he would be able to stay in Aureatia for long. To make things worse, his exceptional bodily physique and extremely dangerous adornments made the people of the city needlessly fearful of him.

"Oh! If it isn't Toroa the Awful! Been a minute, huh?"

"……"

Hearing the voice cut in, Toroa looked somewhat disgruntled as he stopped in his tracks.

The person who brazenly called out to the monster from horror stories outwardly appeared like an aristocrat's child who had accidently wandered into the old town, but he was unmistakably one of Aureatia's Twenty-Nine Officials. The youngest of them all, the Twenty-Second General, Mizial the Iron-Piercing Plumeshade.

"…Mizial? Don't you have government business to attend to?"

"At this point, the military officers're all bored to tears. The talk of war with Okafu and the Old Kingdoms went up in a puff a smoke and all, too. So I thought, hey, why don't I go see Toroa!"

"Am I some rare flower or something to you?"

Mizial cheekily went around Toroa's cart and examined his cargo.

"What's it today, then? Transporting cargo? While you still have all those enchanted swords on your back?"

"Just carrying medicine. I've got enough for the clinic the next block over, so I'm about to go and hand them out there."

The horse wagon loaded with medicinal bottles was undoubtably not something one of the minian races could pull themselves, but Toroa's physical stamina, able to haul this all over the enormous city of Aureatia without a single drop of sweat, was something beyond normal expectations.

"…So let me make myself clear. I don't have time to chitchat."

Mizial invited Toroa to participate in the Sixways Exhibition the very day he first came across him and was rejected. However, since he continued to come visit Toroa whenever it struck his fancy, Toroa had begun to doubt that this young boy in front of him really was one of Aureatia's highest-level bureaucrats.

"Awww. You can rest for a little bit, righ—?"

"Are you Toroa the Awful?" a voice cut in and interrupted their conversation.

A dangerous group had appeared, spreading widely across the road to block it off. A large force, equipped with crossbows, short swords, and hammers, and with two carriages in tow.

Mizial questioned them, making no effort to hide his displeasure.

"......Who're you people?"

"I'm Toroa the Awful."

Toroa stepped forward before Mizial could say another word. He was preparing to respond immediately, just in case his wagon or Mizial were put at risk of being harmed.

"You all have some business with me?"

"We're the Sun's Conifer. We've been entrusted with bein' a sorta neighborhood guard force 'round here. That's why we can't ignore a request from our model citizens, see... Talkin' about you roaming Aureatia all day with all those nasty weapons of yers— and scaring the people. On top of trying to pass yerself off as Toroa the Awful, too, eh?"

"......"

Everything he said was true. Even while residing in Aureatia, Toroa didn't remove his hands from any of his enchanted swords, even for a single moment. Offering protection was, currently, Toroa's calling.

"Not only that, but apparently, you're not a citizen, either, huh? Well, looking like that, you bet I'd believe it. That's why we're gonna step in for those dimwits on the Aureatia Council and drive this dangerous character outta our city."

"As long as the council gives their permission…"

With his hands still in his pockets, Mizial scowled at the armed group.

"Even noncitizens are allowed to reside here for over three small months. Fourth Class, Article II, 'Emergency Evacuation of Sick and Wounded in Wartime.' Toroa's working hard and hasn't built up any criminal history here in Aureatia. You lot don't have the authority to forcibly evict him from the city."

"Quiet, brat. Listen, we're talking to that bum right now. This ain't a problem of laws or approvals. We've received actual demands from the citizens about him. Now, I bet all of us here wanna settle things peacefully. Understand?"

The tobacco-smoking man smiled wide. The weapons of the Sun's Conifer were clearly pointed not only toward Toroa himself but also at the clinic situated behind him.

"……If I leave here, that'll be the end of this."

Throughout his life up until that point, there had been quite a few ruffians who saw Toroa's towering form and tried picking fights with him. He had no plans to abandon Alus the Star Runner's trail, but he could do the same after the Sixways Exhibition event was over, and the wyvern had left Aureatia. He had already thought that if there came a time when his presence invited unnecessary trouble, he'd meekly take his leave. However.

"You think that alone'll settle all this? Hand over the enchanted swords. All of 'em."

"...What did you say?"

"A real dense bastard, aren't we? I'm saying if you give up all those enchanted swords of yers, we'll let you head home unscathed... Don't think I don't know. You may be using a fake name, but those enchanted swords are the real deal, aren't they?"

......*Where did he get that information?*

Toroa inwardly went on his guard. Anyone who believed that he was Toroa the Awful, back from the dead, wouldn't try challenging him in a fight in the first place. On the other hand, anyone who determined he was an impostor taking Toroa's name would likely think there was no chance that the enchanted swords he carried were genuine.

The Sun's Conifer were different from all the ruffians who had picked fights with Toroa before.

"Listen! You're talking to the Twenty-Fourth General here! Me!"

Now appearing to be ignored, Mizial loudly asserted himself.

"Y'know, causing all this fuss right in front of me like this? Knock it off. It makes me feel like I'm being looked down on."

"'Cause we are looking down on you, Mizial the Iron-Piercing Plumeshade. *There's a hero* above us, see. You Twenty-Nine bums... You're bringing 'em all here to Aureatia, tellin' them to enjoy themselves, aren't ya? Huh?"

Stealing the enchanted swords for their own hero candidacy...
So there's someone backing their show of force here.

He had realized for a while that he was currently surrounded. What Toroa was most anxious about right now was the medicinal bottles in his wagon breaking and causing damage to the city and citizens.

Wicked Sword Selfesk. Divine Blade Ketelk. Mushain the enchanted wind sword...shouldn't be a problem.

Immediately afterward, an arrow whizzed right by his face. Raising it with the barest of movements, he deflected it with the hilt of an enchanted sword—a sword composed of a hilt with nothing else. The arrow flew up on top of a roof without hitting any of the medicinal bottles.

"Oh no! I didn't mean to shoot that! Sorry!"

The boorish group member who fired his bow shouted without the slightest hint of guilt. The tobacco-smoking man grinned as if everything was turning out as planned.

"Whoa, whoa, now! We can't go getting violent here, c'mon! Toroa the Awful... Why don't ya hand over those enchanted swords, and we can wrap things up, eh? You'd be in rough shape, right? If, say, this whole part of town caught fi— *Hgnh—!*"

His jaw broke. The fragments of his tobacco, chomped down and torn apart, fluttered into the air.

A throwing projectile, resembling a balancing weight, hit him from below. Mizial the Iron-Piercing Plumeshade. The Twenty-Second General had slipped into the middle of the group in a low, beast-like posture and had already finished his attack.

"It's your fault for ignoring me, really. Right?"

Faster than the ones around him could come to grips with the sudden, violent attack, the next weights had already left Mizial's fingertips, and there came two more sounds of them slicing through the air. The rogues to his right and left had their shoulders, and their hips, broken simultaneously.

"If you hadn't ignored me like that, this wouldn't have happened, now, would it?"

Although the Sun's Conifer had their weapons readied against Toroa, they hadn't predicted the sudden attack. Just how many of their members knew that Aureatia's Twenty-Second General Mizial happened to be a military officer who loved rushing headlong into battle more than anything else?

"You little..."

"What the hell are you doing?!"

He had plunged straight into the middle of the armed gang. A number of fists and kicks flew Mizial's way. Forgetting their original mission there, the rogues reflexively started raising their weapons against the boy.

"Wicked Sword Selfesk."

A storm of wedge-shaped metal fragments swooped in from the flank and deflected all the threatening weapons away.

It may have appeared to them as a sword with nothing but a hilt. Dispersing the length of the blade into numerous wedge shapes and manipulating them with magnetic force, it was the enchanted sword known as the Wicked Sword Selfesk.

"Ah-ha-ha."

Seeing the power of an enchanted sword for the first time right in front of him, Mizial laughed.

Immediately afterward, when he sprang back to his feet with a jolt, he straddled the tobacco-smoking man, unconscious from breaking his jaw, and slammed his elbow into his face four times. There wasn't a single ounce of hesitation in any of his movements.

"Still want to fight?"

"Hngh, augh!"

"*Ah-ha-ha-ha-ha.* C'mon now, what's 'augh' supposed to tell me? How about the rest of you?"

His face stained with blood spatter, Mizial looked out across the rest of the Sun's Conifer. He'd broken the tobacco man's jaw right at the start. There wouldn't be any more orders from their group's central figure.

"......"

"You bastards are pretty dense, huh... I'm saying I'm fine with letting you go, without you suffering any more injuries. For the time being, I'll write this off as a simple brawl. Decide for yourselves; go ahead... What'll it be?"

Sitting up, and coming from fingers on both hands, there was a sound of something slicing through the air. It was a unique weapon that seemed to be two weights connected together with a string.

"W-we're outta here. C'mon."

"Dammit... Snot-nosed little brat, if we had our boss here..."

The rogues vanished one right after another and quietly returned once more to the old town street.

"Ah-ha-ha-ha-ha!"

Smeared with blood spatter and his own nose's blood, Mizial stretched out his arms and legs and went to lie down.

"Hoo boy, it's been a long time since I've gotten to do that!"

"...Mizial."

Toroa crouched down beside him. Thanks to the boy, he was able to get the situation under control without having to use any more of his enchanted swords than necessary. Nor was there any damage to the town. Yet even still...

"You were too reckless."

"Ha-ha, why do you say that?"

Mizial wiped his bloody nose with the sleeve of his luxurious coat, but another stream immediately flowed down.

"...Doesn't that make you mad? Telling you to...hand over your enchanted swords like that. They're the enchanted swords of, the living horror story...himself... Toroa the Awful, right?"

"......"

He was one of Aureatia's Twenty-Nine Officials. He was trying to sponsor Toroa the Awful's entry into the Sixways Exhibition.

That may have then meant that the enchanted swords Toroa kept safe would end up being used by someone else.

"Mizial. I know now isn't the best time, but... Is there any way for me to get citizenship, too? I want it fast."

"Ha-ha."

Mizial was able to understand the meaning behind Toroa's words.

"This? This is just a street brawl... Don't have to feel you owe me."

"You may be right."

Killing Alus the Star Runner. Reclaiming Hillensingen the enchanted light sword. Until that time came, his life wasn't his to live. He needed to fight as a god of death revived from hell.

That was why he never thought about anything like it before.

"...But that sounds like more fun."

◆

The Aureatia cityscape was the ground. The upper floors of buildings were connected with wood or iron footpaths, and the scenery of the old town in particular had a chaotic crisscross of stories going every which way.

So Toroa got through everything all right...... For now anyway.

There was someone lingering on the edge of an iron footpath jutting out into the air. A leprechaun wearing a dark-brown coat.

The old town he gazed down on also had more than half its area hidden underneath the network of crossing pathways, but his azure eyes could clearly see all the way down to the movements of the grains of sand on the ground—everything, all at once.

"...I don't believe it; are you actually worried about Toroa the Awful?"

Catching the voice from behind him, he glanced over his shoulder. Of course, even if it didn't, he could perfectly perceive the approaching person's body shape, their gait, all the way down to their heartbeat. Such was world Kuuro the Cautious saw.

Cresting the stairs was an elf woman with bandages covering both her eyes. Her name was Lena the Obscured.

"Interesting. That's a pretty good laugh."

From the presence of her concealed weapon and her demeanor as she approached, he already knew she wasn't hostile. Therefore, Kuuro replied with nothing but a simple question.

"What do you want?"

The two were not unfamiliar with one another. Previously, Kuuro and Lena had both been agents of the land's largest spy guild, Obsidian Eyes. After Kuuro deserted, Rehart the Obsidian, leader of the guild in the final days of the Demon King era, passed away, and it was said the organization, too, collapsed.

"Oh, come now, like you need to ask. Do you feel like coming back again?"

"...Back to Obsidian Eyes, is it? The rumor that the leader's dead, then, is a lie?"

Kuuro glanced at Lena. The movement of her fingertips. The change in her heartbeat. Perspiration. The pupils hidden beneath the bandages.

"So it isn't a lie, then. Who's Obsidian, now...? Lady Linaris? Got it. That's much better."

"...Kuuro... Cut that out. To be honest, it's creepy."

"We're old friends. No need to hold back, and all."

It was known by the name Clairvoyance. Super sight. Super hearing. A sixth sense. Synesthesia. With any and all superpowered senses combined together in one, he could even find the answer to his questions from the minutely perceived reactions of a living creature, without waiting for them to say a word.

"...It's just as you said. Obsidian Eyes is still alive. In order to continue on the will of leadership she inherited, our lady is earnestly maintaining the organization. Right now, we need your power. The power of the strongest man in Obsidian Eyes."

"Well, you must really be in trouble, then."

Kuuro smiled cynically.

"If we weren't, I wouldn't be asking questions that I already know the answer to."

His past of bloodying his hands as part of Obsidian Eyes was a difficult one for Kuuro to forget. He had taken a gruesome round-about path to discover for himself that piling up corpses wasn't his true desire at all.

"Even still, as a former comrade of ours for a period of time, you need to see your obligations through. Right? Going forward, Obsidian Eyes...will be making strategic moves here in Aureatia. The one who'll know our movements from the very start is you, Kuuro."

"...And you're worried that when the time comes I'll leak that information to another organization, is that it?"

With both hands still in his pockets, the leprechaun gazed at the sky, closer to it now than from the ground.

"Don't worry. What would doing something like that get me? It'd be worth little more than pocket change. I don't plan on joining up with you all again, but I don't intend on taking Aureatia's side, either. No matter which side I'd end up taking, I'd just get forced to take on worthless work."

"You defected from Toghie City. As collateral for that, you must be under obligation to collaborate with Aureatia."

"I paid that back during the Particle Storm incident. You think Aureatia wants to keep eyes that can see all their troop placements, and the location of all the Twenty-Nine Officials, always on hand? The reason they lured me away was simply a precaution against the Old Kingdoms' side using my gifts... They're even thinking that they'd like me gone once I'm finished here—and fast."

He felt the wound in his side. While it was almost completely healed, it had come from being pierced right as the Particle Storm was defeated.

"Actually. To be more precise, I think there are some people actively trying to get rid of me."

The ones who fired on him weren't Aureatia, but Obsidian Eyes. The moment the Particle Storm was defeated, they did so to eliminate any "eyes" that would observe what happened after-ward. They had even planned their operation to ensure Kuuro would point his suspicions at Aureatia in the event they proved unable to kill Obsidian Eyes' strongest man.

Of course, Kuuro couldn't possibly gain the full picture of their network of schemes—however.

"I was shot by an Aureatia soldier."

"That's a laugh. I heard you were wounded during your mis-sion to observe the Particle Storm. So you got done in by those

Aureatia bastards once they didn't have any need for Clairvoyance anymore."

"Seems so. From their mannerisms and the weapons they carried, it had to have been an Aureatia soldier. It took all I had to avoid being killed on the spot, but...I still got a look at their face."

No matter how far away they aimed at him, even from a blind spot, he could see them. Conversely, he hadn't been able to see them up until the moment they shot at him. At that time, Kuuro's senses had only perceived one person, Kuuro himself.

"That day, I *looked at all the faces of the soldiers* who went in and out of the camp. The one who shot me was someone I never saw in camp. Maybe I should think of it as another faction trying to use the observation mission to put an end to me. If they viewed my Clairvoyance as a threat, then why would they even expect their assassination attempt to succeed?

"...It very nearly was successful, wasn't it? You're not able to see as much of your surroundings as you're used to."

"Want to see for yourself if that's true? Zizma the Miasma... He said the same thing. *That my Clairvoyance had declined.* Zizma, part of the same Obsidian Eyes as you lot. Let me ask you, Lena. The ones who tried to assassinate me... It was actually you all, wasn't it?"

His blue eyes looked squarely at Lena. Her heartbeat. Reflexes. Breathing.

However, all he did was ask. No matter how well versed one was in techniques to deceive their own mind, be they a member of Obsidian Eyes or not, he could unmask everything. That was the power of his Clairvoyance.

"……"

Lena's faint smile could only be seen in the subtle move of her lips.

"I don't know, do I?"

Kuuro understood the meaning behind her words. Her reaction neither confirmed nor denied anything.

"…Right. Lady Linaris wouldn't send someone who knows the details of the operation to me on purpose. Besides, even if my guess was off the mark… You also can't say for sure that, since you weren't privy to the knowledge, the operation hadn't actually been carried out, either. As long as this is Obsidian Eyes we're talking about."

"Your senses haven't dulled at all, huh, Kuuro the Cautious. It's very hard for me to believe you've been away from active duty for so long… I really do want you to come back to us, after all. During these past few years, we've lost too many of our comrades."

"…Even still, it's impossible for me to go back. I can't become a corpse anymore."

Kuuro put his index finger up against the back of his neck.

"When they brought me here, they injected me with a blood serum. Since I was formerly with Obsidian Eyes, me being a corpse was Aureatia's biggest concern. You figured that from the start, didn't you?"

"That doesn't matter. Even if you're not a corpse…Obsidian Eyes needs you… Actually. It's better if you're not a corpse. I'm sure our lady would say the same."

"So she really is different from Rehart, then."

He lowered his eyes, mumbling with an almost peaceful glow.

When Kuuro was part of the organization, the young miss was still young. Just what was she like now? There was part of him that wished he had seen her grow up.

"...Bye, then. Give the lady my regards."

"Kuuro."

Lena called out to Kuuro as he turned his back to leave.

"Do you still plan on remaining in Aureatia?"

"...Don't worry. I won't be here for long. I just—"

Footpaths of wood and iron. There wasn't anyone who knew that, in a corner of the tangled old town, there was an unbelievably powerful individual, a cut above the rest. A shura unaffiliated with anyone or any power, whose name wasn't even included among the Sixways Exhibition's roster of hero candidates.

"—have this theater I've gotten real fond of."

◆

A forest, thick enough to block out the sun. Inside a room in a mansion, there was someone listening to Kuuro the Cautious's conversation.

It was voice communication from a one-way radzio Lena had hidden on her. If the receiver had allowed for two-way communication, even without saying a word, Kuuro's Clairvoyance would've have seen through everything just from the sounds of breathing or bodies shifting through the receiver.

...*Master Kuuro.*

Turning the receiver down on the table, the aristocratic young woman cast her eyelashes down. Her skin was white, even among the darkness, highlighting her beautiful features like the moon in the night sky.

Her name was Linaris the Obsidian. The young vampire girl who led the remnants of the land's largest spy guild, Obsidian Eyes.

Lingering next to her was an elderly leprechaun woman.

"Failing to dispose of Kuuro was a big blunder, milady."

The housekeeping governess tasked with looking after Linaris, Frey the Waking, was a veteran from the very first days the guild was established.

She was also the one who had proposed taking advantage of the Particle Storm to assassinate Kuuro. The ones who actually shot him were none other than the field troops under the command of the Thirteenth Minister Enu—one of the Twenty-Nine Officials under the control of Obsidian Eyes.

Kuuro's clairvoyance was waning, and now he could only see a single point that he concentrated on. The plan, formulated off Frey's correct estimation of his abilities, was upset by Kuuro recovering the strength of his heydays, and by the presence of Toroa the Awful there with him.

"If he truly has undergone blood serum treatment, then I believe it will be difficult to control him even with your power, milady... It would seem he has recovered the Clairvoyance powers of his prime. If he simply *thought to do so*, he could see through all of our movements."

An airborne-infecting vampire, capable of placing any living creature under her control simply by getting close to them. As long as the truth about her wasn't revealed to anyone, Linaris's superpower was invincible. From another perspective, Kuuro the Cautious, able to see through any secret, was this power's natural enemy.

With both hands tightly gripped together in her lap, Linaris mumbled.

"Master Kuuro said…that he wouldn't try to interfere with us."

"That is a lie. He went along with Aureatia's operation, and I believe we should consider the fact that he still remains in Aureatia—suggesting that the Aureatia side still has something on him. Milady, your desire not to doubt an old friend…a comrade. I understand it very well. However, Kuuro is no longer part of Obsidian Eyes."

"……"

Kuuro was likely still a champion in Linaris's eyes, having never once stepped outside the organization herself. Much like there were some who still believed the First Party to be the strongest there ever was—and like how many citizens thought similarly of Rosclay the Absolute.

"Do not worry, milady. I will take responsibility and kill Kuuro. I cannot expose you to danger, no matter how small that possibility may be. I suspect, given Kuuro's character…it is not a thing, or information, that Aureatia is using to keep Kuuro in their clutches, but likely a person instead. In which case, I promise to sniff them out and bring them under our control."

"No."

Linaris stood up. The look she sent Frey's way was tinged with something different from criticism or reproach.

"Please, don't do that... For our sake."

Her eyes looked slightly scared, yet with firm conviction.

"Master Kuuro will not try to oppose us of his own volition. I feel simply learning this... Learning that he believes in us...means that Lena's negotiations with him were fruitful."

"We failed to kill him once before. There's nothing worse we could've done to sour his relationship with our organization."

"...Miss Frey. Have you ever seen Master Kuuro *when he's angry*?"

"When he's...angry?"

She recalled Kuuro's face. His expression was always gloomy and sour. Every look a scowl.

However, he was a man who was always indifferent, handling every job he was asked to handle. He never showed a glimpse of truly strong emotions, nor did he expose any deep-seated pain.

"Now that you mention it... I watched him for quite a long time, yet never once have I seen him angry."

"I myself have. Kuuro's anger doesn't come out when someone's trying to kill him. Given my dealings with Master Kuuro... I am convinced. The ones truly in danger......the ones who have gripped a blade barehanded...are the people holding something over his head—Aureatia."

"......"

As long as his eyes were waning, Aureatia had plenty of

opportunities to make use of Kuuro at will. However, now that he had regained his eyes' full power…even that wasn't absolutely true.

"Miss Frey. We believe he has regained his Clairvoyance. Aureatia, at least, doesn't know that fact. I am sure they still believe they can maintain a tight grip on him."

"And eventually Aureatia will find him beyond their control—and self-destruct."

"…That's right."

Frey made no move to tread any further into Linaris's inner thoughts. She simply deliberated over what the girl was holding in her heart.

…Her reasoning that she should avoid decisive hostility toward Kuuro does indeed have some truth to it. Nevertheless… Milady is still unable to erase her fear of losing a comrade, after all.

Linaris's machinations, adhering to a thorough callousness toward their enemies and those who betrayed her trust, also invited danger from being unable to cut down those who were not.

To bring another era of warring chaos to the land. An age for Obsidian Eyes to live in. Thus, she needs to guide everyone there… She needs to ensure we all survive specifically to see this warring chaos. Milady's carried that contradiction within her this whole time… In which case, I cannot let her shoulder this responsibility.

Obsidian Eyes. An organization pulling scheming strings from the shadows, plotting the era's retrograde. Their core was concealed under many layers of secrets.

However, Kuuro the Cautious knew that said core was just one single girl.

...When the time comes...Kuuro will die by my hands.

◆

The small room was tiny enough to faintly make out its features from the light of the lone candle.

It resembled a confessional room—and in fact seemed to have been one before being remodeled—with two chairs facing each other and a round table in the middle. It was all the furnishings the room had.

"...Regarding the Sixways Exhibition matter. The assembly appears intent on holding the matches as true duels."

"Really, now... That'll be rough."

The elderly priest sitting across from Kuze was named Maqure the Sky's Lake Surface. Putting aside his continued relationship with a man like Kuze, he was an intelligent and benevolent leader, deserving of respect and love.

"I wonder why they're going with a true duel in this day and age. It's a barbaric and outdated rule at this point, used for stuff like...a duel among aristocrats or fighting over the monarchy back in ancient times."

"...That's probably all the more reason, I'd wager. To the people, the appearance of the Hero is a huge event on par with the True King's return in the green times. All the more reason to model it after something from that age, and it makes sense as a way to introduce the Hero's power in the people's presence, too."

"They must be out of their minds... Do they plan on making this Hero they've picked out from all these gathered champions turn around and murder them all?"

"I don't want to admit it, but... The citizenry probably want that, too. A large-scale true duel royal tournament like this hasn't been seen, nor will be seen, for several hundred years. It was an era of powerlessness before... The hearts of the people are starved for strength. The heart that desires champion bloodshed and the heart that desires to see the Hero claim victory over it all. They're both still the same heart."

Weapons, skill, Word Arts. The fights would substitute none of them, where nothing would be held back, where each combatant would put everything on the line in the match. Everything, including their life.

That was the agreement inherent in a true duel. There had indeed been time in this world were such a rite was necessary. However.

"...Hold on, now. What's going to happen if the Hero dies during one these matches? Their big debut would be flushed straight down the drain."

"You think they'll die? You think that the True Hero, the one who killed the True Demon King, would die?"

"Other people out there might assume that, but I...I don't feel the same way, honestly. Living people died. Everyone dies eventually."

"In that case, there's another way to think of things."

The elderly priest knew perfectly well that there wasn't anyone else who could hear them but lowered his voice anyway.

"The assembly hasn't found the Hero at all. They're not planning for the Hero to win out over anyone, but they are planning on making whoever ends up winning *into* the Hero."

"Nah, that couldn't be."

Kuze laughed it off, but he didn't have any grounds for his denial.

Nor did he think that his agile mind could pull even with Maqure.

"Well, if that's the case, maybe I've got a chance of winning out in the end, huh?"

"...There's still time to call it off and withdraw your recommendation from the Order."

Kuze understood that this old priest was concerned about Kuze's safety.

Failure could result in death. It was clear from the start as well that, should he win and advance farther, he'd get even more tangled in the schemes and plots at play.

...However, assuming the Hero would be born out of this event, it was already clear to see how things would play out.

The New Principality of Lithia. The Old Kingdoms' loyalists. The Free City of Okafu... Right now, Aureatia was dismantling the organizations that posed a threat to the existing authority. The Order was next. Assistance from Aureatia was openly on the decline, and the populace's continued discontent aimed toward the Order clearly wasn't solely the result of disbelief in the Word-Maker.

The Hero—a true idol and ally of the people, in place of the Word-Maker who failed to rescue society from the threat of the True Demon King.

The fact that the Order was allowed to nominate candidates for the games might have simply been to show the Hero defeating the symbol of the Order for all the masses to see.

"I… I'm serious. I don't have any plans on losing. You know for yourself, Father. I have Nastique with me."

"Think about it carefully. Could you say the same thing when up against Rosclay the Absolute? Or if what Aureatia says is true, and the True Hero does actually exist?"

"*Bweh-heh-heh……* Fair enough, those guys are unmatched champions. Definitely not anyone I could beat, that's for sure."

Kuze laughed flippantly.

He needed to act like that, at least on the surface, or he wouldn't be able to continue on as the Order's cleaner.

Nor would he be able to remain peerless and invincible.

"But here's the question; are all of them peerless champions even while they're eating—or while they're sleeping? And their friends and family, they must be peerless champions, too, right? What about their family while sleeping? Their friends?"

It was Kuze alone who could sense Nastique's presence. The white angel of death had the authority to expunge any sort of being before her.

And most likely, Kuze was the only one for whom such a fighting method was possible.

"Besides… There's a chance that I've got a young disciple out there."

His angel didn't save anyone besides himself. Though he was unexpectedly given a chance to save Cunodey while making his rounds, Kuze had been unable to save his former teacher.

The massacre of Alimo Row was said have been caused by a monster from The Land of The End—however, Kuze knew the truth behind the incident.

In his notes, he had written the name that carried out that slaughter. Uhak the Silent.

Someone Kuze had yet to see—and another butcher of the Order like himself.

"…I get the feeling I'll have a chance to see him in the Sixways Exhibition."

"…Kuze."

"I don't even want to think about it… Just how many kids will be left out in the cold should the Order fall? If someone's gotta do it, then it's me, right? I'm invincible, after all."

The old priest hung his head for a few moments, giving up on the words he went to cast at Kuze.

Then finally, he spoke, as if forcing the words from his lips.

"…………Kuze. Please…… It's all up to you."

To stop them from losing any more of what meager salvation they had left.

To prevent the start of a new age.

"Kill the Hero for us."

There were many forces that had begun making their moves in anticipation of the imperial competition. However, theirs was the most powerless and waning organization among them all.

As they were more than likely to be washed away in the colossal current of the new age on the horizon…they needed to make some move of their own. In order to keep their compatriots alive in the world ahead.

The Order was trying to put its final plan into action.

◆

A garden spread out between the buildings, with a well-managed row of roadside trees. A large metropolis not far from Aureatia, Gimeena City.

In the middle of the roadside trees, there was a huge cargo being transported by a gigant-pulled heavy-freight carriage.

"Hey, be careful carrying that, now!"

The screaming voice belonged to a remarkedly large-built gigant, even among the other gigants. Even on their enormous scale, he appeared like an adult surrounded by children.

"This is real important stuff, okay?! Maye sure you don't get caught on the buildings when you turn, you hear?!"

There had to be some among the city's residents who realized it.

This man, taller than a city tower, was the invincible hero of the Sine Riverstead—Mele the Horizon's Roar.

"Whoaaaa, amazing..."

With Mele's imposing figure, drawing people's eyes just as he walked, right in front of her, the young girl couldn't suppress her amazement.

She was a survivor of the ruins of Nagan Labyrinth City—Yuno the Distant Talon.

...Mele the Horizon's Roar. The Mele, really planning on appearing in the imperial competition...

On the road back from the mission from Aureatia, she was staying a night in the city to get some rest.

She and her traveling companion, Soujirou the Willow-Sword, had separate lodgings, but she was thinking of delivering some hawthorns to the layabout as a snack.

However, when she gazed up at the terrifying champion right in front of her, it awakened her to her own heart, whether she wanted it to or not.

I... I'm trying to kill Soujirou.

Would the Soujirou who cleaved the Dungeon Golem in two, on the day her homeland was destroyed, be able to kill the gigant champion before her eyes?

Yuno's reason for sending Soujirou to participate in the imperial competition was to lure him into the jaws of death and get her revenge for these feelings of hers that she still wasn't fully convinced of herself.

Mele isn't the only one. The Second General Rosclay. Alus the Star Runner. Or maybe even...some far more terrifying monster that was totally inscrutable to someone like me...

It was impossible for Yuno to step into that sort of vortex of shura.

She thought there were certain to be games that required true courage to battle.

"...Ah."

Just how long had she been standing there? Yuno suddenly realized the situation before her eyes.

A thick roadside tree, caught by the heavy freight carriage's cargo, had snapped at the base and was falling toward Yuno.

"Uh-oh."

The dim-witted words slipped out of her mouth.

She was going to die. Here in a place like this. The realization came too late.

"Hey, you all right?!"

Yet things didn't end up that way. A colossal hand grabbed the tree.

Mele the Horizon's Roar, keeping an eye on how the transport was going, handled the unexpected accident with agility wholly disproportional to his massive frame.

He casually placed the broken tree back in place on the opposite side of the road.

"Don't go spacing out like that! You minia are a buncha weaklings, ya know that?! Doesn't take much for you to end up dead, *gwah-ha-ha-ha-ha-ha*!"

"Th-thank...... Thank you......"

Still blinking in surprise, Yuno managed to express her gratitude, but it appeared the legendary gigant had already stopped listening.

Even the scolding he gave to the gigant in the transport unit that exposed civilians to danger was mixed in with laughter. Looking at his demeanor, it seemed that even the grave danger she faced had been utterly inconsequential.

"…What was that?"

Yuno had stopped moving while she stared dumbfounded at the transport team's departure, when suddenly, she heard a young girl's voice call to her.

"Miss, your hawthorns."

"Huh?"

"They fell out of the bag. Are you all right?"

It was an elf child wrapped up in a green robe.

Her pretty turquoise eyes, so clear they were almost transparent, looked up at Yuno.

"See, look, they got some dirt on them. Wash it off and you can still eat it, but minia get queasy about that stuff, don't they?"

"…Sorry. A lot happened at once, and I didn't notice. Thank you."

The three hawthorns she thought were in her bag had fallen out and were soaked in the mud from yesterday's rain.

"Well, looks like I'm going to have to buy some more. I'd be fine eating these, but I was planning on giving them to someone…"

"Hmmm…"

The young girl didn't look particularly interested as she gazed at Yuno.

Then she took out three hawthorns from her own bag and showed them to Yuno.

"Here, have them."

"Huh?! B-but I can't just take the food of a girl passing by on the street like that!"

"But making the trip back to the market from here would be a lotta trouble, right? That tree wasn't even your fault anyway. Ugh, those gigants are so careless and annoying, aren't they?! Seriously, I hate gigants!"

"But…you're the one who paid for these hawthorns, right?"

"…Does it seem that way to you?"

Yuno wasn't sure why, but the young girl flashed her an impish smile.

"This isn't anything to worry about, seriously. Since *I can do anything*, after all."

◆

In the mountains far away from Aureatia stood the Free City of Okafu. Although there were a great many mercenaries living in the city, very few of them met Morio the Sentinel in the central citadel face-to-face.

However, that day, a skeleton mercenary had made a visit to his room.

"Shalk the Sound Slicer, then? I've heard the general story. Well, relax for now."

"No need to worry about that; I'm plenty relaxed as it is. I'm here about the imperial competition, Morio the Sentinel."

Shalk didn't go sit in the chair he was offered. He remained standing up against the doorway as he spoke.

"I had figured there wouldn't be anyone who'd back a construct like me, but apparently there is. I've been given the empty spot that the Black Tone left behind. Sorry to do this mid-contract, but I'll be leaving Okafu."

"…Right. Soldiers are free to find their own battlefield. If you attempted to deliver me to them right now, that'd be a great achievement to present them with, too."

"Save the jokes. I don't intend on allying with Aureatia or allying with you lot, either. Been so from the very start. I just want information on the Hero…the identity of who slayed the True Demon King."

"You think it might've been you, is that it?"

"The way I see it, the Hero who defeated the True Demon King must not know who exactly they are, either. That's why they haven't come forward. Makes sense, right?"

"Though I doubt it's really that simple."

Morio lit his cigar. From the death of the True Demon King up to the present, no one had the slightest idea as to their true identity, even himself, one of the parties actively covering up the truth regarding the True Demon King.

If there was evidence left behind regarding the True Demon King, that meant that somewhere out there in the world was evidence of the True Hero as well. Whether they were still alive—or dead.

That one fact alone was something any living creature in the land wished for, yet no one was able to uncover.

"Shalk the Sound Slicer. Why did you come all the way to Okafu?"

"I told you, didn't I? To get information on the Hero."

"You must've wandered among the other powers that undertook investigations into The Land of The End...save the minian nation of Aureatia. There must've been a reason you didn't first pick the mercenary city that readily accepts constructs into their ranks."

"...You're going to make me say it?"

Morio smiled dryly.

"What? I just figured that sort of future'd be pretty interesting, too."

Shalk might have known from the beginning that Okafu wouldn't actually hand over any information on The Land of The End as laid out in their contract. Perhaps instead, there was a chance he would end up in a fight with Okafu like Kazuki.

"Enough. It's a boring story to tell."

"Let me also ask while I'm at it... Why didn't you go to The Land of The End yourself?"

"......"

"With enough skill to kill Kazuki, you should've been able to step into that hellscape and survive. Even if there was a group scheming to keep you quiet, I doubt they'd be able to keep up with your spear."

Morio the Sentinel was an aberrant visitor and a self-proclaimed demon king who had established an entire nation. He had a more thorough knowledge of the psychology of a warrior than even the warrior himself.

"...Scared, were you?"

"You...may be right."

Shalk didn't reply with a joke.

"I might be scared."

It was terrifying. That's why he needed to know. The truth about the True Demon King and the Hero.

◆

In the town below the citadel in the same Free City of Okafu, a man was visiting a building resembling a small commercial office.

"Phew, I nearly got myself killed quite a number of times on this investigation, I'll tell ya."

A man with a short and round stature, carrying a wooden box on his back. He appeared to be a garrulous man, beginning to speak as soon as he slipped through the door.

"This time really was the scariest of all. Scarier than any battlefield, that's for sure. I've got a true sense of it now, but to think that something like that was alive just a few years ago. It's got to be my only regret about coming to this world, honestly."

"...Thank you for your work, Mr. Yukiharu Shijima."

The young boy sitting on the wooden rotating chair gave a small, seated bow.

He looked no older than a thirteen-year-old boy, but such standards couldn't be applied to visitors. Particularly to the one known as the Gray-Haired Child—Hiroto the Paradox.

The investigation into the True Demon King that Zigita Zogi requested Yukiharu the Twilight Diver was a commission to obtain materials to aid Hiroto the Paradox's negotiations with the Free City of Okafu.

"However, there isn't any need to do any further investigations regarding the True Demon King or the Hero...... For now, I've achieved the goal of this first stage."

"Oh, you sure? If you'd like, Mr. Hiroto, I was thinking I'd use this momentum to start investigating the True Hero, too."

His claim seemed nothing more than big talk, to be so flippant about the mystery that no one across the land had come close to reaching, but it showed just how confident in his abilities he was. The journalist Yukiharu the Twilight Diver was also himself a deviant banished from his original world.

"There's not really any reason to go along with this whole imperial competition hullabaloo, is there? If we reveal the True Hero to the world with proof to back it up, we'll be able to blow their whole scheme out of the water, imperial competition and all. Heck, you could just directly back them yourself, Hiroto. I think the faster, the better here, myself."

"That isn't a very beneficial approach for me."

Hiroto forced a smile. For many years, Yukiharu had been hurrying across the continent as Hiroto's eyes, but that didn't necessarily mean the man understood all the facets of Hiroto's plans.

"That would *result in Aureatia being destroyed*, wouldn't it? The mobilization of Okafu and making use of the imperial competition…is a much gentler, and more peaceful, infiltration than that."

"Oh, come now. Mr. Politician, that's simply another way to say invasion, isn't it?"

"Yukiharu. An invasion is a loss. It only decreases the number of potential supporters. My goal is ultimately—"

…Here in this world, there was even someone trying to turn it into a reality—

An ideal that seemed perfectly impossible.

"—a happy ending. I need to settle things in a way that benefits everyone."

The world's enemy, the True Demon King, who had plunged the whole land into terror, had been brought down by someone.

That individual's name, and whether they truly existed or not, was still a mystery.

Now, with the end of the age of fear, it had become necessary to determine who this Hero was.

Now there were sixteen shura.

Soujirou the Willow-Sword.

Alus the Star Runner.

Kia the World Word.

Nastique the Quiet Singer.

Mele the Horizon's Roar.

Linaris the Obsidian.

Toroa the Awful.

Mestelexil the Box of Desperate Knowledge.

Kuuro the Cautious.

Rosclay the Absolute.

Lucnoca the Winter.

Psianop the Inexhaustible Stagnation.

Uhak the Silent.

Shalk the Sound Slicer.

Tu the Magic.

Hiroto the Paradox.

Now, at present.

"Sixteen all told. I'll share the candidates' information here, too."

Grasse the Foundation Map, First Minister of Aureatia, continued. Sixteen names. More than half of the Twenty-Nine Officials gathered together in the Provisional Chambers were sponsoring a hero candidate, each one confident theirs was the strongest.

They staked their own futures on the victory or defeat of their chosen candidates, themselves staking their life or death on the true duel stage. Thus was the Sixways Exhibition.

"If there's sixteen of them, should we do them in the order they applied? Fine if I start?"

"That'd make things easiest to understand. Then, starting with you, Twentieth Minister. Hidow the Clamp."

In this land, where any and all possible marvels or deviations from the norm were permitted...

...supposing there was just one individual from all the races, from all the combatants out there. That one individual was capable of exhausting all methods at their disposal to survive to the very end, then just what sort of being must that individual be—?

"Alus the Star Runner. Don't really have to explain all this, right? A wyvern who's fully conquered every labyrinth and won every treasure... And actually, cutting to the chase here, if there's anyone out there who's actually killed the True Demon King, it's gotta be someone like him."

Were they a rogue who plundered a multitude of the world's mysteries, crushing everything beneath his greed, and possessed a nigh omnipotent aptitude for everything?

"...Second candidate. Let's get this done with first, then. Eleventh Minister. Nophtok the Crepuscule Bell."

"Ah yes......the Order's recommended candidate. Kuze the Passing Disaster. Said to have butchered several hundred of the Order's enemies as their cleaner. Well... I imagine he'll give it a good run of things."

Were they a stabber who pierced with a single lethal blade, unperceived by anyone else in the world?

"Next, Twenty-Fifth General. Cayon the Skythunder."

"Okay now, for starters, everyone understands what's going on here, right? The main point of this competition is whether these candidates defeated the True Demon King, yes? Why, then it has to be Mele the Horizon's Roar! The champion who kept back the Demon King's invasion of the Sine Riverstead and vanquished the Particle Storm! His achievements are on a whole different level, darling."

Were they an archer who wrought destruction, impossible to

defend against, fired from the edge of the horizon, capturing all creation within his range?

"Twenty-Seventh General... Hardy the Bullet Flashpoint. The next candidate."

"Let me be clear. The story about Nagan Labyrinth City is true. Same with the story of the guy behind it all. A hero no one knows anything about has got to mean it's a visitor who's only come to our world recently, right? Sorry to say, Rosclay, but I'm betting on Soujirou the Willow-Sword."

Techniques that brought a slashing fatal end to any enemy, regardless of their morphology. Were they a blade who strayed from all known laws to the edges of sword heresy?

"Onto the fourth candidate. Thirteenth Minister, Enu the Distant Mirror."

"...Zeljirga the Abyss Web. Formerly of Obsidian Eyes. I can definitively state that, without her defection, our subjugation of Rehart the Obsidian wouldn't have succeeded. Simply by manipulating her threads and without touching her enemy, she can bind, manipulate, and tear them asunder. As far as I am aware, she is the strongest master with them out there."

Were they a scout who controlled a colony of ears, encroaching with intrigue and manipulation from the depths of unknown shadows?

"...Tenth General, Qwell the Wax Flower. Your candidate."

"Ps-Psianop... Psianop the Inexhaustible Stagnation. Um,

well, er… Neft the Nirvana, from the First Party. Everyone knows him, right? He was strong enough to kill him. Oh, um, without using any weapons, too…… He's strong. Far stronger than my full strength, definitely."

Were they a grappler whose aberrant physical form was honed into the ultimate weapon from an accumulation of knowledge and training with an obsession harder than iron?

"Next… Seventeenth Minister. Elea the Red Tag."

"My candidate doesn't have any of the considerable achievements of some of these other individuals. But he is the head of the Sun's Conifer guild, Jivlart the Ash Border. Any resident of the city can attest to his skills. A most suitable candidate to round out the numbers."

Were they a wizard gifted with godlike omnipotence, able to destroy or create all things in nature as they saw fit?

"…Hmph. It's an elimination tournament. Suppose those sorts are necessary, too. Sixteenth General, Nofelt the Somber Wind. What about your candidate?"

"Mine ain't here to fill out numbers, that's for sure. The rumors that he crushed those responsible for the Alimo Row massacre and killed *the* Belka the Rending Quake are all totally true. Uhak the Silent. Well… I bet I'll be able to show you all something interesting with him."

Were they an oracle who rejected the originating curse of the world and killed the mysterious gift of language under one singular principle?

*   *   *

"The ninth candidate is this one, then? Seventh Minister, Flinsuda the Portent."

"*Hoh-hoh-hoh-hoh-hoh!* My little cutie, Tu! Oh, she is *such* a sweetheart, that girl. She obediently listens to anything anyone says; she's always bright and smiling... Oh, silly me, we were talking about strength here, weren't we? Well, she was strong enough to live in The Land of The End, after all~! *Hoh-hoh-hoh!* That girl... Mayhap she didn't find the lingering scent of the True Demon King that scary...? Who's to say, I suppose."

Were they a juggernaut who overwhelmed with nothing more than innocent and artless physical abilities, rendering any and all malicious intent meaningless?

"Twenty-Second General, Mizial the Iron-Piercing Plumeshade."

"Okaaay. But everyone's already plenty familiar with the name Toroa the Awful, right? I don't really think anyone needs to hear me introduce him, to be honest. He's alive and participating! That's it!"

Were they a grim reaper, a successor to a legendary fear, who wielded a menagerie of enchanted swords with perfect precision?

"...Fine, I guess. Twenty-Fourth General. Dant the Heath Furrow's candidate. Explain the situation for everyone."

"...Zigita Zogi the Thousandth. None of the military powers we know were successful in bringing down the True Demon King. In that case, it must have been a military that none of us were aware of until now, that destroyed the Demon King...is one claim to be considered. I... My thought is that Zigita Zogi's tactics, which managed to destroy the Old Kingdoms' army without a single casualty, contributed the most to the Demon King's destruction."

"I went out of order a bit, but Fourteenth General, Yuca the Halation Gaol... You were the last person I expected to find a candidate."

"Well, hoo boy, I was surprised I did, too, honestly. Ozonezma the Capricious. He's a chimera, see? I can't really introduce him like you all have, but... Welp. He's a really strong one, that's for sure."

Were they a statesman who influenced the larger situation without ever standing on the battlefield, using his genius eloquence to turn numbers into power?

"Next. Fourth Minister, Kaete the Round Table."

"Yessir! As you're all aware, the self-proclaimed demon king Kiyazuna the Axle surrendered to Aureatia. Bringing a present with her—the weapon that subdued the Demon King, Mestelexil the Box of Desperate Knowledge. I myself have seen and can vouch for its performance. That should stow any objections."

Were they an architect and a creator constructed by an eminent specialist, whose theory dictated as eternally unable to be defeated?

"Nineteenth Minister, Hyakka the Heat Haze. You're next."

"Right! Shalk the Sound Slicer! Since we were able to reconcile peace with the Free City of Okafu a few days ago, I was able to verify the claim that he killed Kazuki the Black Tone! Extraordinary and faster than his own shadow! His ultimate spear technique leaves no time for a counterattack, truly fit for the designation of strongest!"

Godly speed that left everything and everyone in the dust. Were they a spearhead for whom the reach of their spear meant unavoidable death?

"Harghent's last then. Sixth General, Harghent the Still. How about you?"

"Lucnoca the Winter. *Heh, hwah, ha-ha-ha-ha...* There can't be anyone who hasn't heard the name...... She truly exists! Those claws have shattered champions' swords the world over, that breath...... Wait...... Ah anyway, she's the strongest...... The strongest candidate!"

Were they a silencer whose continued dominion over the final moments of champions throughout history and unwavering, unmatched strength brought despair even to herself?

"That makes fifteen. Now, Rosclay."

"Understood."

Were they an infallible knight and schemer, enlisting help from the very administrators of the games to create an undefeated idol?

"Second General Rosclay the Absolute. It goes without saying, but I will be victorious."

The Sixways Exhibition was about to begin.

It was a golden light.

A sea of illumination brimming over from the opposite riverbank. When the carriage began crossing the bridge, it consumed Kia's sights as it lined both sides of the streets.

Terrestrial light more powerful than the light of any star—and like nothing she had seen in the Eta Sylvan Province.

"That's amazing…! It's like it's still daytime out!"

Kia leaned her tiny body out of the carriage so far she nearly toppled out of it. The nightscape reflected in her turquoise almond-shaped eyes like a mirror.

It was unbelievable. All this light shining up into the dark night sky, long past sunset.

Everyone was still awake. They were working. What in the world could they be doing?

"*Ha-ha-ha*. What d'ya think, lassie?! Aureatia's impressive, ain't she?"

Though her reaction would have certainly earned her a scolding from Elea, the elderly driver responded in good faith. He must've felt a sense of pride for dazzling Aureatia himself.

"You know what those lights there are burning? It ain't animal fat or firewood, I'll tell ya that!"

"Gas! They're gas lamps! Air you can set on fire without Thermal Arts! Through pipes from the Mari Landburrow... Pipes of iron! They're burning those! That's what it is, right?!"

"Well, well, what's this, lass? You're still a wee girl, and you know a whole lot more than me already! *Ha-ha-ha!* Even I didn't know that much!"

Golden light. To think there could be such a big difference between here and the lamps in the towns she had passed through before now.

It had to be because they were gaslit.

"Elea... Er, Professor Viper was the one who taught me! She's the one who saw me off in Gimeena City!"

"Ah, that jaw-dropping beauty, eh? Now you're making me jealous, lassie. If I could do my life over again, I'd want to have a looker like her teaching me, I tell you what!"

"Well, I'm suuuuper glad she didn't come along! If that woman was here, she'd just be annoying me nonstop!"

The carriage continued to run forward, and before long, it flew right into the middle of the otherworldly light.

Unlike the previous dirty roads, they were now on a neatly arranged straight brick road.

This had to be the marketplace. Red. Green. The numerous colors illuminated in the golden gas lamplight, as well as the voices of the people, flowed in from each side of Kia, too many for her to pay attention to each and every one.

"Deluxe Caidehe sheep meat, today only! You won't be able to buy it any cheaper than this!"

"Have you ever seen these?! The true, genuine article! The latest new machinery from the Beyond! Try these 'binoculars' today!"

"Are there any who wish to spend the night at the Blue Beetle?! Come one, come all, we have a real bard from Minatsu Wellspring City performing!"

Everyone shouted in an almost obnoxiously loud voice, asserting their own existence.

Though completely opposite from her quiet and peaceful homeland, the hustle and bustle was still wonderful.

"Hey, are these...? Are all of these actual shops?!"

"Dang right, they are! You ain't see any in the other cities?!"

"But there's so many... W-won't they run out of customers?! Even a whole small month wouldn't be enough to look through them all!"

"*Ha-ha-ha-ha!* They've got plenty! This city here, it's got a whole bunch of people living in it, see! Forget a small month, you could spend a whole year and still not have enough time to see all of Aureatia!"

The carriage stopped. When Kia once again leaned out and looked around, she saw an iron pillar with a small flag projecting out of it.

The checkered flag made a loud clatter as it was lowered with a pendulum mechanism. With this, it guided the flow of carriages going lengthwise and horizontally through the crossroads.

"I-I've never seen anything like that...! Not even in class!"

Indeed. Kia's carriage wasn't the only one. Many carriages were coming and going down the alleyways.

Roads wide enough to allow four carriages to pass on both sides stretched out wherever she looked.

The rare carriage not pulled by a horse passed by Kia together with a puff of white smoke, startling her.

"Aaaah...!"

Said carriage entered into a section lined with residences that towered high up above her.

The appearances of the people living there were all different. The difference didn't come from their diverse range of dress, though. Minia. Elf. Dwarf. Leprechaun. Zmeu.

Were all the minian races in Aureatia...here in the world's largest city?

It was more than just what she had heard in class. This place was filled with the unbelievable and the unknown.

"Look, missy! That there's the royal palace! Queen Sephite's palace!"

"The royal palace...?!"

The carriage had come out into a noticeably larger road. She looked at the building that towered up ahead of her.

It was a very big, very beautiful castle illuminated in white.

All the blinding lights turned the large moat into a mirror image, as if lining the palace with a multicolored sun. A beautiful sight to behold.

A symbol of absolute royal authority, bestowed on the minian races.

A history of radiance and authority, looking down over the ocean-like expanse of business and activity.

It was the lone royal palace in existence, in a world once brought to the brink of annihilation by the True Demon King.

Aw. Kia pitied Elea. She wasn't able to be here next to Kia, looking up at this heavenly palace rising into the darkness of the night sky.

"Wow......"

The admiring sigh was all that slipped out of her mouth.

Kia was going to be spending the next year in this preposterous city.

How much excitement, how many unknowns, could she look forward to?

Before she departed the Eta Sylvan Province, had she imagined this sort of spectacle she was faced with now?

"Sixways Exhibition! Sixways Exhibition! Arrangements are still available! Come to us at Insa Moseo Co. for your tickets!"

"What do you say, miss? How about a Hero commemorative coin?! It'll be the pride of your family for generations to come!"

"Now then, surely you want to save the once-in-a-lifetime sight of the Hero's fighting prowess, right?! Come to Melora Imagining to order your daguerreotype now!"

Along the main road in front of the palace, merchants equally as industrious as those in the market had set up street stalls, and the surging wave of people all but stopped the carriage in its tracks. The words that seemed to be the main focus among all of them were completely new to Kia's ears.

"Hey... Hey! What's this Sixways Exhibition?!"

"Well now, the knowledgeable little lass doesn't know about the Sixways Exhibition?! I'm in shock, I tell ya! It's the biggest Royal Games the palace has ever held! It's a fight, see! A huge true duel tournament, like back in the times of myth and legend!"

"Wooow...! Who's supposed to appear in them, then?!"

"Ha-ha-ha! Why, the Hero who brought down the True Demon King!"

The driver's speech was filled with passion, making Kia think that, even in this amazing city, it had to be something truly special.

She wondered if she'd be able to go and see the games herself. Elea would probably scold her and tell her she couldn't go watch something so barbaric.

I'll go and see them; just watch me.

It would be too boring to come to such a wonderful city like this just to study.

She was going to slip out of her classes, walk through this bustling city nightlife, and witness things she had never seen before.

All sorts of things and events, so many that she'd be recounting them all to Yawika and Thien for the next ten years and still have stories left to tell.

"The winner'll get any wish of theirs granted! That's how incredible the prize is! That's why the strongest champions around are all gathering for it!"

"Seriously?! Then maybe I'll take part in them, too!"

"Whoa now, *ha-ha-ha*! Didn't know I was carrying a tiny little champion in my carriage! But...it's probably best you wait for another ten years, lass! When I say strongest, I truly mean the strongest now! Even Roslay the Absolute himself's gonna be appearing in 'em!"

"Well, I'm the strongest there is!"

A breeze passed through the alley and then through the passenger car.

Kia's golden hair fluttered, dancing on the wind and glittering in the starlight.

Then it flapped violently in the breeze from a deafening explosive rumble. She reflexively looked in the direction of the roar. Overtaking the carriage at a terrifying speed was what seemed like a colossal iron wurm.

"Amazing."

It was Kia's first time seeing the steam-powered vehicle, known as a steam locomotive.

An incredible machine like that, and it was in motion every day. Inside its massive frame, a large number of people were on board. The fuel used to power it was being gathered from all across the land.

People. An innumerable amount of people, keeping all this activity in motion, were living here in Aureatia.

"Aureatia…!"

Kia muttered as she watched the rear of the steam locomotive pass them by with its far greater momentum.

She was positive that there were things beyond her wildest imagination waiting for her.

"This is Aureatia!"

He had the feeling that no matter where he went, he was bound to happen upon the same types of events.

…It had to be a delusion of his. But during Shalk's existence, the same misfortune repeating two or three times seemed like enough consistency to say it had taken up a sizable chunk of his life.

In any case, it happened again here in Aureatia.

Shalk, sitting in the corner of a tavern known as the Blue Beetle and purchasing a glass of undrinkable booze to pay for the seat he took up, was listening to the performance of a cheerful wind instrument and a female bard.

Perhaps because he himself was a skeleton, he didn't enjoy gloomy music. He could've said that this establishment he picked out on the incomprehensible Aureatia streets was at that moment a lucky find.

"Woooow, pretty! Which one should I choose?!"

The first omen that he had made a mistake was the unrestrained and cheerful voice of a young girl.

The young girl looked to be around nineteen years old, her first impression animated and lively. She restlessly waved her long

chestnut-colored braid behind her, gazing at the colors of the bottles of alcohol lined up on the bar's shelves.

"Mister, this one! Gimme this one! The green stuff!"

"……"

The taciturn proprietor, a mismatch to the music in the tavern,
silently began preparing a glass.

The young girl lightly trotted through the crowded tavern inte-
rior and, seeing that the only open seat was the one across from
Shalk, plopped down in the chair without a moment's hesitation.

"Hey, now."

Given the condition the proprietor—the person who should've
originally kept things in check—was in, Shalk took it on himself
to rebuke her.

"…Deep casket whiskey? …At *your* age? If you didn't know,
then go get him to swap it out for something else. One sip's going
to send you under the table."

"Hmm? I'll be all right! Oh, mind if I sit here?"

"Ask that *before* you sit down. If I had a problem with it, I
would've told you."

Shalk thought the girl was like a baby kitten who still knew no
fear. Her long braid, continuing to sway restlessly in sync with her
movements, even after sitting down, in fact, resembled a tail.

"*Tee-hee*, thanks. I'm Tu the Magic. Who're you?"

"Sound Slicer. Shalk the Sound Slicer."

Tu the Magic.

He recalled the names of the participants that his sponsor,

Hyakka the Heat Haze, had told him. It was from earlier that morning, and Shalk hadn't seriously committed them to memory.

However, he felt like one of the participants went by this sort of bizarre second name.

"…You're in a bar, but you don't drink any alcohol? Your ice is already melting."

"Lucky for me, this body of mine can walk around drunkenly even without a drop, see."

A finger peeked out from underneath Shalk's dark-green rags. A true minian skeleton, moving in opposition to biological reason, bleached pure white like a precious jewel.

It was also the reason that, within the crowded tavern, the seat in front of his was the only one open.

Shalk the Sound Slicer was a construct. Save for exceptions like the Free City of Okafu, no matter what town he had traveled to…even one like Aureatia with its racial variety, skeletons were avoided.

"Never know if you'll sober up, after all. If you're fine with this booze, take it off my hands for me."

"You sure? Whoo-hoo, lucky me!"

Tu took the glass in both hands and loudly chugged Shalk's drink.

"Oooh… That's bitter! Still, it's tasty!"

"You seriously think so?"

"Yup! Everyone likes alcohol, right? Krafnir said so!"

"…"

It may have made the girl happy, but he thought that perhaps he shouldn't have carelessly encouraged her.

Although... Despite clearly appearing unused to alcohol, the fact that she could empty her glass like she was drinking down water maybe meant she must've been the owner of an iron stomach.

...Is this really one of my enemies in the Sixways Exhibition? They know my identity and are still acting like this?

Watching her shake her body along with the bard's music, she seemed anything but.

There was a small month left until the start of the games. It may have been a good idea to challenge her here and take stock of his opponent's power. Shalk paid attention to the location of his spear, leaning up against the wall.

"Oh, right, Shalk! There's something I wanna ask you!"

Right as the drink she ordered was brought to the table, an angry quarreling shout came flying from beyond Tu's seat.

"Huh?! You can shut your damn mouth! What does that money I borrowed have anything to do with this conversation?! A pittance like that, and you're getting bent outta shape, huh?! Quit whining about the little stuff!"

"Whoa, whoa, whoa, trying to cheat me, huh?! Go ahead and try it, asshole! Want me to spill those guts out on the table and use that to pay for your damn booze, huh?!"

Shalk heaved a weary sigh.

No matter where he went, he always got caught up in the same type of events.

"Shalk?"

"Yeah?"

While replying vaguely to Tu's inquiry, he stayed cognizant of the brewing trouble. He wanted to avoid getting wrapped up in it should the need arise. Tu, on the other hand, didn't appear to be paying any attention at all.

Shalk could see that one of the men arguing had taken out a small firearm. The man seriously showed up to drink with a loaded gun? He raised the barrel. He thrust it into the other man's neck.

With Shalk's speed, he could've restrained them. Not only could he have rushed over to the seat across the tavern and deflected the bullet, he could have directly stopped the finger before it could even pull the trigger—however, he thought it was best to leave the blackguards free to settle their own problem however they wanted.

Just like Taren the Punished and Milieu the Hemp Drop.

"You can go straight to hell first!"

The clatter of a chair being kicked over. Gunshots. Patrons' shrieks. A stray bullet flew toward Shalk's seat.

Shalk remained silent and looked at the seat in front of him... at the chair his drinking companion instantly vanished from.

He also saw the moment that bullet flying toward him was stopped, without even reaching for his spear.

Tu caught it with her fist. From what Shalk could see, the bullet didn't leave behind a single scratch on the girl's skin.

"Stop!"

Immediately dashing toward them, Tu pinned down both men simultaneously. The brawny men, clearly well acquainted with the world of violence, were each dragged down to the floor by one of the girl's slender arms.

"Everyone here's enjoying the music! This isn't the time for your fight! Don't cause trouble!"

"Hng, augh!"

Tu viewed the two as simple drunks and was trying to show them a little bit of leniency. She took her hands off their throats and declared:

"If you're gonna keep it up, I'll have to teach you a lesson with a good kick!"

"...Tu. Those guys—"

It was when Shalk grabbed his spear and went to stand that the second strange event occurred.

There was the cracking sound of wood being forcibly split apart. Something that came flying from one of the drunks' hands broke one of the lamps behind him. The sound of it breaking stole Tu's attention.

The two both escaped at the same time. One went toward the entrance. The other went to where the projectile had landed— toward the back door.

The back door lay in the deepest part of the tavern, diagonally across from Shalk's seat. Nevertheless, with excessive agility...and mixed with a yawn, Shalk was able to go around and cut him off.

"...!"

"You married to that knife or what?"

Leaning against the wall in the darkness of the back door, he pulled out the item he had stolen from the man before he could reach the back door...the blade of a knife. It was no normal knife. It was an assassin's weapon, equipped with a gunpowder mechanism that fired just the knife's blade out from the hilt.

"Sorry for the rude question, but...you see...I can't think of any other reason why you'd choose this thing here over being pinned down by such a young cutie like her."

"Give it back."

He could guess what happened. This dangerous weapon was thrust at Tu from a blind spot her body had been hiding. The blade didn't penetrate her body, sliding off her skin and getting deflected. This man planned on recovering the evidence and making his escape.

A normal person's body would've been burst open and torn apart, organs and all. Just how had she defended herself?

"...This isn't an easy weapon to get your hands on. Who sent you?"

"Shalk!"

From behind, Tu's voice called out to him disapprovingly.

From over his shoulder, he looked at the girl's stomach. The large torn fabric lined up with the attack she had just been hit with.

"...I'm fine. Let him go."

"I'll make it clear because you don't seem to get it, but this guy tried to kill you."

"Really? It's no big deal. Still, you can't fight with him here, though. Everyone's come here to enjoy the music."

"...Listen."

Shalk was also taking note of the drunk fleeing the tavern while he and Tu conversed.

Exiting the establishment, they split into two in the alleyway. After that, they each divided into three and four more roads, respectively. With Shalk's speed, he could try out all the potential routes and still be plenty fast enough to catch up to the fleeing drunk. He should have enough time to apprehend them and interrogate them about who was pulling their strings.

If he left right now.

Shalk was first concerned with Tu.

"Are you really all right? Treating your wounds is the first priority. Unlike me, you're still alive and all."

"I'm fine, really! Hey, c'mon, don't pull me!"

The feeling of Tu's arm under his bony fingertips—though obviously just the skeleton's quasi-sense of touch—was the same as any normal young girl. There was a softness to her skin, and when he gripped a bit harder, there was a fleshy elasticity.

"......What's going on with your body?"

Ultimately, Shalk's apprehensions had been entirely off the mark.

The skin that had supposedly been hit with two different types of fatal weaponry didn't show the slightest hint of internal bleeding. Tu the Magic wasn't even feeling any pain.

It couldn't have been simply hardness, like dragon scale, that defended her. It seemed like the only possible explanation was that this soft, fair skin possessed a tenacity that neither gun nor blade would pierce through. But then, where did the upper limit of this defense of hers lie?

"*Ah-ha-ha!* I don't really understand the difficult stuff myself, either! But as for me, this body I was born with... Well, you can see for yourself; it's fine. I'm okay."

"Fine or not, you still shouldn't carelessly risk your life like that."

"...Okay. Thanks. Shalk, you're a nice old dude!"

"Old dude?"

Shalk was baffled at himself for his unexpected shock.

He didn't have any memory of who he was exactly.

Of course, that would have been one of the many possibilities left behind, but...

"...I look like an older guy to you?"

"Uh-oh. Not happy to hear that? I like older dudes myself, though."

"Nah, it's fine. Not a big issue. Men who fuss over their age are idiots. More importantly than any of that, though, there's a serious topic to get to."

Hiding the fact and drawing out information from her would have been advantageous for Shalk.

Nevertheless, the long-dead man wasn't foolish enough to throw away his dignity over a small bit of self-protection.

"Tu the Magic. You're a participant in the Sixways Exhibition, aren't you?"

"Yup!"

"That'll speed things up, but maybe don't go around answering so honestly like that. I'm the same. Shalk the Sound Slicer. You realize those two just now weren't any old drunks, too, right?"

"What—they weren't?!"

Shalk held his empty cranium in his hands. This girl was unbelievable.

It had been the same story when she first pinned down the drunks, too. Her frame of mind was leagues removed from a warrior's. Did she really expect to win and advance through the tournament completely off her physical ability and nothing more?

"...When those guys were arguing, a stray bullet almost flew right at this seat. They were aiming for me. There's someone trying to see how we'd handle it."

"Like how you went around to cut the guy off?"

"Nah. No doubt they were looking at you. Bullets and blades. Had to be some intent behind both of them using separate methods of attack—trying to see the limits of your defenses, for example, maybe."

This place wasn't the same type of haunt for scoundrels like Shalk had come across during his roaming.

No matter where he went, he always happened upon the same kinds of events. However, if the same sort of things were happening here in Aureatia, that was beyond the scope of sheer bad luck. An unquestionably abnormal event.

"...Probably one of the other participants staged the whole affair. Sorry."

"That so. But why're you apologizing, Shalk? You weren't behind it, right?"

"I also watched you stop that bullet. I got a bit curious to see how another hero candidate like me'd deal with it. If you had actually died right in front of me, I probably would've felt a bit guilty about it."

Most likely, he wouldn't have. Shalk the Sound Slicer had watched countless deaths, but he had never once truly felt any guilt about it. Because he didn't believe in any firm sense of justice, including the judgment of whether a person lives or dies.

"I see. You're real smart, Shalk. I never thought about that."

Tu flashed a toothy grin, looking unbothered about it all. He felt just a little bit envious of her, moving without any hesitation to save someone else. Because he knew that having convictions meant that one knew oneself.

Still, there's already someone out there trying to investigate our fighting strength. We only learned who was participating just this very morning.

She wasn't paying it any mind, but if he assumed someone was, then the culprit had put things in motion with considerable speed.

Hiring soldiers. Drafting up a plan of attack. Narrowing down the strengths of Tu the Magic's defensive capabilities.

That was a different class of speed that even Shalk's agility couldn't keep up with.

Looks like there's a really shrewd somebody out there.

Even the young girl sitting in front of him had a chance of becoming Shalk's enemy, too.

Or perhaps, he had given her information during this conversation he shouldn't have, leaving himself at an unnecessary disadvantage.

That which he exchanged for a slight sense of dignity might have one day served to force Shalk up against the wall.

"You're a really nice guy, huh, Shalk?"

"Just getting the chance to hold hands with a beautiful girl is enough to hook any man."

"Tee-hee. Was my hand nice and soft?"

"......Yeah."

The Sixways Exhibition was underway. Already, in some hidden place none were aware of.

"Heyo, Hidow! Workin' hard?!"

"Yeah."

"Oh, if it isn't Hidow. Come eat at our place today? I'll serve you up an extra-big plate!"

"If I feel like it."

"*Heh-heh...* You Twenty-Nine Officials, you get to have audiences with Her Majesty, don'cha? Gimme the scoop, Hidow, what's Queen Sephite like? Gotta be a real beauty, eh?"

"I'd say so."

"Yooo, Hidow! We're pumped for the Sixways Exhibition, dude!"

"'Preciate it."

Languidly moving through the wave of people's voices, he passed through the lunchtime plaza. The spray from the fountain wet the tips of Hidow's hair.

Hidow the Clamp, Twentieth Minister of Aureatia. Wearing his hat at an angle and cloaked in a casual aristocratic outfit, his clothing was of a bohemian second son to a well-known noble family. A description he admitted to himself.

However, to the people of society, he was viewed as the Twentieth Minister, one of the members of the minian world's highest governmental body.

...All a bunch of nonsense.

On a long bench in the park, far enough from the eyes of others, he opened up the package in his hands. During lunchtime, Hidow always ate the same shop's sandwiches.

Hope I'll be able to take it easy tomorrow. Aureatia, the Sixways Exhibition... Alus the Star Runner, too. It's all a bunch of nonsense.

Accompanying his rising social position, Hidow was beleaguered with unwanted anxiety. All of it large-scale trouble that he usually didn't need to think about it.

At what point did he end up going down the wrong path? His political position had long eclipsed his elder brother's, the rightful heir to his family's estate. In the life he had envisioned for himself when he was young, things weren't supposed to turn out this way.

Therein lay the reason why he, with his sociable temperament, preferred to take his lunch alone. He needed at least one time a day where he could be released from his position in society.

The soft slices of bread had a uniformly toasted surface and plenty of warmth left.

Within Aureatia, it wasn't a bakery that enjoyed much business, but the moderation in the shopkeeper's Thermal Arts was sublime. The duck meat wrapped up in the bread also gave a luster to the surrounding greens, with the fat melting from its bright-red flesh, and while simple, it was a wonderful meal...

…which was why the presence appearing on the bench behind his own irritated him.

"…What do you want? I'm having my lunch."

The hands on his food stopped for a moment. The physical safety of the Twenty-Nine Officials was supposed to be watched over closely by a large number of soldiers, but there was always the chance it was an assassin sent by another faction.

A weary, worn-out voice replied from the bench behind him.

"With you, it's hard to get you somewhere without anyone else around, Hidow the Clamp."

"…I don't want to take on any more problems than I've already got. Give me a break."

It was the Sixth General, Harghent the Still. Hidow didn't have any tabs on when exactly this man had returned to Aureatia.

Completely opposite Hidow, who had been promoted to his station using the wits and resourcefulness he was born with, Harghent was a military man from a bygone era who had crawled up the ranks after being born in obscurity in some seaside frontier. The nature of his decline put him in the exact opposite position from Hidow's personal career within the Twenty-Nine Officials.

"Sorry… Sorry, but this is one point that I can't afford to back down on. I have Lucnoca the Winter with me, and you have Alus the Star Runner. Both are unmatched dragonkin known across the world as the 'strongest.' In which case—"

"Can we get to the point? You're taking forever here. What are you trying to get at? Telling me to set it up so you and I face off, old man? Seriously… What the hell's wrong with you?"

His patience at its end, he took a bite of his bread.

To him, it was far more important than a conversation with an aging general on the political decline.

"Well, go negotiate with Jelky or Rosclay, then, and try making it happen. If you can anyway. I don't have that sort of authority. This conversation's over."

"Please, I—I...! I need to settle things once and for all with Alus the Star Runner! I swore I'd get my hands on something bigger than him! It's the meaning of my life! I-if it was otherwise, you think a man like me would've been able to bring Lucnoca the Winter back with me?!"

Hidow couldn't care less.

Whatever maudlin sentiments this man had, whatever personal justice, Hidow wasn't interested in the slightest.

He wasn't denying the challenge for any particular reason. He even thought that he'd be fine with it if Harghent went ahead and set things up somewhere behind closed doors. Despite this, anyone and everyone brought their problems Hidow's way, solely under self-serving circumstances. It only worked to expand the range of work he needed to handle.

"Actually, old man? About that Lucnoca... Let me tell you something. Lucnoca the Winter never even had any interest in the minian races to begin with. If she really felt like destroying a settlement, you know what'd happen? Why the hell'd you go and call her here? Unlike you, I have to think about those sorta problems on top of everything else. Now in addition to all *that*, you're trying to make me go along with your selfish nonsense? What the hell sort of thoughts are bouncing around that empty head of yours?"

"......Nothing I did was wrong at all. This land... The strongest being in this land. This all was supposed to be about finding champions who could stand shoulder to shoulder with the Hero...!"

"Ugh...... It's that old, addled brain, I swear... Take a moment to think about things for once in your life. What's the grand idea behind bringing a seriously all-powerful candidate here? Reality is: This candidate crap...... As long as they were famous enough to avoid any criticism from the people, become an ally to the minian races, and be bested by Rosclay, that would've been enough. Instead, you idiots went and decided to gather all these assholes together. Every damn one of you, I swear... Giving excuses like, 'I want power,' or 'I want to be the one to introduce the Hero to the world.'"

He crushed the paper wrappings from his bread in his other hand.

Why—why did he want authority and power that would ultimately be too much for him to control? What was there to earn by rising up in the world without any outlook for what's ahead? Hidow couldn't understand any of it at all.

All he wanted to do was simply live his life freely without having to worry about anything.

If he could live in blissful ignorance, like the city residents that called out to him in the plaza, that was enough for him.

"…You all are always like that."

The general sitting behind him quietly mumbled, still keeping his eyes dropped down to his lap. The tone of his voice was filled with the resentment and anger that had built up inside of him.

"What?"

"Always, it's always how it goes. You lot have the authority to decide anything and everything. Then you try to make us conform to those rules you all create for yourselves. But whenever it comes the time when we're able to make use of those rules better than you all can…you always start talking like that."

Wing Clipper Harghent. A man completely unable to read the current of the times who continued to claim his wyvern hunts as great achievements, done out of habit at this point more than anything.

An obsolete bureaucrat. He wouldn't be considered necessary at all in the coming age. And the creation of just such a future was, most likely, already set in stone.

"'That wasn't really what we meant.' Or 'You should've stopped to think for a moment and realized.' Or 'There's a new rule now.' We never get praised for anything. That's because the power to decide everything is always resting in people like you all. Before the True Demon King showed up, they told me to hunt goblins and wyverns. They said that they were the real evil for attacking settlements and threatening expansion and pioneering. That's why I believed that if I hunted wyverns, I'd be able to rise up the ladder. That's all I did."

"Your brains get boiled? I didn't say any of that."

"It's all the same. No matter who it is, it's the exact same...! Next is the Demon King. Next is the Hero. You people always cleverly say 'That's not what we meant!' I even changed the definition of evil! I lured Lucnoca the Winter, the dragon no one's ever seen, here!"

Hidow could tell that Harghent had stood up. From the bottom of his heart, he truly felt that Harghent was an insignificant and absurd person. A foolish man amplifying his own anger and misfortune with his own words.

Hidow narrowed his eyes and gazed at the grass spread out in front of him. He imagined himself continuing to ignore all of Harghent's words, cutting across the plaza, and taking his leave. There was absolutely nothing this powerless general was capable of. Harghent wasn't going to be involved in any of the Twenty-Nine Officials' decisions from here on out.

"I-I'm talking about...Lucnoca the Winter here! Legendary—and unmistakably the strongest in the land! Why won't anyone commend me?! Why isn't anyone shocked?! What does one need to do to satisfy you people?! Are you people going to tell me giving me a single fight with Alus isn't a reasonable reward?!"

His assertion was so extraordinarily inconsistent, logic that simply seemed to be blaming others for his faults.

Although they could understand each other through Word Arts, Harghent was so eccentric, and so attached to honor and social status, it was almost as if he was a completely different species of creature, with values wholly different from Hidow's own.

......

However. While he couldn't understand him, he grew irritated. He threw down the paper wrapping and shot up from the bench.

"...Hey, old man. What the hell do you know about me?"

For this Sixways Exhibition, who even understood the true reason why Hidow the Clamp, without any shred of ambition himself, immediately threw his support behind Alus the Star Runner?

He was truly apprehensive about the future of these Royal Games. Although he inwardly opposed him, he knew Alus the Star Runner's power better than anyone in the world.

If he hadn't gotten ahold of Alus of the Star Runner before anyone else—

Then someone else would have sponsored him and could have truly ended up winning the whole thing.

Why was Hidow forced to take over roles he didn't wish for?

It was because there were men like Harghent out in the world.

Everyone, the entire world, was filled with nothing but hopeless incompetence. Hidow had wished he could be incompetent.

"You really go and say whatever pops into that pea brain of yours, huh? You're that proud of Lucnoca the Winter, then? You found yourself a legend, and I'm supposed to bow at your feet? Is Lucnoca the Winter really that strong? Listen..."

Simply turning around and glaring at Harghent from underneath his hat was enough to make the general shrink back.

Both of Hidow's fists were trembling; he vividly understood he was putting on a bold front.

He probably could've made the man cry on the spot. The irritation was enough to bring such thoughts to Hidow's mind.

"......"

"Fine. I'll give you the fight you want. Harghent the Still."

Hidow didn't understand why he was so irritated with a weakling like this.

With all the hatred in his heart, he declared:

"I'll send you straight to hell."

CHAPTER 16 ◆ The Matchups

The Eighth Minister, Sheanek the Word Intermediary, was included among the names of the Twenty-Nine Officials for abilities laid out in his second name. He could understand the Order's script, seven different family's systems of nobility script, and two types of scripts from the Beyond.

Studying for many years, even abroad in Nagan Labyrinth City, he was well-known to be a prodigy when it came to deciphering letters and giving written accounts, even surmounting Third Minister Jelky.

Having finished with the work he had been entrusted with that morning, he entered the Provisional Chambers in Aureatia's Central Assembly Hall.

In there was someone still continuing with their work.

"Minister Grasse. I've already sorted all the meeting minutes. How are things on your end?"

"Just wait there a moment."

"…Oh my, are these the pairings?"

Due to his abilities, Sheanek also served as virtual secretary for the First Minister of Aureatia, Grasse the Foundation Map.

The match pairings for the Sixways Exhibition were, until the opening day, information of the greatest, most critical secrecy, but the two of them were in positions that allowed them a look.

"I more or less got consent from all of the Twenty-Nine Officials sponsoring a candidate. This'll likely be set in stone."

"...But...this is—"

"Strange, isn't it?"

"Indeed."

The sense of incongruity, understood with a single glance, was something Grasse had also felt, too.

The period of preparation given to all the participants of the Sixways Exhibition—based on the information that each of them gained from spying on the other candidates...should have created a great amount of opposition and adjustments from among all the supporting officials regarding the pairings. Neither Grasse nor Sheanek had full knowledge of all of these different motives and intrigue. Nevertheless.

"Is it really okay to put Lucnoca the Winter in this position?"

"...If you put it that way, it's the same for Kuze the Passing Disaster. Using an easily beatable pawn like this doesn't make any sense."

"The Twenty-Seventh General really did a good job, didn't he?"

Their interest was centered, naturally, on Rosclay the Absolute.

The authority to decide on this pairing's bracket was the very foundation of his power in the first place.

In which case, the truth behind the list of names was—

"…You came at the perfect time, Sheanek. Can you transcribe this down in northeastern script for me? I can manage to some extent, but after all these years, I've forgotten the grammar, you see. It'd end up eating a lot of my time."

"That's your job, isn't it, Minister Grasse? It's not mine. Especially not for free."

"*Pfft.* Impudent fellow, aren't we? I'll take you out to Fog Phoenix next time."

"Ah well, what else am I going to do? Fine, then."

He smiled slightly and sat down in the seat diagonally across from Grasse.

Grasse let out a brief yawn and then began to read aloud from the top.

Each one would become a pairing to decide all the candidates' fates.

The battle to determine one lone Hero—the Sixways Exhibition.

All eight matches would become the supreme and climactic Royal Games, the likes of which were only seen once in a thousand years.

"Match one. Psianop the Inexhaustible Stagnation and Toroa the Awful."

Ooze versus dwarf.

Unarmed and unlimited, against full-clad swords and pure technique.

"Match two. Alus the Star Runner and Lucnoca the Winter."

Wyvern versus dragon.

A legend-slaying champion and a champion-slaying legend.

"Match three. Ozonezma the Capricious and Soujirou the Willow-Sword."

Chimera versus minia.

Enshrouded visitor hands and an enshrouded visitor sword.

"Match four. Rosclay the Absolute and Jivlart the Ash Border."

Minia versus minia.

The weakest, feigning strength, and the strongest, feigning weakness.

"Match five. Kuze the Passing Disaster and Tu the Magic."

Minia versus unknown.

A spear of mysterious, absolute death and a shield of impenetrable, absolute arrest.

"Match six. Mestelexil the Box of Desperate Knowledge and Zeljirga the Abyss Web."

Golem versus zmeu.

Perfected iron machinery and perfection-destroying shadow mechanisms.

"Match seven. Shalk the Sound Slicer and Mele the Horizon's Roar."

Skeleton versus gigant.

Speed that denied evasion and an attack range that denied evasion.

"Match eight. Zigita Zogi the Thousandth and Uhak the Silent."

Goblin versus ogre.

Reason-controlling tactical strategy and reason-destroying natural law.

"......"

After copying down everyone's matches, Sheanek thought for a brief moment.

"...Rosclay chose the fourth match, after all."

"Handling things as cleverly as expected, it seems. Either the fourth or the eighth. While he's still at full strength and not exhausted from his own match, he can confirm how those in his bracket are battling—and use that info to prepare properly. On top of that, while the next set of matches are going on, he can then prep for the second round, too."

"Choosing Jivlart for his first-round opponent is appropriate, too. The problem is...here."

Sheanek traced his finger along the pairings list. Bringing him pause where his finger landed was the winner of the third match.

The winner would be one of either Soujirou the Willow-Sword or Ozonezma the Capricious.

Presenting a problem here was not the combatants, but their

sponsors. The Twenty-Seventh General held the authority to wield Aureatia's largest contingent of soldiers—the chief administrator of the country's military affairs.

"Hardy the Bullet Flashpoint, eh."

"General Hardy is the biggest challenger to Rosclay's faction. He's about the only one among the Twenty-Nine Officials who'd be permitted to openly fight against Rosclay. He's going to try to crush him with everything he's got, for sure."

"…Ol' Hardy managed to maneuver around and trap Rosclay where he wanted him. Either that or Rosclay plans on stamping out all the factions opposing him at once."

"So you think the idea that it'd be best to clean up everything in the early stages is what's making them apprehensive?"

"Hmm, hard to say."

Grasse and Sheanek were a completely neutral camp within the current Sixways Exhibition.

Though it did mean they were choosing to be disadvantaged within the political strife, for Grasse, who planned to enjoy every moment of it all, his bird's-eye view of the situation was truly the most convenient place for him. With it, he was also able to stand in the center of the games' operations as well.

"What about the thought that they're preparing themselves against Ozonezma the Capricious?"

The opponent for Hardy's candidate, Soujirou the Willow-Sword, was Ozonezma the Capricious.

The one backing this candidate was Yuca the Halation Gaol.

"Yuca's a simple man. He won't be besting Hardy with any stratagems. He's really doing a good job, but he's not bringing any ambition to this kind of fight."

"Today he was apparently serving as Jelky's bodyguard. He doesn't seem to be putting much effort into the Sixways Exhibition, as even Ozonezma's arrival in Aureatia is behind schedule."

"...Then it'll only get harder and harder for Ozonezma to advance to the second round."

With Ozonezma, both his true identity and his actual abilities were a complete mystery, but this fight wasn't going to be an easygoing affair where someone without adequate support behind them could hope to advance.

This would be a true duel. If they fought without exhausting all options available to them, beyond plain fighting strength, they'd be easily outmaneuvered and face defeat in their match, even if their actually fighting prowess was superior.

"Then, for the third round..."

Continuing, Sheanek's finger trailed over to the pairing for the second match.

The two seen as the strongest among all sixteen combatants. Alus the Star Runner and Lucnoca the Winter.

"...One of these two is sure to advance that far."

"I'm thinking the same thing. This...isn't great, either."

"It's impossible to win against a dragon."

Rosclay the Absolute was a dragon-slaying champion. That was how he was seen in the public eyes.

However, should he exhaust every one of his true avenues to victory, the ones unbeknownst to the world at large, would he really be able to win against Alus or Lucnoca?

Whoever confronted them, be it Psianop or Toroa, couldn't possibly be able to hold either of these two dragonkin back.

Let alone Toroa, who had already been defeated once by Alus and had his enchanted sword of light stolen. A man of Rosclay's caliber must have arrived at a similar prediction himself.

"Well, now. Here I was thinking that you'd definitely be able to win one and advance, Rosclay."

Thus, the truth behind the list of names enumerated here was clear.

He hadn't been able to show his strengths at the time this was all decided.

Just what sort of unforeseen circumstances had cropped up, it was impossible to say.

Rosclay the Absolute had failed. He had lost the political battle and was forced into an unwinnable fight.

"Should we wrap things up here?"

The first round of matches.

Psianop the Inexhaustible Stagnation versus Toroa the Awful.
Alus the Star Runner versus Lucnoca the Winter.
Ozonezma the Capricious versus Soujiro the Willow-Sword.

Rosclay the Absolute versus Jivlart the Ash Border.

Kuze the Passing Disaster versus Tu the Magic.

Mestelexil the Box of Desperate Knowledge versus Zeljirga the Abyss Web.

Shalk the Sound Slicer versus Mele the Horizon's Roar.

Zigita Zogi the Thousandth versus Uhak the Silent.

When it came to Mizial the Iron-Piercing Plumeshade's nomination as Twenty-Second General of Aureatia, there may not have been a single soul who could explain the reason why.

He was all of sixteen years old. He was bold on the battlefield and would express his candid opinions during council sessions, but unlike Hidow, for example, he wasn't someone who possessed acumen from the start of his tenure among the Twenty-Nine Officials. At first, he had social standing, and then he was simply driven by that position to acquire the abilities demanded of him.

Around the time the wartime regime known as the Aureatia Twenty-Nine Officials was born, he was merely there occupying his seat. There was some sort of political adjustment between the three kingdoms, and as a representative in name only of a certain family, whose leader died right before the formation of the Twenty-Nine, it was young Mizial who sat in the seat.

It was a ludicrous story, but at the time, there were also rumors that he may have been the illegitimate child of the royalty from the True Northern Kingdom, first to be ruined by the revolution of madness. In any case, at that time, there had been a powerful backer supporting Mizial behind the scenes.

However, during the chaotic, drawn-out war with the True Demon King, the powers supporting him disappeared one after another, and before anyone knew it, they had all vanished entirely.

With this, only Mizial remained. In the Twenty-Nine Officials, even when compared to Hidow the Clamp or Elea the Red Tag, he stood out as young, the youngest bureaucrat of all.

"Pardon me for calling at this late hour! I'm with the Miroffa Farming Tools Co."

"Okay, okaaaay! Gimme a seeeec!"

Mizial replied to the voice outside the mansion, still sunk back deep into the soft chair in his spacious room. He didn't plan on going himself. A servant would head for the door before long.

The other man in the room, sitting down by the fireplace, listened to the exchange, confused.

"Do you have a farm somewhere?"

"Nooope. Why, something bothering you?"

"Well, it's a farming tool salesperson in the middle of the night. Not really the time of day to summon 'em here, is it?"

This dwarf's whole body could be mistaken for a weapon storehouse, his dangerous dress enough to make those who saw it tremble in fear. Even inside the residence of his own sponsor, he showed no intentions of letting a single one of his swords leave his side.

A living legend—he went by the name Toroa the Awful.

"Ah! Hey so, Toroa, tell me. You ever cultivate a field before?"

"It was a daily chore. I'd always wake up early in the morning and begin with tending the vegetable garden."

"Wooow! That's a surprise. What d'you eat? Did you really kidnap bad children, tear off their heads or whatever, and gulp them all down?"

Toroa couldn't suppress a wry grin. How exactly was that tiny father of his supposed to gulp down an entire minia's head?

The legend his father left behind had turned into a genuine fear and taken root in populated settlements. However, parts of that legend included such preposterous rumors and anecdotes that he couldn't hold back his laughter.

The citizens of Aureatia used such stories to frighten children who misbehaved—and even enjoyed fabricated verses that spoke of Toroa the Awful's adventures.

Some sort of fiction, far removed from their daily lives. A monster associated with the fantasy known as enchanted swords. They were all stories totally uninvolved with the citizenry going about living their daily lives.

In the end, Toroa the Awful had been unable to become genuine terror, like the True Demon King.

Contrary to expectations, though, Toroa didn't dislike these diverse range of stories. It made it feel like his father truly had lived in this world—and that even if his path had been one of butchery and regrets, there was a totally unknown someone out there who accepted his existence, too.

"Nothing that could compare with food in Aureatia, but the stuff I ate was probably a lot better than you're imagining. Boar meat soup... Now, that's a favorite. The kind simmered with moonstalks. When potato season rolls around, I'd mash them up and mix them with goat cheese. Then you wrap that in potato leaves. That was another favorite of mine..."

"Hmmm. Kinda boring, huh?"

A bit taken aback from the response, Toroa looked at Mizial.

Still sprawled out on the couch, he was gazing up indifferently at the ceiling.

Even when speaking to the legendary symbol of fear, Toroa the Awful, Mizial didn't show an ounce of self-humility or denigration.

"I mean, c'mon, Toroa the Awful can't be eating normal stuff like that."

"What do you want me to say, then? I can't help it if that's what I actually ate."

"Awww, who cares about the truth. No one's gonna know either way, right? What about saying, like, you dived in the ocean and killed krakens with your bare teeth. Or like you have some enchanted meat sword that sprouts these berries every day that are dripping in blood!"

"...Or that I boil down mandrake poison and drink it with my alcohol?"

"Yeah, yeah, that type of stuff! It's cool!"

Aureatia's Twenty-Second General gleefully cackled.

"It's gotta be stuff like that; I'm serious. I mean, you're Toroa the Awful, after all... Toroa the Awful even came back from hell, right?"

"...........Yeah."

Toroa pictured it. Somewhere out in Wyte was this terrifying monster, and every day he trekked down to the sea to eat krakens. With his mouth split from ear to ear, he'd drain his cup of boiled mandrake poison wine with a broad grin.

That awful monster would roam the night, kidnap bad children—and come back to life even after death to kill those who dared to wield enchanted swords.

"What was hell like?"

"Hell...hell was...... Let's see. Terribly cold, and everywhere I stepped there were blades. A hell where...the ones who accumulated sins of the sword in life were dropped."

With it was one other sight only he was able to imagine.

The image of his tiny father tackling the ordeals of that vast, endless, and far-off world.

For instance......holding on to a single enchanted sword, just like he did when he was alive.

"Powerful and wicked dragons, and terrifying self-proclaimed demon kings...the kind that left their name in the histories—they were there, too. That's why, in order to rise back in this world, I was forced to cut them all down one by one."

"*Hee-hee-hee...!* So, Toroa, you're saying you were able to beat all those guys?"

"I sure am."

Toroa the Awful cut down enemies far larger than himself, one after another.

The enchanted sword streaking though the air like the wind—and that tiny body jumping from the rocky ground surface of swords, racing upside down, and continuously cutting down the fiends of hell all by himself.

This sole answer was the only thing he always firmly believed in, more than anyone else.

"Because Toroa the Awful's the strongest out there."

Deep down in their hearts, the boy and the dwarf were both the same. The two of them liked the tales of Toroa the Awful.

Toroa the Awful knew the reason why Mizial chose to sponsor him.

◆

The dead of night. At an hour when all were asleep, a single-rider carriage departed from Mizial's mansion.

Just as Mizial had requested, its cargo remained loaded.

When he first gained his seat within the Twenty-Nine Officials, everyone around him had viewed it as a nominal position.

It wasn't only a matter of his ability. They didn't think it'd be at all possible for him to bear the heavy responsibilities of being a politician.

However, it was not so. The Twenty-Second General was a mediocre child in most senses of the word, but in one particular way, he possessed talent that far exceeded anyone else. It was clearly this talent that kept his heart true while surrounded by schemes and trickery—and what guided him to military exploits beyond his physical stature on the battlefield.

"...All right, now. No one's around here, right?"

He stepped out of the carriage into a deserted old town plaza.

It was the location where Toroa the Awful and Psianop the Inexhaustible Stagnation agreed to have their showdown.

A match at close quarters where both combatants could display the full extent of their abilities. Aureatia had marked this plaza as a potential location for the Sixways Exhibition's matches, and the shops tasked with furnishing the event proper had chartered the surrounding residences as seats for the audience.

As he checked the condition of the sand he felt under the sole of his shoe, Mizial unloaded the cloth sacks piled up in the carriage bed.

He didn't have much time to prepare. He needed to complete everything before the night was over.

"Hmm, hmm, hmmmm, hmm-hmm, hmm."

Nevertheless, the preparations simply involved scattering the white powder inside the bags over the battleground. Large-scale schemes weren't in his nature, and it was too much of a pain to push the responsibility for making it all happen onto someone else. As a result, Mizial had thought up an act of sabotage that was possible just with his own individual strength.

Something Mizial could handle while humming to himself, while also fully aware he should be making sure that no one nearby found out about his actions. He was a mediocre child in most senses of the word, but in one particular way, he possessed talent that far exceeded anyone else.

It was the talent of self-assurance.

When he attended the Twenty-Nine Officials meetings,

surrounded by a silent pressure that tried to make the young boy conform, he had never once showed any diffidence or atrophy.

Unafraid of powerlessness or futility, he was able to gain knowledge on the power he needed as it interested him.

Even on the battlefield, facing off against a self-proclaimed demon king, he was capable of charging alone deep into the enemy's camp, like a runaway carriage, cutting his way through and taking the enemy general's head with his own Aureatian general hands.

It was because of this talent that Mizial the Iron-Piercing Plumeshade continued to be the youngest, and in some senses the most peculiar, general among the Twenty-Nine Officials.

"......Ah."

The voice didn't belong to Mizial. It was a faint voice, like the whispers of a butterfly, that he could hear from the darkness of an alleyway.

Mizial's hands stopped moving, and he shifted his eyes in its direction.

"Hmm? Is someone there? Heeeello?"

Even after being witnessed in the middle of his sabotage, he showed, what was a fair thing to say, no sense of tension whatsoever. His talent of knowing no fear made even his apprehensions toward his own safety extremely diluted.

If anything, the person who appeared out of the shadows was the frightened one.

"U-um, that's you, Mizial, right?" the voice asked, feeble, like a frail birdsong or an infirmed person on their deathbed.

"I—I wondered what you were doing, um......o-out in a place like this... I-it's late at night, so..."

"Oh. Awww, shoot. It's you, Qwell. Shucks."

He could make out her long bangs that covered half of her face—and the large eyes peeking out through the gaps in her hair. Tenth General of Aureatia, Qwell the Wax Flower.

In complete contrast to Mizial, she was a woman with a feeble demeanor, as if she was always terrified. She was the sponsor of Toroa the Awful's opponent tomorrow—Psianop the Inexhaustible Stagnation.

"...Um, so. That bag. What is it?"

"Lime."

Mizial replied without any hint of guilt. Ultimately, she would figure it out if she traced things back to the Miroffa Farming Tools Co. What he had planned on mixing into the sand on the battlefield was calcium oxide, used as an ingredient in soil conditioner.

"It's been on my mind for a while, actually. What'd happen to an ooze if you poured lime over it? Would it dry up alive, after all? Maybe it'd get burned? Makes you wonder, doesn't it, Qwell?"

"Huh...? Wait, but there, that's where Psianop's going to be fighting, right...? Hold on. Th-that's against the rules, right...? A-am I wrong...?"

The reason he had agreed to fight here in the old town plaza instead of the castle garden theater lay in the characteristics of the soil. The sand was fine enough that he could inconspicuously mix calcium oxide in with it.

Even if the opponent was a martial artist beyond all reason, without a minian body shape, the starting base for his techniques was always going to be the earth beneath his feet. The calcium oxide reaction, producing heat by absorbing moisture, would prove fatal to an ooze during both parts of the process.

"I mean, it won't hurt any of the citizens, right? What's the big deal? Wanna help me, Qwell? It's gonna be fun, trust me."

There was no deceit in his words. Nor did he doubt that Toroa the Awful would come out victorious, either.

It was pure curiosity. He wanted to see if things would play out that way, even for the unrivaled ooze champion. That was his sole reason.

Having spent his formative years with a cold and distant elder, even now at sixteen, Mizial was more childish than other kids his age, and he never corrected his immature behavior.

"Um, well, I—I don't think you should do that..."

"Why? Actually... What're you doing here yourself, Qwell?"

Their positions were of a criminal and an eyewitness, but his attitude made it seem like the exact opposite. At the very least, Mizial didn't think that being seen by her would deal him a significant blow.

Exactly as she appeared at first glance, Qwell's personality wasn't one fixated on gaining power. She shouldn't have been overly concerned about whether Psianop won.

"Huh...? Wait. Th-they said traps and ambushes were all fair game, right? Wh-what then, um...is weird about me being here...?"

"......"

Mizial realized he had misjudged her entirely.

A loud clang reverberated around them.

Mizial finally became aware of the fact that Qwell was holding a weapon. In other words, she came there with the possibility of combat in mind from the start.

The thick blade, seemingly capable of slicing through heavy armored cavalry, horse and all, glittered on top of the stone pavement. It was a long-handled silver ax, boasting such a colossal size that a person of ordinary strength wouldn't possibly be able to lift its handle.

"Um, well, s-so that means...I—I can do that stuff, too, right......?"

"......C'mon now, Qwell! Let's not do this."

Mizial was half smiling while he took out his balance-weight-like weapons, which were suspended from strings.

Holding them between both fingers, the weapons traced slight arcs before they began to spin.

"The Twenty-Nine Officials...can't be fighting among themselves, right?"

He had the gift of self-assurance. He gave his remark knowing well enough the gap in fighting strength between the two of them.

Mizial was in an unusual position among the Twenty-Nine Officials, but Qwell was an exceptional case, in a different sense.

A breeze came, brushing aside Qwell's long bangs, and he got a peek at her other eye for just a brief moment.

It was then he learned that the big, round iris emitted a silver glow.

...She was a minia, the same as the rest of the Twenty-Nine

Officials. At the very least, her outward appearance and government registry dictated as much.

"Ah...M-Mizial. Um......don't tell me...you think, just because we're both members of the Twenty-Nine, you won't get killed? Oh dear..."

"Huh? What......? What're you talking about?"

Qwell's tone still maintained the same shaking helplessness to it, but the ax she gripped in both hands as she spoke took a sharp path upward, instantly raised over her head.

Mizial took a single step backward. Now that he had made an enemy of her, the probability of his sabotage's success was essentially zero.

Below her bangs, she flashed a bashful smile.

"......*Tee-hee*... Just kidding. I was joking."

The Tenth General, Qwell the Wax Flower.

Excluding Rosclay the Absolute, she was said to have the greatest individual fighting strength among all the Twenty-Nine Officials.

"I promise I won't kill you."

◆

The first match, signaling the beginning of the Sixways Exhibition, was held right as it struck midday.

The craftsmen and merchants all finished up the day's work earlier than usual. In the old town, the stage for the first match, street stalls thronged the area for the spectators looking to grab an early lunch before the match, and all the shops that set up there raked in profits that more than offset the tremendous stall tax levied by Aureatia.

Street performers scattered gaudy rainbows of confetti, and the royal winds band delighted the citizenry's ears.

The uproar was more magnificent than any festival held in Aureatia before, but as the time drew closer, little by little...step by step...it quieted down into what was almost a tense stillness.

The first match. Toroa the Awful versus Psianop the Inexhaustible Stagnation.

It was Toroa the Awful. Most people had heard his name in ghost stories from a young age, or someone from a far-off town would claim they saw the aftermath of some butchery, and if it was caused by a gruesome murderer with a single sword, there was always the suspicion that the sword was actually one of Toroa's enchanted blades.

Did he really exist? Was this the genuine article? Just what did he look like?

The air was still and silent, as if frozen in terror. Curiosity accompanied with terror.

A special event to wholeheartedly draw the eyes and ears of the citizens from the first day of the competition. Aureatia's strategy had been minutely planned out, starting with the decision to place Toroa the Awful in the first match.

...Amid the tense atmosphere, someone spoke up.

"It's an ooze..."

It was the entrance to the battlefield on the opposite end of where Toroa the Awful was supposed to appear.

The creature, protected by Aureatian guards as it walked through the crowd, was a transparent protoplasm with no fixed form—unmistakably an ooze.

No one could believe their eyes. This was supposed to be Toroa the Awful's opponent, Psianop the Inexhaustible Stagnation, then?

"…You fought somewhere yesterday?" the ooze, continuing on to the battlefield, asked Qwell walking behind him.

"Eh?! Wh-what?" the Tenth General replied, puzzled. Doing her utmost to avoid contact with the crowd around her, she was casting her eyes, hidden behind her thick bangs, at the ground more than usual.

"Um. How did you know...?"

"Be stranger not to pick up from someone's mannerisms if they had been in a fight the day prior. Combat is an exercise done with one's full body and soul. More marks left behind than just scars and fatigue."

"Y-you got me…… That's right. A little scrap with Mizial… last night…"

The reality that she had, for the past three days, disappeared somewhere for the whole night, did not go unnoticed to Psianop. Her opponent, the Twenty-Second General, Mizial, had been part of Toroa's camp. It was fair to see it as proof that there was an exchange of some pre-match sabotage.

For this past small month, Psianop had been attacked twice by soldiers of unknown affiliation. The other participants were likely in the same situations themselves—so long as they weren't on the side of the perpetrators.

"Then did you lay some sort of trap, Qwell?"

"...I—I didn't do anything."

"You sure about that?"

"Th-the Sixways Exhibition...isn't going to be decided by one's skill, but with trickery, so...," Qwell replied in a high-pitched voice.

However, it was different somewhat from her normal tone, filled with passion.

"I can't think up that sort of stuff, but...I—I can put a stop to it. That's why I stood guard the whole time."

"Schemes are another form of strength. There are times when not fighting is the real victory."

"...But! That's not what *real* strength is!"

Psianop stopped and looked back at Qwell.

The long-handled war ax that she had used across countless battles was trembling as she hugged it close in her arms.

"That's why, Psianop, you...! Y-you wouldn't want to use any tricks, even if they gave you the advantage, right? If—if you're really proud of your mighty strength...th-then all that's, *tee-hee-hee*......nonsense. B-because, it's not genuine..."

"......"

"...I haven't used any tricks. Please believe me."

It wasn't a coincidence that Psianop had met Qwell. He had left his home believing such a person had to be out there.

Someone who brushed aside the brilliant glory of the past, as well as race or outward appearances resembling themselves...

who espoused pure strength, was guaranteed to arise during a long-lasting age of strife. Psianop believed in his own strength, trusting that such a person was bound to choose him.

"Makes no difference."

His enemy was a living legend. He was bound to be strong. There wasn't likely to be anyone who would doubt his strength.

To Psianop, set to challenge the true legend of this age, this "hero," this living legend, would serve as his benchmark.

"I'll win. That's the way I see it."

◆

Slightly earlier in the day.

"Awww... I ended up looking super uncool. A huge failure."

The Twenty-Second General Mizial, returning to the mansion that morning, had both arms and his right toes brutally broken, and after being left unable to use a carriage, he opened up the door and immediately collapsed.

Toroa, hearing the whole picture of his plans to defeat the ooze, was totally appalled, but at the same time, he was impressed that a child like him would think up such a clever trick.

"Sorry, Toroa. It would've been so fun if things went better, too. Definitely can't hope to beat Qwell, either."

"I don't want an apology. I never knew about any of this in the first place."

"That's not what I mean."

Since Mizial's broken arms were in a fixed position, he couldn't even get out of bed with his own strength. The fact that the tone of his voice was completely unchanged from the night before came as a result of his innate impudence.

"Toroa, you came here because you wanted to fight Alus the Star Runner, right? You can't afford to waste your time fighting someone like Psianop, then."

"…That's true. That's the meaning of my existence. I won't die until I can get Hillensingen back."

"It really would've been better to have you fight in the first round, but Hidow had to go and get in the way. I'm not really good with that stuff, to be honest……never have been."

"………Is that what it was?"

He had thought the tournament chart was almost too convenient for him. If he defeated Psianop the Inexhaustible Stagnation, he'd be able to face off against his destined opponent in the second round.

It was all the result of Mizial's pressuring. All for the sake of Toroa the Awful's sole objective. He gave a grim smile. Even given all of that, the idea of trying to easily skip past the first round's fight was an all-too-childish one.

"Psianop…apparently holed up in the Gokashae Sand Sea and spent the whole time on his own, training and disciplining himself."

"…That's not a big deal."

"It is. Since I did the same thing."

How many times had he actually crossed swords with his father? When it came to enchanted sword combat, the answer was zero. If one wielded an enchanted sword, one's enemy would die. Both he and his father didn't want to cut down their only family.

Without any opponents to fight, the days he spent practicing his swings with an enchanted sword all by himself still lingered in his heart.

The tree leaning slightly to the right. The sun rising up, then sinking below, the Wyte Mountains' ridgeline.

Drenched in sweat, and thinking back over the day's results, he'd travel back home with his father, the setting sun lighting the way.

…Within it all was the loneliness found from the spiritual search for truth.

Whether he was facing a lone ooze or not, Toroa was never going to look down on a martial artist like him.

"Will you be able to see the match?"

"Hmm…… I wonder. I'm all banged up like this, and I'd look super lame if someone was carrying me around, too, but…"

"But you want to see me fight."

"…Yeah. Guess I'll go watch."

Toroa gripped his sword. All the swords he held were enchanted, killing any enemy they were brandished toward.

Against an opponent that he bore no malice, would he be able to use them to cut him down?

I can do it.

He had already confirmed he could do just that amid the swirling Particle Storm.

I am Toroa the Awful.

The masses were silent as they watched the two fighters facing each other. They both stayed silent, but the scene was impossible to look away from. The crowd gazed at one fighter with dread, and they were perplexed by the other.

A clear, resonant voice broke the silence.

"Both sides shall agree to the accords of the true duel!"

Standing between both combatants was a solemn woman who appeared rigid and sturdy.

She was Aureatia's Twenty-Sixth Minister, tasked with observing the match, Meeka the Whispered.

"If one of the combatants is knocked down and doesn't get up, or if one of the combatants forfeits the match on their own, the match will be decided. All matters beyond these two conditions will be impartially judged by me, Meeka the Whispered, as one of Aureatia's Twenty-Nine Officials. Any objections from either of you?!"

"Perfect."

"No objections."

The pair, facing each other at close range, responded.

Toroa the Awful hadn't drawn his sword.

Meeka looked over the two of them with a scowl and withdrew to the top of the recently installed stone staircase.

However, for this true duel…given it was between two fighters like Toroa and Psianop, masters of combat at close quarters, an adjudicator like her wasn't necessary to begin with. For this battle, the final outcome was guaranteed to be clear to all who saw it.

"At the sound of the band's gunshot, you may begin."

Everyone took a big gulp and observed the pair.

Someone began counting off in their mind. *Two, three, then—*

"Half a step slow."

"……"

Psianop let out a bizarre murmur.

Toroa the Awful hadn't yet drawn his sword—

A gunshot.

Both of them stepped forward, and a cyclonic dust cloud flew up in to the air.

Toroa appeared to have swung his enchanted sword and missed, long before it would reach Psianop. However, Psianop dodged, far beyond the sword's reach. It was if he could see the slash's elongated trajectory. Maintaining the same movement speed, he slipped through and struck.

Hit soundly in the liver, Toroa's large body was sent flying two whole houses' distance away. Flipping himself upright in midair, he landed on the ground, his feet leaving behind lines on the ground.

"…Your movements just now."

Though he knew it would leave him disadvantaged, he couldn't help betraying his amazement. Toroa was certain there were no records of any other minian race using this enchanted sword, nor should the ooze have had any opportunities to hear about its abilities.

"Do you know about this sword?"

"You were a half step slow to get in your stance. Therefore, the sword's range was a half step's worth in front of you."

It was the Divine Blade Ketelk.

An enchanted sword that elongated the trajectory of its invisible slash beyond the outer edge of its actual blade, disrupting the range of combat at close quarters.

It was impossible to see the whole attack without being aware of its abilities.

Psianop had dodged it.

"Jab punch."

The name of the ultrafast move, sent out at a speed that outstripped the magic sword, was spoken as though he was centering his mind for the next attack.

The martial artist was the one to connect first.

◆

Toroa the Awful never thought he was strong.

He believed he was weak.

Back when he fervently practiced the sword in the mountains, he never once felt that he had surpassed his father. His assumed opponent was, at all times, a singular imaginary enchanted swordsman, and the inexperienced Toroa always ended up bested by his own ideal.

He was a swordsman being used by enchanted swords. This self-consciousness may have been completely contrary to his opponent Psianop the Inexhaustible Stagnation's many accumulated years of believing in solitude that he was the strongest of all.

It was not himself but the enchanted swords he wielded that were all-powerful, along with the enchanted swordsman who used to brandish them.

...Therefore, he couldn't accept defeat. He couldn't sully their ultimate strength with a pitiful failure. With it, he was a man who had given up his weak self.

...He must not have moved perfectly, either.

It was directly after landing the jab. He felt it in his bones before he even took his first breath.

His fastest possible jab, to hit me just as he evaded Divine Sword Ketelk... If I had been struck harder, that would have ended everything.

Though it seemed like a light feint, he could tell that the blow would be enough to rend the average person's torso asunder with a direct hit. Toroa was able to parry its force and get blown back.

Without making a strong opening step, he had cleared their first clash without dying.

Divine Sword Ketelk created an invisible slash that extended out beyond the blade itself. Naturally, the substance-less slash didn't necessitate a strong opening step. Simply brushing up against an out-of-range opponent's space was enough. The wielder could be a child and still be capable of cleaving a fully armored knight in two.

"...Plan on making amends for your backer's skullduggery?"

Another difficult-to-decipher mumble escaped from Psianop.

Toroa the Awful didn't waver. They were five paces apart.

If Psianop tried to back off farther, he'd be in Inrate, the Sickle of Repose's range. If his opening step came from mid-distance, there was Nel Tseu the enchanted fire sword to bring instant death. Or he would bring him down with Vajgir, the enchanted sword of poison and frost.

"If you're trying to create an opening by talking to me, it won't work. If you take a step into my range, I'll cut you down."

"Range? *Pfft.*"

He still hasn't taken his opening step.

Psianop was aiming for the momentary opening when Toroa swung his enchanted sword. Next time, Toroa would take advantage of Psianop's attack to counter with one of his own.

Not yet...

The enchanted sword dangling from a chain on his waist automatically sprang into the air.

"From the start—"

The ooze's strike, twisting in toward him, dug into Toroa's right clavicle as he tried to release his sword for the counterattack.

A semitranslucent pseudopod wrapped itself around Toroa, burrowing under his armpit and constricting both his shoulders.

He couldn't move.

"You've been in *my* range."

"............!"

He couldn't see it.

Toroa had been closely observing him for any indication of the ooze's movements.

Even Toroa the Awful wasn't able to realize the truth until he was hit with the attack.

Psianop should have already started moving a long time ago.

In the Beyond, it was known as the *shukuchi* technique—or by some as the footless way.

Accelerating not by kicking off the ground, but by shifting one's center of gravity. It was a type of martial arts footwork that applies the speed of collapsing down on a focal point to the first initial step. A movement technique that didn't let the opponent read one's opening motion.

Was there anyone in the world who could possibly be able to read the center of gravity of an ooze's physical body, with its constantly shifting form?

"*Hngh... Mgh!*"

"You didn't have your blade drawn at the start. Why? An attempt to make amends for your dishonesty?"

Toroa was gripping Nel Tseu the enchanted fire sword. While still in his stance to slice forward in front of him with it, both his neck and shoulders were completely immobilized.

If there was indeed an ooze martial artist out in the world, then among their limitless possible choices of attack, the technique worthy of the most fear was not their punches. A set structure was universal among all living creatures. Psianop was the only one capable of unilaterally ignoring that structure and destroying his enemy's physical body.

"*Kata-gatame*. It's the name of this technique."

Toroa was unable to move. His shoulder was blocking his own

carotid. While it was based on a technique described in the books within the sand labyrinth, it had changed completely and was now a technique that resulted in death.

Toroa struggled with the end of his left arm from the elbow down, that he was just barely able to move freely. The enchanted sword of fire dropped powerlessly from his hand.

Psianop was right there in front of him yet remained completely unable to slash him. Even his left elbow had its mobility, able sever Psianop in two, cleverly constrained, leaving him no room to resist.

"……!"

The buzz of the crowd grew distant. This was the end.

No, it's not.

His reason for not drawing his sword at the start wasn't a way to address Mizial's dishonesty. It was because that was Toroa's most powerful stance.

Psianop didn't know the shape that Toroa's accumulated training had taken. He was a living weapons storehouse. Cords. Chains. Hinged mechanisms. No matter where the enchanted sword was tied up on his body, Toroa was always a single motion from being able to draw it.

The diverging combat branches afforded by the sheer number of enchanted swords demanded a close-to-unlimited acumen of the wielder. However, the voices of the enchanted swords would tell him which sword he needed to draw next—

"…!"

Psianop instantly withdrew his pseudopod. A silver flash of an enchanted sword passed right through where they had been.

"...Mol...ting!"

Toroa sliced through his own shoulder.

Not Psianop, escaping during the opening directly after Toroa's motion.

The ooze shifted in to punch with the whole of his body mass. However.

"—Graaah!"

Toroa shouted and intercepted the attack with a swarm of stabs, like beams of light. Countless thrusts all occurring at the exact same time.

There was recoil from one of the stabs. He would skewer Psianop al—

"Is that—"

Getting hit by the thrust, Psianop was sent flying. He murmured.

"—a phantom enchanted sword?"

It hadn't run him through. He had definitely been able to stab him, but there was a peculiar response, almost as if all the stress focused at that one point had been swept away. Psianop had simply been sent flying from the force of the thrust and remained unharmed.

For a surprise attack he had sacrificed his own arm to make, it was an all-too-pitiful result.

However, on the one hand.

"...Hah, gaugh!"

There wasn't a single drop of blood flowing out of Toroa's right shoulder, escaped from the hold. The enchanted sword he used himself to slash this part of his body was already loaded back in its sheath, returned in the single motion of his counterattack moments before.

It could make what it cut reverse back as if it had never been pierced at all. If there was one specific situation in real combat to utilize such a special technique, it was to escape from restraints. An atypical enchanted sword, shaped like a machine part component—Gidymel the Minute Hand.

This hidden technique, called Molting, was the only one that could actually materialize Gidymel the Minute Hand's functionality of prolonging or fully rejecting causality.

"......Will you be able to dodge—"

Without even a breath's pause, Psianop went on the move. Toroa had drawn his next enchanted sword. The slash of the blade still proved too far to reach. Though, it was not the elongated slash of the Divine Sword Ketelk from before.

"—from this distance, Inexhaustible Stagnation?!"

An inescapable tempest wind assailed Psianop. Mushain the enchanted wind sword. Psianop couldn't hold his ground where he stood. At the same time, Toroa kicked up the enchanted fire sword at his feet. He triggered its secret technique.

"Gathering...Clouds!"

The heat, flowing into the swirling current of air, birthed flames with a frightening directional range. The buildings of the old town collapsed just from the shock wave. The audience loosed clamorous screams.

He's gone. Where's Psianop?

Toroa swung the enchanted wind sword directly to his side to counterattack.

A needlelike kick descended in from that direction and was repelled after hitting a point along the sword hilt.

The wire that connected the enchanted wind sword to his back was severed.

"Shook up, weren't you? From your own attack."

Psianop had leaped from the momentum of the first gust—kicking off the edge of a building and being assaulted from the sky—and contorted himself into the exact shape of a bullet to break through the air resistance.

"*You're* thinking that you don't want to get the city involved in the fight."

"Quiet......!"

Wailsever. Toroa drew the enchanted weapon with its crystal blade. The sword's vibrations sent out an invisible force, similar to a sonic wave, however, Psianop deflected it with a minimal parry and closed the distance between them. A powerful strike to the chest. Drilling destruction. Breaking through the door of what once seemed to be a merchant's shop, he crashed hard on the pile of old desks.

"*Gnhaugh!*"

The moment the strike found its mark, it had been disrupted

by Wailsever's wave of vibration. He was holding out right on the verge of losing his life.

Psianop spoke.

"You'll send out that illusionary stab again."

The countless piercing thrusts he sent out just as he was getting back up was an illusion from Downpour's Needle. Psianop was no longer deceived by it. He slipped through and evaded the attack.

Movement. The sound of cutting through the air. His sight lines. He was always gauging his enemies, making predictions more difficult than seeing the path of a bullet, yet proving accurate all the same.

It was inches in front of him. The multi-spiral pseudopod sent out a knife-hand strike. He intercepted.

Sword of poison and frost...

The pseudopod, formed into a true blade, tracked an amorphous path and evaded the enchanted sword of poison and frost that Toroa had launched in sync with his opponent's breathing. He blocked the slash closing in on his head with Downpour's Needle. He was blown backward. An instantaneous heavy strike that nearly broke Downpour's Needle itself. Shattering the wooden wall, he was once again lying inside one of the buildings.

In the middle of his attack, Psianop had dodged Toroa's own. With an ooze's body, did that mean he was even capable of evading attacks perfectly timed to strike when his own attack was about to land? Above that, he...had distinctly dodged the enchanted sword of poison and frost.

Just as he had with Wailsever. He was discerning the characteristics of enchanted swords Toroa had never shown him.

"Enchanted swords only have two kinds of functionality," Psianop declared as he smoothly slid out from the burst-open building wall.

"A function that lets you easily hit an opponent—and a function to kill an opponent when it connects. The functions of any sword generally don't go much beyond that to begin with."

This was the unknown member of the First Party.

Deciding to grow stronger by making use of all the things his body was capable of, he had also mastered flustering and inciting his opponent with his words. A technique that Toroa did not possess.

"...Think you'll be able to remain unhit......up until the end?"

The enchanted sword of poison and frost in his right hand. Downpour's Needle in his left.

"Go ahead and try."

"Don't take me lightly. I saw the abilities of that phantom thrusting sword just now. You dazzle your opponent's visual judgment by mixing a thrust attack in with the entrancing illusion and then launch a lethal attack from the enchanted sword in your other hand."

They were in a narrow alleyway, with tall buildings flanking them on both sides. As he continued to speak, Psianop closed the distance between them.

"You centered your gravity diagonally behind you, didn't you? If you pulled out that sword with the long-range slash, you'd probably reach me at this distance. But if I happen to read its trajectory and get in close, you're not going to be able to shift to defense with that sword."

He mercilessly drew in closer. This was the pressure exuded by the ooze, a race none of the minian races had ever concerned themselves with.

"The enchanted swords that can handle both guarding and attacking are that sound wave sword and the two types of illusion swords. But I've already hit the phantom thrusting sword with two of my strikes. I'll be able to shatter it with one more, no matter how well you manage to block it."

There was truth in Psianop's words. Something that the enchanted sword wielder himself knew most of all.

He couldn't block Psianop's attacks with Downpour's Needle anymore. However, Wailsever, with its blade of crystal, would be similarly destroyed if he used it to block one of the ooze's attacks.

"And I'm only two more steps away from being in your range."

Before he had finished speaking, Psianop dashed forward. Toroa stabbed at him with the phantom thrusting sword. While evading the attack, Psianop lightly brushed the cart along the side of the alley.

"Disordered Flock!"

"It's useless!"

Psianop flowed inside Toroa's attack range. He slashed down from above with the enchanted sword of poison and frost. The cart flying in blocked the attack. Toroa's Herculean strength sent the splintered remains of the cart scattering in all directions.

The lethal blade ultimately didn't reach, after all.

Had he calculated the exact trajectory to guard against his enchanted sword and threw the loaded cart up into the air? Psianop had only lightly touched it while he was mid-dodge. Toroa couldn't see at all as the ooze had the complete flow of his power directly under his will.

"If you're trying to tire me out—"

Maintaining his favorable distance, Psianop continued to speak.

A strike. He was trying to seize hold of Toroa's joints, even if he evaded the attack. He could dodge the two punches, aiming at different places simultaneously, but then the fourth, then sixth, attacks would chain together after them. Psianop's movements were completely inscrutable, and with his terrifying mobility, he was always literally one step ahead.

He'd survive at sword distance. He retreated.

"That's because you're panicking. Right, Toroa the Awful?"

"...You're a real chatty ooze...!"

He had gotten out of the *kata-gatame* that Psianop had used on Toroa a few moments ago.

However, when Psianop was using it, the technique was one of instant death. If Toroa had stayed in that position for just another breath longer, Toroa would have been destroyed without any external wounds to speak of or, even worse, ended up dead from the blood flow to his head being cut off.

Should he instantly escape it, he would be unable to close the seam he'd open with his escape.

From birth, the notions of exhaustion and fatigue had been foreign concepts to him.

Nevertheless, the strikes from Psianop the Inexhaustible Stagnation, together with the precision of their force, quite literally surpassed any weapon.

Even the vitality of the monster that came back from hell would reach its limits eventually.

One move was lethal. As he held out against that one move, he was being pushed up against a wall. He was deteriorating.

"Again with the enchanted fire sword. Block with the hilt."

He's holding the advantage.

Toroa cleaved sideways with the enchanted fire sword. With the hit, Psianop evaded the trajectory of the sword's instant death and launched a punch at Toroa. A lighter punch than the one before—however, he was still launched into the air.

In midair, if I defend—

The ooze was right in front of his eyes. The *shukuchi* technique. The flurry of punches he launched right afterward thrust into him. He coughed up blood. A rib broke and cut into his flesh. Another punch came right after.

"Am I correct in my estimation, Toroa the Awful?"

If I could just—just manage to kill the momentum of the hit.

He blocked with an enchanted sword hilt. His arms and central line were all he was protecting.

Everything happened exactly as Psianop had said it would. He had foreseen everything. Whenever Toroa tried to make a move, Psianop was already there, one step ahead of him. If he didn't continue to handle him with his enchanted sword techniques, or without Toroa's tenacious physique, one attack likely had enough power to scatter his body and limbs in all directions.

He's too...strong!

"There's the wall."

With Psianop's single sentence, he knew.

There were words to make him waver. However, it was the truth. Toroa could no longer escape from the impact of his punches.

The ooze was right before his eyes. He couldn't escape.

Death was—

"Not...yet!"

Toroa's giant body flew straight up into the air without any warning. The wedge that had flown up onto the roof of one of the buildings was pulling up Toroa's body itself with its invisible magnetic force as he gripped the hilt in his hands.

The previous punch had been blocked with an enchanted sword hilt. It may have looked like a sword with only a hilt and no blade—splitting the blade from the hilt into numerous wedge shapes and controlling them with magnetic force, the name of the enchanted sword was Wicked Sword Selfesk.

Psianop could instantly maneuver in any possible direction, without betraying any initial motion whatsoever. However, even still, as long as he was a hand-to-hand fighter, there would always be one position that'd become a blind spot.

He's reading—

The enchanted swordsman of horror stories was looking down at the city from the air.

He's reading all my movements. But that doesn't mean he's seen through all my secret techniques.

Causality rejection from Molting. Wicked Sword Selfesk and its main body made from invisible magnetic force. There were secret techniques among his enchanted swords that even Psianop, continuously taking the initiative against any and all actions, couldn't completely see through.

A respite of one second—

In which case, the only way for his enchanted swords to best Psianop...

Let's see how you handle multiple swords at once!

He drew his enchanted sword.

"Wailsever."

He drew his enchanted sword.

"Wicked Sword Selfesk."

He drew two more.

"Divine Sword Ketelk. Nel Tseu the enchanted fire sword."

Two swords for each arm. Every last ounce of his remaining energy needed to be spent on delivering the final blow. Down below, at Psianop the Inexhaustible Stagnation...four swords, all at once.

"Four-chain attack! Song of Feather Swarm!"

The crystal blade trembled, and Wailsever released a vibrating shock. There was some slight interference preventing it from being an effective attack from this distance, but it arrived faster than Psianop could take his opening step. In that second that Psianop was prevented from making his initial move, the Wicked

Sword Selfesk showered him in a rain of wedge blades. Psianop deflected the wedges coming from his right side. It wasn't over.

Raining down on him, mixed in with the hail from Selfesk, was Nel Tseu the enchanted fire sword, thrown from Toroa's hands. It didn't directly hit its mark. However, an intense amount of heat poured into the spot where it landed and exploded—the secret technique Gathering Clouds. Devastating, fatal, power.

Adding to it all, a long-range thrust from the heavens to the ground below. The secret technique of Divine Sword Ketelk, known as—Peck.

A shock wave attack. Blocking him off. An explosion. And then…

All of it… Every single motion was done the instant Toroa jumped into the air and fell back down to the ground.

In other words, it meant it was the same exact moment when Psianop made his assessment.

Psianop *approached Toroa*. With impossibly explosive force, he kicked against the wall and jumped up in Toroa's direction. The only direction where the unexpected course threw off the aim of the thrusting attack—and the explosion on the ground nor the blades closing in on him could not reach.

From the heavens and from the earth, the unarmed and the fully clad swords, face-to-face.

"The long-range thrust… That special technique—"

It was all over in an instant. It was an instantaneous judgment.

Therefore, it was then that Psianop knew. The sword Toroa had gripped in his hand wasn't the Divine Sword Ketelk.

"—was a feint?!"

Yelling out a secret technique and brandishing a sword didn't necessarily mean it was what he had used. The Lance of Faima. Now had come the time he could utilize it properly.

There was viscous sawing sound.

A vibrating slash. Right as they passed by each other, it destroyed Psianop's body, cutting it into tiny pieces of flesh.

"Flapping."

Landing back on the ground, he opened his eyes.

Toroa the Awful heaved a deep sigh.

"*Hng......aah.*"

Psianop's soft body was rent, and the percolating liquid wet the sand of the plaza.

Just what sort of special technique was it?

The Lance of Faima reacted to anything that approached Toroa at high speed.

Using the automatic powers it utilized to hound its target, he turned his wrist right and left over and over again, like a pendulum of terrifying speed, and cut into his approaching enemy with its superspeed swings.

"Just," the heavily wounded Psianop muttered.

The ultimate martial artist, seeing through every attack that came his way and evading them all, was finally dealt a decisive blow.

"...Just, three left."

A terrifying enemy.

The meaning of his low mumbling, like the foreboding of a death god, was clear to Toroa, too. Psianop was counting how many bullets his opponent had left over.

Vajgir, the enchanted sword of poison and frost. Karmic Castigation. Inrate, the Sickle of Repose. There were three enchanted swords Toroa had yet to use in their match. He had never shown this many of his enchanted swords, not even to the Particle Storm, not even to Mestelexil the Box of Desperate Knowledge.

"......You're strong."

No. I'm just weak.

At this point, there was nothing more. His skill was an imitation of a past enchanted swordsman. Simultaneously deploying everything at once had been the sole, extreme limit of his dedication, that Toroa the Awful had arrived at himself.

Even then, even after laying out all the strength he himself could muster.

It still wasn't enough to take his life, huh?

Deploying a total of five enchanted swords' ultimate techniques, and he remained unable to kill one single ooze.

At this point, there was nothing more. *Nothing that he himself could do.*

"...Giving up?"

He wasn't talking to Psianop. The rebuking question escaped his throat.

After using up all his strength, the fight was going to end with it not being enough. If he was a lone fighter, then perhaps it would have been fine to arrive at such an end. But he was shouldering the name of Toroa the Awful.

He couldn't give up.

"Not yet... I'm...I'm still here. Not yet..."

His opponent was unbelievably strong. Likely even stronger than his father. A powerful fighter isolated to the realm of the fantastical.

If he entrusted himself completely to the enchanted swords, could he win? More than he ever had before.

"Don't leave me behind. I... I am, Toroa the Awful!"

Toroa the Awful had never once believed he was strong.

He believed he was weak.

It was not himself but the enchanted swords he wielded that were all-powerful, along with the enchanted swordsman who used to brandish them.

...Therefore, he couldn't accept defeat. He couldn't sully their ultimate strength with a pitiful defeat. With it, he was a man who had given up his weak self.

"Found some serenity of mind, did you......?"

Psianop's voice sounded far off in the distance. Toroa the Awful's breathing was deep and long.

The history of enchanted swords was a history of slaughter. Someone had made them, someone had wielded them, and there was one who cut them all down. Just as fatigue and scars were not the only evidence of a fight, all their histories had clearly been carved inside the enchanted swords. He thought about the scary stories of Toroa the Awful that people continued to pass down to one another.

A monstrosity. He would become an enchanted sword monstrosity.

If such a monstrosity did exist in this world, it wouldn't lose to anyone.

Psianop moved. He acted faster than Psianop's figure was reflected inside his brain's consciousness. Molting. Divine Sword Ketelk's superspeed long-range thrust. It didn't hit Psianop. However, with the superspeed long-range thrust still extending, when he then reaped sideways with the Divine Sword Ketelk—

"......!"

Behind Psianop, a residential building was severed in half from the second floor up. Still keeping the elongated enchanted sword in his hands, Toroa closed the distance himself. Psianop released a lethal punch. Toroa stuck the enchanted flame sword in the ground and sent both himself and his enemy flying with a violent burst of wind.

"You think if you clear your mind of thoughts..."

With it, Psianop was blown backward, in the direction of the debris from the cleaved residential house—

"...that I won't still be able to read them?"

The large mass of a full house floor, moments before it would've made contact with Psianop, shifted its direction directly to the side and dug itself into the plaza. Tearing up all the cobblestones as it went, it crashed into the fountain and broke apart. The audience's screams echoed through the old town.

Such was the power contained within Psianop's punches.

"Graaaaugh...!"

Toroa let out a bestial roar from deep within his throat.

His forward-leaning battle posture lowered even deeper, and the hilts of Nel Tseu the enchanted fire sword and Wicked Sword

Selfesk were thrust into the ground, like the legs of a quadrupedal animal.

◆

He had killed people before.

Though they were bandits who had swarmed in to plunder his father's enchanted swords, he had cruelly killed them, foes someone like Toroa could've handled without any need for death.

In the pages of history, many enchanted swordsmen had stained their hands with mass slaughter. The ones who did so on the battlefield were known as champions, while those who did so in peaceful villages were known as horrifying murderers.

Toroa understood these wielders' thoughts. All enchanted swords existed to cut others down, and the ones who held them allowed them to do that. As long as they held the form of a sword, they'd never once be used to save an enemy's life.

Controlling the enchanted swords gripped in either hand like the legs of a bug, he jumped off the ground, then off the walls.

His right leg reacted automatically to Psianop's intercepting attack, and he cleaved across with the sword attached to it.

The slash had definitely connected and slid off Psianop's surface as though the power behind it had been swept away. The counterattack was coming. Toroa hurled the enchanted fire sword into the air.

Once again, he caused an explosion and mixed himself up in the blast.

Raising his head from his quadrupedal stance, he looked at his enemy. The enemy. The Enemy—the crowd. There were so many people looking at his enchanted swords. So many people looking at Toroa the Awful. Toroa must have looked on the same way himself.

"*Grrrrrrrrr...*"

Kill them all. The voices of the enchanted swords were yelling at him.

That was his true gift—accepting and taking in all the enchanted swords' thoughts. It didn't hurt. His body felt far lighter than when he fought while holding on to his own consciousness.

"...I'm right here."

For reasons unknown to him, his enemy Psianop informed Toroa where exactly he was.

The enchanted swords' bloodlust, scattering among the roars of the crowd, once again converged at a single point.

Twisting his body, he threw Wailsever. It flew faster than a bullet.

"......!"

The sonic wave's impact was repelled. He didn't need to think. Toroa once again threw himself at his enemy.

It felt almost as if his own physical body had become one with the enchanted swords. Nel Tseu the enchanted fire sword. Downpour's Needle. Vajgir, the enchanted sword of poison and frost. Downpour's Needle—

A monstrosity. He would become an enchanted sword monstrosity.

The cluster of slashes he sent out simultaneously pierced through three buildings, destroying them.

The tremendous explosion came three times.

The debris, the fragments, fluttered. Amid the vortex of destruction, unable to even make out his enemy's silhouette, Toroa the Awful was sneering.

"I kill people who simply witness what I do. Innocent people."

As he watched his own rampage, as if the work of someone else, this was what he pondered. Had his father wished for that—and thus done so from the start?

Maybe, in fact, his father had been the same, too.

Had he wanted to ensure that the victims of his enchanted swordsmanship hadn't died in vain?

If that was the case... As long as he, too, remained Toroa the Awful, we would do the same.

◆

That's not it.

Toroa was aware. He had been heavily burned by his own enchanted swords' ability.

If he was his normal self, this wouldn't have happened. His arm automatically drew his next sword. Psianop closed the distance to try to forestall him. From the ooze's flank came wedge blades swarming in like locusts.

The blade of the Wicked Sword Selfesk had been scattered by the previous attack. It had then turned into a storm, swirling in a vortex of magnetic force.

Destruction filled the streets. The roadside trees were hewed before being completely cut to splinters inside its circular radius.

Is this how an enchanted sword fights?

"Unsophisticated! Sophomoric! You're just—"

Psianop irately muttered as he smacked down each of the blades flying in at him. Toroa himself knew the meaning of the ooze's words. It was simply destruction. It wasn't power that could truly defeat his enemy. The enchanted fire sword moved Toroa. To induce an explosion with its maximum size of Gathering Clouds possible—aimed at Psianop.

Engulfing the audience watching the match with it.

I can't do it. After all, I'm just—

Right before it could happen, Toroa punched his own right arm with his left. He sent the enchanted fire sword flying. The explosive flames, bursting in midair, were led toward the canal, running through the iron railing and vaporizing the waters enough to see the river's bottom.

"...Toroa the Awful. You're—"

"...Just using techniques borrowed from another."

"Hmph."

"That's what you were going to say, eh, Psianop?"

Even if he sent the force of the previous secret technique at Psianop, he was convinced it wouldn't have brought him victory.

It was simple destructive force that meaninglessly spread injury and harm.

If he did that, it'd be just the same as when he killed those bandits on Wyte Mountain.

"You're strong. I didn't realize such a master swordsman existed beyond the First Party."

"I'll surpass you."

Toroa's own honed skills, nor his rampage from entrusting his whole self to his enchanted swords, had not been enough to surpass Psianop.

He knew he had to stop clinging so hard to being his own self. But at the same time, he couldn't surrender control over to something outside himself.

Mushain the enchanted wind sword. Nel Tseu the enchanted fire sword. I've lost two. I don't have the time to gather Wicked Sword Selfesk's scattered blades back together again, either. In that case...I have only one way left to settle this.

In the next moment, as Toroa brought his breathing under control, Psianop was closing in. Even after being deeply gouged by Disordered Flock, he didn't think twice at all about rushing back into combat at close quarters. Therein lay his strength.

The enchanted sword of poison and frost.

The automatically counterattacking Lance of Faima's chain was gripped hard and stopped in its tracks. The Disordered Flock technique had hit Psianop precisely because, in that one moment, it was a perfectly unexpected attack. Psianop's pseudopod pulled the chain toward him. He would break Toroa's stance…a goal that the enchanted swordsman had read perfectly. He had already cut off the chain from its base.

Psianop. You're strong. It's not only the fierceness of your offense, either. Right now… I don't think there's anyone in the world who could out-read you.

Psianop continued his merciless onslaught, and Toroa handled his attacks.

Maybe, if I were Alus the Star Runner.

The thought suddenly crossed his mind. He was in the midst of a magnificent battle, so why did he have the composure for thoughts like that?

If he were Alus the Star Runner, soaring through the sky, then he probably wouldn't have kept letting his opponent into melee range—but was that really so?

Psianop had completely read all the enchanted swords nigh impossibly unpredictable techniques and showed that he could rush up into the air without a foothold. Even Toroa would have done the same in order to bring down Alus the Star Runner.

His opponent had read his slash. Sent flying, Toroa's body crashed through a residential house's wall.

They'd either open up space or slip inside each other's range. Reacting with razor-thin room to spare, they both avoided instant death.

…Nevertheless, there was a clear point of difference between the start of the fight and now.

A simultaneous four-point jab. He'll slam the blade from the side and turn it away. Aiming for my liver.

It was the flow of Toroa's thoughts.

"Won't step forward. Drawing attention with a step to the right."

Toroa the Awful's breathing still remained deep and long.

Circling around from the right, Psianop tried to grab Toroa's joints. Toroa could tell.

"As little ground contact as possible, kicking—"

"You think—"

He dodged the incoming blow. He avoided a fatal wound without forcing his slash to meet the attack. Psianop's motions remained impenetrable. Not everything went exactly as Toroa had predicted.

"You think you're going to read *my* movements instead?!"

His technique and enchanted swords were both inherited from his father.

Where then did Toroa the Awful's true strength, his own strength, lie?

No. Dad told me. I should've known from the very start.

That his overly kind disposition took in the thoughts of the enchanted swords and was hindering his own technique.

Toroa had begun to track Psianop's agility as he slipped past Toroa's defenses, not allowing any moment to react.

It was the same feeling he had when he faced the Particle Storm. When Toroa had fought Mestelexil, commanding an endless supply of unknown weaponry, it felt as if Toroa knew everything down to where his opponent's gun barrel would aim next.

I get it. I understand.

He knew that terrifying golem was a child who loved his mother.

Or he understood that the heartless ooze held a lot of pride in his own strength.

He didn't have supernatural senses like Clairvoyance. Nor was the tremendous amount of combat experience accumulated within the enchanted swords the actual memories of the battles he himself had fought and won. However, it was enough to face off against the enemy in front of him and continue fighting.

Toroa the Awful *was able to take in thoughts and ideas.*

His enemy's will, their wishes.

…That's right. My thoughts and ideas aren't necessary. But I know that isn't this the complete picture. There's meaning in having me be here. From this completely limitless accumulation of these enchanted swords' thoughts and ideas…the one truly making the choices is me.

Psianop's fist drew in close to his heart. He suppressed the attack with a side blow from a hilt and responded with the enchanted sword of poison and frost. The pseudopod morphed and, from a tight distance, ripped apart the armor on Toroa's gauntlet. The intuition-led swing followed closely after Psianop's atypical dodge. Shattering a wall, Psianop opened up space between them. Toroa ran in pursuit. A flash of the Divine Sword Ketelk—and the large storehouse above its elongated attack was cut in two.

Psianop once again sneaked inside Toroa's range. But he followed up with Disordered Flock. The ooze handled the attack. Then he dodged. Toroa pulled back moments before Psianop could grab the sword tip.

The sky was above them. Dashing through the streets, at the other end of the numerous obstacles he destroyed or slipped past, he realized he had made it outside at some point.

He could see a carriage in the distance. He knew there was someone watching over the match from inside.

It was Mizial.

He's...

Diagonally in front to his right. Kicking off the wall and coming straight into Toroa's reach. The enemy moved exactly as Toroa had predicted.

...caught up.

The thoughts and ideas he saw...had at last responded completely to the most strange and atypical of martial artists.

At this point, there was nowhere higher to go.

Not for himself.

Nor even for his enchanted swords.

In that case, he'd take in Psianop's thoughts and ideas, too.

Go ahead and read me. All the swords in the world. All the skill throughout history. I'm not alone. Go ahead! Try reading all the enchanted swordsman who came before me!

He sent out Downpour's Needle. Disordered Flock, the illusionary thrusting technique that he had demonstrated many times over. It would hit Psianop's interception head-on, smashing and breaking its true form. He understood that was what the ooze would do.

The trajectory of the phantoms created by the sword grew chaotic, filling up Psianop's entire line of sight with wild abandon.

"...!"

Even if the enchanted sword was destroyed, that didn't mean its abilities were lost. It was a technique aiming *to have the sword broken* from the very start. A onetime-use technique, only able to take his enemy by surprise because of the similar techniques he had aimed at the ooze already—Avian Death.

Then.

Then, Toroa the Awful, with his cords. Chains. Hinged mechanisms.

With every conceivable preparation at his disposal, he could send out all of the enchanted swords, wielding them with his whole body.

"Nest...Descent!"

The thrust he launched, prepared to abandoned Downpour's Needle from the start, was replaced halfway through the motion to the enchanted sword with the forked blade—Vajgir, the enchanted sword of poison and frost.

Naturally, it couldn't be connected through Psianop's evasion, reading all of Toroa's attacks ahead of him.

However, the same wasn't so for the blood from his gauntlet that he had sent flowing through the sword blade.

A drop of Toroa's blood that had passed through the thrusting sword blade fell onto Psianop.

Without the opening in the ooze's presence of mind, that he had pried open with Avian Death, even that one droplet wouldn't have found its mark. He knew, too, that Psianop possessed such a level of skill.

He knew. Therefore, he surpassed him.

"Wh-what did you...?! *Augh...!*"

The protoplasm violently expanded outward.

Psianop's body began mutating into a delicate crystal substance.

The enchanted sword of crystallized corrosion that instantly infected and eroded away any organic body that touched its blade. Even a single drop of blood became a transmission agent.

"Did you think...," Toroa the Awful motioned to the champion, unlike any the enchanted swordsmen of history had ever encountered, "...you'd be able to remain undamaged until the very end?"

"Not...yet!"

During the final moments he would be able to act, Psianop rushed to try to get his enemy in range.

Toroa already knew he'd make this choice. His final enchanted sword was Inrate, the Sickle of Repose.

"Chirp!"

"Spear...hand...!"

A flash of a sword. Psianop the Inexhaustible Stagnation was cut across in two.

The Chirp his father learned was a technique that simply used a grip on the base of the scythe's blade to counter extremely close-range attacks. It may have been too simple of a move to truly be designated the enchanted swords' "secret technique."

However, he had etched Downpour's Needle's Distorted Flock in Psianop's consciousness by repeating it over and over again. It was only against opponents conditioned not to believe the visible illusions before them that Inrate, the Sickle of Repose, raising neither wind nor sound, turned into a true threat, one impossible to counterattack.

"Hrngh...! Hah."

Toroa fell on both knees. When Psianop had gotten past his defenses in the ooze's moment of final desperation, he realized both his knees had been punched with a sharp, piercing strike. Spearhand. Terrifying speed, up until the very end.

Making use of every last one of his enchanted swords, he had won.

He couldn't...

"You can't get up," a voice told him from behind. Toroa held out on his almost broken knees and endured. Why?

A sweat, warning him of serious danger, spouted forth on his back.

"You're able to instantly change weapons by rolling your wrist. Given your need to match your arms up with that movement, for those enchanted sword techniques you use... Their essence actually lies not in both your arms, but the footwork, which becomes your base point to shift your weight. Am I correct in my estimation?"

He went to turn around. In the left edge of his sights, half of Psianop's severed body was melting away.

The half that was afflicted by the enchanted sword of poison and frost.

......*In that one moment...*

His opponent was an ooze. Be that as it may, he made that judgment in that split second?

Had he really cut off the half of his body corroded by poison and made such a sublime read of the situation just to avoid having his core cellular nucleus severed in two by the attack?

Was Psianop the Inexhaustible Stagnation capable of such feats?

No. It was impossible. He couldn't have possibly foreseen Toroa's attack.

No matter how simple of an organism an ooze may have been, it should've been alive after losing half of its body volume.

"*Popoperopa. Parpepy. Peep por ppe. Por pupeon. Perpipeor.*" (To Psianop's pulsation. Suspended ripple. Tie the sequence. Full large moon. Circulate.)

There was no way he could still be alive. If he was a normal ooze.

Toroa had been able to trace his opponent Psianop's thoughts.

"Psi...anop...!"

"You may claim to have risen back from hell...Toroa the Awful."

However, Toroa was not the only one who had inherited the thoughts and minds from another before him—

"This technique belonged to Neft the Nirvana."

There wasn't anyone out there who knew all the methods the warrior known as Psianop had at his disposal.

"I-I'm—I'm Toroa the Awful."

"…I neglected to mention, but in the beginning of the match, I punched through your liver. You likely haven't noticed the pain. You kept fighting through ragged breaths. Much like how you used your illusions to guide my actions, I focused my punches on your upper body, so in the decisive moment, you wouldn't be able to protect your lower body."

"Not……yet! Not yet, Toroa…must…!"

"You'll try to attack me. Turn your shoulder, take your step, and that'll be the end of it."

The technique that used the explosive power of his upper body would be finished with just a half of an opening step. Even from this range.

An invisible elongated thrust, narrowed down to a single point and piercing across long distances—the name of the technique was…

"…Peck!"

"My estimations—"

The foot that took his step slipped off the ground.

With it, he collapsed. With just a half step, Toroa the Awful's sight sunk to the ground.

The Divine Sword Ketelk that was supposed to launch the finishing blow slipped out of his hand.

As if both of his legs had been severed in half, he was unable to stand.

"—are absolute."

♦

"...Looks like you won."

They were in a spot unbecoming of a victorious combatant—the shade of an alleyway, hidden from the crowd. Qwell the Wax Flower had her eyes cast to the ground as always as she came out to greet her hero candidate.

For Psianop as well, it served him better to hide from the eyes of the crowd and the other candidates.

"Didn't I tell you that was my estimation of the outcome?"

"Eh-heh... I—I suppose you did...... But um......in the end there, those Life Arts..."

"Who do you think I am? I stand here having learned the techniques of Neft the Nirvana of the First Party. Whether I am torn in half or otherwise, I am immortal."

In fact, there existed no other living creature with a higher aptitude for cellular regeneration Life Arts than the ooze, almost entirely constructed from simple protoplasm. As long as his internal nucleus was left behind, he could regenerate the rest of his body back to almost perfect functionality. He hadn't mastered Life Arts to Neft the Nirvana's level, but when it came to the relative effectiveness of the regeneration itself, he had almost the same degree of immortality that the lycan possessed.

Toroa the Awful had been unable to anticipate it. Before Psianop the Inexhaustible Stagnation, there had never existed an ooze who had mastered such a skill.

"…I knew it. You can win…! S-since you were able to defeat *the* Toroa the Awful…! I'm sure you'll be strongest of all, Psianop…!"

"I'm told it uses five years."

"……Huh?"

"Before this match, I faced a situation that required me to use regenerative Life Arts on this body of mine. I plan on doing the same in the remaining matches as well. With each regeneration, I lose five years of my cellular life span."

He believed it was a worthy battle to do so.

As worthy as the battle with Neft the Nirvana—or perhaps even more so.

"Um, b-but ooze life spans, um…"

"*Hmph.*"

Psianop chuckled.

He had spent twenty-one years in the sand labyrinth. There were four more matches until the finals, and he had used full regeneration once during his battle against Neft.

An ooze's life span was said to last, at most, fifty years.

"…That dwarf was really strong. If that last sword of his possessed an instant-kill technique, I would have been dead. The true duel accords or whatever might be better for Aureatia's purposes, but…"

The final sword, Inrate, the Sickle of Repose, had been an enchanted sword with functionality that made it easier to hit opponents.

It was precisely because it had come directly after he had sent out the enchanted sword of poison and frost, with its instant death functionality, that he anticipated the final two swords didn't share that functionality—all he could do was hope he was right. Either way, in that situation, an all-or-nothing attack was the only choice to get out of danger.

Toroa the Awful had possessed the strength to force him to choose that singular option.

It might have been his haughtiness as the victor.

However, as a someone who wished for an all-out, decisive fight as a warrior, he truly felt it from the bottom of his heart—

"…I'm glad I didn't end up having to kill him."

Match one. Victory goes to Psianop the Inexhaustible Stagnation.

The night after the first match.

Toroa the Awful was carried to the city's central clinic for treatment. A visitor from outside of Aureatia, Toroa didn't have a regular Life Arts doctor with him, either. It was unknown if the severe destruction of both his knees could be fully healed.

"Maaaan. What a bummer."

The young boy sitting at his bedside looked like he might've been more heavily wounded than Toroa.

He was the one who'd backed Toroa as a hero candidate and shared his defeat, Mizial the Iron-Piercing Plumeshade.

"So you weren't the strongest after all, Toroa."

Mizial smiled, in contrast to his tone.

"…Sorry. That I couldn't become the strongest. I wasn't able to make you win, either."

"I just want things to be fun! Ow!"

With his big stretch, Mizial reopened one of his wounds. A child who acted in such a way without thinking of any of the consequences. Toroa was grateful for his usual carefree demeanor, unconcerned with the seriousness of all his wounds.

"But… You probably shouldn't get too close to me from here on out."

"Why?"

"I lost. Everyone here in Aureatia knows this. They'll be ones like those Sun's Conifer types we met before coming to steal these enchanted swords from me."

Perhaps that itself had been one of the reasons for placing Toroa the Awful's match right at the beginning of the Sixways Exhibition. Supposing he did lose in the opening match, anyone devising up a way to steal his swords would be in a very advantageous position.

Because at that point, he *wouldn't be a hero candidate anymore*— and thus forbidden from being attacked.

"…C'mon, you could smack those guys around even if all your limbs were broken, right?"

"They won't be the only ones. There have to be some who knew the extent of my power and never made a move because of it. Those are the real dangerous ones."

He didn't say it clearly in front of Mizial, but Toroa was likely going to be killed.

Even when limiting considerations to powerful players he knew about, if Alus or Mestelexil, for example, stormed in to attack him, in Toroa's current state, there'd be nothing he could do about it.

Also, there had to be someone behind the scenes of this battle working out schemes too in depth for Toroa to possibly fathom.

He suddenly thought back to the Gray-Haired Child he met

in Toghie City. The face of the mastermind who sent the bandit Elgite to fight him and who likely sent Toroa into the Particle Storm turmoil on purpose.

A guy like him... Does he know about those sorts of behind-the-scenes conspiracies, too?

The Gray-Haired Child had talked big about being able to make up for the power Toroa lacked. He had to admit that, right now, that boy was probably the only one he could turn to for help in the current situation.

It'd be utterly absurd if he had gotten in contact with me, knowing this was how things would end up.

By his bedside, Mizial had, in a rare move, been keeping silent, until he finally raised his head.

"In that case, I'll transport you out of Aureatia. The authority of the Twenty-Nine Officials can make that happen. That way..."

"And how many days will the preparations for that take? Besides, if the person after these is serious, they wouldn't hesitate to chase after me outside the city. You don't need to be so concerned with me. You're not my sponsor anymore, right?"

Toroa hadn't given up. If anything, he needed to keep Mizial at a distance in order to fight it out until the end. It was possible that a marauder could show up in his hospital room at any moment.

"I don't wanna. I'll come by when I want to."

"...Listen to me. I'm saying that you have no obligation to do that."

"We're friends, right?"

"......"

He had always lived together with his father. He had never been deeply involved with anyone else besides him.

His father suggested that when he was old enough to live by himself, he should go down the mountain and find a settlement to live in, but he couldn't leave his father on his own.

Mizial was the first person he had been involved with for this long—and talked to this much.

Maybe he could've counted him as a friend.

"…Scared—"

Suddenly, a completely different voice came to the hospital room.

"—that your enchanted swords'll get stolen? *The* sword-stealing monster?"

"……!"

Toroa had prepared himself for a fight, but when he looked at the man's face standing in the doorway, he lowered his sword.

A dark-brown coat, draped over a man shorter than a child. Blue eyes, dimly peeping out from underneath a flat cap.

Mizial mumbled, taken aback in surprise.

"Kuuro the Cautious."

"Haven't seen each other since the operation at Gumana Trading Post, eh, Mizial the Iron-Piercing Plumeshade? But the one I have business with today—"

"Hey! Been a while, Toroa. We got to see each other again!"

Without waiting for Kuuro to finish talking, a creature resembling a blue songbird flapped and fluttered around Toroa.

Its size and wings were exactly like a songbird's, but every other part of her was that of a minian girl, shrank down to a miniature size. Cuneigh the Wanderer. The guests were acquaintances of Toroa's, after all.

"...With Toroa the Awful there."

"What...do you want with me? A sympathy visit for an enchanted sword monster?"

He had let himself drop his guard the instant he saw their faces, but he recognized again that he couldn't be optimistic.

During the defense against the Particle Storm, Kuuro had been a spotter working as part of Aureatia's operation. There was a possibility he had come to steal Toroa's enchanted swords on Aureatia's orders. If indeed that was the case, he had to fight him.

"I still haven't repaid my debt to you, see. The debt I owe you for saving my life that day. Here I was, thinking I'd try to get out of Aureatia fast, but..."

"U-um. Me too! Me too, Toroa! I wanted to thank you!"

Kuuro the Cautious. He wasn't a participant in the Sixways Exhibition himself, but he wielded the eyes of Clairvoyance, extreme supernatural senses that saw through any and all intrigue and made it impossible to catch him by surprise.

"Until you're fully recovered, I'm going to act as your bodyguard. Any problem?"

"No way!"

Mizial replied instead of Toroa.

"You're amazing, Toroa, seriously! Getting helped out by *the* Clairvoyance wielder himself? That's incredible! *Ah-ha-ha-ha-ha!* Look at you; you have a ton of friends!"

"W-wait… I didn't agree to any of this…"

"Agree or not, I can't have you dying on me, see."

Kuuro gazed at Cuneigh happily flying around.

"Toroa. You're still planning on fighting Alus the Star Runner, aren't you?"

"…That's right. The Sixways Exhibition is nothing more than a method to do that. When it's all over, if he's still alive, I'll take him down, of course. If the enchanted light sword is passed along into someone else's hands, then I'll take them down instead. I think that maybe it's not part of any grudge…or some obsession, but…I just have to do it. In order for me to live my own life."

The strongest enchanted sword, severing any and all matter it touched, Hillensingen the enchanted light sword.

To Toroa, it was a symbol of his beloved father's death.

Until he gripped the enchanted light sword in his hands, perhaps it meant he'd remain unable to accept his father's death as well.

Even now, after his defeat, he remained *Toroa the Awful*.

"Alus might lose."

Kuuro declared, persistently levelheaded.

"His first opponent is Lucnoca the Winter. If there's one among the sixteen that is truly the strongest of all, it's got to be her. That wyvern…also ended up drawing the worst opponent possible for his first match."

"…You really think so?"

Toroa the Awful, to him, always was and would be the strongest. Surpassing the skills of any enchanted sword user in the land, he had continued to stain his blades in battle, until his own existence had passed beyond just legend and into fearful superstition.

"Strongest. Legendary. Champion. Invincible. If there happened to be anyone out there that those words could be applied to...... You already know, don't you, Kuuro?"

In which case, by getting vengeance on the person who killed that strongest of all enchanted swordsman—by fighting against Alus the Star Runner, what was Toroa hoping for?

Did he hope for victory? Defeat?

Even Toroa himself remained unsure of the answer.

"All of those are the exact types of opponents Alus the Star Runner has continued to win out over."

The only plant life was blighted vegetation with shriveled yellow leaves.

It was the only natural life that could be found within the Mari Wastes' surrounding enormous gas field of the Mari Landburrow.

It was a desolate land, with deep crevices running like lightning all over, covered in parched bedrock. The lights of Aureatia, filled with vivacious activity, were supported by this dead land.

With the commencement of the Sixways Exhibition, there was a chance that there would be a battle between two monsters that far surpassed any minia in scale, and thus it was determined there were no better candidates to hold such a battle than here, in the Mari Wastes.

The gas-mining facilities were still a ways ahead in the distance, and there wasn't any minian race zones of activity as far as the eye could see. If there were any eccentrics who wished to spectate what was sure to become a calamitous fight—of course, with the spectator fee becoming tax revenue for the council—amid this terrain, absent any visual obstacle, it would also be possible to watch the flow of the match from a relatively safe and far-off position.

They had provided a special two-day break in between the first and second match. This was to allow the almost full-day ride it took for the caravans full of spectators to reach the Mari Wastes.

It was completely different from the first match. The caravan's rations were enough to cover the spectators' dinner from the night before as well as the day's lunch, and they were all hushed in somber dread, as if watching over a myth.

Then, if the citizens looked through their binoculars or monocular glasses…on one of the two table-shaped plateaus facing each other, they could make out a white silhouette that reflected the sun like cold steel.

Similar to Toroa the Awful, it was a being none among them had ever witnessed before, yet which still exuded a presence that forced all of them to accept she was real.

The strongest being within the Sixways Exhibition. A dragon. A true legend. Lucnoca the Winter.

Absolutely none of them noticed the puny outline of a man standing beside her.

"…I hesitated the whole time."

Aureatia's Sixth General, Harghent the Still, wrapped his entire body up in a thick blanket and was looking down on the expanse of land, split up by dark crevices.

Lucnoca the Winter was a terrifying dragon but also an individual being living within the logic and reason of this world. She didn't constantly radiate cold air. However, the illusionary biting cold from his memories, and the premonition he had of the frigid landscape that was to come, made his body tremble.

"I thought if I told you everything, you and Alus…may no longer be on equal footing. And if winning like that…had any meaning at all. However, I can't let myself think like that, can I? Alus may know about your legend, Lucnoca, but with you being in Igania for so long, you wouldn't know anything about Alus's legend, so—"

"Harghent."

The dragon gently cut in, her clear voice wholly incongruous with her massive body.

"You take such a dreadfully long time to get to the point, don't you?"

"*Hngh…!* I-I'm not…taking that long! Why is it never Grasse or Enu, but always me who's told that…?! Do you really find my words so pointless?! I-I'm saying that, at this rate, you'll be at a disadvantage!"

Lucnoca folded one of her long wings and put it up against her mouth.

A mannerism almost like a minia trying to hold back their laughter.

There wasn't anywhere within Aureatia's borders that could have accommodated her. Because of it, Lucnoca had only made the trip from Igania to Aureatia one day prior.

The white dragon was giddy, as though she was a young girl who had discovered a new place to play.

"*Pfft, hee-hee-hee!* Disadvantaged, is it? Why, I don't mind at all."

"…He has a magic item, known as the Greatshield of the Dead," Harghent muttered bitterly.

He knew, with his own eyes, one part of Alus the Star Runner's fighting style. When it came to the wyvern's thoughts and personality, he was more knowledgeable than any other in the world.

"I don't know the conditions behind it, but he was able to avoid a breath attack with it. It was how he guarded against Vikeon the Smoldering's breath. So that fatal breath of yours won't work with him. You need to think as you fight, or you'll get hit with his magic-item counterattack and lose."

"It'll work."

"Wh-what do you—?"

"I'm saying it's impossible to defend against my breath."

"……Still."

Looking at her demeanor, full of unwavering self-confidence, it conversely brought a feeling of anxiety flitting through Harghent's mind.

—The dragon's breath of Lucnoca the Winter.

It was likely the Word Arts that boasted the greatest destructive power in the entire land, freezing all creation and annihilating the very landscape itself. Nevertheless, she was just like Harghent, in that she had no understanding whatsoever of the full extent of Alus the Star Runner's weapon arsenal.

Although its effects robbed heat, in complete contrast to their normal processes, Lucnoca's breath was still ultimately a type of

Thermal Arts. Was that self-conceit really going to work against the wyvern that butchered a creature of Vikeon the Smoldering's grandeur?

...If I lose, it's over for me. My ambition and my honor will be fully exhausted. That was why I brought along someone who absolutely wouldn't lose—Lucnoca the Winter. I'm sure...... I'm sure I did everything right. But...but still.

His tightly clenched fists were trembling in his lap. It was partly from his premonition of the cold to come, but it carried another reason.

With this battle, something was finally going to be settled once and for all—Harghent's very life.

Alus is strong. The strongest.

He believed so more than anyone else in the world. That was precisely why he decided to fight against him.

He looked at the tall earthen pillar that rose up exactly in the middle between the two large plateaus. As the sun grew higher in the sky, the shadow stretching out along the ground would shrink. That was the signal for the start of the match. For a battle of this scale, they couldn't possibly place any official observers nearby.

At the moment when the shadow totally disappeared, the fight between the world's ultimate two dragonkin would begin.

◆

Aureatia's Twentieth Minister, Hidow the Clamp, was taking part in this fight purely for the sake of Aureatia.

It wasn't because of his own good nature, nor was it out of loyalty for Queen Sephite or the Aureatia Assembly. In fact, Hidow had never once in his entire life been seriously concerned for another person, and he even acknowledged that he himself was a bit of a villain.

He just didn't have any ambition. Simply resolving Aureatia's problems as they came up—and nothing more.

Given that, the fact that he ended up working together with the person who held the strongest ambitions of all, the wyvern Alus the Star Runner, truly was an ironic twist of fate.

"Hey, Alus."

There was a bottomless abyss right below his feet. He was sitting down on the edge of the table-shaped plateau directly across from Lucnoca's.

Alus's responses were always slow, so whenever they'd converse, at the beginning, it would always start with Hidow talking at him in this way.

"This is nothing but a big show."

"............."

"You've known that a while, right? This is just some big festival for those minian race idiots to watch and enjoy all of you fighting. The whole crap about the Hero or whatever is just window dressing. Doesn't it make it all seem so absurd?"

"............Why?"

A small silhouette looked down from an even steeper clifftop from where Hidow sat.

This was simply a question. Alus wasn't offended. He had spent enough time observing this wyvern that he could tell as much just from the tone of his voice.

He looked over in a different direction. The crowding citizens. In the wasteland landscape, they were huddled together like a windblown drift of garbage.

They had come to watch a calamity capable of annihilating them all a hundred times over as if they were on a pleasure trip. Their actions and everything about their lives seemed loathsome and senseless to Hidow.

"Those idiots aren't putting their lives on the line. They can't even solve their own problems by themselves... Heck, they don't even know what their own problems even are, really. You want a country full of idiots like that? Me? I wouldn't."

"...It's all the same," The wyvern blandly replied. There wasn't any emotion in his voice.

"Minian races...wyverns... Everyone's the same, right?"

"So you and I are the same as them, then?"

"......I just have people I like and people I don't like...... Dumb, clever... It's all too nitpicky for me, and I don't really get it..."

"At the very least, minia are like that, let me tell you."

"......Why?"

"It's fine if you don't get it...... More importantly, if you're going to get out, now's your last chance. There's technically an agreement that outlines a penalty of some kind, but the Aureatian army's never going to catch you flying up in the air. If it all sounds like nonsense......forget me and head back home."

Hidow knew his suggestion was a wasted effort.

Alus did whatever it was he wanted to do. Even if it was something that couldn't be measured in gains and losses.

Otherwise, he wouldn't have been able to become a legend who had uncovered everything the world had to offer.

"It's not nonsense at all."

"…You think so?"

"…………It's a match against Harghent…"

It was the same, melancholic mumble as always. However, there was a feeling of delight in his words.

The one he recognized as the greatest opponent of all. The joy to battle against the powerless Sixth General unacknowledged by anyone else.

His gazed was fixed on Lucnoca the Winter—and also not on Lucnoca the Winter at all.

"I seriously don't get it."

Hidow looked at the sky. The sun was close to its zenith. The time was fast approaching.

For a reason as simple as that, a mythical battle was at hand.

All the world, save Hidow, was bound by such a simple rule.

"All of you… I don't get a single one of you."

The pillar's shadow was hidden, and wings buffeted the wind above his head. The dragon had flown into the air.

The start of the Sixways Exhibition's second match was declared. It was exceedingly quiet.

∗   ∗   ∗

The match, the largest-scale fight throughout the games, didn't defy any of the expectations of those who witnessed it, save for those of the similarly all-powerful combatants who would claim victory.

In other words, before the sun could even set, the battle was one that brought eternal destruction to the land around it.

The conclusion taught everyone exactly how terrifying the words *all-powerful* could truly be.

Alus the Star Runner versus Lucnoca the Winter.

◆

The momentum of the silhouette flying out in front of her had the force of explosive firepower.

Even to Lucnoca, having flown from Igania to Aureatia in less than a day, that's what the speed felt like to her.

"Fantastic."

This was not amazement at the speed on display. It was an emotionally charged reaction to the fighting spirit fearlessly coming her way.

Completely isolated by her excessive power, Lucnoca could no longer read how strong or weak her opponents were. In the past, the ones who looked weak were weak, and the ones who believed themselves strong had all been weak, too.

Therefore, though she hadn't noticed herself......she had been waiting for someone to stand in front of her. She grew to only believe in the surest truths of all—the bravery to challenge an absolutely powerful opponent and the recklessness.

Lucnoca the Winter strongly believed that such a heart was far more beautiful than anything else in the world.

"...Now then, Alus. What exactly will you show me, then?"

However, the wyvern, approaching in a straight-lined collision course into Lucnoca's flight path, suddenly changed his trajectory. Arcing up above him, he quickly turned to the south.

Those watching closely couldn't help following him with their eyes.

They ended up looking into the midday sun. He had lured their gazes. Lucnoca folded her wings and suddenly dropped her speed.

The second she lost sight of Alus in the backlight of the sun, her eyes also missed a flash of light. The bullet fired from the musket's maximum firing range flew and hit Lucnoca's cheek.

"*Uh-hoo, hoo, hoo, hoo, hoo, hoo!*"

Feeling the sensation of the gunshot, Lucnoca laughed.

Flying out from the pillar of light, this time she tracked the silhouette diving low inside one of the fissures in the earth. After dilating her pupils and by having her look directly at the sun, now he attempted to contract them again in the darkness.

Lucnoca was aware of the sensation that crawled across her shot cheek. It was branching plant roots, sprouting from the bullet, eating away and corroding everything it touched.

It was known as the Torture Oak's Seed. It was a magic bullet that used the musket's gunpowder heat to germinate a tree that caused immediate organic death.

…But Lucnoca lightly rubbed the cheek being covered with roots with her claw.

"What an interesting little arrow."

That was the extent of the lethal magic bullet, simply peeled off with her dragon scales and falling to the ground, rendered meaningless.

The reason behind the invincibility of dragon scale was not only their hardness. It lay in their insulating abilities.

Alus's previous shot had clearly been aimed at Lucnoca's eye. The eye not covered with dragon scales.

However, Lucnoca knew very well that each and every one of the champions who challenged dragons aimed for the same spot. The dodge she just made with her sudden deceleration was, to Lucnoca, nothing more than a conventional and expected back-and-forth that she didn't even have to think about.

From the bottom of the fissure's abyss, another bullet flew her way. Her claw cut in and repelled it.

Lucnoca the Winter hadn't been aware this "gun" weapon existed, but as long as she possessed physical abilities and reflexes that far surpassed the bullets they fired, any knowledge of it was bound to become meaningless eventually.

It was clear this was another type of magic bullet that would bring death, but the surface layer of the dragon's claws, with its high degree of crystallization, was at no risk of poisoning, and it was impossible for the roots to eat into it.

"Uh-hoo, hoo, hoo, hoo, hoo, hoo!"

She looked down into the abyss running across the land, where Alus had hidden himself. If she launched her breath right there, that would probably have been the end of the battle.

But that wouldn't have been any fun.

How was this speedy little champion going to fight from here on out?

What kind of tricks was he thinking up as he stood before the world's strongest dragon?

What would this Alus the Star Runner, the strongest in this land, do for her?

......*Ah, that's not it.*

Her eyes, twinkling with curiosity and excitement, narrowed slightly.

If he hid himself in the ground fissures, he had no way to escape her breath. That was something that Alus the Star Runner should have been aware of more than anyone else. In that case— the situation was already different.

"Got you......"

By the time she heard the voice, the whip had already been sent off behind her. It traced an angular zigzag, unbefitting a whip at all, across the sky, and grabbed the base of the ancient dragon's right wing.

"Kio's Hand."

The caught section twisted and distorted strangely and began emitting a clicking sound.

Kio's Hand, the magic whip that moved freely of its own accord, had another function to it as well. It would twist anything it wrapped itself around, regardless of the target's strength, and sever it.

As long as he was utilizing supernatural magic items, there were methods he could use to ignore their durability and break through her dragon scales.

"*Uh-hoo, hoo, hoo! Uh-hoo, hoo, hoo, hoo, hoo!* Aaah... How much fun! You truly are fast, Alus! Perhaps it's a sign of my old age, but my eyes can't keep up with you at all!"

".........Really, now...... You're weak, then."

Kio's Hand was still nothing more than a foothold for his next move. While Alus kept one of his three arms pulling on the whip, another arm produced a new weapon. The strongest enchanted sword of all.

It was at that moment the clear voice rang out.

"*Co chwelne.*" (To Kouto winds.)

To those with some knowledge of Word Arts, they understood this was meaningless resistance.

In order to use Thermal Arts for destruction, it was necessary to give them a direction. It was impossible to use them offensively in a direction that would involve oneself in the blast. Alus was now behind Lucnoca, and he locked down her right wing to prevent her from turning her neck around back at him.

Much like a certain visitor had done in a Labyrinth City of the past, even the heat's wake wouldn't reach a person positioned directly behind the practitioner.

Nevertheless, the motion of the dragon's breath attack began and ended with a single breath.

"*Cyulcascarz.*" (Wither and fall at the edge of light.)

At the end of Lucnoca's field of view, there was a gently sloping valley and a waterfront.

There was the red horizon of the wasteland, and beautifully contrasting with it was a blue sky of sparsely scattered clouds.

It was the past several hundred years of the Mari Wastes' changing landscape.

All of it disappeared.

It was as though the five senses held by all life had stopped.

Silence.

Darkness.

Even the spectators viewing from far off in the distance immediately felt the cataclysmic change to the world.

Lucnoca's soundless breath brought the landscape in front of her to a standstill. All that existed there was blinded by white.

—No. It hadn't been brought to an exact standstill. Though Thermal Arts were unaccompanied by any wind or impacting force, the cracked terrain had indeed changed within the raging stillness.

Even the drastic transformation, dyeing the world white by freezing air molecules, was over in an instant. It was chilled, as if the bottom of the world itself had fallen out, yet even more so. The rocky earth had completely contorted black, rippling out as if on the surface of an open sea. Chilled to the absolute limit, below it may not have been solid matter at all.

The construction of the earth, condensed under the terrifying force, flowed like one singular molecule.

"Aaah, Harghent. You said my breath wouldn't work, didn't you?" The ruler of the truly silent world muttered to herself. "Perhaps, in your world, that may have been true. But."

It was horribly quiet.

But. Even with this, the *conclusion* was yet to come.

After a brief pause, it happened.

An explosion like lightning shaking heaven and earth.

The boundless, thunderous rumble devastated the world of silence.

The air, pelting like a raging torrent, surged into the world present before Lucnoca's eyes, and even Alus the Star Runner was swept away by the raging billows, having moored himself to her with his magic whip.

Any and all matter had *fallen* in front of Lucnoca.

The eyes of the wyvern, completely off-balance, and the eyes of the dragon waiting for him to do so mingled together for one moment.

"……!"

"My breath works."

With a downward swipe of her transcendent claws, Alus fell in a straight line down to dead earth.

The lightweight wyvern smashed through the rocky ground just from the speed of his descent.

The champion-slaying legend brushed away the magic whip, torn off from its grip around her right wing, like picking off a piece of seaweed.

She was unharmed.

All the champions who challenged the dragon had tried the same thing.

Lucnoca's breath, shutting the world away in winter, was known even among the children who didn't grow up to become warriors through children's songs.

There were those who came with defenses against low temperatures laid out around them. There were those who carried a magic item that blocked any and all forms of destruction. Yet others were like this Alus before her, using their mobility and tactical skills to try escaping from the vicinity.

Historically, all of them had died.

The absolute and ultimate Ice Arts breath. All air particles within range were made solid.

In which case, the destruction didn't end there. Continued afterward was the explosion of tumultuous tempest winds that tried to flow in and fill the hole the lost world left behind. Even an exceptional creature of the age, Alus the Star Runner, couldn't fight against this reality before him.

…However.

"Uh-hoo, hoo, hoo! Uh-hoo, hoo, hoo, hoo!"

However, Lucnoca laughed. There was only one possible meaning behind it.

"Oh, how funny…!"

She hadn't seen anything yet.

What sort of fighting style did he have left?

Just what kind of tricks did he retain to fight the strongest of all dragons before him?

What would the strongest of this land, Alus the Star Runner, show her next?

"……You're toying with me……aren't you……?"

It was the same quiet, gloomy, and weak voice as usual.

Nevertheless, if someone well acquainted with the wyvern had heard it, they would've been able to guess the singular strong emotion within it, tinged with the slightest degree of anger…

The emotion of "irritation."

"Greatshield of the Dead."

Once guarding him from Vikeon the Smoldering's breath, it was his ultimate form of protection, capable of defending against the strongest dragon claws in the world, as long as the proper compensation was paid.

"…You're bragging. Even……to the guy who's about to kill you."

Alus the Star Runner brandished his next weapon. Kicking the ground, he took off.

…But he couldn't.

The world around them was chilled to the core. The air was heavy. The ground that had once been all rocks was now some sort of black crystal, twisted into a strange pattern by some effect of physics.

"*Uh-hoo, hoo, hoo!* You can't go standing in a place like that, you know."

Lucnoca looked down from far up above Alus's head. Much the same way Alus had to all of the legends he had encountered before now.

Alus tried again to take to the skies. He coughed up blood. The cells in his lungs were being gnawed from the inside. He began to be drastically robbed of his body heat. The landscape after her breath had passed through, as well as the air, the earth, and everything else, was far colder than any ice…than anything he had ever known.

"…Perhaps your back legs have gotten themselves stuck to the ice, hmm?"

The strongest race in the land. The strongest individual among them.

There was no escaping from Lucnoca the Winter's breath.

"*Co chwelne. Cyulcascarz.*" (To Kouto winds. Wither and fall at the edge of light.)

◆

"Y-you…you've got to be kidding…!"

On top of a faraway plateau, Hidow gasped, the color draining from his face.

He had witnessed Lucnoca the Winter's dragon breath with his own eyes. The embodiment of demise itself, completely eclipsing all imagination.

The sight should've been far off in the distance, but he definitely wasn't that removed from it at all. If the area of effect had veered to the west? What if that spot where Lucnoca and Alus had clashed had been even half as close to where he was?

It was cold. The extremely frigid winds, prickling his skin far worse than any snowfield he had visited before, terrified Hidow. The spot showered by the ice breath was so far away from his position. This was still supposed to be the Mari Wastes. However, the current temperature indicated it was no longer.

And it was likely......that it would stay that way from now on.

That fool. Did Harghent know about this?

He couldn't have possibly known. Supposing he had witnessed the attack at Igania Ice Lake, he clearly wouldn't have returned to Aureatia alive. He may have been Wing Clipper Harghent, but Hidow wanted to believe he wasn't foolish enough to know about this and still bring Lucnoca the Winter to compete.

He immediately shouldered the bare minimum of his belongings and called out to the soldier on standby behind him.

"Get the car!"

"H-huh?!"

"Didn't hear me? Steam's running, right? Get the car. We're heading to the caravan."

Hidow turned his attention to the caravan, visible in another direction. The citizens gathered together like locusts. They must have been wildly excited about the shocking scene and the tremendous being that the people of the current era were witnessing for the first time.

"But, sir, toward the caravan?"

"Where else? If Winter's breath is pointed in this direction, it'll kill us all! Me, you, all of them, it's all up to her whims! We don't have any choice but to evacuate! Get moving!"

"But if you leave the area, the Sixth General will be the only one observing the match! If that happens, Lord Hidow—"

"Get. Moving."

Hidow grabbed the soldier by the collar and intimidated him.

The soldier wasn't using his head. No sense of urgency. All of them were like this. He wouldn't stand for it.

Gnashing his teeth, the Twentieth Minister looked over his shoulder to the battle behind him.

Why am I the one who has to think about this stuff?

Hidow was different from men like Harghent. He could think through the results and benefits that went with the choices he made. Even if it may have been so in the moment...he hadn't simply agreed to the fight with Lucnoca the Winter simply out of pride and animosity.

The legend-slaying champion Alus and the champion-slaying legend Lucnoca. Among the participants in the Sixways Exhibition, the only ones that posed a threat to either of them were each other.

They were both out of anyone's reach, beings there was no hope of ever defeating. In order for the minia to put down these two wicked dragons, they needed to make them kill each other and exhaust whichever one was left standing.

Therefore, Hidow had been able to face the first match after completely setting aside the sabotage against Alus he had planned to utilize during the first round. Currently, the Star Runner had control of all the equipment at his disposal. The battlefield didn't impose any limits on his range of flight, and he hadn't been poisoned beforehand, either.

To face off against the strongest of all dragons, he needed to be at his full power.

A purely rational judgment, completely unrelated to Hidow's pride whatsoever.

...He really is the only one who can beat her after all, ain't he?

Lucnoca the Winter's strength went beyond the reach of the minian race's powers of imagination.

You better win here, Alus.

Slipping into the passenger seat of the steam-powered automobile, he spoke into the radzio installed within.

A female liaison responded to his call. It was someone who knew about their operation.

"It's Hidow the Clamp. Get Rosclay on!"

<Lord Rosclay? If you could hold on for a moment, I can—>

"Forget it. I'll leave a message. You tell him, 'Lucnoca is stronger than we anticipated. If Lucnoca wins here, we won't be able to use that process we discussed.' Got that? This might be the last time I'll be able to report in."

<Huh... Then, what about you Lord Hidow? Um...>

"Not important. You got my whole message, right? Tell him all of it now. Rosclay should be able to think of something."

On the horizon, the giant white dragon's silhouette was in motion.

The sight was distorted, almost as if he was looking through a water tank.

It was the temperature difference. Hidow could understand that. The extremely drastic gradient of cold air even changed the speed of light itself.

Was this some other world? A far distant shore, where people were unable to live or trespass. It was as if a frozen-over hellscape had been extracted from the passages of a story and emerged in that strip of wasteland.

"...You think I can die...?!" he warned, speaking to no one in particular.

He'd force all the spectators to evacuate. Think about future steps against this calamity going forward. He would make sure the Sixways Exhibition ended without any mishaps. There was still a mountain of work to get to. He wasn't going to get buried in that worthless work and die like this.

"I can't die now...!"

Together with a puff of steam, the car departed.

◆

Sixth General Harghent the Still was also looking out at the same scene, clutching his knees to his chest underneath his blanket.

The cloudlessly noontime wasteland was now sealed in winter.

It was a time period that existed in the Beyond, when the world died out. Meanwhile in this land, bereft of seasons, spring would never come. Once Winter had visited, the world remained in eternal death.

There was a sense of an unopposable and inevitable end in the cold air that traveled all the way to where he sat.

A temperature of despair and fated resignation, like he had felt in Igania Ice Lake.

...Nevertheless, Harghent looked unblinking at that distant scene.

His eyes were bloodshot and crackled with fire inside the blanket. He was the only one who had believed it.

"Not yet."

Lucnoca the Winter was truly the strongest legend of all.

So strong that she had lost her opportunities to fight. So strong that she was brimming with pride and negligence—and still had more to spare.

"......He hasn't, done it yet...! Not yet...! Not yet!"

He continued to mutter words for no one to hear as his teeth rattled in the cold.

The idea to run away hadn't even crossed his mind.

It wasn't due to his bravery. He never had that choice in the first place.

Alus the Star Runner was putting his whole soul on the line. A contest that would never come again, that Harghent had sunk the piddling remnants of his pride and future entirely into.

He wasn't a sham like Rosclay. He was the only wyvern and the only true dragon-slaying hero in the land. If he could just defeat

Alus in this first round, there would no longer be anyone who could defeat Lucnoca the Winter.

"Alus."

The white dragon once again showered the land with her ruthless breath.

Her attack, aimed down below her, didn't destroy a large area like the one before it.

Instead—a radius of thirty odd meters of the earth collapsed like mud and caved in deep into the ground.

The dragon breath of Lucnoca the Winter didn't possess any physical impact whatsoever.

Such phenomenon occurred simply due to the extreme cooling.

If all the space between molecules, extending several kilometers belowground, were lost in the instant cooling, was it possible for a topographical shift, almost like a meteor crater, to appear?

As it was understood in the Beyond, when under extremely low temperatures, matter didn't maintain its volume. Condensed, pulverized, its entire structure changed completely. In the real, macroscopic world, when that exact phenomenon happened, how did that reality present itself? Even among the residents of the Beyond, no one had seen anything like it with their own eyes.

"...Alus!"

Amid the vortex of ruination, he knew Alus had to be there.

Biting down on his lip hard enough to draw blood, Harghent was trembling.

What emotion exactly was making him tremble, even he himself didn't know.

He simply repeated those words over and over again.

"N-not yet... Not yet...!"

◆

He saw the world behind him crumble away.

Alus didn't fully comprehend exactly what type of phenomenon was occurring behind him. All he understood was that the scope of the attack was far beyond anything he could defend against with the Greatshield of the Dead.

"...Heshed Elis the Fire Pipe's......"

Even after seeing such destruction, Alus the Star Runner...... felt more regretful about losing one of his magic items than the right toe that had frozen and torn off.

When he killed Vikeon the Smoldering, Alus had pierced his flank with a long spear, but what magic item had allowed him to pierce through a dragon's flesh? Even Harghent the Still didn't know the answer to that question.

Heshed Elis the Fire Pipe was a simple iron pipe, not even loaded with gunpowder, but any object that touched its gun barrel would be launched with extraordinary force. As long it was aimed at a gap where their scales were torn off, the magic gun could even finish off a dragon.

He had been faced with a dilemma where instead of using it

offensively, he was forced to use it for an emergency escape. Stuck to the ultracold ground, he had launched himself out from the extinction zone, sacrificing a right toe in the process.

"............"

Inside a small jar, he lit the magic item's—Ground Runner's—flame and refreshed the air around him to stop it from freezing his lungs.

While Lucnoca had yet to find Alus, he checked the workings of his favorite gun. Picked out from among all the mass-produced guns he had swapped in during his long days of adventuring, it was a musket with a nearly miraculous degree of accuracy. Keeping the central mechanism untouched, he specialized the grip for wyvern hands; it was a weapon he placed more trust in than any of his legendary magic items, but—

"...Gunpowder's no good, then."

The percussion cap gunpowder was frigidly cold. Even if he did pull the trigger, it'd likely misfire. At the very least, during this battle, his arboreal magic bullets, poison magic bullets, and lightning bullets were now all unusable.

Kio's Hand, that he had used to twist off Vikeon's arm, had been cut apart, and Heshed Elis the Fire Pipe, used to pierce through his flesh, was lost. The winter of world finality had even killed his lifeless magic tools.

"......I wonder......what sort of treasure......Lucnoca the Winter has......?"

Now that he had lost three different weapons at his disposal, if anything, it made it obvious what his next method of attack should be.

The only method that could pierce through the dragon scales' defenses and take her life in one attack.

Using Hillensingen the enchanted light sword was his only option.

Kicking off the ground with his wounded leg, the wyvern once again flew into the air.

As long as he was up in the sky, where Lucnoca's breath hadn't frozen anything over, he could still fly. While he was flying, his crippled leg wouldn't put him at a disadvantage, either.

There was a clear fact of reality. He needed to get in close, or he would lose.

The all-powerful breath, sweeping death across all the eyes could see, was harder and harder to escape the farther he was from Lucnoca.

Even supposing he could defend against the power of breath itself with the Greatshield of the Dead, the ultracold world left behind prevented the activity of any living creature. Though it may have meant he'd be dealt a lethal blow being caught in the vacuum as before, his only option was expending all his strength to continue attacking from her blind spot.

Lucnoca the Winter came into view in front of him.

He could see her take flight, as if in response to his approach. He heard her clear voice.

"That isn't all you have now, is it?"

Closing in the distance in a straight line, Alus flew at comet-like speeds.

The white dragon hadn't turned her face to him, but she had noticed the presence of her opponent streaking in from the southeast.

"Right, Alus the Star Runner? Ooh, I'm so happy. Very, very, *very* happy, in fact. Everything about you is just oh so delightful!"

Her Ice Arts breath was coming. Alus's wings buffeted the air. A mere moment before it came, the wyvern turned along an acute angle.

He needed to be going at his maximum, life-threatening speed. Faster than Lucnoca's eyes could keep up.

However.

"Co chwelne." (To Kouto Winds.)

—However, Lucnoca caught him directly in front of her.

After their last exchange, Alus had placed Lucnoca at the top among all the other legends he had fought up until now. The destructive scale of their clash wasn't the only reason why. Even when it came to simple physical ability......she was so overwhelmingly superior it was impudent to even compare her to the others.

Why was she able to keep up her activity within this frozen hellscape, born from her own breath?

Why could she face the violent vortex gale, sucking everything into an air vacuum, and not stir an inch?

It was because her body could endure it all.

Dragons were the only living creatures that could possibly survive the aftermath effects of their own dragon breath.

Save for a single young elf girl exception—the Word-Maker never bestowed Word Arts that the user's body couldn't handle.

The strongest physical abilities in the land were even able to follow a silhouette going faster than the eye could see.

"*Cyulcascarz.*" (Wither and fall at the edge of light.) Termination spread.

The view was annihilated in white.

Even if that one breath was to finish things, Lucnoca would still do the same.

As long as she was able to fight without any reservations and with all her strength, just once, then that was fine with her.

No matter how much of a frail wyvern he may have been, just the fact that she had been able to fight without any show of mercy meant that Alus the Star Runner was an irreplaceable presence to her.

The earth once again split open. Even the clouds vanished into mist.

Her Word Arts, ostensibly only supposed to affect the winds, transformed the depths of the earth's crust into eternally frozen soil, simply from the aftermath of the atmospheric cooling. All in a single breath incantation, shorter than the Thermal Arts minia used to produce sparks.

Showered in cold air, the silhouette, just like every single champion before him, had disappointingly vanished.

"*Uh-hoo, hoo, hoo, hoo, hoo...! Uh-hoo, hoo, hoo!* Aaah... it's been a hundred years since I've had a battle like this. Why, maybe even longer than that. I doubt I'll enjoy myself this much *anytime soon* again."

Eventually, another champion would appear who would demand her full power.

Lucnoca would end up waiting in solitude at that Ice Lake, anticipating more than that one encounter.

The vacuum born from the breath's aftermath began to swallow the surrounding atmosphere like a tidal wave.

All of it happened in an instant.

—And if there was someone who knew all of that.

"..............."

If someone had already suffered the aftermath once, then they could match their acceleration with the torrent of wind.

From a blind spot on the dragons' flank.

There existed a magic item called Rotting Soil Sun.

It was a sphere formed from a clod of dirt, and it could launch blades or bullets formed from the mud endlessly fountaining forth. That mud could even, for example...form something resembling a wyvern gliding on folded wings.

In the middle of his ultra-high-speed maneuvering, he used his flight inertia to abandon the substitute behind him and force the all-powerful dragon's sights that were following him to stop mid-pursuit. He made her launch a breath attack at the substitute.

No matter how much kinetic visual acuity, or how fast her reaction speeds were, differentiating between two tiny shadows in a split second, while tracking Alus the Star Runner at his max speed, was impossible for any legend.

"Hillensingen."

Quietly, feebly, he was finishing his mumbling. He always made sure to get his boasting in.

It was his only method of attack that could trivialize the dragon scale defenses and end everything in a single, split-second attack.

Multiplied by the speed of the vacuum winds, as well as Alus's own speed, the attack—

"The enchanted li—"

He collided with something massive.

With a loud crunch, Alus's world dissolved away.

"...Oh my!"

Lucnoca the Winter was slow to notice.

Yet she shouted in despair. "Oh no...! You were still alive?! Oh, heaven's me, what have I done...?!"

The light blade had cut deep, slicing the tip of her massive tail clean through to the bone.

However, that same tail had just slammed Alus to the ground under its massive weight.

"...Why, I truly didn't notice at all! What a terrible failure on my part...! My opponent was still alive, and I wasted my chance! If I had known, oh how much more fun I could have!"

—It hadn't been an attack.

The strongest dragon of all had simply changed her direction in midair.

Her tail, swung around to adjust her position, had just, in a stroke of misfortune, lined up with the trajectory of Alus's attack.

The instant-kill suicide rush, surpassing the efforts of all the other champions in history, was defeated by plain bad luck.

She was too strong. Just moving her body had more than enough power to butcher another life.

She needed to actively try to enjoy herself or else she wouldn't have been able.

"Sorry, Alus the Star Runner! Oh, I'm so sorry…! Let's play some, shall we? Come now, Alus the Star Runner, please…!"

Denying even the fight itself, it was a single sight of desolation.

◆

He had a vivid memory. Just how long ago was it?

The rain that had continued from the night before gradually began to recede, now only intermittently showering.

Looking through the gaps in the wood panels of the crumbling cabin, abandoned on the shoreline cliffs, he spent the whole day gazing at the tide going in and out.

"Hey."

Lifting himself up away from the fissure in the rotted wood wall, that face had appeared again.

Names. Now that he thought about it, the minia all had names. Names that, among wyverns, were only given to the strong and clever upper ranks of the flock.

What was it again?

"Harghent."

"Don't go saying my name so easily like that."

The young boy frantically turned around and looked behind him. He seemed much more worried about anyone from the village approaching the shack than the young wyvern himself.

"If it came out that I was sheltering a wyvern of all things, I could get beaten to death."

"……Really…… Then, I'll……be careful."

"You even know what 'being careful' actually means? That's something *you* gotta do yourself. Why the hell did you break your damn wing anyway?"

Harghent looked at the splint fixed up to his right wing.

As dragonkin, wyverns generally had a strong vitality. Broken bones for them should've healed faster than a minia's, but it seemed like it would still be some time until his would be perfectly linked back together again.

"……? Because I ran into something…"

"Yeah, and I'm asking why the hell'd you run into something. Normal wyverns don't have that stuff happen."

"Because……I'm not normal, then……?"

The young boy scratched his head. At the time, he hadn't been able to answer properly, but looking back, he now understood that his answer to Harghent when they first met had been vague.

Unlike other wyverns, he had unnecessary body parts. One on the left of his torso. Two on the right. This particular wyvern had three arms, unlike any of the wyverns that had been documented up until then.

They ruined his flight stability. He had collided into sea cliffs, normally not something that happened to a wyvern, and broken his wing. That was likely behind it all.

"If you can't fly super well, then the same thing's just going to happen again once it's healed."

"............Maybe......"

"What kind of answer is 'maybe,' huh? Seriously, I don't got a clue what's going on in that head'a yours."

Harghent always seemed to be in a bad mood, but at the time, he didn't understand it at all. Most minians, when looking at a wyvern, were filled with anger and boiling with an urge to kill them.

"You really need a bit more...a little bit more sense of urgency— that you can't keep going on like this, okay? Consider the source and take countermeasures."

"But......I can't fly well......so I can't do that, either, right...? Nothing I can do."

"Then learn how, dammit! The day you popped outta your egg, could you fly? Hell, what about Word Arts? Were you chitchatting with 'em like you are now right from the get-go?"

He struggled to understand Harghent's point.

Were they words of concern for a wyvern like him? They couldn't have been. It didn't make any sense for a minia to do something like that. It hadn't made any sense from the start, when he first sheltered him in this shack.

Harghent sat down and nibbled at the lunch he had brought with him. They were some kind of dried tree nuts and were as crude and wretched as any wyvern's meal. His clothes were fraying all over, and one of the soles of his shoes was beginning to peel off.

"Comes a day for everyone out there, when they're able to do something they couldn't do before. It's growth. Yeah, that's right, growth. You gotta grow, too."

"......Then......what do I do?"

"Huh?"

"Once......I'm able to fly...... What do I do?"

"I mean, c'mon...... Once you're able to fly, you'll be able to get your hands on all sorts of stuff, right? Can get yourself some tasty food, for one, and female wyverns prefer males that're good fliers, right? Not that I got any clue, but... Also, you could even become a big shot in your flock!"

"Hmm... So that's the type of stuff......you want, Harghent......"

"D-damn right I do!"

Harghent's expression grew increasingly dour, and he kicked the nearby wooden wall panel.

The loud sound surprised him, but he was inept at expressing any intense emotions from birth. This surprise probably wasn't made clear to Harghent, either.

"Haven't you ever felt frustrated and humiliated from constantly being looked down on by someone who can't do anything?! Those aristocrat bastards kick us servants around like we're a bunch of useless fools! Both my dad and my mom, too... All they ever did was give these disgusting smiles and ingratiate themselves! I'm different. I'm going to become someone important; just watch... I'll grow up and make all those pompous bastards see how great I really am...!"

"All of that's......"

He cocked his head. Minia logic was strange.

"All of that's about you, though...... It's got nothing to do with me..."

"It's the same thing! It's all the same...! You're alive, aren't you?! Then you gotta have wants, too! Show 'em all that you can fly just as well as everyone else!"

At the time, had he understood that Harghent was seeing himself in the wyvern who had been left behind by his flock?

Whether he did or not, the fact remained that he felt an innocent curiosity toward the intense emotions he was witnessing for the first time in his life, the exact opposite of his own.

He possessed a passion the wyvern himself didn't.

".........Okay. I'll try, then... What do I need to do to grow?"

"......Just have to start with what you can, right...? Ever grabbed something in your hands before? Or moved your fingers independent of one another? Even with your wing injured, you can handle that right now. You add to the number of things you can do, little by little."

"...Then what about you, Harghent? What do you need to do......to become important...?"

"Me?"

The question prompted Harghent's first smile.

"Me, well, *heh, heh, heh*...! I'm the first one among the other guys my age to bring down a wyvern...! So I've got a gift for archery. I'll hunt down more and more of your brethren like this and work my way up to greatness... It'll just be wyverns for now. But someday

I'm gonna be able to take down bigger and better targets, not just wyverns. That's how I'll get to be a general in the kingdom. I'll have enough money to last a lifetime, and everyone'll praise me."

They were, at most, his deepest inner thoughts that could only lay bare to the injured wyvern in front of him. Ambitions that he absolutely couldn't mention in front of any of the other villagers. Just how difficult, how far in the distant future, would it be until he got there?

In minia society, it was shameful. The weak weren't supposed to speak about dreams beyond their station.

The boy held a small bow in his hands. Compared to an adult's bow, its power was much, much weaker.

Nevertheless—even if it was simply dumb luck and had nothing to do with his skill level at all, Proud Bow was still the weapon that shot down his very first wyvern.

"Once I'm a general, I really wanna become a champion! I'm gonna leave my name in history...! I'll even take on a dragon—and bring them down with this Dragon Slayer ballista of mine!

"Hmmm... Pretty amazing......"

His conversational acknowledgment came across almost like a half-hearted reply, but he truly felt that way from the bottom of his heart.

That was why, at that moment, he decided he would try to imitate the young boy.

Because that was surely what it meant to be alive.

"......You're an amazing guy, Harghent......"

◆

There was a continuous, incessant creaking sound.

Though he didn't think he would fail, he may have had some sort of hunch that things might end up this way.

He had challenged more strong opponents than anyone else. He had experienced the limitless possibilities, both fortunate and unfortunate, that occurred when going up against powerful opponents who far surpassed his own stature.

If he hadn't, then he wouldn't have activated Chiklorakk the Eternity Machine.

It creaked with the sound of metallic friction. The sound reverberated from inside Alus's body. A very unpleasant sensation.

In Alus's hazy field of version, first he looked at his right toe. The part of him once thought to be frozen and lost was already being replaced by a peculiar metallic contraption combined from a cogwheel and crank.

Chiklorakk the Eternity Machine, simply a minute gear of unknown composition that was smaller than the tip of a minia's pinkie—yet it was the most valuable item from Vikeon the Smoldering's hoard.

The gear turned the inside of his body. He could feel the sensation from his pulverized backbone as well. In his left thigh and rib. As well as his left wing. The gears were propagating through his body, imitating organic life, and forcibly propelling them to action.

Why the hell did you break your damn wing anyway?

"What was I supposed to do...?" he dimly replied to the inter-mingled traces of the past.

Although accidental, he had been hit with a painfully severe counterattack.

Even the Greatshield of the Dead's defenses were too slow to respond. The item was supposed to be activated in response to the enemy's attack, and since each use brought intense pain and cor-rosion, the shield couldn't be used while also maintaining control of his flight position.

Being swept into the explosive when the attack came was another mistake.

In his normal state, Alus might have been able to dodge the tail attack, even coming in at extreme speeds, right before it hit him. However, in the middle of being swept away, it was impossi-ble for him to change his trajectory.

He had shut out his unrivaled enemy's offense and devoted his everything to the one strike he'd need to turn the tables. That had been the cause of his defeat.

"........Consider the source, take countermeasures. Con-sider the source, take countermeasures...consider the source, take countermeasures...... Consider the source, take countermeasures."

Even now, Alus the Star Runner could do this.

He wasn't able to do everything from the start. He constantly added to the things he was able to accomplish—

First, it was defeating the strongest wyvern in his own flock.

Then the terrifying ogre in the forest. The biological apex of the desert, the wurm. The powerful warrior from a suppression squad. Then it was a champion. A legend. And finally, a dragon.

Alus was smacked out of the air by Lucnoca's attack, but despite that, he had kept his grip on Hillensingen the enchanted light sword. His greed prevented him from letting go of his treasures even in life-and-death crises, leaving him one final method of attack at his disposal.

...Harghent. I'm going to beat Harghent......

He would exhaust every option he had. No matter what sort of treasure he'd have to throw away, he was going to beat him.

Because it was a promise to his only friend.

"...Ahhh, ah... Alus the Star Runner...... You must still be alive, right? After all, you took those claws of mine just fine. This couldn't possibly be enough to do you in now. So please, show me more..."

Unlike moments before, Lucnoca the Winter was grieving.

"I wanted to fight even more. Truly......"

The wonderful champion, Alus the Star Runner, died. In a terribly boring and dull way. So many multitudes of warriors, all making her despondent.

Therefore, it caught her off guard.

"......!"

A sound like a long whistle.

Letting out a shrill cry as it cut through the air, the blade violently flew around Lucnoca's vicinity. It was an enchanted sword, by the name Trembling Bird, but of course, this wasn't an attack.

"*Kysle ko kyakowak. Kestek ko gbakyau—*" (From Alus to Hillensingen. A hailstorm to heaven and earth—)

The instant her attention turned to the enchanted sword's shriek, a shadow closed in on her from directly below. She didn't know the abilities of Rotten Soil Sun. She naturally recognized the figure in the corner of her eyes to be Alus the Star Runner.

Still not intending to make any attack, she extended her claw and instantly smacked the shadow out of the sky.

She shouted in delight.

"Aaah!"

You're still alive, was what she was going to say.

Realizing once again that she had knocked it out of the way herself, she looked as it turned into a splotch on the ground. There was one other thing that had flown toward her from the same direction.

The bullets fired from Rotten Soil Sun didn't start and end with the single shot shaped to copy the wyvern. Alus had sent another small lump of mud hidden inside the other's bulk.

The light overflowing from it dazzled Lucnoca's eyes.

Something then appeared from within the lump of mud—Hillensingen the enchanted light sword.

The claw that knocked the decoy out of the sky was guarding against the line of fire. However, the light blade easily penetrated right through it.

The strongest of enchanted swords, with no possible method of defending against its slash.

The white dragon turned her head away and avoided the flying slash. The twofold and threefold deception was meaningless. Lucnoca the Winter possessed the reflexive speed to immediately move to the defensive after all of it.

"*Kaameksa koikak. Syaskakko kemno. Kairokr aino.*" (Right eye axis. Changing circle. Circulate.) "Trembling Bird. Rotten Soil Sun. Hillensingen the enchanted light sword."

The enchanted light sword pursued her in midair.

Under the effects of Alus's Power Arts, it ran from the front of her neck to the back, burning away her nigh invincible dragon scales.

"Incredible... Oh my! Alus!"

If her dodge had been just slightly less effective, it would've sent a lethal dose through her neck. It was something she had never once received in her long history—the largest wound she ever had.

And that wasn't the end of it.

If the attack cut up her tail, seized her claws, and came from directly below her, she couldn't even shower her opponent in her breath. Because her own enormous body would be included in the attack radius.

"Why, to be able to fight like this—!"

When Lucnoca uttered this, the wyvern champion was inside the reach of her claws. Her breath, her dragon claws, and her tail...... Within this range, none of them could reach him.

Inside his right toe was the magic bullet.

The magic poison bullets of Arboreal Sky Tree, first causing their victim's nerves to rupture. Even when he directly grabbed

hold of it, the physical toe, flesh replaced with iron, didn't possess any nerves to erode. Right now, his own body was a magic bullet, shooting faster than a gunshot across the horizon.

Aiming at her neck, where her dragon scales had been torn off, he would surpass the strongest of all dragons' reflex speed.

"…"

…But he was unable.

The mass of Alus's torso was vertically rent in half.

He lost his entire left wing.

…Lucnoca muttered, dumbfounded.

"…Oh dear. I've done it now."

Then she spit out half of the champion's body she had chomped off.

"Honestly…… How could I act like such a brute?"

The wyvern champion had disabled her tail, slipped through her claws, and even inhibited her breath as he challenged the dragon.

It hadn't been enough. Beyond all of those were her fangs.

On the actual brink of death for the first time in her eternal history, the spinal reflex speed of the dragon's maw far surpassed the maximum direct flight velocity of the strongest of all wyverns.

A reactive speed that even Lucnoca the Winter herself found to be completely unexpected.

It wasn't the sort of personal growth that occurred under extreme situations, like Alus the Star Runner had accumulated over the years.

It was the basic instincts of a wild animal. Like her eradicating breath, nothing but a latent ability that the strongest of all creatures had possessed from the start.

"Why, I didn't know I was so fast."

It was simply that no one had seen her utilize her full strength before.

Even Lucnoca the Winter herself didn't know her limits.

There hadn't been a single person, anyone in the vast, wide world, who had backed her that far into a corner.

"……"

The rogue who had conquered everything far and wide on the horizon had fallen.

Trembling Bird. Rotten Soil Sun. Hillensingen the enchanted light sword.

Together with all his treasures, together with the sparkling brilliance of the world, he fell down into the ruptured earth's abyss.

—What if Lucnoca the Winter's tail attack hadn't accidently caught him?

If he hadn't been wounded by that attack. If his muscles hadn't gone numb in the cold air? If he had thrown his gun away and made his bag lighter…… If he hadn't been born with three arms?

It was he, the one lone wyvern, who was the champion to get the closest to taking Lucnoca the Winter's life.

…I was right.

In the final moments of his fading consciousness, he thought.

…Harghent's an amazing guy, after all……

◆

"N-not yet……"

Harghent stood up and staggered ahead.

Alus the Star Runner had fallen. Down into that deep, dark abyss. To the bottom of the frozen earth.

The severe frost had almost been like death itself, but now he couldn't even bring himself to keep the blanket around him. Without anything to cling to, Harghent shouted, smeared in tears and snot.

"Not yet!"

He would still rise back up again. Alus wasn't defeated yet. Harghent hadn't won yet. Alus the Star Runner was a champion, after all.

He had been his star, grabbing everything he wanted, never daunted by any hardship.

Even if that hardship was Lucnoca the Winter, he knew, surely…

"…Isn't that right, Alus…?! It's not over yet, it's not over…! Aaaaaah…"

His knees buckled in front of the horizon's unchanging stillness.

All that remained there was the cold temperature of despair and fated resignation.

Alus was there. Out in the distance was his greatest enemy. Harghent screamed.

"Someone!"

The elderly Sixth General screamed like a child.

"Someone pull Alus out of there! Someone...! It's Alus! H-he's... He's my friend! Someone! Someone...! Somebody...!"

The voice didn't reach anyone.

Hidow the Clamp, and that giant throng of spectators, had vanished at some point and gone away.

This uninhabited ice field, this scene of desolation itself. It was nothing less than the apex landscape.

"Someone, anyone...! *Hck, hrngh...hngaaaah...!*"

"Aaah, that truly was a delight. Now, Harghent."

Lucnoca the Winter landed down behind Harghent's crouching back.

The dragon, who once prided herself on her pure-white beauty, unviolated by anything...was in pitiful state as she bled copiously from her tail, with her neck wickedly burned and her left claw severed, and yet—

"Come now...! It's *not all going to just end after that*, right? This is barely the beginning of the first round, after all! I'm sure the next one, too...... Of course! There's even stronger champions waiting to give even more wonderful battles, right?!"

In her several hundred years of life, she had never once tasted excitement like this before.

The solitary and removed landscape seemed to glisten in her eyes. She thought that there still remained things she could love about this world.

For her, denied any hope of battle itself, those wounds were exactly what she had wanted more than anything else

"More, more, and more battles like that...! Ahhh, I truly can't wait for the next battle! The next champion!"

Match Two. Winner, Lucnoca the Winter.

HAVE YOU BEEN TURNED ON TO LIGHT NOVELS YET?

86—EIGHTY-SIX, VOL. 1–11

In truth, there is no such thing as a bloodless war. Beyond the fortified walls protecting the eighty-five Republic Sectors lies the "nonexistent" Eighty-Sixth Sector. The young men and women of this forsaken land are branded the Eighty-Six and, stripped of their humanity, pilot "unmanned" weapons into battle...

Manga adaptation available now!

WOLF & PARCHMENT, VOL. 1–6

The young man Col dreams of one day joining the holy clergy and departs on a journey from the bathhouse, Spice and Wolf. Winfiel Kingdom's prince has invited him to help correct the sins of the Church. But as his travels begin, Col discovers in his luggage a young girl with a wolf's ears and tail named Myuri, who stowed away for the ride!

Manga adaptation available now!

SOLO LEVELING, VOL. 1–7

E-rank hunter Jinwoo Sung has no money, no talent, and no prospects to speak of—and apparently, no luck, either! When he enters a hidden double dungeon one fateful day, he's abandoned by his party and left to die at the hands of some of the most horrific monsters he's ever encountered.

Comic adaptation available now!